Luke Eden

DEAD HEAT

A SPEEDWAY NOVEL

Kindle Direct Publishing

50% of the profits from this publication
will be donated equally
between the
Speedway Riders
Benevolent Fund
and
The Darcy Ward Foundation

Published by Kindle Direct Publishing 30 / 11 / 2018

Copyright © Luke Eden 2018

Luke Eden has asserted his right under the

Copyright, Designs

and Patents Act 1988 to be identified as the

author of this work.

This book is sold subject to the condition that it

shall not, by way

of trade or otherwise, be lent, resold, hired out

without the publisher's

prior consent in any form of binding or cover or

electronic means

other than that in which it is published and

without a similar condition,

including this condition, being imposed on the subsequent purchaser.

First published in Great Britian in 2018 by Kindle Direct Publishing.

Cover design by Luke Eden - Speedwaynovel@gmx.com
Cover Photograph by Ian Charles - https://iancharlesphotos.net
Proofread by Simon Cooper - sdcproofreading@gmail.com

Disclaimer - The characters listed on page 205 of this book are entirely fictional. Any resemblance to actual persons living or dead is entirely coincidental. However, except for these characters who are essential to and created for the storyline of the novel, all the other people mentioned are real people who populated the wonderful world of Speedway racing in the UK during the final Elite League season of 2016. This was done in order to lend an air of authenticity to the story. All the riders, staff, owners, officials, helpers and volunteers and associates of featured in the story for this purpose have given their permission to populate this homage to a great sport. Thank you to them all.

DEDICATION

To every speedway rider who has been injured in the pursuit of bringing the excitement of this great sport to the fans who love it.

Without your honesty of endeavour in taking yourself to the limits of safety and beyond, speedway would have no meaning.

This book was written to not only say
"Thank you",
but also to offer practical support. Every book bought by every person will add money to the Speedway Riders' Benevolent Fund
and
The Darcy Ward Foundation.

Thank you to all of you.

ACKNOWLEDGEMENTS

I would like to thank the following people and organisations for helping this book to have legitimacy and credibility by allowing me to use their names or by helping with marketing and sales:

Hans Andersen Adam Roynon Adrian Smith British Speedway Board Barry Bishop Barry Briggs Bjarne Pedersen Brady Kurtz Jan Kvech Brendan Johnson Chris Harris Chris Holder Clive Featherby Charles Wright Chris Whitehouse Danny King Derek Morgan Ellis Perks Graham Drury Tia Woffinden Kelvin Tatum Kim Nilsson Kyle Newman Jake Allen Jack Smith Jason Doyle Jason Garrity Jon Cook John Thomas Justin Sedgman Linus Sundstrom Ludvig Lindgren Mads Korneliussen Mat Ford Mark Baseby Kenneth Bjerre Max Bjerre Neil Middleditch Niels-Kristian Iversen Nigel Leary Nick Morris Nollie Chipchase Ove Fundin Pam Jones Peter Oakes Peter Karlsson Patryk Dudek Peter Ljung Robert Lambert Rohan Tungate Scott Nicholls Sharon Knight SGB (Speedway Great Britain) Speedway Star magazine Steven Massey Sue Bradford Tom Perry Toni Mulas Tony Jackson Wikipedia MMX Events Speedway Riders' Benevolent Fund The Darcy Ward Foundation

Cover Photographer: Ian Charles

A special mention must be made of Nigel Leary and Peter Oakes. To Nigel who offered his help without hesitation when I was stuck and could see no way over or round the mountain. With his connections with many speedway folk through MXX Events and his role on the live centre green mobile mic at Poole Pirates Speedway was able to remove barriers that might have foiled me alone. To Peter for his ability to publicise my work and his willingness to his influence to help get the message to speedway fans. Without their efforts I am sure the finished novel would not have been the same and would have been of lesser quality of storyline. Thanks Nigel and Peter.

CONTENTS

Dedication

Acknowledgements

Chapters 1 to 35

Bulldogs 2016 fixtures and results

Summary of levels of speedway

The basic league rules

Nomenclatures (seen in the results sections)

League Scoring System

Terminology and Slang

List of Characters

The Author

CHAPTER 1

BATTERSEA BULLDOGS TEAM:

Tia Woffinden 9.50
Joe Neal 9.50
Patryk Dudek 8.80
Linus Sundstrom 6.7
Kenneth Bjerre 6.5
Peter Ljung 6.3
Sonny Brent (RES) 3.5
Frankie Chivers (RES) 2.4

ELITE LEAGUE TABLE - Up to and including Tuesday 2nd August 2016

TEAM	M	W	D	L	F
Belle Vue	18	12	0	6	829
Wolverhampton	20	11	0	9	940
Lakeside	20	11	0	9	955
Swindon	20	10	1	9	905
Battersea	17	10	0	7	824
Poole	15	9	1	5	732
Kings Lynn	15	7	2	6	656
Coventry	20	7	0	13	846
Leicester	20	4	2	14	819

Arnie@arniecottrellIt's been a struggle but I think we're really beginning to see the form we've been wanting! The Bulldogs are coming!

Thursday 4th August 2016

Barry Leech was the billionaire business brain and Chief Executive behind the huge international company known as the Leech Group; he was a Bristolian by birth and a Londoner by adoption. Probably the most influential experience of his youthful days in Bristol was his father's enthusiasm for taking him to see the Bristol Bulldogs Speedway team. Even today Barry is not sure whether he actually attended the Bulldogs 1949 record breaking whitewash of the visiting Glasgow Tigers, beating them 70 -14 over 14 heats in the National League, or whether his dad just told him so often that he became convinced he was there. In 2016 Barry Leech continued to pursue his passion for the sport,, in particular to keep alive his fond memories of his Bristol days, by becoming official promoter of the Battersea Bulldogs speedway team which formed a central part of the Battersea Business Park. At six feet three inches tall and fifty four inches around the waist, he was a huge presence in any company. His thick head of professionally styled white hair added to the impressive professional image that had weakened the bladder of many a competitor. He described himself, however, as a wannabe speedway rider who never quite got round to having a go. And the fact was, that in all of his life, being a speedway rider was the only thing he had ever wanted to do that he'd failed to make happen, and even with all his money and the multitude of material possessions that he owned, he knew this still smoldering canker somewhere at the back of his mind reminded him that he would never be truly happy. A self-proclaimed 'man of the people', he was direct in action and speech, made things happen and expected others to be the same.

On the evening in question he was standing on the second bend of the Bulldog's speedway track laughing and joking with fans, cheering everything good about his team and hurling abuse when things went wrong, even to the point of blaming himself and his management when it was warranted. The fans loved him, his employees feared and loved him. Bulldog's riders rode their hearts out for the team he had created because they knew that there was no better deal to be had in the entire speedway world. Battersea Bulldogs was a success and Barry Leech's life was as sweet as it would ever be.

2016 was the fourth season for the Battersea Bulldogs, who were now the second newest speedway team in the British Elite League after Leicester. The Barry Leech stadium was purpose built as a multi-sport venue and provided many design and business ideas that were adapted and adopted for Belle Vue's National Speedway Stadium. It was built to deliver the most up-to-date entertainment package that money could buy and that a veracious public could desire. It's vibrant presentation, state-of-the-art sound and lighting systems together with unmatched franchising opportunities, such as a five-a-side football complex, ten-pin bowling, Laser Quest, a cycle speedway track, go-karting and a modern conference centre, meant that the complex was never silent. Many of the big retailers had opened outlets on the adjoining retail park which meant that there was a steady stream of new faces attending matches after initially visiting in order to do some shopping and noticing that there was a Speedway meeting on a Thursday evening. As a consequence, an average of ten thousand spectators attended every home match making certain that the Bulldogs easily outgunned the rest of the Elite League for income and commercial opportunities. The focus of the speedway business was to ensure the public got exciting speedway and entertainment. In order to attract riders like Tai Woffinden and Joe Neal, Barry Leech briefed the senior team, and the Team Manager Arnie Cottrell in particular, to ensure that the riders always rode the best machinery and received the very best maintenance. This business objective was manifest as a contract like no other in any league in the world. In essence, the riders owned nothing and were exposed to no financial risk. With all their equipment supplied and individually customised, all their maintenance placed in the hands of the best mechanics and engine tuners available who were contracted for exclusivity, travel run and organised from a central office and unparalleled accommodation, even the most junior members of the team felt well looked after and valued. It was only the points target that governed every Elite league teams choices that kept them from creating a monopoly at the start of each season. They were the envy of every opponent who continued to survive from season to season with the input of money from promoters who had to fund it from very limited resources. Battersea Bulldogs were part of the greater and extremely powerful Leech group and received the benefit of the financial clout that a large corporation with profits of £15 billion can provide. Barry Leech's dream was still developing and the first three seasons had seen them qualify for the Play-offs only to fall at the semi-final hurdle. Barry's declared objective was to be Champions in 2016.

Harry Marsh's appearance was in sharp contrast to Barry Leech's. While he did own a suit, there were few occasions that Harry thought warranted bringing it out for an airing. Where Barry shopped in Jasper Littman on Saville Row, Harry shopped in charity shops, where Barry ate in The Dorchester, 100 Wardour Street or Flat 3 in Holland Park, Harry occasionally treated himself and his girlfriend to a Chinese or Indian meal in Notting Hill. As the lead, actually the only, reporter with Speedway FM, he was paid a pittance and was expected to work unreasonable hours. The only redeeming feature was that he loved his job. This internet radio station, which started in the bedroom of its founder Johnny Matthews, had so recently occupied office and studio space in the Barry Leech stadium that they were still moving things in there while broadcasting on a daily basis. The location gave them a newly acquired cachet and confident presence in the speedway world that was attracting more listeners every week. So the only two paid staff, Harry and Johnny, worked long hours to bring their listeners the very best interviews, views and, occasionally, live speedway as many evenings as they could. Johnny published the schedule every morning for the day after when he had looked at the bank balance and taken account of the predicted expenses. The listeners loved the station and participated by writing, e-mailing, telephoning and introducing themselves when they heard Harry was visiting a track for a meeting. So, predictably, funds were always in short supply and Johnny constantly found himself sweet-talking potential sponsors whilst Harry travelled on his old Triumph Bonneville to tracks as far as petrol money would allow. This evening Harry was at the Bulldog's track for their home match against Swindon armed with a microphone and a digital recorder. He had gathered some useable material in the form of a couple of nice interviews with Jason Doyle and Nick Morris, a golden cameo piece with the great Barry Briggs who had called in to see his old Swindon team riding and two very funny 'fan clips' capturing the banter between the Bulldog and Robins fans on the terraces. He had that very nice feeling that comes from being where you want to be, doing what you want to do and he smiled contentedly as he walked through the gates to enter the restricted area of the stadium, little knowing that it was all about to change.

He strolled at a leisurely pace towards the pits in the hope of interviewing Tia Woffinden, composing questions as he went. As he passed the open door to the rider's changing rooms he heard raised voices echoing off the tiled surfaces within. As a reporter, he was professionally nosey, but in reality he was also naturally nosey, so he stopped and listened to the heated exchange pressing the record button on his recorder automatically.

"I never did nothin' honest," he heard Sonny Brent saying.

"You're a bloody liar Brent,"
Harry recognised Steve Hildegarde's voice. Steve had been Sonny's mechanic since they both started at the junior level and they were clearly close friends, or so Harry had thought.

"She's my girlfriend and you thought you could dip your wick when I wasn't looking! Well, you've had the goods and now I'm going to make sure you pay for it," Steve yelled and hit Sonny full in the stomach knocking the wind out of him. Sonny doubled up, fell backwards and sat on the floor gasping for air. Steve stood over him and pointed his finger directly into Sonny's face, "You're a dead man Brent," he snarled, turned and walked away.

"Steve, mate, don't be like that. I didn't do nothing Steve, honest," Sonny was on the edge of tears, "I didn't; Steve, honest!"

Harry walked across to the wall and looked at the track pretending to text on his mobile phone. Steve bowled out of the changing rooms and saw him.

"What are you doing here?" he asked aggressively, clearly wondering if he'd been overheard.

"What?" Harry looked over his shoulder in mock surprise, "Oh hi Steve. I'm texting my Rosie, why?"
Steve visible calmed himself down,

"No, nothing." He squeezed the bridge of his nose, "Sorry Harry, forget it." And he walked quickly away towards the pits.

Harry continued his ruse and waited to see what happened next. Eventually, Sonny Brent came out wearing his Kevlars and carrying his helmet and gloves. Harry nodded a casual greeting,

"Watcha Sonny. OK?"

"Yea, fine," Sonny said neutrally.

Harry kept it going,

"What number are you tonight?"

"Seven again."

"That's ok isn't it?" Harry asked.

"Yea should get a few rides from there."

"I hope so mate," Harry agreed, "Good luck."

"Cheers," Sonny said and started towards the pits.

Harry watched him as he limped away,

"Nothing to read into that," Harry thought, "after all, every speedway rider limps whether he's wearing his steel shoe or not."

Harry grinned broadly as he entered the pits as he saw Rosie Higgins leaning on the low pit wall talking enthusiastically with Tia Woffinden. They both looked up as he approached and waved him over. Rosie was both PA to Barry Leech and his niece. She was efficient and effective; she had terrific people skills, she spoke with a voice that would probably charm and calm a psychopath, warm and without accent.

"Sheer class," as mechanic Johnny Sinclair once commented when he didn't realise that Harry was within earshot. In addition to all this, she was also the most beautiful woman that Harry had ever seen. She had long auburn hair that cascaded onto her shoulders when she wore it down, transformed into a frivolous ponytail when she was playing tennis or doing Zumba, or an austere bun when she pulled her hair away from her face and she needed to be coldly professional. Her lips were fulsome and articulate, normally and naturally shaped into a smile but she could quickly snarl at you or offer a tight mouthed stare that could cool even the most heated emotions. In short, Harry thought as he gazed at her, "Sheer class." He could not believe his good fortune and would occasionally look at himself in the mirror and ask, "Why you? You lucky, lucky man?" Rosie was everything any man could want from a friend, a lover and a stimulating intellectual; but not as a cook. "No," Harry grinned as he approached her, "she is an absolute shocker as a cook!"

"And what are grinning for?" she asked looking at him suspiciously.

"I'm not," Harry replied.

"You are," Tia confirmed.

"Can't a man smile when he's feeling good about things?" Harry said and kissed Rosie on her forehead, "Especially when that man is me and gets to sleep with you."

"Shut it Marsh!" Rosie said glancing at Tia , who smiled broadly and raised his eyebrows.

They had met one warm summer's night in the pits as the Battersea Bulldogs trounced a depleted Eastbourne side during the bulldogs first season two and a half years earlier. Rosie was a great favourite with the riders, the fans, Uncle Barry and after a shaky start, with Harry Marsh. Rosie had asked Harry to leave the pits during the meeting and when he tried to explain that he was a member of the 'press' and as such, had permission to be there; she called him a liar, called for security and had him thrown out of the stadium. "In her defence", Harry was prone to say when the subject came up, "I did look more like a tramp than a reporter."

Rosie always agreed with this and added, "But I did apologise at the next meeting when I saw him." With the ice broken and a moral debt owed, Harry took full advantage and asked this delightful woman out for a meal. Rosie felt obliged to accept and on the agreed night she wore a stylish short dress, high-heeled shoes, visited the hairdressers and selected a reasonably expensive handbag. Harry arrived on his Triumph wearing a vision of a meal at the roadside American style diner just the other side of Potter's Bar.

Tia excused himself by explaining that he needed to speak with one of the young riders before he went out to race and asked that the interview might wait until the end of the meeting when he promised to dedicate fifteen or twenty minutes so that Harry could make a feature article out of it. Excited by the prospect Harry agreed and turned his attention to the match that was unfolding into a fascinating clash as both teams needed the points to enhance their very promising league positions. The wonderful sound of bike engines revving battled with the announcer who was enthusiastically introducing the riders.

"It's time for heat eight and the score sits at twenty to twenty two with everything to race for. So, in the red helmet we have Joe Neal who is looking for his second win of the evening. In blue is our home grown number seven, Sonny Brent looking to improve on his third place in his first race. And for Swindon, in the white helmet it's Nick Morris and in yellow, it's Danny Ayres." The roar of the bike engines, the music from the PA, the cheers of the crowd and the blasts from air-horns combined to create a charged atmosphere that filled the stadium. The riders assembled at the gate and after the usual gardening the Halleluiah Chorus heralded the start of the race. Each rider sat forward on his bike putting weight over the front wheel in anticipation of the acceleration that would try to make it airborne. Throttles were twisted open so that the engines screamed out their power, clutch levers held tight against the handlebars, twitching with anticipation. The heads of Joe Neal and Nick Morris snapped towards the inside post of the starting gate, at the same time, the heads of Sonny Brent and Danny Ayres snapped towards the outside post, all intent on seeing the earliest movement of the starting mechanism and getting the all important fastest start. Joe Neal put a bike's length between himself and the others from the inside gate before anyone else moved and allowed himself to drift out a little on the first bend in order to block the excellent run that Nick Morris was making from the second gate position. Looking over his shoulder and seeing that Sonny Brent was in third place behind Nick Morris, Joe Neal decided to leave his team mate to fight his own battle with Danny Ayres for third place on the basis that Nick Morris was certainly dangerous enough to get past him if he tried to slow-ride the race in an attempt to keep Sonny close. Neal and Morris stretched their lead to almost half the straight by the end of the first lap, while Sonny and Danny were having their own wheel to wheel battle for the all important single point. Danny Ayres was racing in fourth, just behind and on the outside of Sonny as they slowed into the first bend on lap two; he hugged the white line as he opened the throttle to bring his rear wheel round in a broadside. Sonny worked his own throttle trying to hold his line and keep Ayres behind him but he failed to call up enough power to bring the back wheel round and he found himself drifting away from his inside line towards the middle of the track. The situation called for Sonny to control his bike by producing more power and lots of strength. Sonny however, provided neither and his bike controlled him instead as it took him closer and closer to the air fence. Danny Ayres saw the gap open in front of him and grabbed the opportunity by shifting his weight, pulling his bike round, opening the throttle still more to take the inside line and under-cut Sonny to move into third place. Sonny was left wrestling with his machine to keep it away from the fence as it stubbornly described a wider and wider arc guided by a series of deep ruts in the shale, around the ever narrowing bend. He exited the corner at low speed and inches from the final section of the air-fence with his heart thumping and feeling foolish. He twisted back the throttle and gave chase. Danny Ayres crossed the line to start lap three in third place some thirty meters ahead of Sonny. Showing the characteristic determination that made him an instant favorite with the fans, Sonny rode on the very edge of his skill level in his attempt to recover the third place he felt he had given away. Going into bend three on lap three he hurled his bike around the outside of the corner trying to power through the deeper dirt and get his wheels in line sooner than Ayres and thereby effectively lengthening the back straight. It called for significant strength to hold it in the deeper shale but the extra speed was thrilling and he felt the rush of adrenalin that came with moments like this. As he came off bend four he was travelling at a tremendous speed eating up the gap between himself and Danny Ayres as he flew past the start and finish line to begin lap four. Coming out of bend two he was close to Danny and maintaining his momentum. At the end of the straight he was travelling very fast with Danny on the inside line and only five meters ahead. He entered bend three on the very edge of control, edging towards the outside line. Sonny was holding onto the handlebars with a grip that lacked all sensitivity. He hardly dared move anything as he shifted his weight carefully so as not to disrupt his precarious balance. The excitement of the previous adrenalin rush was now replaced with a bowel loosening fear. He could see the deep ruts in the shale coming round the bend to meet him with an inevitability that filled him with dread. He dared not try to move his weight, lean the bike any further over or throttle back. Sonny just gripped the handlebars, held the bike in its existing attitude and hoped that he would get round the bend. For the crowd and Sonny alike, everything seemed to be happening very slowly. Sonny knew he wasn't going to make it out of the bend, but could not do anything to change the trajectory of the bike. The crowd knew that he wasn't going to make it out of the bend as they held their breath watching the inevitable happen before their eyes.

When his front wheel hit the first ridge of deep shale and the trench like ruts, Sonny's speed reduced from fifty miles per hour to twenty in an instant, throwing him forward onto his handlebars and causing the front of his bike to fold up and slide away from him. He went down awkwardly with his chest hitting the end of the handlebars and clutch lever knocking the wind out of him. He hit the air fence slid under the apron at the bottom and struck the wooden barrier on which the whole thing was hung. The impact of rolled him over and spun him round so that he emerged on his back and slid to a halt two feet from the bottom of the fence. His bike twisted in the air, bounced off the top of the fence and came down in a pitching, rolling chaos of raging metal. Sonny's arm was clipped painfully by the footrest and the exhaust pipe scorched across his hand leaving a nasty burn. There was a collective gasp from the crowd and the referee switched on the red lights to stop the race.

Within seconds a paramedic was kneeling at Sonny's side and started attending to him. Within a minute or so other paramedics joined in and they worked together to help the fallen rider and calling for the ambulance. The track doctor was on the scene within three minutes taking over the care of the rider and was seen administrating CPR before a crowd of riders, managers, promoters and pit crew obliterated the view of the disturbing tableau. Over the next forty-five minutes the fans saw all these people venturing over to see what was happening to Sonny and how their demeanor changed from curious to concerned and then to visibly shaken with the dawning realisation that things had conspired to go dreadfully wrong for the young man. Harry managed to get onto the track and stand at the periphery of the scene from where he saw an ashen faced Arnie Cottrell trying to comfort a distraught Frankie Chivers. Barry Leech was there in the middle of the increasingly tragic incident looking on with deep concern etched on his face. Rosie Higgins stood next to him, her arm linked with his as she assumed her role as his niece over that of his Personal Assistant. Harry walked slowly around the edge of the crowd until he came across Steve Hildegarde who he watched for a few minutes. Steve seemed as concerned as everyone else but didn't go in close to see how Sonny was, but then again, he would argue that it was obvious how Sonny was, the paramedics needed space to do their work and didn't need unqualified people getting in the way.

Although the length of time it took to treat Sonny indicated that something serious had happened, it came as a shock when a serious voiced announcer spoke over the PA system to inform the crowd that the match was to be abandoned and that fans should keep the stubs of their tickets in readiness for the rescheduled meeting. After the announcement, some fans left to make their way home, but many stayed and stood quietly knowing that something had happened to Sonny Brent and were not willing to go home until they knew what it was. This was not out of any macabre desire to feed off tragic events, but from a genuine concern for the people who risked their lives on a weekly basis for their entertainment. When one of theirs gets hurt, the people who populate the speedway world close together in support and compassion. The PA crackled again sometime later and the voice of the

Bulldog's manager spoke to the remaining crowd.

"This is Arnie Cottrell speaking to you." He paused to compose himself, "it is with great sadness that I have to tell you that the doctor has officially announced the death of Sonny Brent. Sonny's parents have asked me to thank you for staying here to show your support for their son." He gulped and his voice faltered. After a few seconds he added, "There is no more information available at this time but we will keep you updated via our website as and when anything new becomes available. Thank you for staying and for your demonstration of respect, but there is nothing else to stay for now. Sonny's body will leave in the next few minutes so please leave the stadium quietly and let all our thoughts be with his family tonight." A dark and eerie cloud of silence settled over the stadium and the crowd began to file towards the exits in solemn groups.

CHAPTER 2

Friday 5th August 2016
arnie@arniecottrell
Shock and sadness for the Bulldogs.. Puts what we do into perspective. Condolences to Sonny's family from all of us here

The sky was as heavy as the atmosphere around the Bulldog's stadium as Harry Marsh walked up the stairs that led to the studio and as he passed the door of the adjoining HSE office, Tony Fuller's called out to him. Harry's heart sank, "Morning Tony, what can I do for you?"

The Bulldog's Health and Safety Manager looked exhausted as he leaned his elbows on his desk and indicated for Harry to take a seat, "I've got something I want you to do on your radio programme."

Harry tried not to let his despair show as he prepared himself for yet another 'non-starter' of an idea from an amateur enthusiast who fancied he could present a radio programme. "You look awful Tony, have you slept at all?"

"I slept here," he answered indicating the sofa by the door. "a couple of hours anyway."

"And today's going to be busy as well, I'll bet."

"It's going to be hell," Tony confirmed, "the police will be here again at ten o'clock."

"What about the HSE?"

"They've been here since six."

Tony straightened up in his chair, "Let me tell you what I think we need. Last night was as bad as it gets in our business, but it serves to emphasise that the work we do in HSE is important, even with all the insults we receive."

"Yes, of course, but tell me about it," Harry said sliding onto the office chair and conjuring up more energy than he felt it would deserve.

Tony's idea was every bit as bad as Harry thought it would be. "I think what we need is what I call HSE Hour!" he said, "it's more educational than anything, but it would have plenty of entertainment as well because I know how important that is to you." The reality of the idea was that it would be a vehicle for Tony to tell listeners about how important and difficult his job was.

Harry thought carefully about his response and because he had only known Tony a short time, he wanted to be positive, which, he had discovered on several occasions was trickier than one might think. Tony's ability to deal with the minutiae of life in general and

HSE in particular had been a revelation, verging on a trauma to Harry's creative spirit. What Tony saw as his great strength of paying attention to details, Harry saw as a pedantic, anal retentive preoccupation with trivia. What Tony saw as reducing the risk of his employer being sued, Harry saw as reducing the thrills of the greatest sport in the world to a mundane antiseptic business that would not be worth watching if they were allowed to carry on. Harry had joked with Johnny that Tony would one day issue a decree that all speedway bikes should be fitted with brakes or that only one rider be allowed on the track at a time in order to avoid crashes. As Harry looked across the desk at Tony he pondered on the possibility that the joke might become manifest. "What kind of content do you have in mind for this programme?" he asked neutrally.

Tony sat further forward on his chair, "Well obviously we would need to deal with the dangers of being a speedway rider, but there lots of other equally important stuff like 'pit safety' where we can inform people about the issues that we have to manage on a daily basis."

"That might make an interesting 'one off' item," Harry said.

"I was thinking that it would be a regular item," Tony said, surprised at Harry's lack of insight. "I thought we could also have slot on

Crowd Management where we can alert people to the things we have to consider when we let them through the turnstiles."

He went on to outline several other equally yawn inducing topics. Harry listened with growing dismay,

"You know what Tony; I'm going to take this idea to the next Production Meeting with Johnny and see if we can't do something with it," he said. He got a mental picture of Johnny laughing in derision. "I'm pretty sure it won't make a regular programme," he coughed to clear his throat, "well, not immediately anyway, but there might be some scope for making a short spot in an existing programme. We can get some listener responses on Twitter and Facebook to see if it could sustain its own programme later."

"Ok Harry, that's a bit disappointing though," Tony sat back in his chair, "You see. I'm convinced people will be interested. You know, some people think that Health and Safety is a bit boring, but it's not. It's just that they don't understand."

Eventually the discussion reached a conclusion and Harry excused himself and went next door to the Speedway FM studio where he found Johnny Matthews unpacking the contents of a box. The internet radio station had recently moved into rooms at the far end of the stadium and they still had that 'just moved in' feeling although it was already fully functional. Harry's role as a studio presenter had been extended so that he now fronted a two hour show on Monday, Tuesday, Saturday and Sunday evening and although they were pre-recorded shows it still took him many hours of work on his laptop in cheap hotel rooms and B&Bs to get them ready. The great thing about the relationship was that this left him plenty of time to get to meetings where he could occasionally broadcast live and always record interviews and action for a later broadcast. As he entered, Johnny looked up from his box, "Greetings! Are you ok for twelve o'clock?"

"I am," Harry replied, "but we need to agree the tone and a script." He flopped onto the old armchair that they kept for VIPs. "I suggest we go over it at the ten-thirty meeting because I want to go over and talk to Arnie Cottrell to see what the club are planning to say in their public announcement."

Later that morning, Harry walked across the car park that surrounded the stadium, down past the tractor park where all the equipment required for grading and preparing the track for racing was kept, through the pits and into the administration block, up to the first floor offices where he found the middle aged, portly, soft-spoken and kindly man in a subdued mood, quietly sitting at his desk. Harry could see that Arnie was having a hard time so he walked over and placed his hand on the manager's shoulder, "Morning mate. How are you holding up?"

"I'm ok," Arnie replied, "It's all very sad and horrible, but manageable."

"I guess," Harry sympathised as he pulled over an office chair and sat down beside the other man," I've come over to see if you've had your meeting with Barry yet?"

Arnie nodded slowly, "Yes I have. He's obviously very upset, worried and angry about the whole affair. We've decided what to put on the website and what to do at next weeks meeting. I'm going over to Sonny's parents later today to take his clothes to them and see if they need anything."

"Have they decided when the funeral will be?" Harry asked.

"I don't think so. There'll probably have to be some kind of autopsy before they'll release Sonny's body."

Harry nodded, "I see. You'll let us know when you find out?"

"Yes of course I will," Arnie agreed.

"We'll put out a suitable broadcast when we know the details."

"Sure. What are you going to say today?" he asked Harry.

"We're not sure yet." Harry explained, "We wanted to know if there is anything the club wanted us to include or avoid."

Arnie shuffled among some paper on his desk, "Err, yes," he said, "You can tell them that we will be organising a collection for Sonny's family, we'll launch the sale of wrist bands for that as well as collections. We'd like to hold a memorial service, but that needs to be discussed with his family first." He choked up and turned his head away, collected himself and dabbed his eyes with a tissue. "Did you know he had a girlfriend?" Harry shook his head and Arnie added, "She's pregnant."

"I'll make sure we tell them about the collection," Harry said writing it into his smart phone.

"Yeah." Arnie sighed, "I'm confident that you'll get the tone right," he said quietly.

Johnny had made a change to the schedule and replaced Jenny Howard's usual music and speedway news show with a Sonny Brent tribute that both Jenny and Harry hosted. Neither of them had ever done anything like this and they were both feeling very nervous about the live broadcast on a such a subject. Harry did the first thirty minutes before handing over to Jenny for a spell. Harry sat in front of the microphone and put on his earphones, looking at Johnny in the control booth. They nodded at each other, Johnny switched the studio to 'live' and then gave Harry the thumbs up sign. No music, no glitzy introductions, just Harry's voice solemnly speaking the listeners. "This is Harry Marsh speaking to you from the home of the Battersea Bulldogs Speedway team where last night we witnessed the sad death of Sonny Brent when he crashed during their Elite League match. Each of us knows that speedway is intrinsically dangerous and each week we hear that riders have fallen and suffered injuries that will keep them out of the sport for a few weeks or months and we wish them well, but pass it off as 'these things happen' as, indeed, do many of the riders themselves. But on the occasions when those injuries put riders in a wheelchair for life or worse cause their death, our speedway family comes together to share our collective grief. Our sport is small enough for people to know each other across the boundaries that separate fans from other sports. Riders who regularly move from team to team are our heroes one season and opponents the next. This intermixing creates an intimacy between fans and riders alike so that our common interests and enthusiasms for the sport, and the people who participate in it, are manifest as a sense of caring for each other in times of need and appreciation in better times. Of course, we cheer for our favourites and jeer when a rider goes beyond the acceptable limits, but we also applaud competitors who show skill and daring. For most of us it isn't just about winning, it's about close, exciting racing as well. And this depends on riders who are willing to race close and fast and take risks and give it their all." He paused and gulped.

"Yesterday one of them paid the ultimate price for giving his all and so today we send our condolences to Sonny's Brent's family and friends who will be suffering deep grief over their loss." He went on to tell listeners about the things the club were arranging and how he would keep them up-to-date with news as it became available. The whole programme became a phone-in as speedway fans from all over the country called to share their grief and horror over Sonny's death. Many had personal memories, a few knew Sonny, but most just wanted to express their sympathy and let his family know that they were thinking about them.

This poignant tribute was an enormously emotional and moving occasion and when Harry finally switched off the microphone both he and Jenny slumped in their chairs for several minutes silently holding hands. Johnny bought them both coffees, "That was powerful," he said quietly to them both, "Thank you"

Rosie rang to say that she had listened to it, "It was so touching that I cried."

"Me too," Harry replied.

"I know," she said, "I heard it."

"Oh dear, did you?"

"Yes but don't worry about it, everybody was crying," she reassured him. "Look Harry, Barry has put me in full-time charge of coordinating things with Sonny's family and to make sure we get the whole thing right. So, for a week or two I'll be focused on this."

"Get it right from a corporate viewpoint?" Harry asked suspiciously.

"Yes," Rosie answered, "There are some wider business considerations that need to be watched and potentially dealt with."

"I can imagine," Harry said flatly.

For the next few weeks there was going to be a lot of activity and a lot of awkward questions were going to be asked and some of them were going to uncover issues that might be embarrassing. Tony Fuller was central to all this as he presented the HSE face of the company to the HSE accident investigation team that would be camped at the stadium until they were happy that they had answers to their questions.

When an accident takes place and especially when a death occurs it is incumbent upon the organisation to cooperate with the HSE to discover why and how it happened and how it can be avoided in the future. Tony was now fully engaged in preparing detailed reports designed to educate the management and the HSE about the causes, the hazards and the risks that led to the result; later he would be absorbed in an equivalent report with regards to the future operation. Whilst he would never wish an accident on anyone and indeed his entire job was dedicated to keeping people safe at work, it was evident that Tony was like a pig in shit. Harry was reminded of his Uncle Stan who fought in the Second World War, and when asked how he felt about being a part of it said, "They were the best days of my life Harry my boy, the best days of my life."

Three days later Harry went over to Rosie's office in the admin building to check if she had anything juicy for broadcasting and entered to find her reading a copy of the post mortem report that had been received by Sonny's parents that day,
"It says that it was *accidental death and death from chest injuries*."
"Nothing else?" Harry asked.
"No, nothing else. Just *chest injuries*," Rosie confirmed, "Why?"
"Well I don't know anything about anything really, but it seems a bit generalised and uninformative to me," Harry observed, "I would have expected something more specific."
"I don't know what to expect," Rosie said.

"Well when a man crashes into the air-fence at sixty to seventy miles per hour and dies because of it, I would expect the causes to have been, I don't know, more graphic or identifiable." Harry mused, "I mean; *chest injuries*?"

"Well that's what it says," Rosie explained," You've got to suppose that the professional responsible knew what he was talking about."

"I suppose so," Harry admitted, "Did he have any broken bones?"

"Not according to the report. He had a dislocated shoulder and plenty of soft tissue bruising."

"Hmm," Harry mused. "Makes you wonder how come he died with those injuries doesn't it?"

As Harry walked out of the Administration Offices and down the stairs on the outside of the building into the pit area, he saw Geoff Falk wheeling the mangled remains of Sonny's bike on a gurney to the double doors of the workshop where he left it and went inside. Harry wandered over and took a look at the machine trying to see if there had been a mechanical failure that might have caused the crash, but he couldn't see anything obvious. Geoff returned a minute later with a cup of hot chocolate and raised it to the reporter,

"Hello Harry. Everything ok?"

"Hi Geoff. Yes I think so. I was just looking at Sonny's bike and wondering if there had been a mechanical explanation for his crash," Harry explained.

Geoff Falk looked dubious, "Unlikely, but I was just about to inspect it as part of the Health and Safety Causation Report, so if there is anything, it'll show up then." Geoff swilled the chocolate around the plastic cup, "

"Can I watch you do it," Harry asked.

"Yeah, if you want to," Geoff swallowed the last of his drink, "give me a hand to get it into the workshop," he asked pointing to the gurney.

They found that the front wheel had buckled pretty badly, "Probably due to the impact when it landed after bouncing off the air fence," Geoff commented. Harry nodded and they continued their inspection. Geoff took off the leading link forks, removed the single damper from the left side of the framework and lingered over the damper element of the shock absorbers looking at it from different angles and pushing it in and out.

"Is something wrong?" Harry asked.

"Probably not, but unusually this damper isn't very stiff." He pumped it again to demonstrate, "Look, there's no resistance worth talking about."

Harry took it from Geoff turning it over in his hands. He could see to what Geoff was referring, it was much less firm than one might reasonably expect.

"So what? Is this significant?" he questioned.

"Who knows," Geoff replied, "It's possible but I think improbable that it was wrecked by the crash."

"The front wheel was badly damaged in the nose dive, so this damper could have suffered during that as well, couldn't it?"

"Yes of course it's possible," Geoff agreed, "but the wheel is much more fragile than the shocks. I'm not surprised to see the wheel in this state, but the shocks are designed to take shocks, so I am a bit surprised to see this damper in this state," and he turned it on end and shook it causing it to retract. "That shouldn't happen."

Harry leaned on the bench and asked, "Could it have been deliberately tampered with?"

"That's silly Harry,"

"Yeah, but could it?"

"Yes, it could have been, but then anything could have been tampered with, but who the hell would do that and why?" Geoff said placing the damper with the other bits of the shock absorber unit on the bench. "Given the two theories, I'd say that these shocks were probably damaged during the crash. There was probably a fault waiting to be exposed."

Harry nodded, "Yes, you're right," he said.

Geoff continued to sort through the bits and show them to Harry, "You see," he said, "all the other parts look perfectly good, even the rubber bands are in good nick," and he handed one to Harry. Called a rubber band, it was a robust rubber loop that connected the tubular fork to the rear of the angular rocking bracket. Harry examined it and then placed it on the bench, "What would happen if that damper failed during a race?"

"The rider would find it difficult to control if it were on the bend, a little easier if he were on the straight."

"What sensation would he feel?"

"Well, I suppose the front of the bike would drop sharply and his weight would be thrown forward; after that, it depends on other variables, such as track condition, and speed." Geoff explained. "My guess is that the damper bottomed with some force, that's about the only thing that would do it. But it should hit the bottom with just the weight of the bike, so that's a bit unusual." Geoff continued to examine the bits and picked up the housing looking at the bottom, "A theory, this," and he pointed to the sliding mount at the top of the damper, "wasn't bolted firmly in place; and this scuffing of the paint around the eyelet suggests some movement prior to the crash, so it could have been loose."

"What would that do?" Harry asked.

Geoff twisted the housing to look at it again, "It means that it's possible that the shock wouldn't bottom out on the bump rubber before the mudguard made contact with the tyre."

"And that could happen when his front wheel ploughed into the deep shale?" Harry asked.

"Yes. That loose coupling represents a weakness that could collapse with a heavy impact and that might also explain the lack of resistance afterwards." Geoff said.

Harry kept thinking about Sonny and Steve Hildegarde, their argument and the opportunity the Steve had to loosen the shock absorber. What had Steve said to Sonny "You're a dead man Brent?" Well Steve's words had certainly come true.

Harry thanked Geoff for accommodating him during the inspection and wandered thoughtfully out into the pits where he saw Steve Hildegarde sorting out his tools and placing them neatly into the bright red 'Snap-on' mobile tool box that the Bulldogs supplied for all their mechanics. Harry came up behind him, "Hello Steve."

Steve swivelled round, Oh, hi Harry. What are you up to?"

"I was looking for you mate. We need to talk," Harry told him.

"Do we? What about?" the mechanic asked.

"About Sonny Brent and your argument with him. I heard what you said to him in the changing rooms."

Steve went pale and sat heavily in the plastic chair by the tool box, "Shit. What did you hear?"

"You're a dead man Brent," Harry repeated verbatim. Steve looked up at Harry with an anxious look. Harry went on, "If you sabotaged Sonny's bike you had better admit it to the police. It would go better for you if you did."

"That's bollocks Harry," he spat out, "I'm not bloody doing that! I never did nothing to his bike. I was angry with him and I thumped him in the stomach and, ok, I said a few threatening things in anger. But that's all. I wouldn't do anything like that to anyone, especially a best mate!"

"Even though he'd just screwed your girlfriend?" Harry asked pointedly.

"Yeah, even though he'd done that!"

"Take this as a warning Steve., "Harry said evenly, "If you are responsible, you'd better do something about it rather than let the

HSE investigation uncover something and get the police involved."

Steve stood up indignantly, "Look; I can't do anything about that and I don't know what HSE might or might not come up with. But I didn't do nothing that led to Sonny's death. So get off my back Harry!"

There was nothing left to say so Harry turned and walked quickly from the pits to the studio. He was angry with himself. He should have thought about how to confront Steve instead of going off half cocked. The only result of what he had done was to alert Steve to his suspicions and now he was pre-warned, prepared, angry and resentful. "Great, bloody well done Harry. You tosser!" He said to himself.

That evening Rosie cooked a meal and opened a bottle of wine. So they sat down together to eat and talk. There was a long silence as Harry moved the food around his plate until Rosie asked, "Is the food ok?"

Harry looked up, "Err; yes it is. What is it?"

"Cyanide en croute," she replied.

"It's lovely," Harry said distracted.

"Good."

He came too, "What did you say it was?"

"Beef Wellington with carrots, potatoes and baby sweetcorn."

It was very passable considering Rosie's usual efforts in the kitchen. The gravy was suspiciously lumpy, but the rest was pretty good. Maybe the potatoes could have done with another ten minutes or so; and the vegetables were a little overdone. "Yes, it's great thanks. The pastry's very nice indeed and the beef is very tasty."

"I'm pleased you like it."

"I didn't know you knew how to do Beef Wellington."

"I bought that in Sainsbury's," Rosie said acidly.

"Oh."

Rosie chuckled, "You are a bit of a bell-end sometimes"

"You can say that again," Harry responded.

"You are a bit of a bell-end sometimes"

Harry smiled at her, "Yes I am."

"I take it you've given a demonstration of bell-endedness today have you?" Rosie asked.

"A spectacular demonstration and he placed a forkful of beef and pastry into his mouth and closed his eyes in mock ecstasy, "Hmm hmm! Heavenly."

He told Rosie all about his run-in with Steve Hildegarde and she agreed that he had been at best hasty and, at worst, foolhardy."

By the end of the meal, all the wine was drunk and most of the food eaten, with the exception of the desert that might have been bread and butter pudding. Rosie told Harry about the arrangements the club had made to celebrate Sonny's life at the next meeting. The depression had lifted and they were talking happily when Rosie came round the table and put her arms around Harry's neck, kissed him on the top of his head. In silence she led him slowly to the shower, undressed him and then washed his body very slowly. When she finished, she squeezed the scented shower gel into his hand and pressed his hand against her body. Dried, powdered and naked, they went into the bedroom without a thought for Steve Hildegarde or Sonny Brent.

CHAPTER 3

Sunday 7th August 2016

arnie@arniecottrell
Busy week with police and HSE.. Team spirit is good and our riders are professionals so we will be battling for points

Davy Barns had been a talented, up and coming speedway rider who turned the speedway world on its head when he became British under Twenty-One Champion at his first attempt, successfully defended it twice, took silver in the British Championships in his second season and came fourth in the British Grand Prix as a wild card competitor. Davy had been in coma for almost ten years since the horrific crash in a Swedish Allsvenskan League match three days before his wedding to Rosie Higgins, his fiancée. The wedding they had been planning since they were fourteen years old and at school together which, as many described it, was a match made in Heaven. Rosie had been a regular visitor to the St. Boniface private hospital at Shamley Green not far from Godalming ever since Davy had been transferred from the Queen Elizabeth Hospital High Dependency Unit in Birmingham. Rosie used to visit Davy in hospital on a daily basis immediately after his accident, after a few months, it became a weekly ritual and now it was a monthly habit. She had become a firm favorite with the doctors and nurses there along with several patients who had got to know her well and were delighted when Harry had come into her life and they saw the love that existed between them. She walked through the double oak doors into the elegant Edwardian entrance hall and stood in the spacious lobby with its curved staircase and panelled walls. Nurse Paul Worrall looked up from behind the reception desk and smiled broadly, "Well hello Rosie Higgins! What a nice surprise."

"Hello handsome," Rosie grinned back.

A second nurse appeared in the doorway of the admin office, "I thought I recognised that voice," she said making the sign of a crucifix with her fingers, "Call the ward and warn them, sound the general alert then evacuate the building!" Mary Lambert saluted, "Hi Rosie how are you?" and she kissed the visitor lightly on the cheek.

"I'm good thanks Mary. You?"

"Same as always."

"Oh dear, never mind," and they both laughed.

The smile left Mary's face after a few seconds, "Before you go, have you got a few minutes?"

"Sure," Rosie answered frowning, "Is something wrong?" she asked as she followed the nurse into the admin office.

Mary went round her desk and sat down indicating that Rosie should do the same, "I just wanted to let you know that Davey's parents are here at the moment."

"That's great," Rosie said," I haven't seen them for a while."

"Maybe, but there's a serious purpose for them being here and I don't think you're going to like it."

"What is it?"

Mary hesitated, doubting the wisdom of this conversation, but then decided to go ahead with it, "I shouldn't tell you this, so please treat what I'm going to tell you with care, but I don't want you to hear it when you can't think about how to respond."

"My God, you'd better say it quickly because I'm beginning to get nervous," Rosie said.

"They are discussing the possibility of ending Davy's palliative care"

"You mean switch off his machine?" Rosie was shocked.

"No not technically, we can't do that. But if we cease feeding him it amounts to the same thing."

Rosie was shaking with the emotion that the revelation had aroused, "That's not right, they can't do that, can they?" she asked quietly.

"The short answer is, yes they can. Medically assisted nutrition and hydration can be seen as a medical intervention which puts it outside the basic provision of comfort, which is what we are obliged to offer."

"That's awful," Rosie said, "That's just, awful."

"I just wanted you to know so that you can compose yourself and think about it before you go up there," Mary explained.

Rosie smiled weakly, "Thanks Mary, you're a friend," and she reached out to squeeze the nurses hand.

When Rosie got to Davy's ward she was greeted by Peter and Dorothy Barns who were in deep conversation with Doctor Hammond who had been Davy's doctor for the past five years. Rosie gave no indication of her knowledge of the discussions they had been having and after a few minutes of light inconsequential chat Doctor Hammond coughed and raised the subject of Davy's future. Rosie had prepared herself and remained calm as she listened to the explanation of the options that were open to the family, of which, ceasing nutrition and hydration was one. Davey's mother looked at Rosie through eyes that had shed tears recently, "Rosie please try to understand that we have to think about this," she pleaded.

Rosie was angry, sad, desperate and confused, "I don't know what to say," she said, "how can you be even talking about such a thing as killing Davy?"

"That's not what we're talking about! What we're really talking about," Peter Barns interjected and then caught his breath, "what we're talking about is whether Davy is really alive."

Rosie swung round to face him, "Peter, with the greatest respect, I know you are an intelligent man, so you must recognise a rationalisation when you speak, or are you so desperate to ease your conscience that you don't see it?"

"What do you mean by that?" Davy's father asked with anger bubbling in his voice.

"Well, let's be clear and open about this, if you want to kill Davy it would be handy to have a rational explanation so that you could sit at home of an evening watching television without the ghastly guilty feeling disturbing the entertainment, wouldn't it?"

"How dare you," Peter Barns began.

"But we don't want to," Dorothy interrupted with intoned agony, "we want Davy to live, but Rosie, just look at him."

"So how did this discussion even start, if that's how you feel?" Rosie questioned. "Who raised the issue?"

"I did," Doctor Hammond intervened, "it's part of my duty as a doctor to think about the effectiveness of the treatment and to consider all the possible courses of action. It is also my responsibility to raise this with Davy's family."

"Isn't it illegal to switch off the machine?" Rosie asked.

"Yes of course it is. There are procedures and protocols to be observed as laid down by the General Medical Council and the ultimate decision is made by the Court of Protection or even a High Court Judge."

"I can't believe we are discussing it," Rosie said, "well I for one am against it!"

Peter Barns put his hand on Rosie's arm, "We understand and we will take your view into consideration, but ultimately this decision is mine, Dorothy's and the doctor's to make."

Rosie turned sharply shaking off Peter's hand, "I'll fight it if I can," she said as she strode down the corridor.

Dorothy Barns sobbed, "Rosie, please don't…" but Rosie ignored her entreaties and turned down the stairs with anger and fear in her heart.

As she went through the reception area Mary intercepted her, "Rosie, please wait. Don't go like this," she begged reaching out for her. Rosie shrugged her away but she persisted, "Rosie, for God's sake stop and listen!" she said sternly and grabbed her arm more firmly, "you cannot drive in this state."

That got through the red rage and Rosie turned to face her with tears streaming down her cheeks, "What are they thinking about Mary? Why are they talking about killing Davy after all we have done over all these years?"

Mary put her arms around her and pulled her body to hers, "Shh." She whispered in her ear, "I know how it must hurt. We are just talking about it. Nothing is going to happen in a hurry, if anything happens at all."

Rosie laid her head on Mary's shoulder and sobbed until she was silent and empty. They stood there for a few minutes, "I loved him so much and for so long," she said eventually.

"I know you did. I saw your love for him. It was deep and still is," Mary said softly.

"Not as much as I did I'm afraid." Rosie confided.

"No, but that's ok too. You have to live your life. You have the right to do that and Davy would have wanted that wouldn't he?"

Rosie sobbed, "Yes. Yes he would." She stood up with head bowed, "I suppose I was admitting that Davy was gone when I allowed myself to fall in love with Harry."

"In a way that's right isn't it," Mary agreed, "but that's natural in these circumstances." Rosie raised her head and looked at Mary, "You're a good person Mary Lambert," and she kissed affectionately.

Mary smiled sadly and took Rosie's hand in hers, "And you, Rosie Higgins are one of the nicest, gentlest people I have ever had the privilege to meet." She let go of her hand and brushed her skirt down, "You'd better wash your face before you leave."

"Yes, I bet I look a sight don't I?" Rosie said," I'd better go back and talk to Peter and Dorothy as well."

She spent a few minutes in the toilets and returned looking much fresher and went straight upstairs and found Davy's parents where she had left them. They looked up at her approach with anxiety in their eyes. Davy's mother said, "Rosie," and held her hands out. Rosie flew into her arms and held her hand out for Peter to take, which he did willingly.

"I'm so sorry," Rosie apologised, "I'm so sorry." And they all cried together again and held each other.

That night Rosie lay with her head on Harry's shoulder and cried herself to sleep. Her emotional attachment to Davy was still strong although not as strong as it had been when she would have described it as love. She now reserved that word for Harry and meant it every bit as sincerely as she had when she thought of Davy that way. Harry was amazingly without jealousy when she spoke about her feelings for Davy. He listened, sympathised and supported her in the way she was feeling about the decisions that the Barns family were trying to make and understood the high emotions she felt at the moment. And he did all this without making it about him and his needs. She loved him for that.

CHAPTER 4

Tuesday 9th August 2016

arnie@arniecottrell
Big week! Poole v Wolverhampton, Bulldogs v Leicester. Must win to take advantage of one of our main opponents losing.

The morning dawned bright and sunny and Rosie woke Harry with coffee, "If you get up now I will have Angels on Horseback waiting for you by the time you are showered and shaved," she bent down and put her lips right by his ear, "but you must shift you arse immediately," she whispered.

He opened one eye and looked at her face so close to his, "You temptress. Get thee behind me," he croaked hoarsely.

"I am discovered!" she whispered in mock horror and then bent even closer allowing the breath from her nostrils to blow lightly into his ear knowing it would drive him crazy.

"Angels on Horseback my child," she said seductively and pulled the duvet
off the bed exposing the naked form curled in the foetal position. "so get out of bed and ablute with all haste."

"Ablute? There no such word."

She smiled coldly, "There is now, so go and do it!"

They sat over breakfast talking about the coming day and discovered that the prospects that faced them were all depressing. Rosie had a meeting with Sonny's parents to discuss the funeral arrangements and what the club wanted to do to pay tribute during the service and then afterwards at the wake. Barry Leech was keen to hold the wake at the stadium that bore his name and at the club's expense. Harry had a programme to record and was considering going straight off to the meeting at Torquay where Rye House were visitors in their clash between tenth and eleventh in the Premier League. He had then planned to stay somewhere overnight and carry on down to Wimborne Road to catch Poole's Elite League meeting with Wolverhampton before coming back to London on the Thursday in time for the Bulldog's match against Lakeside. The other strong pull was the visit of Darcy Ward and his wife Lizzie and their Q&A session after the meeting. "What time will you be finished with Sonny's family?" he asked Rosie.

"Probably about lunchtime. Why?"

"Do you fancy coming down to Torquay with me and maybe onto Poole the next day?"

Poole? That's quite close to Swanage isn't it?" she asked.

"Yes, it's just down the road a few miles, why?"

"In that case, the answer's yes! I'll have to alter a few plans but that will ok. I'll organise a car and pick you up at the stadium."

"Sounds good to me," Harry said raising his tea cup as a salute.

"And I might have an idea that will lift the atmosphere even higher," she added.

Harry's eyebrows arched, "Oh yes? What is it?"

"A surprise," Rosie replied, "and by definition, you will not know until I decide that you should. I need to make a phone call to see if I can make it happen."

They drove on down to Torquay and arrived about an hour before the meeting started. Rosie was visibly shocked at the condition of the venue. It could not be called a stadium; it could hardly be called anything other than a hole in the ground with a track in the bottom of it. She stood by the dilapidated entrance gates with her mouth open taking in the impoverished state of the rusted metal tables with shreds of plastic curling up where people had tried to peel the cracked surface off and the bare metal frames of the seats that, at some point in the past had been involved in a fire and were completely devoid of covering. And in a surreal juxtaposition, a sparklingly modern mobile kitchen was serving fish and chips, burgers and hotdogs amongst many other delicious looking alternatives. Rosie supposed this was an independent trader and not owned by the club and she was right.

Harry asked, "Would you like a drink Madam?"

"I would be delighted," Rosie answered, "Where?"

"Over here, if Madam would care to follow me," and Harry indicated a wooden shed with a wooden decking patio. "If you would care to choose a table, I will get the drinks from within."

To be fair to the Torquay club, the shed was a double shed and inside it was a perfectly passable club house with a bar and a couple of games machines. A few fans sat in cheerful groups drinking beer and discussing the forthcoming meeting. When they finished their drinks Harry suggested a tour of the stadium. This involved no more than a walk along a path that took them on an upward slope around the third and fourth bends to the top of the grass bank that overlooked the back straight, dipped down to a lower level on the first and second bend and on round at track level on the start and finish straight where most of the six or seven hundred strong crowd were gathered.

The track was small and tight but appeared to be in good condition. The fences, however, were not of the air fence variety and looked as if they would do some damage to any rider that got involved with them.

Harry smiled at Rosie's reaction to it all, "Welcome to the National League," he said putting his arm around her shoulders.

Rosie looked around her, "Harry, I've been to National League venues before and they're better than this."

Harry agreed, "Yes, I suppose this is the worst. It's hard to see how it stays in business. The fans are passionate and loyal but the management don't seem to want to, or aren't able to, invest in the infrastructure. It's a great shame."

"It must be hard to get sponsorship too, I don't suppose there many sizeable businesses in the region who could afford to put enough money into this to make much of a difference."

The fans were beginning to drift in and by the time the meeting began, the small venue seemed full, a great atmosphere was generated and the racing was exciting and close with plenty of overtaking.

"Cup of tea?" Harry asked Rosie as they passed a two-berth caravan with its end window tilted open.

"Why not," she replied and grinned widely as a man handed two plastic cups of tea through the window to them together with a cheerful, "Sugar?"

They carried their teas down and round towards the first bend to watch the racing. The crowd there was about four deep and they had some difficulty seeing the races so they moved to the slightly higher ground on the second bend. Jamie Crompton was the rider of the night with a maximum of fifteen points from five rides for Torquay, although Rye House scraped a 44 to 48 point win on a night of exciting racing that had the fans chattering between races.

"I think this track offers some the best racing in all the leagues even though it looks like a load of rubbish," Harry commented, "It never fails to deliver."

As he spoke these words, he became aware of something happening up by the first bend where they had been standing at the start of the meeting. A heated debate seemed to be taking place between a couple of fans and one of the security staff in a high-vis yellow jacket. Harry excused himself and moved slowly towards to the small group that was forming.

"I've been going to speedway for thirty years and coming here since it opened and I've never had anyone say anything to me about it before!" the short stocky man remonstrated.

"I can't help that sir. The rules are the rules and I've got to ask you to stop using them."

"There's lots of people that use boxes and step-ladders like mine to watch the speedway over the heads of the crowd," the fan pointed to three people doing exactly that over by the second bend, "with no racked seats or terraces, how are we supposed to see if you're stood at the back?"

"It's a health and safety policy now sir, so we're not going to allow it any more." Harry realised that this was Jim Norman the new Health and Safety Manager at Torquay who was making an issue out of people using step-ladders to get a clear view of the racing.

"As far as I'm aware," the man said, "there's never been an accident involving any of these sorts of things in all the years we've been doing it."

"That's beside the point sir. The fact is we have run a risk analysis on it and it comes out in the red band and that's high. Apart from that, it's a risk that our insurance company is not willing to entertain, so you'll have to get down and stay down," Jim Norman told him assertively.

"It's bloody ridiculous!" You can't do this; I'm going to watch the speedway from up here just like I have done for the last fifteen years."

"You are not going to do that sir because if you try I will have you ejected from the stadium." Jim threatened.

Harry watched as the interaction degenerated into insults and threats until Jim Norman finally spoke into his radio and asked for two security officers to attend. In front of the whole assembly of spectators the shamed fan was escorted, along with his offending three step step-ladder, under the old wooden stand and deposited in the car park. Harry quietly followed and caught up with him as he was putting his steps in the boot of his car.

"Excuse me sir," he said, "I couldn't help witnessing what happened back there. My name is Harry Marsh, I work for Speedway FM and I'd like to interview you with a view to broadcasting a piece about it. Would you be willing to do that?"

"Too true I would," the man said, "My names Rick Berkley."

Harry got an animated interview which encapsulated how Mr Berkley felt about the incident both from a health and safety angle and from the point of view of the way in which he was made to feel picked upon and foolish in front of the spectators, many of whom he knew well. "You saw how many people came round to support me didn't you?" he said angrily, "It's Health and Safety gone mad; that's what it is, Health and Safety gone stark raving mad!"

Harry went back into the stadium after the interview through the machinery park that butted up to the second bend at the Nutbush Lane track and went looking for Jim Norman. When he found him, Jim Norman didn't want to give an interview, so Harry decided to give him a bit of space and let the temperature cool down a bit. It was after heat 15 that he ran into the Health and Safety Manager again, "Mr. Norman, I really would like to get your views on the issue from earlier so that I present a balanced piece, otherwise it'll just be Mr. Berkley's views that get aired."

"Whose Mr. Berkley?" asked Jim Norman.

"The punter you threw out earlier. The step-ladders?" Harry said.

Jim Norman thought about it for a moment and decided that, if this Harry Marsh was going to broadcast something on the subject, he had better be represented otherwise it could be very one-sided and misinterpreted.

The Torquay HSE Manager, was a man who knew his own mind and saw it as a duty to tell others what he thought about every and any subject. He was a living embodiment of a man who presented his opinions as facts and seemed to have an aversion to grey areas that might start to cloud his conviction. His ability to selectively listen to others enabled him to formulate judgments and decisions that had all the benefits of speed and apparent clarity and all the disadvantages of depriving others of opportunities to contribute,creating new and different problems while solving the original difficulty. With those who disagreed or differed from him, Jim Norman was protected from their stupidity by what Harry called the 'disease of certainty'. The worst symptom of the disease afflicts the patient with the capacity to be absolutely certain that they are right whilst actually being wrong. It is a blessing for the patient that an accompanying symptom prevents them suffering a complete self-esteem meltdown. This symptom usually manifests itself as the ability to delude oneself that either the other person is an idiot and occasionally may require the skilled application of post rationalisation to explain away anything that appears to be a mistake on the patient's part. It is almost a mandatory requirement of anyone who wishes to work in HSE or act as a sports referee. Jim Norman had all of this in spades! To those who agreed or were aligned with his personality, ideas and values, he possessed the 'God like' qualities of being able to supply clarity and direction. To those who thought differently, he was stubborn, authoritarian and bullying.

"So what do you want to know?" he asked Harry testily.

"Just tell me what happened from your point of view," Harry suggested holding out the small digital recorder so that the Health and Safety Manager could speak into it.

"Ok," Jim Norman said relaxing a little, "We have been aware that quite a few people have been bringing step-ladders and boxes to the stadium in order to stand on them to get a better view of the racing. It's our view that these represent an unacceptable health and safety risk to the public and that we should stop it forthwith. We put this to the Management of the club and they felt that they should be guided by our expertise. What you saw tonight was me putting that decision into action."

"Aren't some people are going to find it difficult to see this as a risky activity? I can remember people doing it when I was a youngster; they've been doing this for years now."

"That's not really the point is it? People have been doing all sorts of things for a long time. That doesn't mean it's not dangerous."

"How many accidents are you aware of that involve people standing on boxes and step-ladders at speedway meetings?" Harry asked.

"There are no figures that I know of, so I can't say." Jim Norman answered.

"Have you ever seen or heard of such an accident?" Harry pressed.

"I don't need to have seen or heard of one to know that it's an unacceptable risk. It's obvious isn't it?"

"Well the very lack of evidence suggests that it is not a risk of any substance." Harry persisted.

"We don't think of it like that. Just because no evidence has been gathered doesn't mean that there isn't any somewhere." Jim Norman insisted feeling himself being forced into a corner.

"On that basis," Harry queried, "You shouldn't be surprised if people aim criticism at you for spoiling things in the name of specious safety. You know the commonplace comment about Health and Safety gone mad?"

Jim Norman, irritated by this remark, came back with energy, "What you people don't seem to understand is that we have a legal responsibility for the welfare of the public. That can't be taken lightly and certainly won't be compromised because ill-informed trouble makers make comments like that."

"Of course not Mr. Norman and I'm not suggesting that anyone should be placed in danger, but surely some of the responsibility should be placed on the individual members of the public you are trying to protect."

"And when you do that," Jim Norman declared, "They do things like we had tonight."

"Isn't that the point though?" Harry argued, "They are happy to take whatever risk that represents. Couldn't you ask them to sign a rider that vindicates you from any responsibility?"

"That's not the way Health and Safety works. It's our job to formalise the way things happen at public events. We can't have people doing whatever they want, it would cause mayhem."

"I think that many people will see you as a kind of policeman who is spoiling their enjoyment of an event they have paid good money to see. How do you respond to that?" Harry continued.

"Their payment enables them to attend the event. It does not entitle them to become a danger to themselves and, more importantly, to others." Jim Norman said pointedly.

"How will they become a danger to others?"

"Well," Jim Norman's eyes rose to the sky in exasperated disbelief, "Suppose the steps malfunction in some way and the person falls off the steps and hurts someone else? They may trap their fingers; they could even lose a finger in such an accident."

"I suppose those things are possible, but the question is, who should be responsible for that and who should say whether people can do it or not." Harry said.

"The answer to that is simple, "Jim Norman answered, "I am and as long as we live in a litigation society, people will not be able to stand on things at my speedway track."

"Is that really how you see it, your speedway track?" Harry asked.

"You know what I mean, don't start to twist my words," the Safety Manager said.

"Let me ask you why you felt the need to eject the man from the stadium."

"That's straight forward enough. Our policy is that of zero tolerance on people who cause trouble inside the stadium."

"In what way was he causing trouble?" Harry enquired.

"He wouldn't do what we were asking him to do."

"I watched what was happening and I thought Mr. Berkley wanted to talk about the issue, but you didn't seem to want to listen. Do you think that's what added to his irritation and caused him to be a little more belligerent?"

"As far as I was concerned there was nothing to be discussed, he had to get off the step-ladder and that was that."

"So, his non-compliance with your order was the real issue that got him ejected?" Harry pressed.

"Well, non-compliance with the safety policy is enough to warrant ejection." Jim Norman hesitated for a moment, "Look Mr. Marsh. Things will be changing around here from now on because Health and Safety matters in business and clubs like this and we have to take it seriously. There are legal constraints and issues that have to be imposed and the fans are going to have to get used to that fact, whether they like it or not."

The interview came to a sudden end as Jim Norman turned and walked away. Harry switched off his recorder and tapped it fondly, this was gold, pure gold."

CHAPTER 5

Wednesday 10th August 2016

arnie@arniecottrell
A win tomorrow over Lakeside will keep us in contact. If Poole beat Kings Lynn it'll stay very close at the top!

Harry and Rosie decided to drive down to Poole to catch their meeting with Kings Lynn in the evening, but Rosie had an agenda that would take up the afternoon. "I want you to meet someone special, well special to me anyway."

"If he's special to you then he's already special to me," Harry said.

"Shut up you silver tongued romancer. You going to meet my Uncle Max. I think you'll like him. He's weird. Wonderfully weird," she told Harry. "Of course, he's a complete embarrassment to the family and there are several who would really like him to die quietly but he seems to have other plans."

"Can't wait," Harry said, "is he related to Barry?"

"Brother."

"I see."

"Yes, you probably think you do, but reserve judgment."

The drive took them past Poole, on past Wareham, through the heart of Purbeck Stone country with its beautiful villages, delightful cottages, functional quarries and stone masons, over the rolling hills and down into the lovely coastal town of Swanage. This beautiful seaside resort was a revelation to Harry and he instantly fell in love with the quirky mix of Victorian and Brutalist architecture. As they entered the town they approached the pretty little railway station that is home to the Swanage Railway Trust and some lovingly preserved steam and diesel engines along with their period carriages. Harry insisted that they stop and take a look. They had a cup of tea in the old railway carriage café and watched the engine as steam issued from various vales, pipes and secret places that could not be seen without getting down and under the machine. "Oh my goodness," Harry waxed, "just suck it in. The steam, the oil, the….the soul, the smell!"

Rosie's eyes rose to the ceiling, "I'm going to have rethink my choices of perfume in the light of the last twenty four hours. Do they make Au de Castrol?" She looked sternly across at Harry, "I didn't know you were a railway enthusiast."

"I love engines of any sort!" Harry explained through a mouthful of toasted teacake, "I'm not really bothered about what they're connected to, but I think Steam engines are one of the greatest joys in life. They're real works of art as far as I'm concerned."

Rosie nodded, "And on that note," she said rising from her seat," Let's go and see my Uncle Max."

They drove through the town and parked outside a small art gallery next door to a quintessential seaside shop called Bill's Bits.

"On my," Harry started, "just get…."

"Don't!" Rosie pointed a long elegant finger at him.

"I was just going to say…"

"Don't, just don't," she laughed.

Swanage is a long time haven for artists of all disciplines and persuasions. It boasts music festivals and events of many hues from folk, blues, jazz to classical music and five or six commercial art galleries which tend to be full of landscapes, mostly of Swanage and Old Harrys Rocks. Uncle Max was a long standing and notorious member of the artistic community that worked and lived in this creative environment. His home was a combined studio and shop for creating and selling his work. It was a gathering place for artists and musicians and characters of unconventional leanings who, like him, tended to disrupt and disturb the conservative elements in the community. His shop was fifty meters from a small pebble beach next to the Pier Head which, in keeping with the spirit of the town, proudly sported a wonderful mural that provided great photo opportunities for visitors. Harry and Rosie approached the entrance to the shop only to find a notice posted on the inside of the window stating,

'CLOSED
due to lethargy brought
on by old age and whiskey'

"Don't take any notice of that," Rosie said knocking firmly on the glass of the door. The face of a bearded man appeared around the edge of a doorway at the far side of the shop that led to a back room and smiled hugely. The man, who must have been in his mid-seventies with white hair like Albert Einstein, spectacles like John Lennon and a beard like Karl Marx, started across the shop wiping his hands on his multicoloured shirt which had obviously cleaned his hands, brushes and pallet knives over many years. He opened the door and opened his arms very wide, "Rosie, Rosie, Rosie my dear. How wonderful to see you," and he planted a kiss on her cheek.

"Uncle Max, this is Harry Marsh. Harry, this is my favorite Uncle, Max."

They shook hands, "Would you like a cup of tea or coffee or maybe something stronger?" Uncle Max asked.

"Coffee will be fine thanks," Rosie replied.

Max was tall and thin, he wore brown corduroy trousers, paint spotted suede shoes and a collarless shirt under his working shirt with red braces. While he made the coffee, Harry looked around the walls of the studio on which were hung about twenty abstract paintings presented in simple white frames with pale gray mounts. Most of them seemed to have been done with broad brushes, pallet knives and, Harry thought, maybe fingers. The colour combinations were often surprising but Harry found himself strangely attracted to them. If someone had suggested that they might use them together, he would have doubted their taste, but they worked in execution.

"I love your colours," Harry told him as he took his coffee from the artist, "The colours are…are…unexpected."

"Thank you Henry," Max grinned at his diplomacy, "I've had a lot of people say things like that. I think it's because I'm red – green colour blind. But I know my colour theory, so I trust in that and get on with it."

Uncle Max explained how he had exhibited all over Europe, the States and Asia and sold through various agents in a dozen countries, "although the interweb is proving very useful nowadays," he said, "but I like Swanage, so I stay here and sell direct from the studio when I want to."

"Yes we saw the sign," Rosie put in, "you are dreadful you know."

"It amuses me my dear and adds to my image as an eccentric artist."

"But you are an eccentric artist Uncle Max," she said.

"It's just an act," Max replied.
"It might have been once, but not now, now I'm just a drunken old artist."

Harry turned from one of the larger paintings, "Do you sell many Uncle Max?"

"Henry, you must call me Max please. Sell many? Not really, but I don't need to sell many to maintain my standard of living," and he took a sizable drink from the tumbler of whiskey he had poured while making the coffee.

Harry and Max walked around looking at paintings and eventually Rosie who had gone off to make fresh coffee came back and handed another very large whiskey to her Uncle Max. "Bless you my child," he said taking it from her. "She's the only one in the family who accepts that I drink too much without making any judgments. I'm thankful for that of course. The rest of my family would love it if I kicked the bucket and leave them what they mistakenly believe is my fortune." He grinned wickedly and winked, "Rather irresponsibly, I have spent it all," he laughed and demolished half the whiskey in the glass.

"So, you are still working?" Harry asked.

"Of course," Max said, "Being an artist isn't like having a regular job. It is what you are and always will be."

"I'm don't really know anything about art," Harry admitted. "and I don't want to offend you by being too personal, but I can see the prices you ask for your work; they are very expensive, at least to my mind £20,000 is an awful lot of money, but you don't seem to have a standard of living the reflects that kind of income."

"Well I did say, I've spent it all," Max replied grinning back.

"He's playing with you Harry," Rosie commented from her comfortable position on a large sofa, "tell the poor boy what you do with the money Uncle Max."

"I keep some of the money to live on, and the rest goes to charities."

Harry's eyebrows rose in surprise, "That sounds wonderful, how much are you able to donate?"

"It varies from year to year, but I guarantee that at least seventy-five percent goes to charity. I don't need very much money to be happy, I don't spend my time wanting things," Max explained. "You strike me as a man cut from similar cloth, am I right?"

"I don't know," Harry replied, "I don't own very much and I don't yearn for things."

"It's one of the things I like best about him uncle." Rosie chipped in, "I've had to buy him some clothes, his flat was very small and his job doesn't pay very well but he does it because he loves it. The only thing he has that worth anything is an old Triumph Bonneville motorcycle"

Harry turned the subject back to the artist, "Do you mind telling me how much you gave to charity last year?"

"I don't mind at all," Max responded and he thought for a few moments, "I painted five works last year so I should say those works raised about £150,000 for some charities and I kept about £50,000 I should think. So, you see, I still had plenty to live on."

"Do you ever think about how much you could have if you'd kept it all?" Harry asked.

"Occasionally, but then I think about the greed and avarice involved in that way of thinking, and the troubled mind that comes with worrying about losing it all or the anxiety that comes with hording it; that's not for me thanks."

Harry liked what he heard but could hardly believe that it was actually working and said this to Uncle Max.

"It's not particularly surprising, it's just that I don't need to make a profit," Max said, "the reason it feels like an uncomfortable idea, or even impossible is because the big business and politics have brainwashed us into thinking that there are no other alternatives to capitalism and communism. There are more and more 'not for profit' organisations starting up and I think it will become a very common method of working. Organisations like Spinux and Wirewolf are huge now and work because of the volunteers who offer their skills for nothing. They wouldn't do that if they thought they were lining the pockets of shareholders who are only in it for the money."

"Well I think it's great sir, I really do."

"What about Speedway FM, are you in it for profit?" Max asked.

"I'd say we are 'not for profit' but not through choice," Harry joked, "but I am going to have a conversation with Johnny about this."

Uncle Max finished off his tumbler of whiskey and wandered across the room to find the bottle, "What kinds of art do you like Henry?"

Harry looked at Rosie who just grinned at him, "I don't really know much about art," he replied.

"Not many people do Henry," the artist agreed," but that doesn't stop them talking about it at length."

"I like the Pre-Raphaelites, the Impressionists, Pop Art, Art Deco and Art Nouveau," Harry offered.

"All the popular movement then?" Max responded.

"Yes I guess that's right, I only know what I see on television or in magazines. I suppose they're popular for a reason though, aren't they?" Harry asked.

"Well put. There's a lot of truth in that." Max agreed.

"Do you always paint abstract?" Harry asked.

"Yes. I've got a camera for the other stuff." Max replied and then added, "It seems it's the best way for me to get out what's inside."

"That's important to you is it?"

"It's the only thing that is important to me. Everything else is superficial."

"Aren't you just being contentious when you say that?" Harry asked.

Max turned to Rosie, "I like your boyfriend," he said, "To the point. Direct and he's not scared is he?"

Rosie smiled broadly, "I knew you would," she said with satisfaction.

The elderly artist went on, "No I'm not just being contentious. I do mean what I say. Oliver Wendell Holmes wrote, 'What lies behind you and what lies ahead of you are nothing compared with what lies within you.' I believe that. So I try to paint what is within me." He laughed shortly, "Mind you, looking at some of the paintings, that might seem a bit disturbing." The elderly man took a big swig of whiskey and swilled it round his mouth, "If I'm not here to communicate and participate, what the hell am I doing here?"

"And what if a person doesn't get a chance to express it, what if something happens to stop them?" Harry asked.

Max frowned, "We all get our opportunity, but if you're not on the look-out for it, I suppose they could come and go without being taken," he finished his whiskey, "but life is circular isn't it so you could catch it next time round. Just be ready to jump on when it's your turn."

Harry sat listening to Uncle Max, "Where there is life, there is hope," he mused.

"Very much so," Max agreed. He walked to the window and pointed out at the scene, "Look at that," he said, "The sea, the birds, the seaweed, the flowers, grass, butterflies, bees, the wind, the sky. They've all got one thing in common. Like us, they're all alive. We, with them, are all part of the same process of living.

It needs to be respected you know." Rosie and Harry looked out of the window and pondered his words. "Is that a bit soppy and green for you two?"

Rosie turned to him and said, "No. No it's not. In fact, it might be very timely."

"I guess it might depend on what you call life," Harry put in.

"Go on," Max invited.

"Well, what about someone who is in a coma and is considered to be in a persistent vegetative state?"

"I take it you're asking whether or not their machine should be switched off." Max asked.

"In essence, yes."

"I imagine the medical people are talking about quality of life as a way of deciding?" the elderly artist went on.

"Yes," Rosie answered.

"And who will decide what that means?"

"A High Court Judge finally," Rosie replied.

"Is that supposed to be reassuring?"

"I think so."

"This is close to you isn't it?" Max enquired.

"Yes," she responded simply.

"But?"

"But, I don't have legal say in the decision. My opinion is valued but it is only one of several opinions and mine differs from the decision makers."

"I see. Well, it is a decision that must be made on the basis of deep conviction otherwise it will return to haunt those who make it." Max said.

Harry looked at the artist, "Have you ever had experience of anything like this yourself?" he asked.

Max sat thoughtfully, "Yes I have," he answered eventually, "My wife; Rosie's aunty was similarly struck down not long after we were married. She was involved in a terrible road accident and hovered between life and death for several weeks until I eventually to succumbed to arguments that said I should agree to cease keeping her alive by mechanical means. She was not in a coma and would have died of her injuries eventually."

"Did you, do you ever regret your decision?" Harry asked.

"I'm not sure regret is the right word. Certainly I have had, and still get pangs of guilt. Your comment about 'where there is life there is hope' resounds like a bell tolling in my mind." The trio fell into a thought filled silence. This was broken when Max, looking at his empty glass and rising to replenish it, said "Presumably there is little prospect of this person coming out of the coma?"

"On the basis that anything is possible, he could," Rosie said, "He probably won't; but he could."

There didn't seem to be anything else to say on the subject so Rosie made more coffee and poured yet another whisky for Max. They discussed their love of Speedway, Battersea Bulldogs, Sonny Brent's death and Harry's job as a radio reporter.

"And this is not broadcast using radio frequencies?" Max enquired.

Harry explained, "No, we broadcast over the internet which is entirely different."

"Do you have to have a license for that?"

"No," Harry went on," because we are not using any radio frequencies."

"I see. I think I see anyway."

Harry started to explain again, but Max raised his boney hand, "It's ok Henry, I don't understand but let's leave it as a mystery for me to wonder at." Changing the subject abruptly he waved his hand around the walls, "I'd like you to choose any one of these paintings and have it with my love."

They offered resistance, but he was insistent and they chose a small, energetic and colourful piece that would go well in the bedroom.

"So where are you going to now?" Uncle Max asked them.

"Poole are riding against Kings Lynn tonight and I'm going to cover it for the station," Harry told him.

"Why don't you come with Uncle Max?" Rosie asked with enthusiasm.

"It sounds splendid and normally would love to, but tonight I am giving a talk on American Abstract Expressionists to the local U3A. He saw the blank looks on the youngster's faces and explained further, "University of the 3rd Age. It's a load of pensioners who want to keep their education going. Actually it's a brilliant idea and it's international."

"And tonight it's you?"

"Yes. I chose the subject with a bit of devilment in me. I can't see them naturally falling in love with Jackson Pollock, can you? But I think they might go for Mark Rothko. I bet they won't ask me again!" and he laughed out loud at the thought of it all,

As they went to the car Harry turned to shake hands with the artist, "Thank you," he said.

"For what?" Max asked genuinely.

"Your thoughts. They helped."

Rosie kissed him on his cheek, "Yes they did. Thanks."

"I am pleased. I hope you will come and see me again."

"I would love to do that," Harry said and meant it.

"We've had a wonderful time my darling Uncle. Next time we come down to Poole for the speedway, we'll come and collect you and take you with us."

"Oh, that sounds absolutely marvelous!" Max enthused.

"That'll be a Wednesday," Harry added.

"Which Wednesday?"

"Not sure at the moment, but I'll call you and let you know when we know." Rosie said as she slid into the driving seat of the hire car.

"It'll be soon because it's part of my job," Harry told him.

Uncle Max winked at him, "Some job eh?"

"I know," Harry grinned back.

Max stuck his head through the car window and kissed Rosie, "You make sure you keep your hands on Henry." he told Rosie, "He's a good one," he added in a whisper.

"I know," she whispered back, "and he's called Harry."

"I know that," he retorted pulling his head back from the window.

There are few pleasures to match a warm summer's evening at Wimborne Road. The sun slowly setting behind the restaurant stand, the sound of seagulls, and the view across the bay. Harry savoured the moment and drank in the intoxicating atmosphere, the twilight and his favourite sport as the crowd began to fill the old stand and to filter round the earthen bank above the first and second bends where they could look down on the track from their elevated position. The smell of hot dogs and burgers from the mobile kitchen, eating chips with those wooden forks that had that awful dry feeling in your mouth, and drinking tea while leafing through the official programme to see who would be racing who in what heats all contributed to the feeling of well-being and quiet excitement. Fans browsed in the converted graffiti style painted shipping container that doubled as a very effective club shop where they presented themselves as do pilgrims approaching the object of their divine journey, to take reverential delivery of their copy of the that weeks' Speedway Star. And then the almost mind-altering sounds and smells of the bikes as the mechanics started to prepare the set-up for the first races. Harry turned to Rosie and grinned from ear to ear, he could not have been happier than he was that night.

They had a very successful evening as Poole comprehensively beat Kings Lynn 65 to 25 in a match where the Pirates were superb while the East Anglia team dipped well below their normal form and suffered some poor luck to boot. Brady Kurtz on 11 paid 14 was selected by Darcy Ward as Rider of the Night over his higher scoring team mate Chris Holder. Harry got an excellent interview with the team captain who had continued his improving form with an outstanding 14 paid 15 to inspire from his Captain's position and dominate the meeting.

They had stood on the second bend for most of the evening where they were able to see through to the pits and record some atmospheric stuff for inserts behind the interviews. It also gave them an opportunity to see and talk with the Poole riders who loved to sit on the viewing platform by the pit fence in order to watch the racing. Rosie was less impressed with the regular showers of shale that pelted them and the clouds of red-brown dust that swept over them as the bikes sped round the bend and off up the back straight. Harry just laughed and dismissed her complaints, "It's an important part of the experience!" he shouted at her over the noise of the engines. "Anyway," he added, "if you stand here you can drink in the intoxicating smell of methanol." He raised his nose higher and inhaled, "Oh man, just get a load of that!"

Rosie curled her lips with disdain, "Oh shut up!" she said.

"You uncultured philistine," Harry replied, "For your information I have seriously considered producing aerosol cans of that aroma especially for speedway fans who suffer withdrawal symptoms during the close season."

"Rosie laughed out loud, "Yeah, right"

Harry looked hurt, "If someone else did it, I'd buy a dozen immediately!"

The Q&A with Darcy had been an emotional affair with strong feelings of love and genuine affection filling the room. Harry managed to grab a couple of minutes with him afterwards and was impressed with the way this popular star had come to terms with his new way of life and wanted to act as an inspiration to others who suffer life changing injuries. "You know, I think Darcy is even more popular now than he was before his accident," he told Rosie when he met her in the bar afterwards, "people have really stepped up to support him. It's great."

Finally, Harry and Rosie met with Mat Ford and Neil Middleditch to get their thoughts on the clubs push to catch Wolverhampton and Belle Vue at the top of the Elite League. He was also very interested in their pleasure at Bjarne Pedersen's return to the team and his pragmatic and supportive philosophy to riding at reserve.

CHAPTER 6

Thursday 11th August 2016

Harry spent Thursday morning with Rosie, sleeping late in her Notting Hill flat, making love, eating a slow breakfast, reading the newspapers and drinking coffee. They talked about Uncle Max and laughed at his insistence on calling Harry, Henry. They also admired his commercial acumen and were thankful for his wisdom. Rosie talked to Harry about Peter and Dorothy Barns and the matter of withdrawing Davey's nutrition. Harry was genuinely upset about Davey's prospects and Rosie was touched that he felt that way and a great deal of clarity had come from this and the conversation with Uncle Max. She knew now with a certainty that she didn't want it to happen.

Thursday afternoon's show was pretty much back to normal with the exception of a few calls and the announcement of the funeral date for the following Monday morning, the sale of sonny Brent wrist bands from which the proceeds would go to the Speedway Rider's Benevolent Fund and the intention to have a one minutes applause at the beginning of the next meeting. In addition, Harry broadcast the HSE interview with Jim Norman and Rick Berkley and didn't need to edit very much to achieve the controversy that he always felt was built into it. As a consequence the lines buzzed with texts and emails absolutely pouring in. Most of them in condemnation, and a few in support, of Jim but Harry gave them a balanced airing and sensed there might be the potential for something on the theme along the lines that Tony Fuller had suggested. He decided that he would talk to Johnny about it and develop the idea further.

Later that day, Harry was returning to the studio having had coffee with Rosie in her office. As he ran up the stairs to the studio to collect his crash helmet a voice boomed out, "Walk, don't run!" Harry stopped dead in his tracks with shock. It had been a long time since anyone had addressed him in the style of a school teacher. Tony Fuller sat behind his desk scowling at him through the open HSE office door, "I want a word with you," he said tightly.

Harry stood still and collected his thoughts. He determined that he would not play the compliant or rebellious child to Tony's critical parent, but that he would rather try to stay calm and rational. Tony Fuller pointed to the chair opposite him. "Sit down a minute."

Harry's hackles rose effortlessly at this patronising display from Tony, so he thought it best to buy some time before engaging with him, "Give me a minute mate while I put my stuff in the office and I'll be with you." Harry said moving towards the studio door.

"Make it quick then, I haven't got time to waste!"

"I will Tony, I know how busy you are," Harry called ducking into the kitchen area and grabbing the kettle, "Do you want a drink Tony?" He knew this was mischievous, but he couldn't resist it because, even though he knew he shouldn't, he did actually enjoy playing the rebellious child. More to the point, he knew that he should not be doing this to Tony Fuller because Tony had no resistance to getting hooked into the predictable roles which would only lead to grief for both of them.

"Not just now! Just get on with it will you?" Tony's voice was strained with frustration.

Harry made himself a coffee and controlled himself. His anger and frustration had gone now so that he felt able to manage whatever was about to come. He strolled across the hall and into the HSE Manager's office with a pleasant smile and a steaming mug of coffee.

"Now, what can I do for you Tony?" he asked with a broad smile, "You seem agitated."

"You are way out of line mister!" Tony snapped, "And we expect an apology."

"We?" He raised his eyebrows, "to whom are you referring?"

"The HSE of course. How dare you try to make fools out of my colleagues?"

"I'm not aware that I have done that. Are we talking about Jim Norman at Torquay?"

"Don't come all innocent with me and try to be clever, you know I'm talking about the interview you put out today. Jim was seething."

"Did you hear it Tony?" Harry asked.

"No I did not!"

"I'd have thought it would be difficult to make any kind of judgment about the content if you haven't heard it."

"Well obviously Jim told me about it. He was on the phone as soon as we opened up this morning, complaining to me."

"Why was he complaining to you?" Harry queried.

"He wanted me to tell you what we think about what you did and get the broadcast stopped"

"Well I suppose any feedback is always helpful, but what a shame he didn't feel able to talk to me directly," Harry said, "Anyway, whatever made him think that you had any editorial influence in Speedway FM?"

"He assumed that I could…." He spluttered to a halt.

Harry's eyebrows went travelling up his forehead again, "I see. Well that was a mistake wasn't it? But never mind, no harm done."

"What you don't seem to realise is that we don't like what you did," Tony said trying to re-establish the dominance he felt that he had lost.

"Yes I do Tony. Jim let me know immediately after the interview."

"And you still went ahead with the broadcast? How dare you?"

"It didn't take any courage on my part. I did it because it was good material that reflected differing views about a subject that had raised some real passion on the night. Unfortunately, Tony came across in a bad light because he behaved badly."

"I'm telling you now. Don't do anything like that again or you and I will have a major fallout," Tony fumed.

Harry looked around the room, stood up and walked over to a rather nicely presented football referee's whistle suspended in a clear acrylic block. He picked it up and examined it carefully. Tony watched him attentively. "This is a lovely thing isn't it," Harry observed holding it up so that he could examine it before placing it gently on the desk in front of Tony Fuller. "If I recall correctly, you were presented with this when you retired from the FA and gave up your role as a referee. I am right aren't I?"

"Yes, yes, but what the hell has this got to do with…."

Harry raised his forefinger, "Bear with me Tony and I think it will become clear enough." Harry sat down again and took his time, "As a referee," he continued, "I imagine you become accustomed to being in charge of things, telling people what to do and expecting them to obey. And if they objected or questioned your judgment, you had the power to punish them. Am I about right?"

"Well yes, but…"

"Again, stay with me Tony," Harry held his hand up to stop him, "As a retired referee you probably realise that you can no longer expect people to react to you in the same way as before."

"No. Yes. I realise that." Tony agreed.

"Quite," Harry nodded, "and yet you think you can call me into your office and chastise me like some child that has misbehaved. In addition, you think I should quietly do as I'm told." Harry leaned forward on the desk, "I want you to understand my position so that you don't make the same mistake again." Tony shrank back in his chair and Harry went on, "You are not a referee of my job, my life or my anything. You have no jurisdiction over me and you are not my parent. Therefore, if you wish to keep my friendship, you will never speak to me in that way again." Harry sat back in his chair, "I hope that I have my position clear for you because I would hate it if you mistook my quiet calmness as a sign of softness or weakness." Harry stood up, "Good to chat Tony. I'll see you tomorrow," and he walked out closing the door behind him.

After an hour of editing and drinking coffee with Johnny, Harry wandered over to the admin building to see if any more news had emerged about Sonny's accident. As he entered, Barbara Finch waved him over; she was a cheerful, bespectacled, dark haired woman of about fifty, who was the popular Bulldog's Office Manager, "Come here my dear," she said and took his hand in hers, "I just wanted to say that we were all so impressed and pleased with your tribute programme for Sonny on Wednesday. It was so touching and…..and, just great."

"Thank you Bar, I felt it went well and that we got it about right," he replied.

"Spot on! Barry was delighted with the tone," she added.

"I'm pleased about that; it was an important programme to get right." Harry said and then, changing the subject, "Do you have a copy of the 'post mortem report that I can look at," he asked.

Bar sorted through some papers on her desk, "Yes," she answered, pulling an envelope out of the pile, "But you can't take it away."

"I won't. I just want to see exactly what is written." Harry said. After a few minutes he looked up from his reading, "It really isn't very informative is it?"

"What do you mean?" Bar enquired.

"Well it says that the cause of death was chest injuries and the verdict is accidental death. I thought there would be more details."

Bar took the report and looked at it, "Hmm, I don't think this is unusual. I think the term 'chest injuries' is quite common in situations like this. Why, what's the problem?"

"No problem, at least not one that I can put my finger on. Just a strange feeling that all has not been explained. Who were the medical staff who dealt with this?" Harry asked.

"It's on the sheet behind the report," Bar answered.

Harry found the name of the Coroner and two nurses which seemed legitimate and according to the way it should be.

Bar came back to him, "Harry, from track staff point of view, the St John Ambulance team on duty that evening were, Ted Robinson, Julia Raglett and Bernie Thorpe, does that help at all?"

"I don't know, maybe. I think I'll have a chat with them if that's ok with the club? Are they going to be here this week as well?"

Bar looked at her screen, "Yes," she confirmed, "all three of them will be here on Saturday night. What are you after Harry?"

"I wish I knew. Maybe nothing at all. Just an over active imagination I expect." He responded, "There's something niggling me."

"What kind of niggle?" Bar probed.

"I wish I knew," he sighed, "All I can say is that I was surprised and shocked when they told us that he'd died from what looked like a crash that most riders would walk away from. On the other hand, we've all seen accidents that looked innocuous but resulted in bad injuries. It could just have been very bad luck for Sonny."

"Hmmm," Bar thought for a moment, "Have you thought about contacting Dirt Track Films to see if you can view their footage of the crash. You know they film every meeting."

Harry walked over and kissed Bar on the forehead, "Bless you, you are a marvel. That's exactly what I'll do."

Harry called Johnny on his mobile as he left Bar's office, "Just letting you know that I'm going over to the Dirt Track Film offices on Totterdown Street in Tooting Beck. I want to see if they have any footage of the Sonny Brent crash. I'll be back soonest."

Dirt Track Limited was a company that had a license to film all the Elite League and Knock-Out Cup meetings at all the tracks in the UK and offer the edited results for sale at the tracks involved on a shared profit basis. Harry was ushered into Susan Hawley's office. She was responsible for Editing and Post production, but Harry had known her since she was PR Manager at Lakeside some years before. After the usual inconsequential chat, Harry asked, "I really want to know if you have the footage of the Sonny Brent crash from the Bulldogs and Swindon meeting."

"Yes we do," she responded, "Why?"

Harry asked, "Would you mind if I took a look at it?"

"No problem. Are you interested in anything particular?"

"It's difficult to say really. It may turn out that there is nothing to look for at all," Harry responded.

Susan found the relevant file and brought it up on a monitor on a free desk. She quickly found the incident and left Harry to view it. He watched the race from the start trying to see if there was anything related to the working of the bike, but there wasn't, or at least, nothing that he could see. He watched as Sonny's front wheel hit the deeply rutted shale and got stuck in the channel rather than riding over it. He saw

Sonny's weight thrown forward and his chest driven with force into the handlebars. He saw that Sonny was pinned there by his own forward momentum and the rapidly decreasing speed of the bike. He saw the bike steer into the air fence and watched it ricochet through the air in a high arc twisting and spinning like a gymnast and he saw the front wheel collapse as the bike hit the track nose first and the shock absorbers dig into the track before themselves collapsing like a disassembled pile of scrap metal. Harry made a note on his pad, "inconclusive on shocks issue." Upon hitting the air fence, Sonny was propelled over the handlebars and catapulted like a rag doll onto the track again. Sonny hit the shale awkwardly, which is probably where his collarbone was broken. Then Sonny rolled over twice and lay still. Within ten seconds a paramedic arrived by his side obscuring Harry's view of Sonny as he attended to the stricken rider. He could only see Sonny's legs as he lay on the track, "Is this the only camera angle you've got Susan?" he called across the room.

"'Fraid so Harry, sorry."

Frustrated he continued to observe the scene closely but he could not see what treatment the paramedic was administering, only that Sonny appeared to be responding with some movement of his legs. It took almost a minute for the other two paramedics to arrive by the time one of them had run burdened with equipment from the opposite bend on the far side of the track and the other had come from the crowd where he had been dealing with a fan who had shale in his eye. Harry thought that the second paramedic must had been Julia Raglett and that she seemed immediately concerned because, having knelt by Sonny, she almost immediately stood up and signaled urgently for the ambulance to attend. Harry supposed that Sonny must have been close to death at that point judging by Julia's reaction and the fact that the first paramedic was continuing to work on Sonny, presumably still applying CPR. Harry asked Susan to join him and view the footage herself a couple of times. "What do you think?" he asked after the second viewing.

"It's very difficult to say what's happening there." Susan said, "I think it was a bad enough crash to cause serious damage but beyond that, I couldn't say what's happening there."

"Something's not right," Harry said biting his lip. "Why did it take so long for the second paramedic to get to Sonny? I mean, it was almost a minute! Why didn't the first paramedic call for the ambulance straight away?"

"I don't know the answers to your questions Harry."

"I know you don't Susan and I don't expect you to. I'm just thinking out loud that's all."

"You know what it's like Harry." Susan said, "The second paramedic had to go right across the centre green and she was carrying a lot of gear. The first paramedic was probably giving CPR the whole time and thought that was the best response given that the others were on their way."

"Would he give CPR if the rider was suffering from life threatening chest injuries? I mean, wouldn't that make it worse?"

"I don't know Harry, I'm not a paramedic," Susan said, "What did the post mortem say?" she asked.

"Chest injuries and accidental death. But that's just plain uninformative."

"Maybe it's just a case of 'it is what it is,'" Susan responded, "You may wish it was more, but it isn't."

"Yeah, you're probably right," Harry pondered, "Thanks for letting me see that footage. It did help to see it."

"My pleasure Harry, any time."

"On a lighter note. Will you be up for the Lakeside match tonight?"

"Oh yes we'll be there, I expect we'll bump into each other at some point," she said smiling.

Thursday 11th August 2016

They arrived at the stadium just after six o'clock to get Harry's set up completed early so that he could speak to the paramedics. He found Julia Raglett checking the first aid boxes in the First Aide room at the bottom of the storage yard and approached her, "Julia Raglett?" he enquired.

The auburn haired woman of about forty years looked up from her work with a broad and genuine smile, "Yes I am." And she reached out to shake hands.

"I'm Harry Marsh from Speedway FM," Harry smiled back, it was impossible not to.

"I recognise you," Julia said, "What can I do for you Harry?"

"I wondered if I could ask you a few questions about the Sonny Brent accident last week."

Julia frowned, "What kind of questions?"

"I want to try and clarify some things that I find confusing."

"Is this for broadcasting?" Julia asked with concern.

Harry shook his head emphatically, "No, absolutely not. This is just my own personal concern and probably ill-founded and of no consequence, but there are some things that are on my mind." The paramedic looked a little defensive but agreed to hear his questions. "I understand that 'chest injuries' is the term often used in post mortem reports as the cause of death. Is that true?" Harry asked her.

"Yes it is. It usually means that no specific cause could be identified," Julia explained, "but that no foul play was suspected."

"Would you give CPR if you knew that someone had life threatening chest injuries?" harry asked.

"It's a judgment call Harry. If the paramedic judges that the victim is at high risk of dying if CPR is not given, then, not giving it offers a higher risk than giving it. It's not an easy one."

"No, I can see that," Harry answered thoughtfully. "When you saw Sonny, did you think he had injuries that would result in his death?" Harry asked.

"That's somewhat academic Harry," she responded, when I arrived Sonny was already dead."

Harry was stunned, "Already dead?"

"Yes, Bernie had checked for a pulse, not found one and was administering CPR when I got there."

"Did you check it as well?" Harry enquired.

"Yes of course and when I confirmed it I called for an ambulance and we applied CPR until it got to us and the doctor took over." Julia looked hard at the reporter, "Look Harry, Why are you asking these questions? Are you trying to imply something?"

"No I'm not," Harry said back peddling quickly, "but I do have a feeling or maybe an instinct that I cannot shake off. Something is wrong. Having said that, I don't have any expertise or knowledge on which to base any theory." He scratched his head, "I'm probably wrong but if I don't at least ask a few questions I think it will come to haunt me."

"In the light of your lack of experience and knowledge, I'd be inclined to tread carefully if I were you; you could do some real damage and hurt some good people." Julia then thought it better that she didn't discuss it any further and Harry accepted that decision.

As he stepped outside the medical room he found Bernie Thorpe checking the supplies in the ambulance. He stopped looking into the back of the vehicle where Bernie was working, "Hi, it's Bernie isn't it?" he asked cheerfully.

A tall well-built man of roughly thirty to thirty five who looked as if he attended the gym occasionally turned from his task and smiled, "Yes that's me. Who wants me?"

Harry introduced himself and then said, "I'm doing a bit of radio with regard to Sonny Brent and wondered if I might have a quick chat with you, as you were the first on the accident scene?"

Bernie looked dubious, "Well, I don't know. We shouldn't really discuss that sort of thing with the press."

Harry reassured him that he wouldn't use anything for broadcast, "It's just background stuff I'm looking for," he said.

Bernie reluctantly agreed to answer a couple of questions as long as they weren't going to get him into any trouble. Harry thought he would keep it general, "What sort of responsibilities does a paramedic have when something like happens, is there a system or something?"

Bernie told him, "Yes, there's Dr. ABC, a process, a systematic approach if you like."

"What does that mean?"

"It means Danger, Response, Airway, Breathing and Circulation. It's what we call the primary survey and it's a quick way to find out if someone has any life-threatening injuries or conditions. If you follow it, you can identify conditions and deal with them in order of priority.

"Is there a secondary survey?" Harry asked.

"Yes, that's for dealing with trauma and is really for dealing with causes. You don't get to that until you've dealt with the immediate life-threatening stuff. Fortunately, most of the time speedway's about cuts and bruises, twists and sprains, but occasionally it's broken bones and last week was a dreadful first for me."

"It must have been a shocking experience," Harry sympathised, "can you tell what kind of injuries you're going to encounter in advance?"

"Not really," Bernie replied, "Certainly nothing you can depend on. When a rider locks up and gets a tank slapper he will often land head first and awkwardly. This commonly ends with a broken collar bone, but that's about as predictable as it gets."

"When you saw Sonny Brent crash did you think it was going to be serious or what might be wrong with him?" Harry asked.

"No not really," Bernie recalled, "when he didn't get up immediately I just got there as soon as I could."

"I imagine your Dr. ABC kicks in automatically?"

"Oh yes that's vital. It helps avoid mistakes."

"What exactly do you do?" Harry enquired.

"Well if the rider isn't moving, check for a pulse. If there is one, check airways are clear, if his injuries aren't obviously serious, like broken limbs, put him into the recovery position. If they are, call the ambulance, and then try to make him comfortable and offer reassurance."

"So, when you got to Sonny what did you have to do?"

Bernie frowned at Harry, "I gave CPR."

"CPR?" Harry asked in surprise.

"Yes. You see, when I got there, Sonny was already dead."

Harry was stunned by this news, "Already dead?"

"Yes, when I checked for a pulse, I didn't find one; we were unable to bring him back with CPR or the defibrillator in the ambulance.

"So what killed him?" Harry asked.

Bernie shook his head, "I don't know Harry. I'm not a doctor but my guess is it could have been any of those knocks he received. Have you seen the post mortem report?"

Harry confirmed that he had, "It just says that he died from chest injuries."

"Yes I know," Bernie said, "Not particularly helpful is it?"

Harry was troubled, "But I thought he was alive because just before Julia got there, I thought..."

"No, he was dead when I arrived. He obviously died instantly," Bernie said.

Harry was about to speak again but decided against it, he was obviously mistaken and he wasn't in any position to dispute it with a paramedic who was actually there. Instead he said, "Hey listen Bernie, thanks for your time. I need to make tracks and I'm sure you need to get on."

"No problem Harry," Bernie answered cheerfully, ""You should think about doing a bit about paramedics on your radio show sometime."

"Good idea," Harry agreed and meant it, "maybe I will."

CHAPTER 7

Thursday 11th August 2016

arnie@arniecottrell
Busy times for Bulldogs let's hope we can just think about speedway tonight. Good luck Bulldogs!

The meeting against Lakeside was a close affair, with the West London side losing 47 to 43, but taking a well-earned league point with them. The whole evening started with a minute of total silence for Sonny Brent and an emotional few words from Arnie Cottrell who spoke with feeling about Sonny and the sort of boy he was to know, and the potential he had to be a good rider. Arnie's sadness was a tearful and moving manifestation of the way everyone in the stadium felt and Harry was reduced to tears by the genuine and dignified response from the fans in the crowded stands.

He got an excellent interview with Jon Cook and Kelvin Tatum who bounced off each other superbly to make a lively and entertaining five minute slot. Harry felt confident that their honest and contentious appraisals of the performances of the Hammers and the Bulldogs would stimulate opinions from listeners. His interview with Tai Woffinden was a gem that would please Johnny because it would attract lots of downloads on their new podcast application. These and watching speedway took his mind away from his conversations with Bernie but when it had all finished, the conversation came back with vivid recollection as, later that night, he and Rosie were relaxing with glasses of red wine before going to bed. Harry nursed his wine gazing into the middle distance, "Something on your mind darling?" Rosie asked.

Harry's mind returned to the room, "Yes and no," he replied, "I had an interesting couple of conversations that were intended to bring clarity but they had exactly the opposite effect."

"Go on," Rosie encouraged.

Harry paused for a moment thinking about where to start, then said, "Sonny was dead when the paramedic got to him on the track."

"That's awful,"Rosie replied, "but, so what?"

"The 'so what' is that I thought Sonny was alive when Bernie Thorpe got to him. But he says that it wasn't so."

"What makes you think he might have been alive?" Rosie queried.

"Well, when I watched the video footage at Dirt Track yesterday, I thought I saw Sonny's legs moving."

"I've heard that peoples' limbs sometimes move after death, sort of spasms or something," Rosie said.

Harry took a gulp of red wine, "I saw Bernie Thorpe administrating treatment. I don't know what treatment he was giving and I saw Sonny's legs moving, I didn't think they were spasms though. I thought he must have been in pain."

"How sure are you about that?" Rosie pressed.

"Well, I was very sure having watched it several times and having got Susan Hawley to watch it a couple of times as well, and she agreed."

"Are you saying that Bernie Thorpe's lying"

Harry looked perplexed, "It's difficult because either way I'm saying something is wrong. Either he is lying, or he made a serious mistake. I can't see a positive explanation."

"But why would he lie?" Rosie questioned.

"That's what I've been rolling over and over in my mind since we got back. I keep coming up with outrageous, almost fiction like scenarios."

Rosie curled her legs under herself on the armchair, "Go on."

"He would lie if he had something to hide. It could be that he made a mistake that resulted in Sonny dying there on the track."

"Well, that's possible isn't it?" Rosie said.

Harry rocked his head from side to side slowly, "It's possible, but improbable," he said.

"Why so?"

"Because he's a professional, because he didn't have much time."

"How much time do you need?"

"Ok, point taken, but I could see what he was doing, well not what he was doing, but that he was doing something."

"So, he did it deliberately then?" Rosie suggested.

"No of course not. Why would he do that?"

"I don't know," she replied, I was joking."

CHAPTER 8

Friday 12th August 2016

arnie@arniecottrell
Lakeside took us close last night. They definitely look like a top 4 team! It was a great meeting and 3 points in the bag

On Friday morning they gathered for Sonny Brent's funeral. His parents had wanted a quiet affair with just family and a few invited speedway friends; in the event more than a thousand people lined the road to the church. Speedway fans from Plymouth to Glasgow and Edinburgh came to offer their sympathies and support. Sonny's mother and father were touched beyond words and it was Barry Leech who spoke a few words of thanks to the gathered throng. The service was very low key and simple with Sonny's younger brother speaking a few words about his older brother and hero. Arnie spoke about the loss of such an up-and-coming talent and his genuine liking for a thoroughly nice young man. His body was buried next to his grandparents' graves and a bouquet of flowers in the shape of a winged speedway bike wheel. Harry and Rosie kept towards the back of everything and maintained a quiet dignity as the sad and sorrow-filled affair came to a touching and fitting end with Sonny's mother, father and younger brother standing alone by the grave. Harry was relieved not to have had a live show that day, so he was relieved of the onerous task of appearing cheerful for his listeners.

That afternoon Harry and Rosie decided to visit Davy's parents in Guildford so they called them and arranged to be there at about two thirty in time for a sandwich and tea. As Rosie had predicted, Dorothy Barns had prepared an awesome array of daintily cut sandwiches with corned beef, ham and Dijon mustard, smoked salmon, and four different cheeses from which choose. A choice of Earl Grey, Darjeeling and Green tea got them through to the cake course which was as sumptuous as the first course, but Harry was equal to it and ate everything that was offered. Their conversation was polite and neutral throughout although Harry discovered that Rosie had lived in Lancashire for a part of her life, went to school in Lancaster and lived in the nearby village of High Bentham which, by coincidence, was where he had attended a vintage motorcycle convention with an old BSA and sidecar he had renovated. Eventually Peter Barns lit his pipe and looked around to gather everyone's attention.

"Now then Rosie and Harry, I don't suppose you've called round just for a social chat, have you?" he said as an invitation to open up the thorny subject of Davy's future.

Rosie coughed to clear her throat, "Well sir. I wanted to talk to you about Davy and your proposal to withdraw his food and thus bringing about his death."

Peter Barns looked vexed, "Now Rosie, let's be clear about this, we don't want to argue again, do we?"

"I understand that sir. And I don't want to argue, but I would like the time to understand the way you both feel about things."

"That's more than reasonable," Peter Barns replied.

Encouraged, Rosie pressed on, her voice shaking a little, "So what are your thoughts now? Do you still want to stop treatment?"

Peter Barns sucked on his pipe and let the smoke slowly rise out of the corners of his mouth before blowing a cloud out into the living room, "Ok, let's be very clear. The notion that we want to do anything doesn't describe the way we feel. Neither Dorothy nor I wake up in the morning thinking, 'I want to end Davy's life'." He paused to gulp down the pain that had grabbed his throat, "There isn't anyone in this world who loves our son more than we do. When I wake up in the morning I think about what it would be like if Davy woke up today. What would I do what would I say to him? My dearest wish is that he will wake up and I can have my Davy of old back, my lovely son, my little boy who loved me as much I love him. This part exists in my mind that dreams about a miracle happening. Another part of my mind exists where reality reigns, where miracles don't happen and dreams don't come true. In this world it is unlikely that my Davy will reawaken and even if he does he won't recognise me and won't be able to function in any meaningful way. In the real world he either dies without reawakening or awakes as a vegetable, or some incapacitated variant between the two. In this world it is conceivable that Dorothy and I will die before Davy and we leave his sleeping body or bewildered mind to a lonely existence in some institution somewhere where no-one will ever visit him." Peter went quiet and looked down at the smoking pipe in his hand.

Dorothy Barns coughed, "That sums up my thoughts and fears as well Rosie. When I am in that dream world, I want to keep the machine switched on, keep it going; I haven't wanted to visit the real world for fear of having to facing the truth. But it's unavoidable and when I do go to the real world, I have to admit that we should stop his treatment and I hate myself for thinking like that." A tear ran down her cheek and she dabbed it with a hanky.

Rosie and Harry listened with clear empathy, "I can see both these worlds exactly as you describe them," Rosie said softly, "and I also see how and why you get to where you are," she paused and swallowed hard, "but these definitions you use to describe the different worlds are false in themselves. They sound plausible and we are sucked into them by their apparent logics, but both of them are fantasies." She took a deep breath, "The only reality is what is happening now, Davy is in a coma and nothing has changed for him. We can be certain that one day things will change for him or you, or both and that's when a decision may need to be made. If you terminate his treatment the only change on offer to him is that he will die." Another tear ran down her cheek. Harry reached across, took her hand and smiled gently at her. Dorothy Barns wept silently whilst Peter looked solemnly at Rosie and quietly puffed at his pipe. After a few moments Rosie stood up and said, "Thank you for listening to me. I won't come again, well, not for this purpose anyway. I hope you will take my views into account when the time comes to make a decision."

Kisses were exchanged at the door and Peter hugged Rosie. "You're a good person Rosie. Davy would have been the luckiest man in the world if he had married you." He turned to Harry and shook his hand, "And if you do the right thing by this young woman, you'll be the luckiest man in the world. We wish the best for both of you."

As they pulled away from the front of the Barns' house, they saw the couple standing by the curb arm in arm, waving goodbye with the weight of the world on their shoulders.

Thursday 18th August 2016

arnie@arniecottrell
The victory over Lakeside team put clear air between us and fifth place. We need to press on, but no Joey this week!

Joe Neal's absence due to a wrist injury put a dent in the evening for many fans, but it did mean that the Bulldog fans had an opportunity to cheer for Tai Woffinden due to the application of one the stranger rules in speedway, where a rider from a direct opponent can ride for your team. In many other walks of life the term, *conflict of interests* would certainly apply and personal motivations would be questioned. Of the match, little can be said as Leicester offered meagre resistance and were consequently demolished 58 to 32 with Tai Woffinden scoring 12 points + 1, Patryk Dudek with 11 + 1, Linus Sundstrom on 10 + 2 and Frankie Chivers at reserve with a creditable 5 + 3. Leicester's Ludvig Lindgren on 8 was their only heat winner and the rest of the team was lusterless in both energy and performance. In a successful attempt to lift the communal spirits Barry Leech offered reduced admission to £10 for adults and made it free for children. This gave the whole stadium a high pitched volume that built as the evening went on and even though the racing was processional in nature, the children added an excitement that would otherwise have been lacking. The race of the evening came from Patryk Dudek who, starting with a fifteen metre penalty, caught and passed Andy Winters on the first lap with a stylish sweep around the outside of bends three and four, hunted down Nicolas Kaminski by bend three of lap two and battled ferociously to get past a very skillful and tricky rider. Coming down the back straight with inches between them and both keeping close to the fence Kildemand showed tremendous courage by holding his nerve on the outside while Kaminski gave no quarter and offered no racing space. As they entered the third bend, Kildemand, who was no more than half a metre behind in third, switched from the outside to the inside to undercut the Leicester rider brushing Kaminski's back tyre with his front. The stadium erupted into a cauldron of boiling cheering and air horns as he took second place from the Leicester rider by half a wheel to finish behind his team mate Peter Ljung. Barry Leech could be seen standing on the first bend with a broad smile on his face, waving with the other fans and shouting until he went hoarse and lost his voice.
Saturday 20nd August 2016

arnie@arniecottrell
Oh what a night! We were stupendous! Everyone is so stoked here we can't wait for the next meeting!

Life quickly got back to normal, and a week later Harry had visited Cradley Heathens for the Golden Hammer meeting on Tuesday, then across to high flying Birmingham for their Wednesday meeting against a struggling Coventry side in the National League and back to London for his Thursday show. Listeners were still talking about the Sonny Brent tribute that he put out the week before and it became clear that he had touched a national nerve when he heard what other fans had been doing to honour the passing of the young star. He was quite emotional when he finally switched off his microphone and vacated his chair for Jenny to start her programme. Johnny had a coffee waiting for him as he dropped onto the sofa and sighed deeply.

"OK mate?" he asked Harry.

Harry picked up the coffee and sighed again, "Yes I'm ok. A bit churned up from some of the phone calls, that's all."

"I heard them; there was some great stuff there, very emotional." Johnny said. Like all producers, he loved it when people got emotional on air, angry, crying or ecstatic. He always wanted real emotion coming over the radio, tears were the stuff of dreams to all broadcasters, not just Johnny.

Harry drank his coffee, "Yeah. Well we really got under the surface with some of them," he looked into his mug and pondered for a moment. "What would you think if I told you I was nursing a suspicion that a mistake caused Sonny Brent's death?"

"I'd say, tell me more, but be careful," Johnny warned, "You can't go around saying things like that unless you got some bomb proof evidence."

"I know that and I don't really have any evidence at all, but I think Bernie Thorpe may have accidentally caused Sonny's death."

"Hmm, that's a very big claim," Johnny responded.

"That's why I'm talking to you about it. I don't want to go off half-cocked. I'm thinking that I should go back to Dirt Track today and take another look at the footage of the crash. Will you come with me?"

Johnny shook his head, "I can't mate, not today. I'm standing in for Ricky; he phoned in ill at lunch-time."

Harry went over to Dirt Track alone and Susan Hawley set up the file again and he watched the footage through several times to try and see what happened. By the end of the fifth viewing he had no doubt about what he was watching. He couldn't see as much as he wanted, but it was enough to convince him. Harry called Susan over and asked her to take another look. "Just watch and tell me if you see Sonny's legs moving while Bernie is treating him," he invited her.

Susan watched it three times and then turned to Harry, "His legs are definitely moving during the time he was being treated."

"So," Harry asked, "does that mean that Sonny was alive when Bernie first got to him?"

"Yes, I think so. He was alive," Susan answered.

Harry's heart missed a beat. Now there was someone else who had seen what he had seen. "What would you say if I told you that he was dead before any paramedic got to him?"

"I'd say you were wrong. Why are you saying that? What's this about Harry?" Susan asked.

"The paramedic you see treating Sonny told me that Sonny was dead when he got to the scene," Harry told her.

Susan looked blankly at Harry, "Jesus. Really? Why would he do that when it is so obvious that he wasn't?"

"I don't think he has thought about this video footage and because he was kneeling in front of Sonny he thought people couldn't see what was happening," Harry said, "and because Sonny was close to the air fence, the crowd on that side couldn't see anything at all. So maybe he thought it wasn't as obvious as it is to us. I can only think that he made some kind of mistake in his treatment and Sonny died as a consequence."

"Wow, that's a hell of a mistake to make," Susan said quietly, "but what sort of mistake could he have made that would have killed him? I mean, all they have to do is check the airways and look for broken limbs don't they? How can you kill someone doing that?"

Harry considered this, "I don't know, but in some ways that makes it worse. I don't know enough about it."

"What do we do about it?" Susan asked.

"Nothing rash," Harry answered, "I imagine we will report our suspicions to someone appropriate at some point, but I'd like to take some advice first so if it's ok with you, can we leave it until I've done that?"

Susan Hawley nodded, "Yes of course. I'll leave it to you. Naturally, the footage is available to anyone who needs to see it."

Harry bade her farewell and made his way back to Notting Hill in thoughtful mood.

Tuesday 23rd August 2016

Harry went to Isle of Wight to see the Warriors battle with Birmingham in one their many uber-competitive matches that never fail to thrill their fans. The two clashes between James Cockle and Jack Parkinson-Blackburn were the highlight of the evening with other superbly exciting moments. Most memorable were the races that pitted Jack Smith and Brendan Johnson, and Tom Perry and Mark Baseby against each other. Warriors managed to win but Birmingham only just missed out on a point as they went down fifty to forty. Graham Drury and Barry Bishop were full of praise for the quality of riding from both teams and between them they gave Harry a capricious and humorous joint interview that would be sure to excite listeners to ring in with Graham having managed both teams to League titles in recent years. Harry ran a little experiment by collecting a series of interviews with fans in the crowd between races. He thought that, when edited into the show, they would provide some very entertaining moments. As the show got back to normal with more general speedway topics he felt that it was a good time to introduce some changes as Sonny's death began to recede in the minds of the fans.

Wednesday 24th August 2016

Harry had a quiet night in with Rosie. They talked about his video viewing with Susan Hawley. Rosie was surprised and concerned when she heard the outcome of the session, "What are you going to do?" she asked.

"I'm not sure," he replied honestly. "Report it to somebody I suppose."

"I guess," Rosie agreed, "it will ruin his career as a first aider. Does he have a day job?"

Harry shrugged, "I don't know, but I can't let that affect my judgment. He might kill someone else if he carries on."

They agreed that he should talk to Julia Raglett and let her decide how to handle it.

ELITE LEAGUE TABLE - Up to and including Tuesday 23rd August 2016

TEAM	M	W	D	L	F	A	Pts	+/-
Belle Vue	21	14	0	7	988	877	49	111
Poole	20	13	1	6	1004	815	44	189
Swindon	24	13	1	10	1092	1073	44	19
Battersea	23	11	1	11	1020	890	43	130
Wolverhampton	23	12	0	11	1068	1019	42	49
Lakeside	24	13	0	11	1130	1060	40	70
Coventry	24	9	0	15	1028	1156	30	-128
Kings Lynn	19	7	2	10	798	912	25	-114
Leicester	23	5	2	16	946	1142	18	-196

Thursday 25th August 2016

The Battersea track saw Coventry visiting and Harry was down in the pits early as mechanics were working on the bikes. He settled himself in the visitors side of the pits, chatting with whoever he could grab, corner or cajole into an interview. He had often put interviews with 'spanners' into the show and received good feedback from listeners who seem to love the less politically correct approach and the different 'behind the scenes' slant that they brought to the microphone. He had a fascinating half hour with Chris Harris' mechanic, who took him through the set-up that Chris thought would bring him the best chance that night on the Bulldog's track. The intricacies of the relationship between the various influential parts of a speedway bike can seem like a 'black art' to the uninitiated and Harry came away from his session a lot better informed.

As he strolled along the pits towards the Bulldog's side, Harry thought about how much better he would have been as a rider if he'd had knowledge like that in his head, but the truth was, he knew nothing compared with other riders of his own age. What he did know now, was not to dwell on past disappointments, but he wished he'd taken a bit more of an interest, instead of just wanting to ride the bike as fast as he could. He had an interview planned with Joe Neal and his mechanic Billy Knapp, and as he made his way through the rather stark and utilitarian storage yard that every speedway track tries to hide away from the public, Bernie Thorpe appeared from around the corner and Harry stopped in his tracks. He considered for a moment that he might confront Bernie right there and then, but Bernie just nodded and smiled as he walked past. Harry turned and watched him walking away as he made his way across the yard, weaving between small groups and mechanics pushing the bikes onto the track ready for the presentation, before turning right into the First Aid room. Harry knew full well that this was neither the right place nor time to have that kind of conversation and anyway, he had an international speedway star waiting for him up in the admin office. As he walked on he became aware of movement in the storage area where the two large gas tanks and the waste oil tanks stood side by side. There crouching by the waste oil tank was Steve Hildegarde.

"Steve," Harry nodded curtly to him.

"Harry," Steve reciprocated.

"Busy?" Harry ventured trying to offer a rather feeble olive branch.

"Yeah, just getting rid of the old oil" Steve replied, turning back to the large tank and screwing the cap back on. He stood and wiped his hands on a cloth from the back pocket of his Bulldog overalls.

"Who are you spannering for tonight?" Harry asked.

"No-one," Steve explained, "I'm a spare mech tonight."

They walked round to the pits together, where they split up and Harry went in search of Joe Neal and Billy Knapp.

The interview with Joe and Billy would be the monthly feature interview on the Bulldog website and would also appear somewhere in the Speedway FM schedule. What was really nice about this was the way Joe and Billy bounced off each other with great humour. They were just starting on the subject of Joe's continued absence from the Grand Prix series when a massive explosion rocked the building and people started shouting and running about. Harry, Joe and Billy went out onto the balcony that overlooked the pits and the second bend and saw great plumes of smoke billowing and drifting through the pit stalls like a thick fog engulfing everything. Huge flames shot skyward on the far side of the pits. Riders and mechanics were hurrying down towards the offices and exit onto the track. Harry decided to wait where he was rather than add to the confusion and allow the medics do their jobs. Bar came running up the stairs to the balcony, stopped when she saw the three of them, "Harry, will you call the fire brigade and tell them we have a large fire? I'll go and open the back gate ready for when they arrive. Tell them that," she called out as she made her way back to the stairs.

Harry said he would and added, "What happened Bar?"

"The waste oil tank has exploded! It's a real mess round there, that thick black smoke is the oil burning if we don't do get it out soon, we think the gas tanks will explode!", and then she was on her way down the stairs.

"Is anyone injured?" Harry shouted after her.

"Yes, one of the mechanics was round there testing the clutch on a bike and got the full blast," she stopped to call back.

"Who was it Bar?"

Bar was already running backwards down the last two steps, "John Sinclair!"

Harry froze with shock, Bar shouted, "Harry! Fire brigade!" She made the shape of a telephone with her hand up to her face.

For half an hour it looked as if a serious fire might take hold and spread into the main body of the pit area and even the main office building. The fire fighters, however, arrived within ten minutes and brought it under control pretty quickly. Meanwhile, for the second time in three weeks, the fans were asked to leave in an orderly fashion. Harry went down into the heart of the malaise to see if he could help, but he wasn't needed and would have simply been in the way. He saw the paramedics treating many of the people who had been on the periphery of the explosion. He saw Bernie Thorpe in a dirty yellow high vis jacket, his face marked by soot and smoke tending to a mechanic's gashed forehead. Julia Raglett was talking to Sam Thomson, the referee so he waited for her to finish her conversation. As Julia turned away from Sam he jumped in quickly, "Julia how is John Sinclair," he asked.

Julia stopped and looked at him sadly, "He's dead Harry. He was killed instantly."

CHAPTER 9

Friday 26th August 2016

arnie@arniecottrell
Disbelief and sadness. Johnny Sinclair died this week in a tragic accident. Confusion and hurt hangs over us again

The morning dawned on a bleak scene. "I want all department heads in my office at ten o'clock tomorrow morning," Barry Leech demanded, "and I want a detailed situation report covering all departments, actual damage, human, material and economic. I want predictions and projections about implications for the Speedway club particularly and the whole group generally, with any specifics of negative spikes, and a profile to show where we are vulnerable by area. I want the Health and Safety team all over this from now. Get Tony Fuller up here now and tell him I want to know what the worst is that we're looking at." Bar made a note of all his demands and then waited, "and get Rosie in to tomorrow mornings meeting. I want her to co-ordinate our own internal investigation. You can work with her until this thing is cleared up." He paused, "Is that alright with you Bar?"
"That's alright with me."
"Good," he said with finality, "that's it then."

Everybody connected with the club turned up to work, Harry and Johnny joined them to lend a hand. The far end of the pits was badly damaged both by the explosion and then by the fire. Health and Safety officers were everywhere, and everyone was told to make themselves available for interview. The police arrived and applied the same conditions to them all. By the time they had finished it was nearly five o'clock in the evening. During his interview Harry had told the police that he had seen Steve Hildegarde in the storage area crouching by the waste oil tank. When it became clear that the explosion could have been deliberately set, the police decided to take Steve in for questioning and kept him for twenty four hours at the police station. His interrogation had included officers from Project Griffin of the National Counter Terrorism Security Office, who made the Met boys look like pussy cats. Upon his return he was interviewed by HSE officers from Claxton Street who were just about the final straw for the weary, sleep deprived mechanic. By the time Barry Leech called him into his office Steve was outraged, in a state of near collapse and incapable of coherent thought. Barry put him in his Rolls Royce and sent him home with orders to sleep, but this did little to placate, Steve who was swearing revenge against the whole world, but Bulldogs particularly and Harry Marsh specifically. Harry sat in the office listening to the live broadcast that Johnny was fronting when Bar came in and sat down.
"Have you got any coffee Harry? I badly need one," she said.
"Certainly," he replied and filled the kettle. "You look troubled," he observed.
Bar drew her hand back through her hair, "I am, I just had to get out of my office before I blew a gasket and said something I would regret later."

Harry placed the fresh coffee in front of her," What's been happening?"

"What hasn't been happening?" she complained, "We are being hit from every side. HSE are saying that there's an outside chance we might be closed down, the police are saying we might be prosecuted, the share price for the group has gone into free-fall and the Speedway Control Board are getting involved, although; to be fair to them, they were very understanding and offered support, but still it's another bureaucratic process that needs to be navigated. Barry is asking for minute by minute updates, all the riders are making noises about loss of earnings should they miss their meetings in Sweden and Poland and the police suspect Steve Hildegard of causing the explosion deliberately so he may be charged with who knows what?"

Harry looked in the cupboard, but it was empty all bar a packet of digestives, "Biscuit?" he offered. Bar looked at them and then looked up into his face and laughed out loud, "You blithering idiot Harry!"

They both laughed until their stomachs ached and they could laugh no longer. Eventually they settled down, drank coffee and Bar talked about the pressure of the day. She had HSE looking into everything, the police looking into everything and Barry looking into everything and, of course, the press who wanted to look into everything.

"Sitting here is like being in a haven of tranquillity and calm" she told Harry.

"You can come here anytime you want to Bar, you'll always be made welcome."

"Thanks Harry, that means a lot."

He wanted to know things but didn't want to add to the pressure, "Can I ask you a question about the explosion?"

Bar nodded, "Of course you can. I'm not sure I know much more than you already know though, she replied.

"Why was John Sinclair round by the gas tanks?" Harry asked.

"That's where they go to bump start the bikes when they're testing them before the riders take them out. It was terrible luck on him, I mean being there at that time."

"You're right there," Harry said, "is there any information about what caused the explosion?"

"HSE think there might have been a leaking valve that caused the gas to escape, but they don't have a cause for the ignition," Bar explained, "The police have not ruled anything out. So, their investigation in ongoing, the terrorist crowd think it could be a terrorist-based attack."

"Wow, are they working together on this?" Harry asked.

"What do you think?" Bar replied.

"I see." Harry's eyebrows travelled north. "Are the valves and all that sort of thing examined on a regular basis? I mean, with Tony Fuller on the case I would have thought they were checked on the hour."

Bar agreed, "Yes. Tony is very diligent with all that kind of thing. And it's a legal requirement which any business ignores at it peril nowadays."

"So, it's hardly likely that a valve would fail without being spotted before an accident could take place."

"Well, that's the idea behind inspections. What are you getting at?" Bar asked.

"I'm not getting at anything. I'm just trying to understand, that's all." But Harry still had a vivid memory of Steve Hildegarde crouching at the waste oil tank which was next to the two gas storage tanks. He made a mental note to have a look at all three of those tanks before he went home.

The mess was unmitigated with charred partitions, scorched clothing, helmets, body armour and gloves, buckled tool boxes, and general smoke and flame damage scarring the far end of the pits. The melted plastic guttering hung like strands of melted cheese dangling from a pizza all the way to the ground. As he rounded the corner Harry was faced with utter devastation. The ragged edges of the exploded waste oil tank looked like macabre teeth jutting out of a metal mouth where it had erupted.

"It's lucky that the Fire Fighters managed to put the fire out before the tank had emptied." The words came from Mike Hopkins, who was one of the HSE officers that worked for Tony Fuller.

"What do you mean?" Harry queried

"If that tank had emptied while the feed line was burning," Mike explained, "it would have created a momentary suction and the flame would have been sucked into the tank where there would have been an almighty explosion. We would have been picking bits of tank out of the Thames, or worse out of someone's living room."

"My God that would have been terrible."

"For everyone." Mike said, "For the householder, we could have been looking at manslaughter. For the club, we would almost certainly have lost our operating license."

Harry nodded and walked over to take a look between the tanks. There was a smaller tank between them, bolted to the wall, "Is this the waste oil tank?" he asked Mike Hopkins.

"Yes, the old oil is put there and once a week it's taken away for safe disposal. A bit of a pain and expensive; that's what caused the thick black smoke last night."

"Where do you think the fire started?" Harry enquired.

"Right here," Mike Hopkins said pointing to a soot covered tap at the bottom of the waste oil tank and immediately next to one of the gas tanks, "and here's where the leaking feed line is, or was," he added indicating a melted tube.

The discussion was interrupted by an angry voice. "What the hell are you doing round here Marsh?" It was Tony Fuller in his element, in full HSE uniform and an ego the size of the grading tractor and shining as bright as his pristine high vis jacket. He was marching across the yard hell bent on a confrontation.

"Hello Tony" Harry said cheerfully, "what a mess eh?"

"Never mind that! You shouldn't be here, this is a restricted area! There is evidence here and you're contaminating it! Now clear off!" Tony was incandescent and puffed up with his sense of importance.

Harry stepped from between the tanks, "I'm on my way," he nodded to Mike Hopkins, "Thanks Mike, very interesting." As he walked away, Harry could hear Tony Fuller chastising the HSE officer. He felt a bit guilty about that, but he wasn't going to be answerable for Tony's behaviour as well as his own.

He went straight to the admin offices and sought out Rosie and Bar, "Are you going to get home tonight?" he asked and hoped it didn't come out sounding like a bleating man who wasn't getting his way.

"Debatable," Bar answered and hit the return key on her computer, stood up and moved Harry out of the doorway. "Excuse me," she said, "I've got to get to the printer." Rosie was absorbed by the content of her computer screen but put one hand in the air to indicate that Harry had been noticed and should wait. He sat down at an empty desk, picked up a local newspaper and started to read it. The headline shouted out from the front page, "Two deaths put the Leech Group on everyone's blacklist!" Harry read on:

> 'Yesterday represented the blackest day in Leech Group history. The company, owned entirely by the multi-millionaire entrepreneur Barry Leech, has only ever known the energy and enthusiasm that comes from sustained success over a long period. Having steered the group through the depths of the Credit Crunch and the following recession and realised significant growth when other giants of commerce and industry have either sunk without trace or suffered serious losses, Mr Leech is now experiencing some pain of a different kind. He is being deluged with criticism that accompanies the tragic events that have occurred in his speedway enterprise. Leech group shares dropped fifteen percent on the Stock Exchange as the market opened on Monday morning. Experts predict a significant loss in confidence if the charismatic chief executive doesn't act quickly to address the cause and the impact of the deaths that are the blight of the Battersea Bulldog's Health and Safety reputation. The current HSE investigation is raising questions about Barry Leech's focus. Some are openly saying that he is distracted from his 'core' business by what is essentially a 'hobby.' Mr. Leech says he will issue a statement on Tuesday morning when he has reviewed and spoken with the various bodies involved in the investigations.'

Harry folded the paper and lay it on the desk. Rosie looked over to him, "Pretty bad eh?"

"Yeah, looks like it," he replied, "Is it as bad as it sounds?"

"Oh yes, maybe worse." Rosie confirmed, "We've got to get confidence back and we've got to do it tomorrow at the press conference."

"I see," Harry said, "I don't think you'll be home tonight either."

"No chance," Rosie answered without looking away from her screen.

An idea came to Harry, "Rosie? Do you think Barry will let us broadcast the conference?"

"What? What do you mean?"

"Can we broadcast it live?" he said, and slipped in a chancer's afterthought, "I mean exclusively."

"You paparazzi scum!" Bar called across the room, "just looking for an opportunity to profit from scavenged morsels."

"Harry affected an East London twang that, for some reason he associated with journalists, "'Old on luv!" I'm just doin' mi job! Anyway, I have a responsibility to broadcast anything that's in the public interest."

Rosie laughed out loud for the first time in a long time, "I had a word with the old man and he says yes, but not an exclusive you greedy, greedy man."

"What!" Harry leapt to his feet, "I was only joking, I think."

"You should be careful what you wish for," Bar put in.

"What is Barry going to say?" Harry asked.

"We haven't decided yet. We're still doing the research. We've got a meeting scheduled for eight thirty this evening, after that we'll put the presentation together. Whatever it is, it'll be about regaining confidence in the whole group by getting the response to this small but important and tragic glitch right and appropriate to the circumstances in which we find ourselves," Rosie said.

"Steady and dependable eh?" Harry mused.

"Basically, yes. He's had everyone in today and read the riot act." Bar revealed.

"How have they responded?" Harry asked.

"The way most people always respond when Barry Leech says 'jump!'" she smiled, "they ask, 'how high?' and then jump higher than that."

Rosie joined in, "They're frightened, angry and resentful but mostly, they're determined. He spelled out in very basic terms, so that it was easy to understand, the impact on the business if we don't get it right," she turned back to her laptop, "and we can't afford for the share price to drop any further. Simples."

Saturday 27th August 2016

The giant broadcasters such as the BBC and Sky took upwards of two hours to set up their equipment and run through their checks, whilst Johnny and Harry consumed ten minutes, seven of which were spent trying to open the jammed zip on the carrying case before pressing the "on" button on their prized Zoom portable recorder. But none of this could dent the thrill that they felt at being present for the most important broadcast in which Speedway FM had ever been involved. When Barry Leech walked into the room, he faced the BBC, ITV, Sky News, Fox, BBC Radio, and several other global players, all the financial journals that matter and Speedway FM. Barry stood in front of the array of microphones and started to speak with quiet confidence and visible assurance.

"I'd like to thank you for coming here today although I am aware that there is a degree of interest in what I am going to discuss today. I am saddened by the circumstances that have forced me to hold this conference, for it has involved the loss of two young and promising lives. The young men who have died this week were both employees of my company and more importantly, my friends. The nature of speedway in general, and I hope, Battersea Bulldogs are an exemplar of this, is that of close relationships born out of our love for the sport and the deep respect in which we hold the riders who risk their lives for our entertainment and the mercurial skills of their mechanics who demonstrate their skills in a kind of alchemy that produces bikes of the highest quality. We talk about the speedway family and at times like this it is evident that this is a real entity and not just the product of deluded and overly romantic minds. Battersea Bulldogs is not like any other business in the Leech Group. It was started for different purposes and I take a personal interest in the hour to hour running of it. As a result, I know each and every person who works here. I understand the concerns that investors have about my apparent preoccupation with the Bulldogs and I can see that this may give the impression of a lack of focus on other parts of the group, but I am here to reassure everyone that my passion for the Bulldogs, as real as it is, does not take my attention away from the rest any more than other businesses would. My passion for running businesses is as strong as it has ever been and will be maintained for many years to come." He went on in this vein for another thirty minutes, providing financial evidence to support his claims and assertions. At the end of it he invited questions and was so bombarded that he had to ask for order and invite specific people to ask their questions. Most were about the financial strength of the group and the share price, but one was speedway related when Barry was asked if he would be selling the Bulldogs. Barry eyed the questioner with a glare that might have turned him to stone, "Why are you making me an offer?" he decided to joke, and the audience erupted with laughter. He leaned forward on the lectern, "Did you come in late and miss the first half hour? Everything I have said in the last hour should have told you how I intend to direct my business group to even bigger financial prosperity and how the Battersea Bulldogs are an important part of the that group. That's the long answer. The short answer is, no," he paused to let it sink in before continuing, "Look, I have spent twenty long years planning and preparing this speedway team. From first discussions with the local council to buying the land and getting planning permission, I have developed the best stadium outside of Wembley and a handful of football stadiums. In addition, I have negotiated revolutionary contracts that benefit the riders so that they can focus on what they are good at and not worry about non-riding issues such as maintenance, accommodation and access to the very best mechanics. We have raced for two and a half seasons and have done really well. I love this sport, I worked hard to get it where it is today, and I will not be walking away from it; that's a promise." As the door closed behind him the place erupted again with chatter between reporters, people on mobile phones and technicians packing away their expensive equipment. Harry heard Johnny speaking into his mic, "So there you are speedway fans, that was Barry Leech speaking live from the Battersea Bulldogs conference facility. The scene, as you may be able to hear from the background noise, is one of excitement, energy and activity as journalists respond to what they have heard this morning and file their reports. Our Skype channel will be open in ten minutes and Jenny will be taking your calls to gauge your reactions and opinions on the Battersea Bulldogs situation. If you can't call us, please contact us on Facebook or Twitter and we will feature your contributions live and also during the live broadcast from Monmore Green where the Bulldogs are meeting Wolverhampton tonight." Johnny sighed and put down his mic and high-fived Harry with a whoop of delight, "What a coup!"

Harry and Johnny switched off their equipment, put it in its bag and left the big boys to pack away theirs into lorries and vans while they headed back to the studio. As they passed the pits Steve Hildegarde walked out of the stores carrying some bike spares which he placed on his tool gurney and bent down at the side of the bike on which he was working. Harry watched expecting to see some sign of furtive behaviour, watchfulness or anxiety but none was forthcoming, Steve looked perfectly normal and relaxed. Harry changed direction and headed towards the mechanic.

"Hello Steve, how's things?" he asked pleasantly.

Steve looked up from his work, "Hello Harry. We're all pretty gutted about Johnny Sinclair of course, but then you probably think I did it don't you?" Harry spluttered for a few seconds, until Steve turned back to his work, "Sod off Harry."

That evening Rosie was beginning to show the strain. She looked tired and drawn as she lethargically moved her food around her plate.

Harry watched her as they dined in silence, "You OK?" he asked after five minutes.

She was touched by his concern and smiled weakly, "I'm pretty tired darling and under quite a bit of pressure at work," she said placing her hand on his and squeezing it.

"I'm here if you need me, you know that don't you?" he said.

"I do know that, thank you," she replied, "That's what helps me to be strong."

"I know it's tough but is there any news from the HSE yet?"

"Yes, and its quite disturbing really," Rosie answered, "They think there could have been an electrical fault."

"Where, on the gas tanks?" Harry asked.

"There or the waste oil tank. The fire damage was so great that it was inconclusive. Whatever, the leaking feeder pipe provided the conditions to make it into what it became, a tragic accident and a killer."

Harry sat thoughtfully pondering the options and then asked, "Did they say how it happened?"

"No." Rosie replied, "But they're coming back tomorrow."

CHAPTER 10

Sunday 28th August 2016

arnie@arniecottrell
Big match last night! We needed more to stop Wolves but we were not good enough, they really are a great team this year!

Harry's radio show was tempestuous and manic as people phoned, texted, emailed and Twittered in such numbers that the system crashed and the station went off the air for half an hour. Harry made a plea to listeners to only contact the station if they had something new and different to offer, in order to keep the volume of traffic down. He kept people on the line to represent the different views and fed new contributors into the debate. It was an excellent programme that hit the main issues and was full of controversial comment. Johnny was delighted with the results, even the breakdown thrilled him, "It's brilliant," he enthused, "Think about it Harry, small time internet radio station is closed down because it was so popular! We could make the national papers, certainly the larger locals and local television and radio. I'll bloody well make sure we do!"

Harry was packing his rucksack ready to make an unusually early exit when his cell phone started to vibrate, it was Rosie, "Hello darling, what's up?"

Rosie's voice was so full of emotion that she was finding it difficult to speak, "Oh Harry it's so awful. Peter Barns just called me and told me that he and Dorothy have decided to cease Davy's nutrition. They're going to do it Harry. They're really going to do it!"

Harry's heart sank, "What did you say?" he asked.

"I pleaded with them not to do it. I told them that it doesn't make any sense, that it's wrong!" her voice choked and she began to cry uncontrollably.

"Where are you now?" Harry asked her.

"In the office," she sobbed.

"I'm coming over now, put the kettle on and make two cups of tea."

They sat at Rosie's desk drinking tea and eating custard creams that someone had left behind. Harry could see that Rosie was deeply affected, so he leaned towards her and put his hand on the back of her neck, "Do you want to tell me about it," Harry asked gently.

"I told him that I was appalled and he said that he was sorry about that, but it didn't change their decision. He said that he was sorry that I felt that way and hoped I could respect their reasons for deciding the way they have. I told him that I couldn't do that because they have essentially decided to kill their son and rationalised it in their minds."

"That sounds like pretty tough talking," Harry said, "how did he respond to that?"

"He told me that he had lots of people to inform and that he had to get off the phone so that he could get on and do it. Then he went," Rosie replied.

"That doesn't sound good," Harry said.

"No, I know. The thing is, I was the first person he called." Rosie explained.
"What do you want to now?" Harry asked.
"I want to go over and see Davy."
"I'll take you," Harry said, "I don't think you should drive at the moment."

When they arrived at the St Boniface Hospital Harry stayed in reception while Rosie went up to Davy's ward. Mary Lambert made him fresh coffee and saw him into a comfortable waiting room with a television, newspapers and magazines and then she went with Rosie to see Davy. As they walked she told Rosie, "I've heard the decision. Listen, nothing is going to happen quickly so don't get to jumpy about it. This is a long process and could easily take a year, maybe two."

Rosie was comforted by this news and felt the panic that had been bubbling inside her start to subside, "I still don't like it Mary. What do you think about it?"

"It doesn't matter what I think about it," Mary answered.

"It matters to me," Rosie retorted, "Your opinion means a lot to me."

Mary thought about it for a moment, "Well, I don't like it either Rosie but I can't say that officially."

Rosie understood that, "I realise that it would cause waves if that was known."

"You bet," Mary confirmed. "I know that you are very upset about it now. But do you have any idea what you might do?"

"I'm definitely going to try and persuade them to change their minds." Rosie said. "I thought I would write to someone about it."

"You could do that," Mary replied, "but remember they are all intelligent experts who understand the arguments all too well and they will make their decisions based on the clinical evidence and the ethical issues. They will not be swayed by emotional pleas. So don't go down that route, try to come from an angle that will grab their attention in a positive way," Mary advised.

"I will Rosie assured her, "can I go in and see him now?"

"Of course you can," Mary said, "I'll come by in about half an hour and see how you are."

Rosie sat by Davy and took his thin bony hand in hers, holding it gently and looked at his gaunt face. She remembered how it had once been so youthful and full of health, but now it was lined and the skin was pulled across his cheeks bones and his brow. He would smile so easily and laugh at the silliest things that she didn't think were funny even though she would laugh as well. Rosie smiled at this memory and said, "Hello Davy, its Rosie. How are you my darling?" She laid her head next to his on the pillow as she sat next to the bed and smelled the scent of coconut and lychee from the shampoo they used to wash his hair. Rosie kissed his forehead, "When are you going to wake up Davy?" she whispered in his ear, "Please wake up my darling, it's really important that you do." She kissed his hand, "Davy, if you can hear me, please give me a sign, anything my sweet, anything will do." Rosie sat there quietly holding Davy's hand, watching his face for anything that would cause her to get a nurse and tell them that he was alive. She didn't know what to say, what to do or what to think any more. Mary came in eventually and asked if she wanted to come down and have a cup of tea. "What time is it?" Rosie asked.

"It's nearly midnight," Mary told her.
"Oh my goodness," Rosie was shocked, "I should go home. Oh my, what about Harry? Where is he?"

"Harry's fine," he's waiting for you downstairs."

CHAPTER 11

Thursday 1st September 2016

ELITE LEAGUE TABLE - Up to and including Tuesday 31st August 2016

TEAM	M	W	D	L	F	A	Pts	+/-
Belle Vue	23	15	0	8	1078	967	52	111
Wolverhampton	26	15	0	11	1004	1127	52	189
Poole	23	14	1	8	1092	948	47	193
Battersea	24	13	0	11	1069	931	47	138
Swindon	24	13	0	11	1068	1124	44	49
Lakeside	25	13	0	12	1130	1117	40	70
Coventry	25	10	0	15	1028	1089	33	-128
Kings Lynn	22	8	2	12	798	1066	29	-114
Leicester	25	6	2	17	946	1238	21	-196

arnie@arniecottrell
We welcome Kings Lynn tonight. With Belle Vue meeting Swindon it could be good news for us, but we must win.

The following Thursday brought rain in the form of a miserable drizzle. The grey clouds hung low over Battersea like uninvited guests who resist all suggestions to go home. Harry worked his show in the afternoon and came out of the studio pleased but unexcited. Johnny looked disappointed, "The trouble with you," Harry observed, "is that you have got too used to ground breaking, high impact, edge of your seat journalistic radio. Anything that falls short of those standards, which you now consider to be the norm, simply disappoints and will no longer do."

Johnny agreed with this and admitted, "Yeah yeah, the next thing you'll be telling me is that there is no perception without contrast and that you have just dished up a load of contrast for me." He put his hand on his friend's shoulder, "I have to say though that our listener figures are to die for, at the moment. I've had two meetings this week with potential advertisers."

"Add the new sponsor you got the other day and it's been a good week for the station," Harry said.

"It certainly has," Johnny acknowledged, "but at what cost? I'd sooner have John and Sonny alive than any number of sponsors and advertisers."

"Yeah right," Harry agreed and they stood for a moment not knowing what to feel when something good had come from something so bad. Harry broke the uneasy silence, "Come on Johnny, I'll buy you a sausage sandwich and a mug of tea at the Tony's mobile café."

The rain eased in the afternoon and a drying wind blew across the stadium so that by six thirty the track was in near perfect condition for racing and any doubts about the meeting going ahead were dissolved. As the riders for both the Bulldogs and Kings Lynn were being introduced to the large crowd, the rain started again and came down solidly for fifteen minutes changing the conditions considerably so that the riders and mechanics had to work frantically to change the set-ups on the bikes to better suit the slick surface. Heat 1 was won by Tia Woffinden with almost the length of the straight between him, Niels-Kristian Iversen and Robert Lambert, who took second and third by team riding Peter Ljung into fourth. Heat 2 was a precarious affair with the two relatively inexperienced reserves pairings treating the corners with so much caution that they were hardly managing to get their bikes to slide, which meant that they had increased difficulty keeping control of their machines and found themselves constantly fighting to keep away from the fence. In their following run out, all four reserves showed a bit more courage and consequently Frankie Chivers and Lynn's Carl Leech fought out a spectacular battle for three laps until Frankie was filled in and had to back off

For the first half of the meeting, the scores varied by only 4 points, with both teams having taken and retaken the lead. It rained a little before heat eleven and added yet another degree of difficulty to an already very slick track. Frankie Chivers was sitting on his bike waiting for the tractor to leave the track after grading. Tia Woffinden, Joe Neal and Patryk Dudek were visiting each of the second string riders in turn to check they were feeling ok and that they had a set-up that made sense in the changing conditions. All three of these Grand Prix stars were world class performers who knew the value of teamwork and sharing knowledge. Frankie Chivers, who was sitting in the corner of his pit stall while his mechanic made adjustments to the bike, looked up from his seat to see Tai approaching with Harry Marsh in tow.

"How's it going Frankie," Tai asked cheerfully.

"I'm good thanks," Frankie answered, watching Tai carefully as he dared to use Grand Prix rider's nickname.

Tai sat down next to the teenager and explained that Harry was recording some typical conversations behind the scenes. They talked about the weather and how the normal racing lines would change in the current conditions and discussed the rutting on bend one towards the outside.

"You'll need to get pretty aggressive and ride hard into the corners. If you are too tentative the track will control you and you'll end up in the fence. Just remember the bike performs best when the back wheel is spinning and that takes power. In these conditions and when it's under enough power, you will have to bring the back round much more deliberately and be brave with the throttle so that you get plenty of speed into the back wheel. That will keep you away from the fence. It might be worth using the longest wheel base available to you as well".

"I've got Jezz adjusting it to make it short at the moment" Frankie replied.

Tai took a look at what Jezz was doing and said to Frankie, "I can understand that you're looking for some more speed, but this track is very tricky at the moment and you know it's much more difficult to slide the bike on the short wheel base unless you've had a lot of practice with it."

"I do want more speed," Frankie said.

"You'll get more speed by sliding the bike and getting the back wheel spinning faster on the bends. This way," he said pointing at the bike, "the speed you gain on the straights will be lost on the bends."

Frankie nodded, "Got it Greg, thanks."

As they left Frankie to think about the advice, Harry pulled Greg over to a relatively quiet corner of the pits, "Can I just get a bit about the advice you gave him please?"

Greg agreed and they talked about the fact that a speedway bike is designed to perform at its best when it's going sideways and essentially skidding around the bends.

"That's right," Greg confirmed, "everything from the centre of gravity to where the engine is positioned on the frame and more is taken into account. They don't much like to be simply leaned over on bends at speed like Moto GP." Greg explained, "Hey, let's go and see if Frankie put the advice into practice."

For the first two laps of heat 12 Frankie Chivers followed Greg's advice to the letter and found himself in a creditable second place behind Mads Korneliussen and some three or four lengths ahead of Troy Bachelor and Linus Sundstrom who were receiving all the wet shale that Frankie's back wheel threw at them. On the first bend of the third lap, Korneliussen made a concerted effort to overtake and by sliding under Frankie on the inside, forced him out towards the deeper shale where the ruts were deep and mushy. Frankie came out of the bend in second place but considerably shaken by the experience. His anxiety was such that he left the inside line wide open and, not surprisingly, the experienced Korneliussen accepted the opportunity gratefully and simply kept his front wheel on the white line and slipped inside as they went into the third bend. The Swede controlled his speed and allowed himself to drift closer to Frankie who was trying to hold his line next to him. At the apex of the bend and at the very moment when Frankie should have opened the throttle further creating more wheel spin and trusting Mads not to actually ride into him, he became fearful and tentative allowing Mads to push him wide into the ruts of deeper shale that were lying in wait. Frankies front wheel slotted into the first rut and followed the curve for a few metres until his back wheel entered the deep shale and found the extra grip it afforded. With the sudden acceleration, his front wheel rose in the air until it was nearly three feet off the track and he was out of control. Panic gripped the young rider and he followed his instinct to open his right hand and release the throttle. This caused the bike to decelerate at an alarming rate, slamming the front wheel into the track and unbalancing Frankie to such an extent that he veered right towards the air fence. He turned the throttle to gain speed and attempt to bring the rear wheel back round to the right, but succeeded only in driving hard towards the fence. All of this drama was acted out in front of Kings Lynn's Robert Lambert who had placed his faith in a strategy that took him wide round the outside line at nearly twice the speed of that which Frankie was travelling. To his horror, he saw Frankie's 's bike kicking and vaulting towards his line with no chance of taking avoiding action. All of Robert Lambert's options were bad so he chose the least worst by sliding off his bike by laying it down on the track and letting go of the handlebars so that his momentum fuelled heavy metal bike might slide away at a greater speed than his lighter body.   In some ways it would have been better if Frankie had just crashed into the fence and had done with it.   In the event, the agony was prolonged as Robert Lambert's bike caught him and threw his bike onto a different trajectory so that it now described a long arc that, while it took him ever closer to the awaiting barrier, it also offered a tantalising possibility of escape; but it was a possibility that was never to be realised. As he approached the last section of the relative protection of the inflated wall Frankie realised that he was destined to crash.   With lamentable poor fortune, the moment he passed the end of the air fence, his handlebar caught the part of the crash barrier that was made of wooden boards and jarred the steering, pulling the handlebars out of Frankies hands and turning it directly into the first of these solid obstacles. With all his commercial wisdom Barry Leech had sold the space for advertising and, as in so many cases like this, there is humour inside every tragedy. Frankie smashed into an advert for a group of injury lawyers who promised to get you financial rewards for any accident that wasn't your fault. Frankie didn't see the irony of this as his bike pivoted on its front wheel causing the back wheel to lift high off the track with such force that he was catapulted violently over the fence onto the greyhound track while his bike bucked across the track like an angry bronco. Considering the spectacular nature of his crash, He came out of it remarkably unscathed, although the almost mandatory broken collar bone would keep him out of racing for a few weeks. A collective sigh of relief went up from the crowd, staff and riders alike when he eventually stood up nursing his shoulder and waving to the crowd before climbing into the ambulance.

Barry Leech stood by the pit gate with Arnie Cottrell looking as if a great weight had been lifted from his shoulders and muttering, "Christ, I thought we got ourselves another death then, that's all we needed," he said as he turned and walked back into the pits.

Ten minutes later the heavens opened and torrential rain submerged the track, forcing the referee to call the meeting off with the score standing at 46–35 after 13 heats, which meant that the result would stand. Even though the Bulldogs took a valuable 3 points from the meeting, a depressed atmosphere settled over the stadium as circumstances continued to inflict problems on the club for the third week running.

Harry and Rosie were sitting in the bar watching the rain slant across the empty stadium when the referee, Sarah Johnson, came by to wish a "Good night," to those stalwarts who were gathered in the Bulldog Bar for a final drink before going home. Harry watched her as she dashed through the pits dodging under cover occasionally to speak with mechanics and riders who were still clearing their gear in the stalls. He'd noticed before that she had a good relationship with the personnel of the various teams, which was different to the more distant relationships that some other referees seemed to have established. Harry suggested that he and Rosie should go home to Notting Hill and when they had finished their drinks they set off across the pits towards the staff entrance. They saw that the lights were on and so stopped off at the first aid room to say, "Goodnight," to Julia Raglett who was packing equipment into cases so that Bernie Thorpe could store it in the ambulance that was parked outside at the bottom end of the carpark.

"Are you on your way home?" she asked the pair.

"Yes, just got to pick up our helmets," Harry explained.

"I don't envy you a motorcycle ride in this weather," Julia said with a scowl.

"No, it's pretty dire isn't it," Rosie agreed.

Julia handed the last box to Bernie who took it out to the ambulance.

"While I think about it," she said to Harry, "I've been mulling over your idea for an interview with a paramedic and would like to tell you what I've come up with. Are you around next week, say Friday morning?"

"Yes, I might be able to manage that" Harry replied.

"Good, both Bernie and I are interested in getting involved. Say, about eleven o'clock?"

"That's great with me," Harry agreed.

They set off from the studio to collect their equipment when Rosie said, "Harry, would you mind if I took the tube? I don't fancy riding home in this weather."

"Ok, of course. You go ahead. I'll bring your helmet and gloves in the pannier."

Rosie left through the staff entrance and Harry carried on towards the studio. As he passed the ambulance he saw Bernie loading the boxes into their compartments in the back of the vehicle.

"Evening Bernie," Harry said poking his head through the open rear doors.

"Oh, hi Harry," Bernie looked over his shoulder, "You going home?"

"Yep, just on my way. I'm meeting Julia a week on Friday in the morning to chat about an interview. She says that you might be interested."

Bernie stopped and turned, moved his soaked high vis jacket along with a first aide box onto the floor and sat on the seat in the back of the vehicle, "Yes, I'd be keen to do it. It sounds exciting."

"That's great, can you make the meeting?"

"No, I'm afraid not, I'll be working then, but Julia can bring me up to speed," Bernie said cheerfully.

"That's good then, sounds like a runner to me," Harry said as he came out from the shelter of the ambulance. He was pleased to find that the rain had eased a bit and the wind had dropped, "Hey, it's improving out here!" he called to Bernie.

"Brilliant!" Bernie replied, "I've nearly finished here, so I'll get going before it starts again. Cheers!"

Johnny Matthews was still in the studio editing material for Jenny Howard's show the next day and inevitably he and Harry found a couple of jobs that required discussion which soaked up about twenty minutes before Harry felt able to collect his and Rosie's stuff and shut up shop for the night. He went down the stairs and turned to shout goodbye to Johnny from the small hallway and, as he did so, he glimpsed something on the floor as it caught the dim light. Over by the under stairs cupboard where the cleaner's kept their various brooms and mops he saw a small red disc on the floor and he went over to look at it, "Find a penny, pick it up and you'll be...." Then he stopped the rhyme because he saw that it wasn't a coin; it glistened, not because it was bright, but because it was wet. Harry bent down to put his finger on it and discovered that it was fresh blood.

He looked around the floor of the dimly lit hallway and saw several other, larger spots and smears of blood that were all over the wall and the floor in the corner opposite the cupboard door. Harry hesitantly reached out and turned the door handle and opened the door slowly. It was dark inside, so Harry clicked the switch to illuminate the cupboard. A dim bulb light came on and lit a small space that was filled with a broom, a mop, dustpan and hand brush, buckets, waste sacks, cleaning liquids and the dead body of Sarah Johnson. Harry jumped back with shock and let out an involuntary shout that attracted Johnny's attention.

"Is that you Harry?"

Harry stumbled backwards into the hallway, "Johnny," his voice was more of a squeak "get down here quick."

Johnny came down the stairs, "What wrong mate?"

Harry pointed towards the cupboard, "Look!"

Johnny got to the door and stopped in his tracks as he saw Sarah lying grotesquely in the blood that had poured from her cut throat, "Oh my God!" he whispered hoarsely, "How the hell, what, who did this?"

"It's Sarah Johnson, the meeting referee," Harry told him, "I'm certain she's dead, there's so much blood, but you'd better go and get Julia Raglett and Bernie Thorpe quickly."

"Of course," Johnny said moving backwards towards the door but unable to take his eyes from the gruesome scene.

Julia entered with Bernie and Johnny a minute or so later and took responsibility, "Call Doctor Rodgers and get him here immediately," she told Bernie, "Harry, call the police. Johnny go and make some hot fresh tea." She bent down by Sarah's inert body and started looking for any vital signs.

Barry Leech arrived during the activity, white faced and agitated, "What the hell happened?" he asked Harry and Johnny.

"I found her," Harry explained, "She's been stabbed."

"Stabbed? She's dead?" Barry asked, "How? Murdered?"

"Dead yes, I think so. Her throat's been cut," Harry said.

"Shit! Shit! Shit!" Barry spat out the words and turned away and walked outside pacing up and down the car park. He returned a couple of minutes later, "Harry? Does she have any family?" he asked.

Harry thought for a moment, "I think she has because she showed me a photograph of her daughter and son."

"Find out please, contact them and her husband if she has one and I'll speak to them," Barry said, "Poor woman, poor kids." He went back outside and made a call on his mobile phone then he returned to the hallway.

Friday 2nd September 2016

Barry Leech stood in front of a room full of staff and spoke in a low measured voice that intoned the seriousness of the situation, "Three dead people and three families who are wondering what they might have done to deserve what's happened to them. If it weren't so tragic it might be a sick joke." He looked round at the people in varying degrees of shock and mourning, "Can anyone throw any light on what is happening here? Why it's happening. Are we being targeted? Is someone responsible for all of this? Are we just unlucky and it's all random chance?"

"He was so angry and frustrated and incredibly sad," Rosie told Harry later as they sat in her Notting Hill flat.

"What happened then?" Harry asked.

"He demanded answers."

"What did people think about that?" Harry enquired.

"I imagine they went off to start answering his questions. That's what I did anyway." Rosie replied, "What about you? What have you been doing?"

"I've been with the police for most of the day. It's surprising how long it takes to tell the story when they want to go into every detail."

"Yes, I suppose it is," Rosie said quietly.

Later, when Rosie had gone to bed, Harry sat alone eating cashew nuts and drinking whiskey as he contemplated what had been happening over the last three weeks or so. He drew diagrams and made notes to see if he could detect a pattern. Two accidents and one possible murder: one very promising speedway rider with a mystery around when he died, one mechanic whose luck ran out when he was in the wrong place at the wrong time. One speedway referee who was killed for, what? There was no evidence that she had been robbed and she had not been sexually assaulted ,so Harry was left devoid of useful ideas. "Well, there's one obvious link," he muttered to himself, "Pretty fair bet its speedway related. But why? What motive?" and that's where his mind went blank. "Steady Harry, you might be in danger of seeing things that aren't there. Step carefully." He poured another large measure of whiskey and looked at the light through it. One name kept coming back to him, that of Steve Hildegarde. He had been in the area where the gas storage tanks were and could easily have rigged something to blow the electrics on the waste oil tank. He could have pulled the feed pipe off the gas tank. He could have sabotaged Sonny's bike. He had threatened Sonny before his death. Harry drew a circle around Steve's name as if that added weight to his case. The outstanding question with regards to Steve was to do with his whereabouts when Sarah Johnson was killed. Harry was certain that he was at the track that night, although he hadn't actually seen him. Harry decided he needed to investigate further, to either place him at the scene of the crime or eliminate him as a suspect.

Saturday 3rd September 2016

Harry went to the studio but could do very little because the stairwell was a crime scene and was sealed off until further notice, plus very few people were actually at work. He found Arnie sorting through the post that had poured into the club as a response to all the troubles. Arnie looked gaunt and haunted as if he was carrying the entire weight of the issues on his own shoulders, "Morning Harry," he said managing a weary smile, "What are you doing here?"

"Dunno really, Arnie," Harry replied, "just seemed better than being at home."

"I know what you mean mate," Arnie agreed, "but there's very little to do here either."

Harry nodded, "Shall I make some coffee?"

"That'll be nice thanks."

As he busied himself at the mini kitchen that Arnie had made in the corner of his office, Harry asked casually, "Was Steve Hildegarde working on Thursday night?"

Arnie consulted the staff rota on the wall, "Yes, he was spannering for Linus. Why?"

"Oh, no reason particularly. It just occurred to me that I didn't see him that's all and I wondered if he'd missed it or something."

"No, he was here," Arnie said turning back to the post.

"Shame about Danny," Harry said switching the topic.

"Yeah," Arnie replied not looking up, "it's his collar bone again; third time."

Harry put Arnie's coffee down on his desk, "If he doesn't watch it, he'll just have more scar tissue than bone."

"Now there's a thought to play with," Arnie laughed shortly. "I'll tell him when I see him today. He's coming with me when we go up to Swindon for tonight's meeting."

That afternoon Rosie and Harry went to see Barry Leech at his huge house on the outskirts of the village of Hook Norton near Oxford. The official version was that he had decided to work from home, but the truth was that he needed to be away from the spotlight, away from the pressure and the news teams that were even now parked at his gate. He looked a diluted version of the normally strong, self-assured business man he had been a month ago. He had dark shadows under his eyes and his skin had taken on a waxy, tight consistency. He was a worried man and he looked to be near the end of his tether. Both Rosie and Harry were shocked when they saw him. Barry had come to the large oak front door as Harry brought his Triumph to a halt on the deep gravel. When she saw him, Rosie jumped off the pillion seat and rushed over to her Uncle and hugged him. They went into the drawing room and sat down on two of the sumptuous old Chesterfields that were dotted around the room. A maid bought them afternoon tea in the form of beautifully cut, crustless triangles of brown bread with the thinnest slices of salmon Harry had ever seen, "It was so thin that I wasn't even sure if there was any there at all," he revealed much later. These were accompanied by fingers of toast with sliced pilchard, slivers of cucumber and a garnish of parsley, home-made scones, cream and raspberry jam. Rosie swooned over the selection of teas on offer. She cooed as she sorted through Bai Hao Yin Zhen or Silver Needle, Lung Ching or Dragon's Well, Tai Guan Yin, Black Tea and Green Tea amongst many others. "How do I choose?" she moaned.

Uncle Barry smiled, "Just start with one and move through them." He might have been a rough diamond, but he knew about the refined things of life. Barry sat sullenly on one of the sofas, "Arnie tells me that the police are all over the stadium again today."

"Yes, they are," Harry confirmed, "They began arriving as we were leaving."

"They've made it a murder case you know?" Barry said.

"Yes, so we hear. It's hard to see a cut throat as anything else really," Harry ventured.

"I can't get over the number of incidents we've had recently," Barry told them.

Rosie sipped her green tea, "I know, I never heard of such a weird run of coincidences"

Harry took one of the toast fingers, "I don't like coincidence as an explanation. Maybe the first or possibly the second could have been accidents, but the third one certainly wasn't. However, consider this possibility," Harry looked at Barry, "Suppose Sonny, Johnny and Sarah's deaths were not accidents, suppose they were deliberate acts of sabotage."

"But what motive could there be?" Rosie joined in.

Harry looked back to Barry, "Do you know anyone who might have a vendetta against you, and wishes you or your business some harm?"

Barry laughed out loud, "It would be a long queue if we ask them to form one."

"I see," Harry said with surprise.

"I've made plenty of enemies over the years and some of them might want to harm me, but not by doing this. It's too extreme and none of them would bring innocent people into it."

"Certain?" Rosie asked.

"Certain," Barry said firmly, "Some of my business competitors are well capable of organising something like this if they wanted to, but the kind of things I've done that might make them angry are business deals with the occasional bit of sharp practice. I think all of them would just put it down to experience and move on; I would, in their place. We are much more interested in making money than getting this kind of revenge." He took a sip of tea, "These are not the actions of disgruntled business acquaintances. If you're right, we're looking for a deranged mind."

"What about non-business acquaintances?" Rosie enquired.

"I can't think of anyone that I've upset that much."

"Do you know Steve Hildegarde?" Harry asked.

Barry looked surprised, "Yes of course I do, why?"

"I can connect him directly to the first two deaths and I can speculate about his motivation for them but, as yet, nothing for the third death," Harry explained.

Barry frowned, "Do you really think he could do those things? He hardly seems the type to me."

Harry shuffled in his seat next to Rosie, "I'm trying not to rush to judgment because there are gaps," he said, "I'm lacking authenticated motives for Johnny and Sarah, but I can see he had opportunity and means for them."

"Along with several hundred other people," Barry observed.

"Yes, well....but the several hundred didn't threaten to kill Sonny Brent because he made love to his girlfriend."

Barry was thoughtful at this revelation, "What do you think we should do about it?"

"Nothing at the moment," Harry answered, "if we raise a fuss at this stage we could scare him off or end up in court for defamation of character or something. Either way we should be careful."

I'll certainly keep an eye on him," Barry said agreeing with the sentiment.

"If we don't do something we risk him potentially killing again," Rosie warned, "What about suspending him from work for the duration of an investigation?"

"It's possible," Barry admitted, "but a bit heavy handed without some kind of official ratification, like a police investigation."

"True enough, but I think we should dig around a bit and find out what his movements were at the time of Sarah's death," Harry suggested.

"Ok that makes sense," Barry agreed.

"How long will it take?" Rosie asked.

Harry thought, "I should think we could do it by end of business on Monday."

"Ok let's do it," Barry confirmed, "let's meet on Monday evening after the office closes to discuss any results."

CHAPTER 12

Monday 5th September 2016

arnie@arniecottrell
We are trying to keep things normal under abnormal circumstances. Once again sadness and tragedy are upon us. Hard times

Harry was at the track by eight o'clock on Monday morning to prepare the afternoon show so that he could start investigating Steve Hildegarde. He spoke in general terms to all the mechanics except Steve and from these conversations he established that Steve had indeed been working with Linus Sundstrom and had been in the pits for the entirety of the meeting. A couple of mechanics remembered that he had hung around with some of the team members in the bar after the meeting. Of that group, all remembered Steve leaving with them and being with them all evening apart from going to the toilet.

So, an inconclusive morning suggested that Steve was behaving normally throughout the evening, but he could have left the bar long enough to commit a murder before returning to drink with his mates. The charitable side of Harry thought it was unlikely, while the suspicious side thought it was perfectly possible. Harry spoke to three stewards who were around, but none could recall anything that placed Steve near the studio entrance. One of them remembered that an ambulance had been parked near there, but could not place Steve Hildegarde there. The ambulance was usually parked outside the First Aid room on the east side of the stadium where Julia and Bernie always restocked it before finishing for the night, however something was rattling in Harry's brain, but he could not form it into anything informative.

He rang Julia Raglett and found her running a training course at Overstone Road in Hammersmith, "What can I do for you Harry?" she asked.

"Have you got a couple of minutes so I can ask a couple of questions?"

"For you Harry," she answered, "Yes I have, but I only have a few minutes, I'm due back in session soon."

"Thanks. Ok, straight in then," Harry said, "I'm trying to find out what people may have noticed on Thursday evening so that I can confirm or eliminate a theory about what happened."

"Why are you doing this Harry? Isn't it a job for the police?" Julia asked.

"Ideally yes," Harry agreed, "but I'm under suspicion and there don't seem to be any other candidates emerging to challenge me."

"Why are you under suspicion?"

"Because I found Sarah's body, so I could have done it and used the discovery as a cover-up."

"But you didn't do it, did you?" Julia queried.

"No of course not!"

"Good; ok, well fire away."

"Do you remember that the ambulance was close to the studio entrance on Thursday night?" Harry asked.

"Yes, I do. I parked it there. We were restocking the medical boxes ready for the next meeting."

"Can you recall seeing anyone around that area while you were doing that?"

"No...just me and Bernie. I passed Sarah Johnson as she was going to the car park."

"What were you doing?"

"I was going to lock up the medical room," Julia explained.

"Was she ok then?"

"Yes, she was. She wished me 'Goodnight' and flashed me a big smile, "I asked her if she was coming back soon and she told me that she was due back in a month. That's not going to happen now though."

"What time was that?" Harry pushed on.

Julia thought about it, "I don't know but it was about half an hour before I got the call to go to the studio hallway and that was at 22:47. Bernie and I packed the stuff away and spoke to her in the stadium by the First Aid room in the pits. We carried stuff over to the ambulance and Bernie started packing it away."

"I remember speaking to him just after I agreed to meet you about the interviews and told him about them." Harry recollected.

Julia agreed, "That's right, I took the last load over and he told me about your conversation. That was when I saw Sarah."

"What, when you were in the ambulance?"

"No not in the ambulance, I'd just started walking back to the First Aid room from it when we spoke."

"So, Bernie was still in the ambulance?"

"Yes, he was packing the boxes away." Julia confirmed.

"Do you think he saw Sarah?" Harry asked.

"I would have thought so. Sarah kept walking and we were calling to each other as she was trying to get out of the rain."

"I think I should talk with him as well, maybe he saw something," Harry said.

"Well if he did see something, he will have told the police about it," Julia pointed out.

"Well yes, I guess so, but I'll ask anyway. You never know I might jog his memory." Harry replied, "Where can I get hold of him?"

"He'll be at work until the next meeting."

"Maybe I can go to see him there, where does he work?" Harry asked.

"'Sofa City' over in Paddington, Julia said, "I suppose you'll get him there."

Harry thanked her and rang off. An hour later he was waiting to see Bernie on the sales floor of the large furniture store. When he arrived, he was surprised to see Harry.

"What do you want?" he asked suspiciously.

Harry told him, so Bernie ushered him through the store, "Come out the back, we can talk in private there." They went into a small empty office, "Ok, what do you want Harry?"

"I want to know if you saw anyone or anything when you were in the back of the ambulance on Thursday evening."

Bernie thought about it for a few moments but concluded that he did not see anything or anyone, "Other than you of course," he pointed out.

"Well it was just an off chance," Harry said, "How long did it take to restock the boxes?"

"I think it was about ten minutes after you left and then I went straight to the bar. It's horrible to think that it all took place not more than thirty or forty yards away from where I was working. I'm only sorry that I can't help you, but as I say, I was busy inside the ambulance."

"Did you talk to Sarah as she passed the ambulance?

"No, I didn't."

"Can you remember Sarah passing the ambulance at all?"

"No I can't but, as I say, I was busy and I did have my back to the doors."

Harry nodded. "Right…look, thanks Bernie. I'm sorry to have troubled you at work," Harry said, and he thought, 'Is that a lie he just told me? If so, I wonder why?"

"That's ok Harry," Bernie said interrupting Harry's thoughts, "If I remember anything I'll tell you," Bernie and Harry went back onto the sales floor and across to the entrance doors. Harry rode back to the Battersea Stadium in a thoughtful mood. Bernie was an unlikely suspect, but Harry suspected that he had lied about Sonny Brent and now he had might have lied again about not seeing Sarah. Julia had spoken with Sarah close enough to the ambulance so that Bernie must have heard them speaking? Surely? What couldn't be denied was that Bernie was in very close proximity to both Sonny and Sarah at the moment of their deaths.

Harry headed south directly from Sofa City, turned off the Bristol Road and rode up the thread of road that led to the Oak Tree Arena at Edithmead in time for a Skype meeting with Barry and Rosie, who were sitting in the Bulldog's Boardroom back in London. He told them about his conversations but majored on the ones he had with Julia and Bernie. Barry said that he would get the team to dig around some background information with regards to Bernie and Steve to see what, if any connections there might be before they started working with the Bulldogs.

"To reiterate, we may have something of a motive for Steve Hildegarde. You may recall, I overheard him threaten Sonny Brent. He actually said, 'You're a dead man Brent.'"

Rosie frowned, "You're pushing that a little bit too hard for me if you're suggesting that puts him in the frame for John Sinclair's and Sarah Johnson's deaths based on his threat to Sonny."

"I'm suggesting that he may be capable of killing a person," Harry retorted.

"That doesn't hang right. Steve isn't the kind of person to go that far. Anyway, if we prosecuted everyone who said things like that, we would have courts overflowing with brothers and sisters, parents and friends," Rosie observed.

Harry sighed and Barry slumped back in his chair, "So what we've got then," Barry said, "is two suspects who both had opportunity and means, but no apparent motives. Plus, each of them can only be connected to one death and both of those connections can easily be disputed. Plus, only the last of the deaths is considered foul play. Is that right?"

Rosie pursed her lips, "Put like that, it all seems a bit flimsy doesn't it?"

"Little wonder," Barry added, "that the police appear to be very quiet about it all. They've interviewed Steve, Bernie, me, Harry and you Rosie, not to mention almost every other employee and they haven't found a clue or connection worth a mention."

"I suppose it looks bleak," Harry agreed, "and although we certainly can't go accusing either of them at this stage, I still think we should get the team to do more research though."

They all agreed on that, "What about you Uncle Barry?" Rosie asked, "How are you coping?"

Barry Leech in his office was a very different person to the Barry Leech at home. In the business environment he was strong, decisive and self-confident, "I'm fine," he said, "I admit that the third death is a hammer blow that I'm not sure we can survive, but we'll fight until we drop. We won't just fall over."

"Is it that bad?" Rosie asked with concern.

"The share price is dangerously low for the group and the individual companies so we are beginning to mount potential defences against hostile takeovers from other big players. The speedway team is vulnerable because it receives so much finance from the group."

"I didn't realise," Rosie said thoughtfully.

"Hey, that's how business is done," Barry said with a hint of excitement in his voice, "that's why I love it. The strong will survive while the weak will go to the wall. That's life."

"Well, it is in the capitalist world, it's not like that everywhere is it?" Harry retorted.

"Survival of the fittest applies to everything," Barry stated.

Rosie stepped in to intercept this exchange, "I haven't seen any papers today, what kind of things are they saying?"

Barry and Harry got the message and took the route out that she was offering them, "They're reasonably gentle actually. I was expecting them to take the opportunity to slate us," Barry answered.

"That's good then," Harry said.

Barry agreed with reservations, "Generally, yes you're right, but obviously they can't yet justify being brutal from a business angle but I think my competitors will have plenty to say this week if the share price doesn't change direction."

"How far will it have to drop before you really do become a target for a takeover bid?" Harry asked.

"Not very far now," Barry answered, "if we lose another ten pence, you'll see the vultures circling, twenty or thirty pence and the jackals will start arriving, fifty pence like we did on Friday, and they'll start biting chunks out of us."

"Your conference should have helped shouldn't it?" Rosie asked.

"Yes, but that was only a short term tactic just to give us a bit of breathing space, but that's pretty much wiped out now we've had another death. It will have knocked confidence in my ability to manage the situation that I built in the minds of the shareholders and the media," Barry took another sip of tea, "having said that, the papers have been gentle with me today, I was going to say compassionate, but they're never that with anyone."

"I saw journalists and TV cameras around today," Rosie said.

"Yes, we've been the focus of quite a bit of attention. We even made the national news this lunchtime. With any luck a bigger story will come up this afternoon to keep us off the evening news."

"Let's hope so," Rosie said, "Obviously I'm not wishing a disaster on anyone."

"I never realised that this sort of thing would have such an effect on the entire group's share price," Harry commented.

"Oh yes, but that's more to do with the level of confidence that investors have in me personally. Big business is driven by the competence of the Chief Executive specifically and the Board in general. If I appear to be vulnerable or weak, people think that I've lost control and they'll ship their money out pretty quickly. You see, shareholders are super sensitive to anything that might suggest the Board of Directors might not be good enough to manage their money." Barry laughed quietly to himself, "One positive effect from all of this is that speedway is getting lots of exposure in the national media. I would fully expect the gates to go up as a consequence. Morbid isn't it?"

"The public do have macabre taste, the more gruesome, the better." Harry responded.

"What about the Bulldogs?" Rosie asked, "Will they be ok?"

"They should be fine," Barry confirmed, "I can disconnect them very easily from the rest of the group and I can finance them personally if I need to, just like any other promoter and any other speedway team."

"What do the riders say about it all?" Harry enquired.

"Supportive," Barry replied, "I spoke with Arnie this morning and he told me that he has received emails from all of them with messages of encouragement and support. They are all tentative about saying anything in public and have stayed away from commenting on social media, although they've all sent their sympathies to Sarah's family."

"So, we need to keep our fingers crossed this week." Rosie said.

"Yes, offer prayers, gifts for the gods, sacrifices, whatever you think will work," Barry said. "We can say for certain that, whatever it's like, this time next week it will be different."

CHAPTER 13

Tuesday 6th September 2016

arnie@arniecottrell
Still in the top 4! I'm delighted with the team character. No meeting for us this week but watch out for Poole and Swindon!

With his Skype meeting finished, Harry tried to turn his mind to the Somerset Rebels and their meeting with Sheffield Tigers. As he stepped out of the office he'd borrowed for an hour he was the target for questions from curious and concerned staff and a few fans who recognised him. He eventually managed to become an anonymous member of the public by retreating into the café and sitting in the corner with a polystyrene box of chips and chicken strips; he needed time to think.

"Hello Harry! What are you hiding in here?" Kevin Hinchcliff, the Rebel's Health and Safety Manager, asked with a mischievous grin on his face.

Harry jumped with surprise, "Just grabbing a bite to eat and a tea Kevin. How are you?" Harry answered standing to shake his hand.

"I'm good thanks mate," Kevin answered, "Looking forward to a good meeting tonight. Of course, we are going to try and get through it without killing anyone," he laughed at his own joke.

"Ouch!" Harry said and sat heavily in his plastic chair, "let's hope you achieve that, otherwise that remark will go beyond tasteless and be plain offensive."

"I don't mean any offence Harry; it's just my way mate, what am I like?"

Harry nodded, "I understand Kevin, an arsehole?"

"What?" Kevin's eyes looked narrowed and wary.

"Hey, don't mind me. I'm just joking."

"No but seriously," Kevin pushed on through the awkwardness "it's been bloody awful up at Battersea hasn't it?"

"To say the least," Harry agreed.

"It's shot your safety record to bits. I bet Tony Fuller's livid isn't he?"

"Why should Tony be livid?" Harry asked.

"Because it makes him look like tool," Kevin retorted.

"Yes, I suppose it does reflect poorly on him especially in the circles you lot move in."

"Too true."

"Well, you know Kevin, Tony is feeling pretty upset at the moment, but it's got nothing to do with what's happened to his reputation or his position in some HSE league table." Harry said deliberately, "No, the reason he is upset is because there are a lot of people who are in great pain, feeling a sense of loss and grieving."

"Well yes of course he does, but I know Tony well as you do, and the HSE league table means a lot to him. He'll be hurting," Kevin chuckled knowingly.
"Anyway, it was such a shame about Sonny Brent, I liked him. He was a really nice lad."

"Yes, he was," Harry agreed dryly.

"Mind you," Kevin went on, "he showed another side of his character when he rode here as a replacement for our Jake Allen and few weeks ago."

"Really? In what way?" Harry was intrigued.

"He had a real bust-up with his mechanic and they came to blows on the track," Kevin explained with some relish. "Yes, Sonny gave him a good right hook that knocked him off his feet. Oh....what was his name?"

"Steve Hildegarde?" ventured Harry.

"That's right, Hildegarde," Kevin said, "they had to be pulled apart otherwise they would have gone on with it."

"What were they arguing about?"

"I'm not sure; I heard that it was a woman, but that was just gossip."

"Right," Harry nodded as his suspicions were confirmed. So the argument he had heard in the changing rooms at Battersea had been going on for a while.

This conversation was to play on Harry's mind throughout the evening. He went down to the pits and grabbed a couple of interviews with Andy White and Jason Priestly and a lively and humorous interview with Tony Jackson, the Workington Manager. But the disturbing image of Sonny and Steve fighting on the track persistently returned. Deep inside, Harry wanted Steve to be innocent, but this latest information didn't go in his favour.

Wednesday 7th September 2016

After the Wednesday afternoon broadcast Harry rushed over to Rosie's office and they took a hire car to Swanage, picked up Uncle Max and went straight back to Wimborne Road to see Poole against Coventry in their rerun meeting after the abandoned match on the 25th August. Krzysztof Kasprzak on 12 points and Chris Harris on 9 points were the strong backbone of the Coventry side, but this was not enough to compete against a Poole team that was determined to maintain their strong second position in the league. Chris Holder on 12 points and Hans Andersen on 11 + 1 points headed four riders who scored solid 9s and a 7 +2, while the rest of the Coventry team members performed below their green sheet averages.

Chris Holder and Brady Kurtz put on a display of superb team riding to keep Danny King and Jason Garrity in third and fourth place to gain a 5 - 1 heat win and started an avalanche of Pirates scoring that saw them enter heat 13 with Chris Holder and Hans Andersen with an 8 point lead to defend against Chris Harris and Adam Roynon. It was the race of the night with Holder getting to the first bend in the lead from the inside gate with Harris right on his back wheel. Roynon was desperately looking for a way past Andersen, but the veteran Swede kept his racing line to stop any opportunity of passing. Holder tried to slow the race down so that his team mate could get up alongside him, but only managed to block Andersen and in so doing provided an opportunity for Roynon to slip past on the outside into third. Holder decided to leave his team mate as the threat from Harris and Roynon became acute. He tried to pull away up the back straight, but Harris had other ideas. Holder hugged the white line putting his front wheel on the grass, while Harris trailed his leg and took his bike into the deeper shale on the outside line looking for grip and then cutting back sharply down the inside of Holder as he let the inside line go and drifted away towards the middle of the track to cover Harris's original line. Holder's choice allowed Harris to get his front wheel ahead as they entered the first bend on the third lap. Both riders were riding at their best and raced wheel to wheel for the next lap going into the fourth lap side by side having both held the lead and lost it twice. Behind them Roynon and Andersen's battle was such that they gained on the leaders to such an extent that all four riders went across the start and finish line to begin lap four with only ten metres between first and last. On the first bend Chris Holder had the inside line with Harris just outside on his shoulder and the other two side by side on Harris's back wheel. Roynon's greater momentum behind the slower Holder and Harris forced him to throttle back and cut to the inside line. Andersen drifted out and away from the potential overcrowding just as Harris, in attempting to stay out of Holder's way moved out as well. The situation was tense and Andersen was given two simple choices; continue to be driven out and hit the air fence or, shut off the throttle and get out of the way. The experienced campaigner chose the latter and dropped back to fourth place. Harris came out of the bend in good shape and very close behind and on the outside of the Australian. The question that Chris Harris was asking himself, was whether or not his opponent would leave the gap open between himself and the fence as they sped down the back straight where the spectators sat in comfort behind large windows, drinking and eating as they watched the dual. Harris's superior pace out of the second bend meant that he rapidly gained on Holder, closing the gap to nothing as he aimed his bike at the narrowing gap before it closed. Chris Holder is the consummate competitor but, more than that, he is a sportsman who wants to race rather than risk lives, so he left enough space for a man and bike to squeeze through between him and the fence - if he dared and was good enough. Harris certainly dared and proved good enough as he and Chris Holder clashed elbows on the one side and Harris's rear tyre scorched the wooden fencing, leaving a black scar. Going into the third bend Harris's extra speed put him ahead, and as Chris Holder turned his bike sharply to get his wheels in a straight line he felt the presence of Adam Roynon driving hard around the white lined inside track and Hans Andersen close by and charging. As they passed the finish line all four riders were only a few feet apart with Chris Harris first, Holder second, Roynon third and Andersen fourth. The crowd were in a frenzy of excitement and cheered all the riders as the two managers sent all four of them round again on a lap of honour. The track announcer was shouting with the thrill of it all, "That's what I call speedway! That's why we all love this sport! That's why we come here!"

The interviews that Harry got with each of the riders made one of the best features he had ever broadcast. He was able to present the race from the point of view of each rider in their own words and fascinating perspectives. He also got several recordings of fans talking excitedly about it and the riders which blended beautifully with the rider's contributions. Johnny called it a 'masterpiece' and turned parts of it into a trailer for the Saturday round-up show that Jenny fronted.

That night Rosie, Harry and Uncle Max stayed at the Red Lion in Wareham where they were greeted like old friends. They talked until late about the night's speedway, "It was sensational!" Uncle Max waxed lyrical, "I loved the sound, the sheer noise of the bikes! The smell was just exquisite; I couldn't get enough into my lungs! The riders are so brave, and reckless, and..and...and, well skilful! Thank you so much for taking me to see that."

"Would you like to go again?" Rosie asked.

"Yes, I would! I can still feel the pressure in my chest from that wonderful race with the four riders who did a lap of honour. It's given me an idea for a painting when I've finished the one I'm doing now."

"Well, we can't wait to see that can we Harry?" Rosie said.

"True enough, we'll try to get down again to see Poole." Harry said, "But that may be the play-offs at the end of the season."

"Do you think Poole will get to them?" Uncle Max asked.

"It's a relatively safe bet, they pretty much always do."

Thursday 8th September 2016

The next morning they motored slowly down to Swanage and discovered that Uncle Max had been working on a twelve foot canvas that took up a whole side of the studio, "What are you going to do with it?" Rosie asked.

"Sell it." Uncle Max replied.

Harry was looking at it with his head on one side, "What's it about?"

"It's not about anything Harry. It's an abstract piece based on textures and complimentary colours. I want it to dominate the space it hangs in."

"Well the size will ensure that," Rosie laughed.

Uncle Max punched her arm, "Hey saucy!" Harry was looking blankly at it. "Don't worry about it Harry," the elderly artist laughed, "it hasn't got any meaning. It's just a big, ballsy, colourful mass of rough and smooth textures and, most importantly, it's paid for."

Harry grinned, "I might have guessed."

"It's not always like that, most of the time I just paint whatever I want and hope someone buys it. This is different; it's a commission that came from a client who wanted something in warm colours and a large size to hang in the reception area of his offices.

"I like the choice of colours, the subtlety of the different reds and oranges," Harry said.

"Yes, they match the furniture."

Harry eyes rolled to the ceiling, "I'm going to shut up!"

"As long as I sign it and it meets his two criteria, he will be a happy bunny," Uncle Max said.

"If I wanted one, how much would I have to pay for it?" Harry asked.

"Just over forty-five thousand pounds

"Wow! Who the hell would pay that kind of money for a painting?" Harry asked in astonishment.

"A Russian oligarch."

"That's impressive."

"It's handy," Uncle Max smiled.

They walked through to the shop made some coffee, poured a whisky for Uncle Max and sat down on the sofas that were scattered around the room.

"So," the artist asked, "What's been happening in your world?" They told him all about the deaths, "My God, that sounds terrible and very scary."

Rosie nodded, "It's getting scary, I find myself wondering if there are going to be any more."

"That supposes that the deaths are connected and in turn raises the issue of them being deliberate." Max said, "Do you think they are?"

"We're not sure, but there is some circumstantial evidence that makes us think they might be." Harry said.

"That's terrible," the elderly artist leaned forward, "What is the evidence?" Harry and Rosie took him through the entire story, ending "I'm beginning to look at perfectly ordinary people and see them as potential murderers. That, in itself, is pretty scary."

Max sat back on his sofa and sighed, rubbed his eyes and took an Uncle Max sized sip of whiskey, "What is Steve like as a person, do you know him well?"

Harry answered, "Reasonably well, or should I say, I thought I did. I always thought he was a very pleasant, enthusiastic young man, who works hard and loves his job."

Uncle Max asked, "Have you altered that opinion?"

Harry thought about this, "No I don't think I have but I am suspending judgement at the moment. I mean, his fight and his argument with Sonny takes the shine off the image I had."

"Of course it does, but you couldn't see any faults, so who could have lived up to the image you had? He's a young man who's had a fight and an argument with his best friend over a girl. That doesn't sound out of the ordinary to me, or am I being overly charitable?"

"What about his presence between the gas tanks on the day of the explosion?" Rosie put in.

Max thought for a moment, "He said he was emptying waste oil into the oil tank didn't he?"

"Yes," Harry confirmed.

"On what basis do you choose to disbelieve him?"

Harry was disconcerted by the question, "I have no reason to disbelieve him other than all these thoughts and things that are hanging around," He answered honestly, "and he was in the vicinity of the explosion."

"Hmmm, does that sound as thin to you as it does to me? What if he was innocently emptying the oil as he said he was? How many other people went there for the same purpose or equally prosaic purposes?"

Rosie stepped in, "Uncle Max! Stop beating Harry up like that."

Harry answered, "It's alright, I'm ok with it. It's actually helping."

The elderly artist leaned forward again, "Have you tried looking at it without the bias of judgement? Have you ever been certain that you are right only to discover that you are wrong?"

Harry laughed shortly, "Touché. That one struck home."

Uncle Max looked sympathetically at Harry, "I'm not trying to score points Harry."

"No...I know you're not. It's just that some questions can be uncomfortably relevant."

They fell into silent thought for a while. Eventually Max said, "I'm not even sure you have any evidence against Steve at all. What you seem to have is a set of interpretations of behaviour all of which hang off the fact that he had been angry with Sonny over his girlfriend. Be careful that you aren't shoe horning the rest into a convenient package that condemns him."

"Hmm. So, I'm seeing what I want to see?" Harry asked.

"Yes, I think you might be!" the artist confirmed, then he stood up abruptly and walked over to the whiskey bottle, "Enough! You know what to do."

It seemed to bring a natural end and a little later, as they stood by the car saying their 'goodbyes' there was a close feeling amongst the group. As he slid the painting onto the back seat of the car Harry thought how much he liked Uncle Max and that the elderly man seemed to have taken a shine to him. They shook hands, "Thanks again Uncle Max, you've made me think."

"Thanks for being interested enough to ask me what I thought."

Rosie kissed him on his cheek, "See you soon, you old rascal. We'll pick you up next time we are down here."

"I look forward to that my dear."

CHAPTER 14

Thursday 8th September 2016

ELITE LEAGUE TABLE - Up to and including Tuesday 6th September 2016

TEAM	M	W	D	L	F	A	Pts	+/-
Belle Vue	25	16	0	9	1178	1053	55	125
Wolverhampton	27	16	0	11	1280	1169	55	111
Poole	25	15	1	9	1235	1037	51	198
Battersea	25	14	0	11	1103	987	47	116
Swindon	26	14	1	11	1188	1157	47	31
Lakeside	27	14	0	13	1265	1197	44	68
Coventry	26	10	0	16	1119	1248	33	-129
Kings Lynn	24	9	2	13	996	1068	32	-172
Leicester	26	6	2	18	1063	1295	21	-232

arnie@arniecottrell
We welcome Leicester and although they are having a hard season at the bottom, we need to be at our best to get the points

Back at the Barry Leech stadium things were neither better nor worse on Thursday. The police had gone but the HSE were still working on the fire prevention system and ploughing through the SOPs. The staffs were still under enormous pressure, supplying information or trying to get the pit area repaired and ready for the next days' meeting. Rosie was in the office by seven o'clock that morning, in order to catch up from Wednesday and Thursday's excursion to Poole and so that she could prepare for the nine o'clock meeting. Harry got in at about eight thirty and tidied up the interviews from the Poole meeting in the editing room. Johnny rolled in at eleven o'clock, made coffee and put a mug in front of Harry, "How's things?" he asked.

"Good, I think," Harry replied, "I've got about half an hours work here and then I have to see Julia and discuss the paramedic's interview."

Johnny sipped his coffee, "That's a good idea. I'd like to see that included in the next couple of weeks if we can. I think it has potential."

By the time he'd finished the editing it was lunch time and then he met with Julia before going onto his live programme which, thank goodness, was only an hour in length that week. He went over to the admin offices hoping that Rosie had finished work for the day as well, to discover that although she had finished she also had a plan to go over to Peter and Dorothy Barns' home to see them and discuss the outcome of their meeting with the legal people involved with the case. Harry didn't feel that he could contribute to such a meeting, so he decided to slide out of it, go home and chill out with a bottle of whiskey and a microwave meal.

Peter and Dorothy Barns were very formal when they entertained visitors even when they call in at short notice, so Rosie found herself sitting in their lounge while Peter opened a bottle of wine and Dorothy prepared food in the form of nibbles and malt loaf. They sat in silence drinking and eating until Rosie asked, "What was the outcome of your discussions with the legal department at the hospital?"

Peter put his wine down on a coaster that had a photograph of the Sagrada Familia in Barcelona printed on it, "Nothing of any import I'm afraid. It was really about setting out the basic case, although the hospital lawyer did venture a view that, due to the length of Davy's coma, it would probably not meet with any significant opposition."

Rosie composed herself before speaking, "I want to understand. I want to try and see the situation from your point of view so that I don't feel the way I do at the moment about your decision. Please tell me how you see Davy and what goes through your mind when you are thinking about turning his machine off, which at some point is exactly what you will have to do."

Peter and Dorothy Barns looked at each other then back to Rosie. They were clearly troubled by the whole subject and found it difficult to talk about it. "We love Davy," Peter said eventually, "he's our son".

"No-one loves him more than we do or ever will." Dorothy added

"I know," Rosie replied quietly.

Peter continued, "So everything must be viewed from this perspective. We see our beloved Son lying year after year in this heart-breaking, unresponsive state and physically deteriorating," he gulped a sob back, "and it destroys us a little bit more each time we visit him. Every time we leave the hospital we cry for him and ourselves. There are no winners in this. The longer it goes on, the more futile it seems to us. We talk about what it would be like if Davy woke up and was mentally sound and as bright as he was before. How long would it take for his muscles to reconstruct, if ever they could? Would he be in a wheelchair for the rest of his life? If he was, how happy would he be? If he is brain damaged, what kind of life would he have?" He stopped to hold back tears that were threatening to emerge.

Dorothy took over, "We are getting older and will reach a stage when we cannot look after Davy if he were at home, so we see a future where he lives in a hospital or a home until he dies."

Peter Barns came back in, "So either way, we can only see a lonely, empty life filled with pain, sorrow and frustration, lived as a disabled person who'd had a life of activity and action. When we think about it, we feel responsible."

Rosie sat quietly thinking about what they were saying to him. Uncle Max's words came to her, but she could see why and how they had come to their conclusion, "Can you see any circumstances whereby Davy could lead a happy and full life?" she asked.

They both shook their heads and wept silently holding hands to give each other strength and support.. Rosie believed them and reached across to take their hands in hers. They sat like this without speaking for some time. Rosie felt closer to them now than she had ever done, and she didn't want to argue with them anymore but she also felt that it was not the end of the story.

She got home at nearly midnight and slipped into bed next to Harry. He awoke from a deep sleep, "Oh, hello, who are you?" he yawned.

"The woman who's been following you for the last two years."

"Well, welcome to my bed." he whispered sleepily, "how are you anyway?"

"Tired," Rosie told him.

"Kiss?" he asked and she bent over him and kissed on his forehead.

"And you?"

"Drunkish," he said, "I may have imbibed well but not wisely."

"Hmm," Rosie put her mouth to his ear, "I love you when you're sleepy," and she kissed him again.

"I love you all the time," he retorted.

"You know what I mean," Rosie snarled and started undressing.

Harry's eyes slowly closed and he slid gently into a deep sleep.

Saturday 10th September 2016

They spent Saturday relaxing together and enjoying an idle life of eating, drinking, making love and watching DVDs until four o'clock when it was time to get ready for the Bulldog's meeting against Leicester. A large crowd had rallied to Barry Leech's call for support during these hard times and with an hour to go, the fans provided a noisy and lively atmosphere as they filled the stadium with the wail of air horns, clappers and whistles. Harry was busy collecting interviews from riders in the pits and broadcasting general descriptive reports to paint pictures for the listeners. He saw Barry and Arnie leaning on the pit gate chatting together, "Hi both, how's things?" he asked.

Barry looked round, "Hello Harry," he replied evenly, "Moderately well considering everything. We have a fabulous crowd, so a big tick in that box. We have a fine sunny evening, so another tick there too, no-one has died yet, so a massive tick there, but there's plenty of time yet. I just want to get to the end with everyone going home safely."

"Amen to that," Harry concurred.

The meeting was a great spectacle with the Bulldogs scraping a narrow victory and Leicester taking a point for staying within six points of the home team. Barry Leech was visibly relieved when the last spectators left the stadium leaving only the staff to clear things away and riders to shower and head off to their various destinations.

Harry caught Susan Hawley from Dirt Track films and had a conversation with her about the arrangements to pick up some DVDs he had ordered. He also wanted to speak with Johnny before they left and found his friend in the studio clearing away papers. They talked about Monday's upcoming show and agreed to try a new feature that Harry had been thinking about. They locked up the office and went down to the car park where Johnny went off to catch the tube train and Harry went in the opposite direction to track down Rosie. There were no staff left in the main stadium as he walked down towards the tractor park but he could see that the office lights were still on and that Rosie was up there still talking to someone.

As he strolled down the car park outside the studio he saw the ambulance with its rear doors open and walked over to say 'hello' to Bernie Thorpe, who he supposed would be packing away the gear ready for the next meeting. When he got there, the vehicle was empty and Harry just walked on by, guessing that Bernie was in the first aid office with Julia. As he started through the gate into the machine park he thought he saw someone between the grading tractor and the large water cart, but no one appeared so Harry cut down towards the vehicles to take a look. He was sure that he saw a shadow move as he approached the grading tractor, so he quietly moved down the side of the great vehicle and, as he did so, a sharp and powerful blow landed behind his right ear. Harry heard the dull sound of wood clunk against his skull and felt his eyeballs jolt in their sockets as he slumped against the side of the tractor. A second blow caught him across the back of his head and he fell to the ground dazed and hurt. Someone dragged him across the rough concrete surface leaving him collapsed some fifteen meters in front of the tractor. He saw no-one as he lay there trying to stay conscious and make sense of what was happening. Large lights snapped on and blinded him with their glaring brightness, a diesel engine burst into life with a deep rattling rumble, the smell of acrid exhaust drifted into his nostrils and somewhere distant voices were shouting. The lights started to close in on him and to his horror he realised that the tractor was driving towards him. Harry tried to get up, but he could only drag himself slowly backwards slower than the oncoming tractor was approaching. The distant voices were getting closer and he thought he heard Rosie shouting his name. His slow progress was halted when he came into contact with the water cart and he realised that the tractor was going to crush him.

Harry tried to shout for help but all he could manage was a small pitiful squeak. The large vehicle continued to roll slowly towards him and he heard the splintering of wood and the metallic scraping sound of the team trailer being crushed by the left front wheel of the tractor. The lighter frame of the trailer stood no chance against the much larger vehicle however, and it was sufficient to affect its steering and deflect the tractor slightly off its original trajectory. With the lights less blinding than before Harry could see that the giant tyre was only meters away from his legs. Harry tried to move, but his body didn't respond, instead it just sat there in front of the approaching machine. Harry closed his eyes and prepared for the pain to come when a huge grinding and screeching of metal erupted in front of him and the engine noise changed into a stuttering and laboured vibration. He opened his eyes and saw the vehicle on top of him, let out a screamed as it stalled and stopped on top of his foot and then he blacked out.

He came to a minute later and became aware of several voices calling out and shouting instructions and people standing over him. The tractor park lights had been switched on and Harry looked up at the huge side of the vehicle towering over him.

"Get that tractor off him!" Barry Leech's boomed out.

"Wait," Arnie shouted, We can't just move it, we might do more damage to his leg."

Barry leaned over him, "Harry? Can you hear me?"

Other voices, "It's trapped his foot"

"It must have smashed it to bits!"

"We could just reverse it couldn't we?"

"He's a lucky bastard!"

"Who did this?"

"Harry? Can you hear me?" Barry's voice came through all the others, "What happened? Who did this?"

Harry felt very ill indeed, "Is Julia still here?" he asked just before he passed out again.

Sunday 11th September 2016

He came round in hospital in the early hours of the morning and found Rosie sitting by his bed. He opened his eyes and the morning sun was streaming through the window, bathing the whole room in warm light, "Good morning," Rosie said in a voice full of relief. Harry rolled his head over slowly and winced with pain. She smiled gently, "Take it easy cowboy, you've probably got a bit of a head, eh?"

"You can say that again," he whispered hoarsely, "drink please?"

Rosie poured some water into a plastic tumbler and put straw into it so that Harry could drink. She told him how they had got the tractor off his foot, "You are the luckiest individual in the world you know. Do you know what a pattern profile is?"

Harry nodded and wished he hadn't, "I can guess," he said quietly.

"Well, the fact that this was a brand new tyre meant that the tread was deeper than your foot was thick and your ankle sat neatly inside the hollow between the treads. You've got some bruising, but nothing broken. Your head probably came off worse than your foot."

Harry touched the sore spot just behind his right ear and then the very tender spot on the back of his head, "Lucky eh?"

Rosie's eyebrows arched in surprise, "Harry, apart from the possibility that you could have been killed, by either the blows to your head or under the wheels of that huge tractor. That wheel was within an inch either way of crushing your ankle to the extent that you might have lost your foot completely."

"Bloody hell," Harry whispered.

"You really do not have any idea how close it was do you?" she asked.

"No," he admitted.

"Did you see who it was that tried to kill you?" Rosie asked.

"Kill me?"

Rosie looked stern, "Yes, kill you. You were struck from behind on the head with a wooden stake, twice," she stated, "then, whoever it was tried to run you over with the tractor."

Harry lay looking at the ceiling for a moment, "No I don't have any idea, he said quietly.

Harry was discharged from hospital after forty-eight hours when the doctors were satisfied that his head injuries were not likely to lead to anything life threatening. As he signed his discharge papers the nurse said, "You feel dizzy, headaches, vomiting, you get in touch with us immediately. Understood?"

"Understood," he replied compliantly.

Rosie insisted that he spent the whole week at home and the only people allowed to see him were the police, Johnny and Barry Leech. He was asked lots of questions by all three but had very few answers and none that threw any light on the identity of the likely perpetrator. Barry was full of sympathy and regret, "I should have arranged protection for people," he said.

"Don't beat yourself up over this Barry," Harry advised, "until this, it was not certain that there was some kind of link between all the incidents."

Barry appreciated these words, "Yes, but it is now." He mused.

"But why you, Harry?" Rosie questioned.

"Well, I suppose you've been asking a lot of questions lately, maybe you got a bit too close for someone's comfort," Barry offered.

"Which puts Steve and Bernie right back in the frame," Harry pondered.

Barry told them that he had added another level of security to the current company's contract and that it included some undercover duties, so that every day there would be at least one and often more employees of the security company watching over things at the stadium. "Obviously I haven't made anything public, so

I'd ask you to be discreet about this." Rosie and Harry assured him that they would respect his wishes, "Are we allowed to know who they are?" Harry asked.

Barry shook his head, "I'd rather you didn't know, they specifically asked me not to reveal that."

"Ok," Harry nodded, "I should think it will be pretty obvious to us now we know this much. There aren't that many people around a speedway stadium on a none-match day and we know everyone who's normally there."

"Maybe," Barry answered knowingly.

Johnny came round every day on his way home from work where he was filling in for Harry. On Wednesday he came in enthusing about a girl he'd met who had auditioned really well and he thought would make an excellent presenter, "She's called Bethany Joseph, her radio name is Bet and I'm going to try her on your show this Friday," he told Harry.

Although he knew it was immature and not worthy of him, Harry felt a little stab of jealous resentment towards this young woman who he'd never met. "Oh… that's good," he said, "I hope she does well."

"I'm confident she will do great," Johnny replied with a big smile.

Johnny came round on Friday evening and listened to the show with Harry. Harry had to admit that she was an excellent presenter, "Am I under threat?" he asked Johnny half-jokingly.

Johnny laughed out loud, "No chance! I can't get rid of you! You know too much."

Harry's magnificent black eyes subsided over the next five days to the point where he looked as if he had slept badly for a few nights. The swollen lumps from the blows to his head settled down in those days too and the stitches dissolved leaving hardly any sign of the cuts. So when Harry returned to the Bulldogs stadium the following Saturday evening for the Bulldog's Elite League meeting with Coventry, he looked fairly presentable and walked with only the last vestiges of a limp.

Wednesday 14th September 2016

The circumstances surrounding Swindon's fate should be acknowledged at this moment. With two matches left, the Robins required only one point to qualify for the play-offs.

arnie@arniecottrell
Big night for everyone- good luck to all! Come on Belle Vue!

14th Sept Belle Vue 52 v 40 Swindon

With Belle Vue guaranteed a place in the play-offs and Swindon looking for 1 point, the home side wanted to finish the league stage with a display to thrill their fans while Swindon only needed to stay within 6 points to secure their place. Jason Doyle and Justin Sedgman launched their assault right from the first heat with a 5 – 1 win, but it was short lived as Richie Worrall and Joe Jacobs pulled it straight back in the second heat. In the fourth and fifth heats, Belle Vue extended their lead to 6 points and from that moment, Swindon were struggling to limit the damage. The truth was that all the Belle Vue riders contributed good scores while only Rohan Tungate provided consistent resistance for Swindon with even Jason Doyle and Justin Sedgman fading towards the end.

arnie@arniecottrell
I'll never wish bad things for anyone, but good luck Lakeside!

Thursday 16th Sept Lakeside 58 v 35 Swindon

Once again, the Robins just needed to stay within 6 points to reach the playoffs. But Lakeside were merciless and dominating throughout the meeting and, but for the magnificent Jason Doyle on 15 and the impressive Charles Wright on 9, Swindon's embarrassment would have been total. Kim Nilsson on 13 and Scott Nicholls on 10 paid 13, spearheaded an excellent team effort as, for the second night in a row, Swindon were outgunned by the consistency of their opponents.

Swindon fans, management and riders alike can take some solace from the fact that none of this failure to perform took place as the last act at the Abbey Stadium after such an illustrious history there, although, unexpectedly, it was the plans that were embarrassingly demolished rather than the lovely old venue. However, it cannot go unstated that this sudden decline resulted in an enormous opportunity being firmly kicked into the long grass with careless abandon.   All those connected with the Bulldogs were astonished by their good fortune and while they still had points to gather at Coventry two days later, there was definitely a feeling of thankful providence in the pits that evening.

ELITE LEAGUE TABLE - Up to and including Tuesday 12th September 2016

TEAM	M	W	D	L	F	A	Pts	+/-
Belle Vue	27	18	0	9	1278	1138	61	140
Wolverhampton	28	17	0	11	1332	1210	58	122
Poole	27	16	1	10	1341	1114	55	227
Battersea	26	14	0	12	1133	1047	47	86
Swindon	26	14	1	11	1188	1157	47	31
Lakeside	27	14	0	13	1265	1197	44	68
Coventry	27	10	0	17	1160	1300	33	-140
Kings Lynn	25	9	2	14	1025	1229	32	-204
Leicester	27	6	2	19	1103	1347	21	-244

Thursday 15th September 2016

arnie@arniecottrell
Three riders missing and guests don't get their averages. Regular riders score below their average and we got a spanking.

A lot of people wanted a piece of Harry that Thursday evening and he was genuinely surprised and touched at the out-flowing of good wishes and friendship that followed his accident, for that's what the deliberately worded public notice called it. Amongst all the attention and conversations Bernie Thorpe made time to come over and speak with Harry and wish him a speedy recovery, but Steve Hildegarde made no such approach, so he went and sought him out. Harry found him working on Patryk Dudek's bikes when he walked into the pits and made a bee-line for the rider, ostensibly to speak with him, but mostly to let his presence be noted by Steve. Peter parted Harry's hair to look at the scars and bruises at which point Steve looked up from his work and took time out to join them, "That looks like it was a heavy crack you took there Harry," Steve said with what appeared to be genuine sympathy and concern. He seemed completely relaxed about Harry's presence and after a couple of minutes he went back to changing the chain on Peter's bike.

The match with Coventry was not the straightforward affair for the Bulldogs that some had predicted with the Bees stealing an unexpected 10 point win at 41-51. Even with Joe Neal and Tai Woffinden scoring twelve point maximums, Chris Harris bagged 12 paid 13 and the Coventry team scored consistently well to make the difference on the night. The Coventry team sported two replacement riders for the absent Kenneth Krastanak and Jason Garrity who had clashing commitments with their Polish teams, but showed a closeness of spirit that was impressive. Heat 11 was one of those that many years later fans would still say," I was there." When the tapes went up, Tai Woffinden made a great start off the outside gate with team mate Peter Ljung hot on his tail. Chris Harris went into the first bend just ahead of his team mate for the night, Justin Sedgman, and what unfolded was reminiscent of Darcy Ward's fabulous victory in Bydgoszcz in heat 15 of the 2014 Grand Prix when he not only undertook a Titanic battle with Nick Pedersen for second place, but also conquered Tai Woffinden to beat him on the last bend of the race. Tai Woffinden glided down the back straight with Ljung and Harris almost touching as they gave chase. Through bends three and four both Ljung and Harris rode lines that took them within inches of the fence and as they exited bend four Chris Harris's bike rose on its rear wheel and took him almost to bend one. Ljung and Harris swapped places three times on lap two while Tai rode steadily and stylishly round the inside line of the track nursing a secure lead. In an exhibition of masterful bikemanship, the two protagonists refused to give an inch to each other and as they entered bend one of lap four Chris Harris found some exceptional grip on the very outside and, riding inches from the fence, he was able to get his wheels in line and extend the back straight to release the momentum he had built up, leaving Ljung back in the distance. Such was Harris's speed that he now found himself within passing distance of Tai Woffinden who was still hugging the inside line. In a spectacular and exhilarating drive around the outside line, Harris came around Woffinden at tremendous speed for which Tai had no effective response and had to watch as Harris flew past him in the last twenty meters to win the race.

Harry and Rosie were standing by the pit gate when the break was announced after heat 11 and patted Chris on his back as he rode back into the pits. The intermission signaled a welcome break for all the officials so when Julia, Reg and Bernie met from their different positions around the track as they came in for a cup of tea they saw Harry and came over to ask after his health. "Let's have a look at those bumps and bruises," Julia said and all three of them examined the bruised and sore areas on Harry's head. Again Bernie seemed perfectly natural and sincerely concerned about Harry's plight.

So, by the time the evening was over and he had met both suspects, Harry had to admit that neither of them was guilty of attacking him. "Either that or one of them is a bloody good actor," he said to Rosie afterwards. The whole event had a strange feel in the sense that security was clearly intense, the usual but significantly enhanced private security was present, plus the police presence was increased and very visible. Harry thought that, if he were the attacker, he would keep a deliberately low profile that night. He went to Rosie's office after the meeting to get an elevated position and, with the lights turned off so that he could observe without being observed himself, he watched the mechanics packing up their gear and stowing it in the workshops, the riders going into and out of the changing rooms, the police patrolling the different areas of the stadium, the private security also patrolling the same areas as the police and the paramedics packing their equipment away into the first aid room and restocking the ambulance by the tractor park. He watched all of this with a feeling that nothing was going to happen that night, and so it proved. Eventually, each group left the stadium until only Harry, Rosie and a skeleton security staff remained. When Harry and Rosie left they reflected on the fact that this was the first time in three weeks that the Bulldogs had managed to run a meeting where no-one was killed, injured or nearly murdered.

CHAPTER 15

Saturday 17th September 2016

arnie@arniecottrell
Not good to drop a point at this stage with Swindon on our tail. But we still have 4th place! Phew!

The next day Rosie had been summoned to work, while the police visited Harry at Rosie's flat in order to relate their findings from their investigations in the attack on him. They had no identification and no-one had seen anybody enter or leave the tractor park at the time of the incident. There were no finger prints, other than those of the designated drivers, and no DNA that was significant. The wooden pole also proved as indecisive as the tractor. "I'm sorry to say, sir, we have searched everywhere we can and there simply isn't anything that gives us a lead," the detective said, "but rest assured we will keep looking."

"Thanks," Harry answered, "that's very reassuring."

"I realise that does nothing to help you feel safe, but let me ask you again, can you think of anyone who holds a grudge against you or has any reason to dislike you enough to try to kill you."

"It's not just me is it? I'm just the next one in a series, but this time who ever it was failed. I was lucky, that's all," Harry said.

"Well, you must appreciate that, officially, that's not the way we view it. The evidence points towards one deliberate killing for which we have no motive and two accidents, at best death in suspicious circumstances. Of course, we remain open-minded and if something arises that causes us to reassess the cases, then that's what we will do."

"So what about linking the attempt on my life with the killing of Sarah Johnson?"

"Yes, that's exactly what we are thinking, but we can't speak in those terms until we have some evidence to support it."

"Have you spoken with Steve Hildegarde and Bernie Thorpe?"

"No sir, not in connection with this."

"Why not?"

"I have no more reason to select them for interview than I do to choose anyone else, other than your suspicions that they are somehow connected with the three deaths, and as I say, that's very much your theory, not ours."

"So what do I do now?" Harry asked the police man.

"I wish I had a concrete answer for you sir, but I don't. You should be vigilant and not take any risks such as wandering about in deserted places in the dark or at least make sure you are accompanied if you do. Keep a watchful eye for anyone who seems to be taking a particular interest in you or your movements etc. And, report anything to us, no matter how small."

Harry nodded, because he did understand that this man was doing his best, "I will," he assured him.

"Picture the scene," Rosie said, "Uncle Barry sitting behind the table in the boardroom of his office in the NatWest building in the very heart of the UK Financial centre. He is furious, frightened and feeling shat upon." Rosie spoke as if telling a story. "When I arrived," she went on, "the rest of the Board were assembled and seated in descending order of seniority, that's why my seat is furthest from the head of the table. All of us were waiting to find out why we had been summoned at such short notice and all of us knew it wouldn't be for a trivial purpose."

Harry poured a cup of coffee, "So why had you all been summoned?"

Rosie paused and took a sip of her own coffee, "Uncle Barry had received a blackmail note," she said simply.

"What?" Harry was shocked.

"Barry Leech is being blackmailed."

Harry sat with wide eyes, "Wow! Does that provide the missing motive for the deaths?"

Rosie nodded, "Yes it does," and she took a piece of paper out of her handbag, unfolded it and held it out, "interested?" Harry put out his hand to take it from her, but she snatched it back, "You can't use it you know."

"I know that," Harry said, keeping his hand outstretched. Rosie put the photocopied letter into his hand. It was printed from a computer Harry supposed.

> *Mr Leech, by now you must be aware that I can and will carry out any threat I make. Sonny Brent, Johnny Sinclair, Sarah Johnson and Harry Marsh are all testament to that.*
>
> *Twenty-five million pounds on Monday 26th September following this letter will stop it all. I will contact you with payment instructions. I am giving you ample time to prepare payment so any delays will result in a failure to comply or any attempts to subvert this venture will result in the death of more of your employees.*

Harry looked up from the letter, "Wow! This is red hot," he said, "did Barry inform the police?"

"No, he didn't," Rosie responded.

"Why not?"

"Because he and the Board are agreed that this could bring the group to its knees if it got public and their view was that telling the police is tantamount to going public."

"I see," Harry said, "I mean, he's probably right, but all the same. They must be breaking the law by keeping it quiet like this. So what is he going to do?"

"Set it up so that they can pay if they have to, or not if they decide not to."

Harry thought that keeping all his options open sounded about right for Barry Leech, "And do you think he will pay?"

"We are talking about Barry Leech."

"He doesn't intend to pay, does he?"

"No."

It doesn't give us much time does it?" Harry said.

"Much time for what?" Rosie asked.

"Time to find the blackmailer," Harry answered, as if it were self evident.

Johnny sat back in the only office chair the studio owned, "Ok," he said to Harry's request for time off, "We can't give you total absence during the speedway season, but how will two thirds suit? I'll ask Bethany to do your shows, she did a great job last time," and he winked at his friend.

Harry made the shape of a crucifix with his fore fingers and grinned, "Thanks Johnny, it'll be worth it."

"Of course it will, that's not in doubt," Johnny agreed, "we'll get an absolute exclusive story, you'll be a hero and Bethany will become an experienced broadcaster. What's not to like?"

Harry turned to Rosie, "That's agreed then, I only have to do three shows a week and then I can spend two thirds of my time on the search team, if you'll have me."

Rosie was pleased, "That's great but we don't have much time so we need every person who can help." Rosie said she'd cleared a desk for him and a meeting was arranged for his arrival.

Barry Leech had given Rosie a free hand to select anyone she wanted for the 'Search Team' and she took him at his word by taking the entire Senior Management Team of the Leech Group, indeed, the four managers who were identified as talent to be developed for a future Board. Ben Charles, the Bulldog's Business Manager, Nik James the Facilities Manager, Sam Donovan the Logistics Manager and Jenny Murphy the Public Affairs Manager, all welcomed the opportunity to work with Harry.

"Ok, where do we start?" Rosie asked the assembled six strong 'search team' They decided to put two on the broader search that included the whole world and focus the other four on the two suspects who were already in the frame. Rosie laid down the ground rules, "We are looking for anything that will confirm or eliminate them, any little thing no matter how small should be brought to the team. It may be that your tiny bit is a key that links with other small things to make a whole picture."

She looked round the team, "Let me emphasise something right from the start. If working hours, time off and fairness of work loads are of any concern for you, I think you are in the wrong team. So now is the time to bale out if you can't work round the clock for seven days a week with unreasonable amounts of work to do until we are successful, or Barry pays the blackmailer." She waited to allow people to make their decision. When no one did she clapped her hands and said, "Ok, I've identified some tasks that we can get out teeth into and I'll explain what I'm looking for now so that everyone knows what everyone else is doing." This was a good start for Rosie as Team Leader and everyone was impressed with her style, directness and organisation. "I'm pairing you up so that you can bounce off each other and reduce the chances of missing anything." She took an A3 sheet of paper on which a task instruction was written in large letters and pinned it to the notice board above desk one, on which two computers stood waiting. "Nik and Jenny, I'd like you to make a file on Bernie, his work, social media, qualifications, hobbies, family and friends, just see where it takes you and cast the net wide."

Rosie pinned up a second sheet above desk 2, "Ben and Sam, I'd like you to focus on Steve Hildegarde in the same way and create a file for us. Harry and I will take a broader look at other potential suspects and map the evidence we do have to see it as a whole." Rosie paused and looked around the group, "This is how it is," she said with determination, "Barry and most of the Board don't want to inform the police about this blackmail, but there are members of the Board who are very uneasy about the legality of that approach. This means that there are three possible outcomes to the work we are doing here, one, we find out who it is and intercept this business somehow. Two, we fail before the ransom has to be paid and the Board have to decide what to do. Three, the minority Board members raise enough noise to force Barry to tell the police and the company lives with the fall-out from that. Plus, the blackmailer will probably be alerted to this and takes retribution as he or she has promised. So, the only two solutions that stay clear of any more killings are, number one, we discover who it is and, number two, Barry pays the ransom. We want number one." She picked up her papers and stacked them neatly, "Let's work for three hours on family and friends data and then take a break before coming together to review progress and we'll follow that pattern while it bears fruit. Let's go."

After three hours they took a break to ease their aching eyes and Harry took the opportunity to nip back to the studio to check how Bethany was getting on with the show. On his way across the stadium he ran into Julia Raglett, "Hello Harry," she greeted him cheerfully.

"Hello Julia," Harry returned, "what are you doing here?"

"I was at a meeting with Tony Fuller looking at some of the HSE issues that are going to affect the paramedic team." She saw Harry eyebrows go on one their upward journeys, "You may well look like that," Julia laughed. "You're not one his favourite people, are you?"

"No, I'm afraid I'm not," Harry admitted, "Why, did he say something?"

"He made it known that you are definitely HSE enemy number one and that we should be careful what we say to you."

"I can understand that, given where he's coming from. Who was at the meeting?"

"Tony, Bernie, me, someone from HSE headquarters and the HSE Manager at Torquay," Julia replied.

"That'll be Jim Norman," Harry offered.

"That's right," Julia confirmed, "he's no fan of yours either. What have you been doing to them?"

"Well, I may have been a bit naughty, but they're so sensitive and precious." Harry said, "Anyway, how was the meeting?"

Julia pursed her lips, "Hmm, yes, well it was ok I suppose. Some positive actions came from it for us, but my goodness, it's like pulling teeth trying to get off the small stuff isn't it?"

"Yeah, I can imagine," Harry agreed.

"Is there anything that Tony and Jim don't have firm and definite views about?"

Harry laughed heartily, "I shouldn't think so. You could never accuse them of being ambiguous could you?"

Julia guffawed at this and they both stood laughing together, "Well, every circus needs a clown."

Harry chuckled as they went their different ways.

CHAPTER 16

arnie@arniecottrell
Good win at Lakeside. I hope now that 4th place is just between Bulldogs and Swindon now.

The first review of the search revealed very little, "It just takes time to wade through all the dross to find anything that is in any way useful," Ben Charles explained, "we suggest that we work for longer between meetings, that way we might come back with better quality information."

Rosie agreed to this, "Ok, that makes sense, we had similar issues as well. Let's hear what we have got so far."

Sam Donovan stood up and switched on the computer screen so that it projected onto the wall, "Steve's got three brothers, Matthew, Martin and Simon," he explained, "Matthew is younger than him by five years so he's only sixteen and is still at school. Don is just over a year older than Steve and he has his own stall selling DIY goods and tools at Borough Market. He seems to be a regular sort of bloke, good job, married, two children. Martin is the oldest of them all and he is a house husband whose wife has a career whilst he looks after the home and the children. Mum and Dad are happily married, as far as we can tell, very proud of their kids and both are keen on speedway as one might predict. That's it I'm afraid." Sam concluded.

"Ok, thanks Sam and Ben. It is what it is." Rosie responded and she turned to the others, "Right, let's hear from Nick and Joe."

Nik James switched the projection to show his screen, "Not much to report on Bernie. We got everything we have from Facebook and Twitter because we couldn't find anything anywhere else. Bernie is thirty-seven years old, English, born in West Bromwich in the Black Country. Both his parents are dead; his father, Bill died five years ago at fifty-five from a heart attack, his mother, Helen died three years ago, aged fifty-nine from lung cancer. He's got two brothers, Patrick and Jimmy. Patrick is thirty-nine and lives in Japan, working for Sony. He's got two children and has a Japanese wife and seems settled there judging from his Facebook exchanges with Bernie. Jimmy is forty-two years old, single but in a 'same sex' relationship with an Australian; they've lived in Sydney for five years and seem happy. Bernie has been with the St Johns Ambulance on and off for fifteen years. He's worked as a sale assistant at Sofa City for the last year. He moved to London ten years ago and lives in Camberwell since he started with Sofa City. He plays tennis occasionally at Camberwell Tennis Club where he is a member. And that's about it," Nik said switching off the projector.

"Ok, "Rosie said," that's quite useful as far as it goes. Now we need to do some research and go down to the next level of detail on these issues, but also spread the net wider.
Let's meet again tomorrow afternoon. Say four o'clock?" They all agreed to this and went straight back to work.

Johnny called Harry to ask if he could go back to the office for half an hour to listen to a couple of interviews that Bethany had edited, "I just want to give you the opportunity to ok them before they go out," he explained.

Harry was thoughtful as he wandered slowly through the stadium complex. His conversation with Julia that ended with him making a joke at Tony Fuller's expense had been playing on his mind. Tony was an easy target for people's ill humour and insults, but it was unworthy of him to fire at that target and he knew that Tony was hurt by the continual sniping about HSE. "Bad Karma comes from bad thoughts," Harry said to himself and he decided to do something about it the next morning.

Saturday 17th September 2016

Instead of going directly to the studio Harry diverted and knocked on Tony Fuller's door.

"Come!" Tony's voice commanded from within. Harry opened the door and smiled, "What do you want?" the HSE Manager asked through clenched teeth.

"Have you got a few minutes, Tony?" Harry asked calmly.

"I'm very busy," Tony snapped back.

"I know you are," Harry sympathised, "but this is important and I would like to get your thoughts on something that is HSE related."

Tony sat up straight in his chair, "Right, well you'd better sit down and take the weight off your ankle, how is it anyway?"

Harry sat down opposite Tony, "It's good thanks. A bit sore but that's all."

"You were very lucky indeed that night you know," Tony said.

"Yes, I know," Harry agreed folding his hands on his knees, "Look Tony, do you recall about a week ago you talked to me about having some HSE stops on Speedway FM?"

Tony nodded, "Yes, it was twelve days ago," he corrected Harry and sat forward a little on his chair.

Harry sensed he had Tony's attention, "Do you still think it will work?"

"Yes of course. I'm convinced they will be really interesting to speedway fans," he said, rearranging his pens in the desk tidy and moving the pencil sharpener a millimetre.

"Well we think so too, and we think we should run a couple of pilots to see how they are received by listeners. If you are willing?"

Tony was engaged now! "Yes, yes I am. How do you want to do it?" he asked.

Harry smiled cheerfully, "I was thinking that we could do a ten minute interview on my show." Harry proposed.

Tony recoiled at the suggestion, "What, like you interviewed Jim Norman you mean? I don't think so! Thank you."

Harry held his hand up to placate him, "No, no not like that at all. This is an informative piece not like Jim's, which was a news item. It's completely different."

Tony relaxed a little at this, "Oh well, I don't want HSE ridiculed or made to look foolish, that's all."

"I know that Tony and you have my word that I will treat it with respect." Harry promised.

When they parted they had a plan, shook hands and smiled at each other. Harry was confident that he could steer this so that it would make at least two short and interesting slots and actually thought that there might be scope to make it a regular feature as long as he controlled it through the interview approach. He was convinced that Tony should never be allowed to broadcast live or worse, on his own.

"Shall I put a few ideas down on paper?" Tony asked as Harry walked towards the door.

"No need for that Tony. I think you should be asked live on the day so that your responses can be fresh and spontaneous." The last thing he wanted was a Tony Fuller PowerPoint presentation over the air.

"Oh ok, if you think that's best."

"I do Tony, I do. It's live radio and it will be great."

"I think I might be nervous though, so some preparation might help that."

"I'll look after you. I'll prompt you with questions and rescue you if you dry up mate.

Tony suddenly changed the subject and asked, "I'm just going to make some coffee, would you like one?"

This was a first and a very good sign that things might be on the mend. Harry stopped in the doorway and turned to look at the HSE Manager, "Yeah, ok Tony. I'd love a coffee thank you." He went back into the office and sat down again at the desk, "White, no sugar please."

They sat talking and drinking coffee inconsequentially for a while.

"Where do you live Harry?" Tony asked.

"Notting Hill most of the time. I kind of live with Rosie in her flat. What about you?"

"Colliers Wood," Tony told him, "I've got a house there."

"Are you married?" Harry asked.

"Yes. Thirty-five years."

"That's great," Harry said meaning it, "Any children?"

"Oh yes, we've got two children," Tony answered, "A son and a daughter."

"How old are they?"

"Brian's thirty-two and Irene is twenty-nine."

Harry began to see Tony in a different light, as a husband and a parent. "What do they do for a living," Harry asked.

"Brian is a geologist with an American oil company working in Kazakhstan and Irene doesn't work."

"That's nice," Harry said, "Is she married?"

Tony looked down suddenly and said, "No she's not married. She still lives at home with Monica and me.

CHAPTER 17

Saturday 17th September 2016

arnie@arniecottrell
Well done Belle Vue last night, great win at Coventry! They'll get top spot now. We want 4th and will work hard for it

The team came together at four o'clock as agreed and Rosie asked Ben to go through the information they had pieced together since the last meeting. "We've managed to cover most of all the areas that we think we are interested in, but if there are any gaps, please flag them to us so that we can go back and cover them. He began, "First, let me go over the extra stuff we have on Steve's brothers of which there are three, these being, Matthew, Don and Martin. Matthew is sixteen; he attends The Basildon Upper Academy where he is studying for seven 'A' levels. He's got a weekend job at Loaf Around, a sandwich shop in Basildon. His hobbies are playing Xbox games such as FIFA soccer and Battle Zone. He is mad keen on speedway, probably through Steve's connections here. He has never been in any trouble with the police and he doesn't appear to have a girl friend or be in any romantic relationships. He looks pretty much like your average teenage boy who likes sports, computer games, hanging around with his mates and social media."

Sam stepped in at this point, "Second up is Don the market stall holder. He left school at sixteen with four GCSE's and worked as a barrow boy for a trader and graduated to his own stall in Borough Market when he was seventeen. He socialises with friends mostly at The Ship on Borough Road which is his local, he lives on Stones End Street. He is married to Sue and has two children. He drives an eight year old Mercedes Vito van that doubles up as a people carrier and his work vehicle. He is a mad keen West Ham fan and has held a season ticket for the last five years. He has had a couple of run-ins with the law and was arrested for some minor offences connected with handling stolen goods. Apart from this, he seems to be an ordinary family man who likes to propagate the image as a bit of a wide-boy."

Ben stepped back in,

"Third is Martin, a 'house husband, whose wife is a prestigious London barrister with a very successful practice, while he looks after their children and the home. They live in Royston, Hertfordshire in a very expensive house, whilst their children attend Jarrotts private school as day pupils. Martin is twenty-nine, plays golf, tennis and squash and leads the kind of life most people can only dream about. He has never been in trouble with the police and he was educated at Oxford, where he met his wife Stella." Ben and Sam fell silent and waited for questions and comments but nothing was forthcoming, so Ben went on,

"Steve himself offers a very interesting background. He left school at sixteen with some poor GCSE grades and flirted with Technical College, then dropped out. He got a job with a small garage on the corner of Freemantle Street in Southwark and learned everything about engines. It seems he was a particularly good student and ended his time there after two years when he went on to work at Wilfred Smiths motorcycle shop, where he had the opportunity to get involved with grass track which naturally led into the speedway world. He worked as a tuner for two years and still tinkers with private work, but now he is contracted to Battersea Bulldogs he restricts it to favours for friends and if he charges anything, it's at mate's rates. He has had quite a few scrapes with the police because of his strong connections with the Inter City Firm which is a gang associated with West Ham Football Club. His reputation there is for being at the head of the attack when they engage other gangs. He appears on the police list of notable members and used to be one of the first to get pulled in when there's trouble. He has been closely linked to three very serious injuries inflicted on opponents who spent time in hospital. It seems to be a kind of sport that everyone involved sees in just that way. They take injuries as a matter of course and battles are pre-arranged with the opposition by coordinators who are in telephone contact with each other. It has to be said that he has an impeccable record here with the Bulldogs apart from threatening to kill Sonny Brent and, with that in mind, we think this strengthens his position as a suspect because he obviously has a violent streak running through his DNA."

"Finally," Sam chipped in, "to Bernie himself. He is thirty-seven, a qualified paramedic which enables him to work in public areas. He left school at seventeen with nine GCSEs and three A levels that got him into the Faculty of Medicine at Southampton University. He dropped out during his second year and later joined the ambulance service. He now works for a private medical company as a paramedic and on a part-time basis for us. He's never been in any trouble with the police and doesn't appear to be in any relationship of any sort. Outside of speedway and the occasional grass track meeting, Bernie doesn't have any hobbies as far as we know."

"It's a bit thin isn't it?" Rosie said.

"Yes, it is," Sam agreed, "it's all off Facebook, we couldn't find any other source."

An air of underlying disappointment hung around them as they discussed the content of the presentations for about twenty minutes before breaking back into their subgroups to continue their research, "Not very inspiring was it?" Rosie said to Harry when the others had gone.

"Well there's the stuff about Steve and Bernie." Harry said.

At that moment the door opened and Gillian, Barry's secretary walked in, "Sorry to disturb you, but we have just received another note from the blackmailer."

All the team stopped working to look at her with rapt attention, "We have to deposit twenty-five million pounds in a Swiss bank account by close of business on Monday," she clarified, placing a photocopy of the letter on the desk and leaving the room.

Rosie picked up the letter and read it silently, "Well that's what it says with the account details. I imagine that will be impenetrable by arrangement with the bank," she said.

Nik James nodded his agreement, "we've had occasion to use Swiss banks and their reputation is predicated on their iron-clad security. We won't get any satisfaction if we try to explore that route."

Harry looked quizzical, "Even if they know that the account is being used to store blackmail money?"

"Even that," Nik corroborated.

The blackmail note really flattened the group's energy levels and they had to work hard to get back into their research knowing that the pressure had just been substantially increased. Later that afternoon Harry and Rosie were walking across the complex to grab a breath of fresh air when they saw Tony Fuller drive a converted Ford minibus into the rider's car park at the back of the pits and start to unpack a tail lift from the back. Harry wandered over, "Afternoon Tony do you need any help?"

Tony looked round, "Hello Harry, I'm fine thanks, I'm used to doing this on my own, I've been doing it for a few years now," he nodded towards the figure sitting in the back of the vehicle, "You haven't met my daughter have you? Our conversation put it into my mind that I had been promising to bring her here for a long time now, but kept putting it off, so I thought I'd do it today."

Harry looked into the rear of the Minibus and saw a woman in her early thirties sitting in an electric-powered wheelchair that was secured to the floor by clamps. He smiled at her and her face lit up with a delightfully broad smile in return and she waved awkwardly, so he waved back hesitantly. Tony saw Harry's indecision, "Cerebral Palsy due to oxygen deprivation at birth," he said quietly, "her name is Irene."

Harry moved so that she could see him better, Hello Irene, my name is Harry."

"Harry works on the radio here at the stadium," Tony added flicking up the spring clams from her wheels. She turned her chair and rolled it onto the lift held out a hand that trembled unsteadily to shake Harry's hand and said with difficulty in a slurred and clipped but understandable voice, "I am very pleased to meet you Harry,"

Harry looked into her warm and friendly eyes, "I'm very pleased to meet you too Irene," and he took her hand in both of his, "Have you come to look around the stadium," he asked.

"Yes, my dad works here so he said he would bring me down to see it." She replied.

"I work in the office next door to your dad's office," Harry said.

"That's nice. Do you look after people as well?" she asked.

"I hope so Irene, but not like your dad does. His is a much more important job than mine."

"What do you do Harry?" she questioned him.

"I make radio programmes for speedway fans," he responded

Irene's head jerked and wobbled almost constantly and she struggled to control her body and speech, "That sounds like an important job to me," she said.

"I suppose it is," Harry agreed.

When Tony had finished with the van he excused himself and Irene and took her down towards the main buildings in the stadium area. Harry watched them thoughtfully and a lump came into his throat as Tony pointed to the tractor and grading machinery, then he wheeled her over to the edge of the track and showed her the canter lever stand. He wiped her mouth with a tissue and made sure the blanket was keeping her legs warm. Harry saw a very different Tony Fuller and felt ashamed of himself and strangely proud to know Tony. He turned away and went upstairs to the studio in a very emotional state.

In retrospect, Harry thought that his lacklustre contribution to the meeting was somewhat detached and allowed Johnny to do most of the talking. Afterwards he rang Susan Hawley at Dirt Track films, "Have you had any luck getting any of the DVDs for me Susan?"

"Not yet Harry, I can't find anything you asked for."

"What about getting anything from Sky?"

"I could, but it's the same problem," she explained, "I still have to watch every race because they, like we, haven't indexed the footage like that."

"In addition," Harry ventured tentatively.

"Y-e-s?" Susan drawled slowly.

"If you can find anything footage of the Special Olympics?"

"Is that the same as the Paralympics?" Susan asked.

"No, it's not, "Harry replied, "the Special Olympics are run for people who have suffered different kinds of brain related accidents and conditions, I think. Plus, I need it for tomorrow."."

"You don't want much do you?" Susan grinned and thought about it for a moment, "I think you might mean 'learning disabilities', Let me give you a telephone number of someone who might be able to help you. His name is Paul Holdean and he works for Mencap."

Harry met Paul Holdean that evening after work and told him about his need to have some film footage of the Special Olympics for the next day. Paul said that he had some stuff that might suit the purpose and gave him a promotional DVD that they used with prospective sponsors and some personal video footage from the 2012 Olympics in Leicester. Harry thanked him, promised to return the discs and, stopping only to pick up some beers and pizza, he rode back to Battersea to join the Search Team at work.

CHAPTER 18

ELITE LEAGUE TABLE - Up to and including Tuesday 19th September 2016

TEAM	M	W	D	L	F	A	Pts	+/-
Belle Vue	28	19	0	9	1330	1178	64	152
Poole	28	17	1	10	1394	1153	59	241
Wolverhampton	28	17	0	11	1332	1210	58	122
Battersea	29	17	0	12	1190	1082	50	108
Swindon	29	15	1	13	1263	1267	50	-4
Lakeside	28	15	0	13	1323	1232	47	91
Kings Lynn	27	10	2	15	1112	1323	36	-211
Coventry	28	10	0	18	1201	1348	33	-147
Leicester	27	6	2	19	1103	1347	21	-244

Sunday 18th September 2016

Rosie and Harry went back to the Search Team room and found all of them hard at work, half exploring every aspect of Steve and Bernie that occurred to them, the other half developing scenarios and strategies that didn't involve Steve or Bernie.

"What have we got?" Rosie asked Sam Donovan.

"Nothing substantial," he admitted, "I think Bernie did it and I think he smothered him on the track."

Nik heard this and turned sharply, "Not even close Rosie."

"You could see his legs kicking out as it was happening," Sam added.

Nik shook his head vigorously, "What you saw was simply convulsive post death muscle spasms. That's very common in a recently deceased corpse. No, my money says Steve rigged the shock absorbers to collapse and then let the crash take its course."

"You'd lose you money then Nik. Too much left to chance. The likelihood of that crash leading to death is massively against the odds."

Rosie raised her hands, "Ok, cease! Let's not jump to conclusions. I know it's tempting but we need to be systematic, it's too important to get wrong."

They were all feeling the pressure and all were coming up with absolutely nothing. After lunch they were visibly beginning to flag until Barry called by for a few minutes, asked lots of questions, poured encouragement into the mix and said a few words of inspirational common sense, "I know this kind of analysis can be tedious and can get you down. You have to look at everything because you don't know where the piece if information is that you do want," he paused, "It reminds me of when I was selling door to door in nineteen eighty three. I'd be standing alone in the middle of a housing estate, soaked by the drizzle, miserable on a dark, freezing February evening. Everyone was sitting in their lovely warm homes watching EastEnders and Coronation Street and I had to persuade them to open their doors, let in the cold air, invite me in and buy what I wanted to sell them. When you been out for an hour or so and no-one has shown the slightest interest, your head goes down, your shoulders slump and the thought that comes into your head is, 'I think I'll go home.' Of course, if you do go home, you're definitely not going to sell anything," he paused again, "This is what I used to say to myself, 'somewhere down this f******road, behind one of these f****** doors is someone who wants to buy one of the f****** things I'm selling. All I've got to do is f****** find them!'," Everyone laughed, "It's the truth! Of course there was someone who wanted to buy from me; the problem was, I didn't know which door they were behind, so I had to knock on every door until I found them. If you let the situation get you down, you lose concentration and you will miss the sale because of it. If you can't change your attitude around, you might as well go home. We don't know what or where this information is, but there will be something, somewhere; all you've got to do is find it. Stay positive, keep knocking."

When he left the room the energy levels were back up to the top and people were raring to go again. Harry leaned back in his chair with a smile on his face, "A fascinating and remarkable man."

"Of course he is," Rosie retorted, "You don't do what he's done without having some qualities like that."

Harry nodded slowly, swung round in his chair and started hitting keys at his computer.

At five o'clock, Rosie persuaded them to stop long enough to eat a sumptuous selection of Chinese food she had delivered from Golden City just round the corner on Battersea Park Road.

Tuesday 20nd September 2016

Thursday dawned on a search team that was beleaguered, desperate and in need of a stroke of luck. Harry sat in the office with the team trying to think of something to change the dynamic. Depression and a rising sense of panic were driving the energy levels to a dangerous low. Harry leaned back in his office chair, swivelled right round with his knees up. Rosie saw him out of the corner of her eye and winked, "Hey buster," she said.

"It's not working is it?" he said.

Rosie shook her head, "Not really. We keep running in to the same dead ends. And now we're running out of things to try."

Sam pushed back from his screen and took his glasses off to rub his eyes, "There's an old Appalachian Mountain saying that fits this situation nicely," he observed.

Joe looked up, "Oh yeah oh wise one, what's that then?"

"If you always do what you've always done. You'll always get what you always got," Sam recited.

They all laughed, "So let's change what we're doing then," Harry said. "Let's come from a different angle," he said deciding to run the video of Sonny's crash for the whole group. He ran it three times and then they discussed it, and all agreed that Sonny appeared to be alive when Bernie got to him. "And yet, Bernie claims that Sonny was dead when he arrived," Harry told them.

"For my part," Joe put in, "I think Bernie is lying."

"You realise you're accusing him of murder or manslaughter?" Rosie asked.

"Yes, I do," Joe said decisively, "I don't think he was giving heart massage and I don't think he was trying to help him. My guess would be that he smothered him and that's why we see Sonny's legs kick as he struggled. That wasn't muscle contraction."

"Rosie stepped in again, "Just wait a minute everybody before we go running off with a rope to hang Bernie with. The medical staff are all agreed about the cause of death and we come along, not a medical qualification amongst the lot of us, and we pronounce the cause of death as murder."

"Of course you're right about all that," Ben Charles said, "but where did the medical experts get all the information from with regard to the events of the crash and what happened immediately afterwards. From the paramedics who attended Sonny, in other words, Bernie Thorpe. Whenever we discuss it, we end up talking about Bernie Thorpe, that must be significant."

Barry spoke, "We need to get to Bernie as quickly as possible before he can wreak any more havoc."

"I admit that Ben's got a good point, but we cannot simply accuse him or treat him as if he were guilty. He might be perfectly innocent." Rosie railed. "And don't forget, Steve's got one hell of a record of planned violence that, as far as I'm concerned, puts him firmly in the frame."

"Whatever, I assume you're not going to pay, are you?" Harry asked Barry.

Barry shook his head, "I don't want to, but, it's not that easy is it?" and he changed the subject, "Rosie tell the police all of this and then they can get going and arrest Bernie."

"I certainly will not do any such thing," she asserted, "I'll call them and tell them what we have come up with, for what it's worth."

The police were less than impressed with the information that the team had uncovered and although they said they would look into it, they also said that the team were not offering them any evidence, so taking the step of arresting Bernie was not one they felt able to make.

Barry Leech was furious, "Well, what about taking him in for questioning?"

"They didn't think they would do that either, but they will look at the video footage again to see if it met the criteria required for it to be considered as evidence." Rosie told him.

"In the meantime," Barry snarled, "he could be out there threatening to kill someone else if I don't pay him twenty-five million pounds!"

"The police were adamant that it was not established that Bernie had sent the letter although they are taking the letter very seriously and a team is dedicated to the case," Rosie explained to her boss. "The truth is that they have no evidence that the deaths are linked."

"That's ridiculous!" Barry steamed.

"All they're saying is that they are keeping an open mind." Rosie explained.

"Well if we are right, they're going to feel pretty guilty and foolish if another person dies," Barry spat out, turned and stormed out of search team's office.

Harry stood looking at the door that Barry had just slammed, "Hmm, well I think we'd better stop messing around then."

Rosie looked at him, "And what do you mean by that?"

"Let's confront him at the meeting tonight and see what he's got to say for himself."

"And get killed?" Joe said.

"He won't do anything in such a public arena, even if he was inclined" Harry answered.

"Really?" Joe questioned, "Ok, but let's just stay clear of the tractor yard eh?"

SEMI FINAL PLAY-OFF 1st LEG

21st September 2016
arnie@arniecottrell
This is the sharp end! Everyone here is so excited to be riding against the very best.

POOLE V WOLVERHAMPTON
(1 to 5)

Heat 1	Holder	Kurtz	Karlsson	Lindgren	5 - 1	5 - 1
Heat 2	Ellis	Newman	Howarth	Clegg	5 - 1	10 - 2
Heat 3	Thorssell	Masters	Pedersen	Lindback	1 - 5	11 - 7
Heat 4 re-run	Newman	Howarth	Buczkowski	Proctor	4 - 2	15 - 9
Heat 5	Karlsson	Kurtz	Ellis	Clegg	3 - 3	18 - 12

Poole came out to the initial heats with massive energy and determination and by heat three Wolves were in trouble and something needed to happen quickly. Thorssell and Masters found the answer and delivered a 5 -1 heat win to stop the haemorrhage and put them back in touch. Ty Proctor's fourth place in heat 4 allowed Poole to make a 6 point difference which remained after heat 5. To this point Antonio Lindback's return to Wimborne Road had not delivered against the expectations and hopes.

POOLE

C Holder	3					
B Kurtz	2*	2				
B Pedersen	1					
K Buczkowski	1					
A Lindback	0					
A Ellis	3	1*				
K Newman	2*	3				

WOLVERHAMPTON

F Lindgren	0					
P Karlsson	1	3				
J Thorssell	3					
Ty Proctor	0					
S Masters	2*					
M Clegg	0	0				
K Howarth	1	2				

SEMI FINAL PLAY-OFF 1st LEG

BELLE VUE V BATTERSEA
(1 to 5)

Heat 1	Dudek	Sundstrom	S Worrall	Zagar	5 - 1	5 - 1
Heat 2	R Worrall	Chivers	Bjerre	Jacobs	5 – 1	10 - 2
Heat 3	Sundstrom	Cook	Hancock	Fricke	2 - 4	12 - 6
Heat 4	Nicholls	Chivers	Neal	R Worrall	3 - 3	15 - 9
Heat 5	R Worrall	S Worrall	Dudek	Bjerre	1 -5	16 - 14

The Bulldogs were missing their 6 pointer Peter Ljung for this vital meeting and had to rely on the 'rider replacement' facility to overcome the gap. Their response to being one man down was to launch themselves at Belle Vue and they caught them by surprise, building a 10 – 2 lead by heat 2. But the Aces are a tough team this season and they bounced straight back to end the first five heats with only a two point deficit thanks to a fantastic Worrall double act that got them a 5 -1 heat win.

BELLE VUE

M Zagar	0							
S Worrall	1	2*						
M Fricke	0							
S Nicholls	3							
C Cook	2							
R Worrall	3	0	3					
J Jacobs	F							

BATTERSEA

P Dudek	3	1						
L Sundstrom	2*	3						
J Neal	1*							
T Woffinden	1							
K Bjerre	1*	0						
S Chivers	2	2						

SEMI FINAL PLAY-OFF 1ˢᵗ LEG

POOLE V WOLVERHAMPTON
(6 to 10)

Heat 6	Masters	Lindgren	Buczkowski	Pedersen	1- 5	19 - 17
Heat 7	Holder	Thorssell	Lindback	Proctor	4- 2	23 – 19
Heat 8	Buczkowski	Newman	Howarth	Karlsson	5- 1	28 – 20
Heat 9	Proctor	Kurtz	Howarth	Ellis	2- 4	30 – 24
Heat 10	Lindgren	Newman	Lindback	Karlsson	3- 3	33 – 27

Heats 6 through to 10 ended with an equal share of the points after a roller coaster set of heats where the scores got wider and closer at every turn. Both teams were now fully engaged and only Poole's faster starting was the difference. Freddie Lindgren had found the formula for success and produced significantly improved results.

POOLE

C Holder	3	3				
B Kurtz	2*	2	2			
B Pedersen	1	0				
K Buczkowski	1	1	3			
A Lindback	0	1				
A Ellis	3	1*				
K Newman	2*	3	2*	2		

WOLVERHAMPTON

F Lindgren	0	2*	3			
P Karlsson	1	3	0	0		
J Thorssell	3	2				
T Proctor	0	0	3			
S Masters	2*	3				
M Clegg	0	0				
K Howarth	1	2	1	1		

SEMI FINAL PLAY-OFF 1st LEG

BELLE VUE V BATTERSEA
(6 to 10)

Heat 6	Zagar	Woffinden	Neal	Cook	3 - 3	19 - 17
Heat 7	Nicholls	Woffinden	Sundstrom	Fricke	3 - 3	22 - 20
Heat 8	Neal	R Worrall	Chivers	S Worrall	4 - 2	26 - 22
Heat 9	Nicholls	Dudek	Chivers	Jacobs	3 - 3	29 - 25
Heat 10	Zagar	Woffinden	S Worrall	Sundstrom	2 - 4	31 - 29

The score over heats 6 through to 10 ended where it began with regards to the point's difference. Both teams battled on equal terms over these five heats with three 3-3 drawn heats and a 4-2 heat win to each team. At this stage Scott Nicholls was unbeatable and Belle Vue were beginning to look more and more confident about their ability to take this match.

BELLE VUE

M Zagar	0	3	3					
S Worrall	1	2*	0	1				
M Fricke	0	0						
S Nicholls	3	3	3					
C Cook	2	0						
R Worrall	3	0	3	2				
J Jacobs	F	0						

BATTERSEA

P Dudek	3	1	2					
L Sundstrom	2*	3	1*	0				
J Neal	1*	1*	3					
T Woffinden	1	2	2	2				
K Bjerre	1*	0						
S Chivers	2	2	1*	1*				

SEMI FINAL PLAY-OFF 1st LEG

POOLE V WOLVERHAMPTON
(11 to 15)

Heat 11	Holder	Thorssell	Kurtz	Masters	4- 2	37 – 29
Heat 12	Newman	Howarth	Ellis	Clegg	4- 2	41 -31
Heat 13	Lindback	Holder	Masters	Lindgren	5- 1	46 – 32
Heat 14 rerun	Proctor	Buczkowski	Thorssell	Pedersen	2- 4	48 – 36
Heat 15	Holder	Lindgren	Proctor	Lindback	3- 3	51 - 39

Heats 11 through to 13 saw Poole apply that competitive edge for which they are renowned and as a consequence they pulled out a 14 point lead that looked very unhealthy for Wolverhampton. They managed to squeeze out a 4 – 2 heat win and in heat 15 they held the out of character Lindback, to get second and third and so keep the score to an ominous 12 points. In the history of the play-offs, no team had ever overcome a 12 point deficit.

POOLE

C Holder	3	3	3	2*	3	14+1
B Kurtz	2*	2	2	1		7+1
B Pedersen	1	0	0			1
K Buczkowski	1	1	3	2		7
A Lindback	0	1	3	0		4
A Ellis	3	1*	1			5+1
K Newman	2*	3	2*	2	3	12+2

WOLVERHAMPTON

F Lindgren	0	2*	3	0	2	7+1
P Karlsson	1	3	0	0		4
J Thorssell	3	2	2	1		8
T Proctor	0	0	3	3	1*	7+1
S Masters	2*	3	0	1		6+1
M Clegg	0	0	0			0
K Howarth	1	2	1	1	2	7

SEMI FINAL PLAY-OFF 1st LEG

BELLE VUE V BATTERSEA
(11 to 15)

Heat 11	Cook	Neal	Dudek	Fricke	3- 3	34 - 32
Heat 12	Chivers	R Worrall	Bjerre	Jacobs	4 - 2	38 - 34
Heat 13	Cook	R Worrall	Sundstrom	Dudek excl	1 - 5	39 - 39
Heat 14	Zagar	Nicholls	Neal	T Woffinden	1 - 5	40 - 44
Heat 15	Cook	Nicholls	Sundstrom	Neal	1 - 5	41 - 49

Heats 11 through to 15 saw Belle Vue impose their quality on the Bulldogs with three magnificent 5 – 1 heat wins in heats 13, 14, and 15 that pole-axed their opponents completely. Scott Nicholls remained unbeaten on a night when the Manchester side had to weather a determined attack at the start of the meeting, stabilise the situation through the central portion of the match and then finally dominate in the final stages. Battersea will look back on this meeting and wonder how, with their three world class riders available, it was down to Frankie Chivers at reserve to top their scorers.

BELLE VUE

M Zagar	0	3	3	3				9
S Worrall	1	2*	0	1				4+1
M Fricke	0	0	0					0
S Nicholls	3	3	3	2*	2*			13+2
C Cook	2	0	3	3	3			11
R Worrall	3	0	3	2	2	2*		12+1
J Jacobs	F	0	0					0

BATTERSEA

P Dudek	3	1	2	1*	0			7+1
L Sundstrom	2*	3	1*	0	1	1		8+2
J Neal	1*	1*	3	2	1	0		8+2
T Woffinden	1	2	2	2	0			7
K Bjerre	1*	0	1					2+1
S Chivers	2	2	1*	1*	3			9+2

CHAPTER 19

Thursday 22th September 2016

It was a subdued and sombre crowd that filed out of the stadium lamenting the result as Harry and Rosie made their way nervously towards the fist aid office with the intent of finding Bernie Thorpe. When they got there it was anticlimactic, because Julia informed them that Bernie had called in that afternoon and told her that he couldn't make the meeting.

"Did he say why?" Harry asked.

"Yes, he said that he had an upset stomach and didn't want to risk spreading it to others, "Julia answered, "That's the responsible approach even if it creates a bit of fluster close to kick off. Why do you want him? I'll probably see him tomorrow at our even training session."

"Oh, nothing important," Harry replied, "I just wanted to set a time to meet for the interview, I thought we'd do a bit with you as individuals and then together. We can pick it up next week."

Julia was satisfied with this and left it at that.

"So, what are we going to do now?" Rosie asked as they walked towards the admin offices.

"My gut says, go to his house to see him," Harry said.

"I'm for that if you are," Rosie said.

"Let's do it."

After finding Bernie's address in the office files they went, in the Ford Focus that Rosie had hired for the week, to Twickenham to find his house. When they arrived they found it locked and in darkness, it seemed that Bernie was out. They went right round the back of the house to convince themselves that he was not there. They stood on the patio looking in through the kitchen window, "What do we do now?" Rosie whispered.

"Wait here and report in to Barry every half hour," Harry replied making it up as he went along.

They found an unlocked garden shed at the bottom of the large lawn and set up a look-out post in there and waited. Rosie called Barry and set up a monitoring process to give and get updates, but the first three calls revealed nothing because nothing happened. After three hours Rosie asked, "What makes you think he's coming back here tonight."

"I'm not sure about anything, but I can't think why he wouldn't come back," Harry answered, "It's not like he knows that we're on his trail. So if I were him, I would go home." Harry sat on a wooden box and squinted across the lawn. "Anyway, where else would he go?"

Neither of them could think of anything in answer to his question. It was just past one o'clock in the morning when the kitchen light came on and both of them jumped with the shock of it. Hearts pumping and adrenalin flushing their brains, they watched attentively as Bernie Thorpe walked past the window.

"Stay here and call Barry," Harry said opening the door and stepping outside the shed.

"Where the hell are you going?" Rosie said in a rasping whisper.

"I'm going to see what he's up to." Harry responded.

"Well I'm coming with you then," Rosie said.

"No, you stay here in case."

"In case what?"

"In case it goes pear shaped," Harry said.

"Why should it go pear shaped if you're not going to do anything?"

Harry was stuck there, "Yea, well, I'm just going to look ok?"

"Make sure that's all you do otherwise Bernie will be the least of your worries." Rosie threatened. "Got it?"

Harry winked at her through the crack of the shed door, "Yeah, got it." And he closed the door softly.

Rosie saw him trot across the lawn in a crouched posture using the shrubs and trees as cover. Although he felt exposed Harry knew that as long as Bernie stayed in rooms that were lit from inside the house, he was safe from discovery.

Harry got himself close enough to the house so that he could see what Bernie was doing. Bernie occupied himself with domestic chores as he made a cup of tea, put some bread in the toaster and boiled a couple of eggs. He left the kitchen and went into the lounge where he turned on the television and drew the curtains. Harry watched all this with growing anxiety as he thought about what he might expect a killer and blackmailer to be doing the night before a ten million pound transaction. It passed through his mind that they might be observing an innocent man while the real culprit was making his nefarious arrangements to sting Barry or injure some unsuspecting victim. Harry had moved round the house and could see through the narrow crack in the curtains that Bernie was watching television and tucking into boiled egg and toasted soldiers. He made his way back to the shed and brought Rosie up to speed with the mundane details and his concern over whether they had the right person.

Rosie stood firm, "Harry, for God's sake!" She rasped in a loud whisper, "we established the motive, the means and the opportunity for each killing and they all fit Bernie Thorpe! It's him! We are in the right place at the right time. Let's keep him in our sights and make sure he doesn't do any more harm when Barry fails to pay." She hesitated, then kissed him on the lips, "Don't go soft on me now Harry Marsh."

"You're right," Harry agreed, "Have you phoned Barry?"

"I'll call him now with this update about his eggs and toast," Rosie giggled.

"And tea." Harry added.

"And tea," she repeated. When she finished telling Barry Leech she said, "He's ok with all that and says that he will await instructions from us before doing anything."

For the next hour they intermittently watched Bernie watching television and began to wonder how private detectives could do this for a living. Then things changed.

Bernie washed the dishes and began turning out lights. Either he was going to bed or he was leaving. Harry and Rosie watched as he put on his coat and went out of the front door. Carefully, they made their way round the side of the house and saw Bernie get into his old silver Honda Civic, reverse off his drive into the street and drive away past their hire car. They trotted down the pavement and got into the Ford to give chase. They caught him as he waited at traffic lights at the Finishing Post roundabout at Sunbury, where Bernie turned left and headed south down the M3. At the Bracknell turn-off he took the A322 right through Bracknell and exited up the Warfield Road and onto Maidenhead Road. Harry and Rosie were beginning to doubt the wisdom of their venture again when Bernie turned down Drift Road and after a while left down a track into dense woods. Rosie drove past the track and stopped two hundred metres up the road.

"What to do now?" she asked.

"I think we've got to go down the track as well," Harry replied, "The question is. Do we drive or walk?"

"He'll see our lights if we drive," Rosie offered.

"Yes, but what happens if he drives out on a different route and our cars up here?"

"Good point smart arse. We'll have to go down without headlights," Rosie said.

"Are you ok with that?" Harry asked

"I'm ok with it, let's see if I can actually do it." And she slipped the Focus into reverse and swung it backwards across the road, then into second and gunned it in the direction from whence they came.

It was a narrow path that passed between varieties of deciduous trees that was a natural area devoid of any straight lines and with branches and trunks that have lain where they fell. The track was formed of two deep furrows that were a product of many vehicles and this was a great aid in the darkness as the wheels of the focus found the edges and self-corrected back to the centre. Rosie drove very slowly so that the engine noise was almost silent, so that she could stop quickly if they came upon Bernie unexpectedly and so that she could follow the strip of sky that showed where the tree tops left a tell tail gap. They looked for a place to hide the car without knowing how far Bernie had travelled down the path, so they logged likely places in case they might have to back track. Eventually they saw the brighter light of open ground coming through the trees, so they knew they were close to the edge of the woods. They turned off the path and parked the car between three bushes that offered very good cover. They walked through the trees without going back to the path until they reached the edge of the wood and crouched there looking across an expanse of grassland. A hundred meters away was a cottage outside of which Bernie's Honda was parked. The lights inside the living room were on and the curtains roughly drawn together. Rosie and Harry stealthily made their way to the end of the house and hid in its shadow. They agreed a plan whereby Rosie went around the back of the building whilst Harry went to the front, they would meet back in the shadow in ten minutes.

Harry went to the living room window and found a small crack at the bottom of the curtains through which he could see Bernie working on a laptop at a desk. He was surrounded by papers that Harry could not identify, but judging by the way in which they were laid out it was clear they were in some kind of order or relationship to each other, although he was unable to identify what that relationship might be from his position. When they met again they crouched in the lee of the external stone chimney that formed a substantial part of the end wall of the cottage and Rosie told Harry that had also seen Bernie through the window on the opposite side of the room. She also saw the paperwork, but she had been able to read what was written across two of the sheets, "I couldn't see them all" she whispered, "because they were overlapping each other, but some were laid on the back of the sofa by the window. One pile was headed Banque Cantonal de Zurich with what I think must have been an account number and a password, but I couldn't read those. Next to that was a similar sheet headed Eight CIC AG Suisse, which I've never heard of, but I imagine is a private bank of some sort. My guess is that there is something like fifteen to twenty such sheets each representing different banks which must be set up to transfer money between them, in order to make it disappear."

"Harry nodded agreement, "I've heard of Eight CIC AG and you're right, it is a Swiss bank."

Rosie frowned, "Why all the paper work? Why not do it on the computer, it would be much easier."

"And easier to discover afterwards if the police got their hands on it," Harry offered.

"I guess. Oh my God," Rosie gasped, "That means we've got the right man!" She took out her mobile and rang Barry Leech's number with the intention of giving him their location, "We're going to have to be very careful indeed," she whispered to Harry.

"Much more careful than you've been to date," Bernie Thorpe said calmly from behind them. Harry turned quickly and came face to face with both barrels of a shot gun. Rosie dropped her mobile behind her and into some deep grass growing at the foot of the chimney, turned slowly round and faced Bernie. "Well, well, Harry Marsh and the lovely Rosie Higgins." The Bernie said in mock surprise.

CHAPTER 20

Friday 23th September 2016

arnie@arniecottrell
Working hard to find the way to lift ourselves onto the higher level needed to stay in contention for the play-offs.

The Board Room of the Leech Group head quarters on Old Broad Street in the City had been converted into a mission control room with five senior police officers, two professional hostage negotiators, three concerned and worried company board members, three members of the finance department, two senior people from Barry's personal accountants, four secretaries, a psychologist, a psychiatrist, two councillors and a forest of computers, monitors, printers, and other assorted IT paraphernalia. Barry Leech looked at the computer screen and read the latest message from Bernie Thorpe and wondered where all this was going to end. He didn't mind the money; he had plenty, but he did mind the way it was being taken from him and this had initially made him very angry and belligerent indeed, but this was greatly tempered by the vicious nature of the violence that Bernie Thorpe had used to try to ensure payment would take place. Indeed, people were very surprised at how much he had been affected by the whole affair; the normally strong minded and resilient business man had been personally damaged, and it showed. Since he was a boy, he had always wanted to be successful as a businessman. He had run businesses as a child by selling drinks and old toys at the garden gate to any member of the passing public who would part with money, and plenty did. As a teenager, his first stall in the market taught him what made people tick, what turned them on and off, what attracted them and what deterred them. Even though his businesses had grown enormously in size and complexity, he always felt that the principles he had learned in the market never changed. His parents had been so proud of him when he made his first million and they were so made-up when he treated them to their favourite Chinese food at The Good Earth on the Brompton Road as a celebration. He was a pragmatic man who understood that there were two sides to everything, that there would always be positives and negatives in every situation, that success and failure are close neighbours, that happiness would give way to sadness and visa versa and that there were consequences attached to everything, but if someone had told him that his riches and success would one day be the direct cause of a series of deaths, he would have refused the opportunities he was so pleased to have taken.

He looked at the Chief Superintendent Law "Why?" he asked, "why would he kill those people before making any demands. Why didn't he tell us what he wanted with a warning that he would kill if we didn't pay."

The policeman sat down beside the businessman, "I don't know sir. There are several possible explanations, but the reality is that we don't know, and unless this man decides to tell, we may never know."

"He's made it so personal. He chose people who were connected to my business, people I knew, and people I care about. I mean, that's deliberate isn't it?"

"Yes sir, I think it is, but I also think that there is something deeper that we don't know about, some underlying motive that's driving this crime."

"Do you have any idea who he is yet?"

"No sir, we haven't, but in a sense it doesn't matter at this stage because he is talking to us directly and by doing that we should be able to find his location."

"Do you think he knows that?" Barry asked.

The policeman looked circumspect, "I hope not, but he appears to be pretty bright, so…"

At that moment Barry's secretary Gillian came over, "Mr Leech, check your emails, you've just received something."

Barry clicked on his unread inbox message and watched as Bernie Thorpe's most recent missive opened in front of him.

> Attached are the details of accounts into which you
> will deposit the sum of money identified on the
> attached schedule. You are to do this in exactly the
> order, the amount and the time specified. If you
> stray in any way, I will assume that you are deliberately
> sabotaging the program and I will deal out retribution
> accordingly. I am monitoring every transaction in real
> time. Once again, I urge you not to test my resolve in
> any way. I want to hurt you as much as you have hurt
> my family. The financial pain will be significant but
> bearable but the emotional pain will stay with you forever.

Barry opened the attachment and found the schedule – it read:

> Monday 3rd October 2016
> 1100 (GMT) deposit Euro: 29,497,883.
> Euro: 881284 to the following = CH94 0077 2001 6538 5495 2
>
> 1700 – You collect hostage: place: To be advised
> Person: To be advised

DO NOT DEVIATE FROM THIS SCHEDULE.

Barry looked away from the screen to Nik James, "What am I looking at here?"

"It's a Swiss IBAN format sir. Essentially a very fast way of transferring money globally from bank to bank, I should think he might have several of these that will activate upon receipt. It's very difficult to trace and the Swiss are hot on confidentiality."

"What do all the numbers mean?" Barry asked.

Nik sat down next to him, "Ok, look at this long string of numbers. CH is the ISO, or international country code, for Switzerland, 94 is the IBAN check digits, 00772 is the bank identifier, 001 6538 5495 2 is the account number."

"So we know the bank and the account number?" Barry asked.

"This one, yes," Nik confirmed, "but that's the last we'll see and hear of it I'm afraid."

"Bastard!" Barry hit the desk hard.

"The irony is that we've had occasions to be pleased with the process," Nik added, and Barry's head swung round sharply so that he glared at Nik.

CHAPTER 21

Friday 23th September 2016

arnie@arniecottrell
Looking forward to the run-in now. I think we can really break through into the big time.

Bernie sat on a box in the garage that had been converted into a passable gymnasium and looked down on Harry and Rosie tied firmly to the wall bars some ten or so feet apart. "This could be very useful indeed," he said pleasantly as he pulled the rope very tightly around Harry's ankle, "you have saved me so much time. In the event that your Uncle fails to deposit the money I now have the perfect hostage with whom I can motivate him. How can I thank you?"

"Let us go," Harry suggested.

Bernie laughed genuinely, "That's very good Harry, but seriously, Uncle Barry is a hard-hearted bastard, so I did have a niggling worry that he might test my resolve by not paying on the basis that I wouldn't kill again, despite all the evidence I've provided. He'd have been wrong about that, but with you as my prize," he said looking at Rosie, "it makes it superbly personal doesn't it? I see it as a good omen that you came to me"

Rosie looked directly into Bernie's eyes, "You're wrong about him, he never would doubt your ability to kill innocent people. You've established a good track record on that front," she stated, "and if you can be wrong about that, you could be wrong about other things too."

"Of course you're right, but I can't imagine that even the ruthless Barry Leech will allow his niece to be killed so that he can save money." He carried out a final check on the knots around her hands and ankles and said, "Look, I'd love to stand and chat, but I've got some final admin details to see to, so I'll leave you for a while."

Bernie went out to the Honda, took out the boxes of paper files and carried them through to the living room and placed them on the table, propped the shotgun against the desk and fired up the laptop. There were elements of satisfaction and dissatisfaction connected with Harry and Rosie, one the one hand it meant his identity was discovered, on the other, he had gain some serious leverage. He opened a new email account and typed the only message that would be sent on it, for he simply opened a new account for each message and then abandoned it afterwards.

> Let me update you on the latest development
> Mr Leech. Rosie Higgins and Harry Marsh
> are my guests having failed to accomplish their
> mission to track me down and stop me. The only

thing they have achieved is to get themselves
tied up and become my hostages. So now you
know who the hostages are that you will collect
when you are in compliance with my conditions.
This was not what I planned, but it comes as a
superb opportunity for me to make you suffer
even more than I had hoped. Even though you
have stayed well clear of the victims of the misery
you have caused, you will be made to feel the
pain and anguish you deserve.

.

When he regained consciousness, Harry's head was very painful when he moved it. They were sitting in semi darkness with just the dawn light filtering under the metal garage door.

"Morning Harry," Rosie spoke out of the murk.

Harry squinted to see her, "Morning." He grunted, "What time is it?"

"I don't know, but it must be around five o'clock judging by the light outside."

"Where's Bernie?" Harry asked.

"He went about half an hour ago. I suppose he's back in the lounge." Rosie replied.

"How tight are you tied up?"

"You should know, you tied the knots," she said, "Too tight to get any movement. What about you?"

"It feels very tight, but I'll try moving around and see if there's any give." Harry said.

Both had their arms tied akimbo and about a meter apart so that they couldn't reach one hand with the other. It was extremely painful after an hour or so in the same uncomfortable position.

After a while the linking door to the house opened and Bernie came in to check their tethers. "Ha! Ha! I see you've woken up," he said pulling the straps that held Harry's spread-eagled hands, "Good man, you haven't moved much have you?" Satisfied that both of them were well tied he returned to the house.

It was lighter now and they could see more of their environment, "Can you see anything that we can use and can reach?" Harry asked. There were weights in the far corner, a treadmill, a multi-gym, a static bike and a small quantity of sundry home maintenance items on three shelves on the wall to the side of Harry.

"Can you see what's on those shelves over there," Rosie asked nodding towards them.

"No, I'm too low."

They sat looking around the garage desperately for anything that offered and kind of opportunity for escape. The wall bars were a classic school design, built in sections with vertical wooden beams and horizontal poles that slotted tightly into them. Both Rosie and Harry were tied to the same horizontal bar and to his amazement Harry noticed that his left hand and Rosie's right hand were tied in the same section which potentially meant that they could reach each other if they could each slide along the rail by some eight or ten feet, if they could move at all.

"Rosie!" Harry whispered, "Can you slide your left hand along the bar it's tied to?"

Rosie saw immediately what he was considering, "I'll try," she said and after some initial resistance the tether moved little by little if she yanked her arm strongly back and forth painfully.

Over the next twenty minutes they both worked their respective hands towards each other while anxiously hoping that Bernie wouldn't return and discover them. Eventually, they were, by this time stretched to their fullest distance with Harry's right hand and Rosie's left hand pulling painfully against the vertical uprights while their arms were stretched apart to their fullest extent so that it felt as if they might be pulled out of their shoulder sockets. Their other hands were reaching along the horizontal bars towards each other but fell short by inches; it might as well have been a mile. Harry said, "Let's go back and see if there's any movement in the vertical supports. We need about four inches," he said.

So, agonisingly, they reversed the process that had got them so close but yet so far away from their goal. Twenty minutes later they were back where they had started. Both examined their respective wooden uprights and Harry found a small amount of play that could be measured in millimetres. They hadn't heard a sound from the house for almost two hours and hoped this meant that Bernie was asleep. Harry put his foot against the vertical support and pushed against it. Nothing happened, so he tapped it with his heel and still nothing happened.

"Just kick it as hard as you can!" Rosie whispered loudly.

"What happens if Bernie hears it and comes in?"

"We'll think of something," she retorted, "Kick it Harry!"

He gave it a kick with his heel with all the force he could muster and felt the support move. He gave it another few kicks and got it loose until it moved freely at the bottom and then the door opened, the light was switched on and Bernie came in, "What the hell are you doing?" he snarled looking around the garage and pointing the shotgun at Harry's head. Harry flinched involuntarily at the sight of the two barrels inches away from his face.

"We were trying to attract your attention, "Rosie said angrily, "Given that you refuse to answer our calls!"

"You haven't been calling," Bernie snapped back.

Rosie laughed out loud, "My God man, you're the one with the gun so you don't need to lie and pretend that didn't hear. We've been yelling our lungs out!"

Bernie walked over to her looking as if he were going to have an argument with her and then thought better of it, "Well, what do you want?"

"A drink, you bastard, we're dreadfully thirsty!" Rosie's deception had the advantage of being true, making it very believable.

It was Bernie's turn to laugh out loud, "You stupid bitch, stop worrying being thirsty and start worrying about whether you'll be alive in a few hours." He turned and stormed out of the garage slamming the connecting door behind him.

Harry and Rosie were just about to resume their escape attempt again when the door opened, and Bernie appeared with two plastic bottles of water one of which he put next to each of them, "Enjoy, you haven't got long now."

They both looked at him with hatred in their eyes, "Bastard," Rosie shouted, "how are we supposed to drink them?" Bernie turned in the doorway and smiled as he switched out the light leaving them once again in semi darkness.

Rosie's head fell forward, "Bastard," she repeated.

"I imagine he thought about that before he brought them in," Harry observed.

"He's still a bastard." Rosie muttered.

Harry got back to work trying to move the wooden support. He could get about three inches at the very bottom, but he needed four inches movement at the level of his and Rosie's hands, which was a good three feet higher. His heart sank as he thought he would never be able to move it the distance needed and he flopped in his seated position.

"Come on Harry don't give up now," Rosie urged.

"I can't see how this will work; the horizontal poles prevent the upright from moving sideways because they are glued into the joints." Harry told her.

Rosie looked at the joints by her side and grabbed one with her hand and with difficulty she tried to give it a twist. It moved and not only that, it went right through the support for she saw the whole bar turn down the next section. "Harry, chin up, test whether the horizontal bars go all the way through the support like mine do."

They did, and Harry calculated that he needed to move the bottom of the support some twelve inches if he were to gain four inches at their hand height. In the event, it was more than that and Rosie managed to get some movement at her side too.

With no surety that this had been enough they made their laborious and painful progress back towards each other again. After twenty or so minutes they were at a point where their hands could just touch. Rosie's fingers were long enough and nimble enough to reach the strap around Harry's hand. With anxiety riddled patience she managed to peel an edge back on the synthetic strap and then make that into a slightly more pronounced raised edge, eventually she could get the end of her finger farther under the strap and get some further movement by pulling upwards thus making room for her to pull the strap through what was now a loop. After some forty or fifty minutes Harry's left hand was free and he untied his right hand and then set Rosie free as well. They discussed their fight or flight options as they drank the water Bernie had left. Basic instinct for both of them was 'flight' but they knew that Bernie would simply find another unsuspecting victim and they would lose the killer. So 'fight' it would have to be.

They listened at the door but could hear nothing, "Whatever we have to do we'll have to do it fast," Harry said, "he won't be holding that shot gun, but the moment he knows we are free he will reach for it and then it all gets extremely difficult."

Rosie nodded to show her agreement, "Yes, up until then it will just be very difficult."

"Let's arm ourselves to even it up a bit and then we'll try to rush him," Harry suggested. They looked round the garage and found a 'Z' bar and an 'curl bar,' took the weighs off them and wielded them like light sabres, except that Harry's 'Z' bar looked ridiculous, "I catch him round the ear with this, it won't matter what it looks like, he pointed out.

Rosie agreed, "We need to take some care. We could kill him with these."

"If he picks up that gun, that becomes a real option," Harry replied.

Rosie said, "We'll open the door slowly and quietly, then listen again to see if we can locate him, agreed?"

Harry nodded and eased the door ajar looking through the crack into the empty hallway. All was quiet, so they opened it to its fullest extent and stepped into the house. The kitchen door was open and they could see that the room was deserted. The lounge door was closed but they could see light showing under it where the old floorboards were worn enough to form a shallow footfall dip even with a carpet. Rosie pointed to it and put her finger to her lips. Harry signalled for her to open the door and that he would enter first brandishing the 'Z' bar. Rosie moved to the door slowly, put her hand on the handle and mouthed, "One, two three," then yanked the handle down while Harry pushed the door open.

Bernie Thorpe was seated facing the wall at a computer desk. He spun his seat round in surprise as door flew open and Harry rushed into the room and leapt over the sofa with Rosie in close formation. He grabbed for the shot gun and rolled out of the office chair in one movement but caught the edge of the desk causing him to fumble his grip. Harry shouted, "Hold it Bernie!" and raised the 'Z' bar in readiness for striking. If Bernie could have stopped rolling, he probably would have done, but his momentum was such that it took him into a full rolling fall onto the floor. He turned the fall into an avoidance manoeuvre and managed to get enough purchase on the shot gun to take it in the same direction as his fall so that it clattered to the tiled floor at the side of him. Harry saw the danger and leapt across the space between them dropping the 'Z' bar as he did so. He collided with Bernie knocking him away from the gun but sliding away from it as he did so. Bernie was the first to recover and lunged at the weapon before Rosie could get involved. As his hand grasped the barrel of the gun he twisted his body so that he was facing Harry and tried to bring the shot gun around to bare it down on him. Rosie heaved her bar at Bernie and shouted at him, "Get back you bastard!" The end of the bar caught Bernie a glancing blow on the shoulder which was enough to prevent him from aiming the gun directly at Harry but was also enough to cause him to press the trigger and discharge one of the barrels. The room was filled with a deafening boom, a cloud of thick smoke and a cartridge full of shot that, by some miracle, missed everyone in the room, but destroyed the bay window leaving a very large hole. In the confusion Rosie bolted for the door and escaped down the hallway, through the front door and out to freedom. Bernie brought the barrel round and pointed it in Harry's face, "Sit down," Bernie ordered him in a controlled voice, "or I'll blow your face off."

Harry complied and sat on the floor where he had landed. Bernie sat on the floor with his back against the wall resting the barrel of the shot gun on his arm, "Now, where would you suppose your girlfriend has gone?" he mused.

"If she's got any sense," Harry said breathing heavily from his exertions, "straight to the police."

Bernie nodded, "I think you're probably right." He thought for a moment, "In that case, we should consider moving." He stood up slowly, "Ok Harry, I don't want to kill you yet, however, if you try anything at all, I will blow your arm off. I urge you not to test me on this." Bernie took Harry back to the garage, got him to tie his own feet to the bars and then tied Harry's hands to the bars as well, checked all the knots and said, "I'm not going to be long so I doubt that you'll have time to do anything, but always be mindful about how valuable your arm is to you."

This time there was no way Harry could work anything loose although he certainly gave it his best shot in the short time he had. Bernie returned within half an hour and placed a sack over Harry's head tying it uncomfortably tight to ensure that it could not be forced over his chin. Trussed up and tied, Harry was loaded into the Honda and lain face down over the prop shaft arch behind the front seats.

CHAPTER 22

Friday 23th September 2016

arnie@arniecottrell
Thank you for all the support we get, it helps us overcome the problems in the club and maintain our push for success

Barry Leech looked like a man who had aged twenty years in the last few weeks. His beloved Rosie was now in mortal danger and her future was in his and a murderers hands. The twenty-five million pounds had just become irrelevant compared with her safety, as he realised that she was the most important thing in his life. Rosie's parents died from carbon monoxide poisoning while on their second honeymoon on a skiing holiday when she was seven years old and it was Auntie Mavis and Uncle Barry who took her in to live with them and bring her up. When Barry's wife contracted breast cancer and died, it was Rosie who was there for him and helped him get through the worst nightmare of his life. He felt lonely and empty as he sat looking at the view from his private office at the top of the Leech Tower waiting for the next part of the beating that Bernie Thorpe was handing out to him. The door opened and Gillian entered, "Here you are Mr Leech," and she ushered in Uncle Max.

He threw his army great coat on a chair and hurried across the room to Barry, who turned in surprise, "Come here my dear boy," and he took him in his arms. Barry sobbed as his brother hugged him and they both stood motionless as Gillian quietly closed the door and left them alone.

They released each other and Barry held Max's shoulders at arms length and looked at him, "I'm so glad you could make it, I can't tell you," and he hugged him again.

Eventually they sat down in the comfortable leather armchairs by the coffee table, "Right, now bring me up-to-date," Max said.

"If you wait about five minutes, I'm going through to the Boardroom for a briefing session with everyone. You can come with me." Barry said.

The Chief Superintendent indicated for everyone to be seated at the Boardroom table and shuffled a wad of papers into a tidy pile in front of him. "Bernard Thorpe appears to have had a varied and interesting life. For starters, that's not his real name. He changed it from his family name of Garnet. So Bernard William Garnet has a military background. He spent nine years in the RAMC, that's the Royal Army Medical Corps, working as a Corporal where he was the first line medical support for the soldiers of G squadron during their first tour of Afghanistan. He returned from that and worked in Leamington Spa for Lock Security for two years, ending there as a supervisor, before moving to London and getting a job a year ago under his current name, Bernard, Bernie Thorpe with Sofa City on a lower salary and effectively a demotion. At the same time he volunteers to work for the St John Ambulance and asks to be attached to the Battersea Bulldogs. Added to this, his name change took place just before his move to London"

Sam had been looking very thoughtful throughout this report, "There's a connection to be made here somewhere or somehow. There's something familiar, but it's evading me for the moment," he said looking into the middle distance then shook his head, "Nope; it's gone."

Chief Superintendent Law coughed and went on, "So where does this take us? We are developing some thoughts about this beginning to look like a planned move in order to get attached to the Bulldogs. So far the theory has legs but it has to be born in mind that we do not have a motive that amounts to anything. So as a leader of the team, I have to warn against leaping to any hard and fast conclusions."

Sam's eye lit up, "Got it!" he said with satisfaction. The others all looked at him curiously. "I've made the link that was worrying me." He laughed shortly, "It was your reference to 'leader' that did it Chief Superintendent. The consultant that ran our Leader Training Course near Chipping Norton was called Garnet."

"Yes, Michael," Joe confirmed.

"We all attended as a team remember?" Sam asked them.

Ben laughed, "Will I ever be able to forget it? Dorchester is burned into my memory banks. It was a great course!"

"That's right, Michael Garnet," Nik remembered, "A good man. Do we still use the company?"

"I don't think so, I haven't heard anyone talking about them for a while now."

"Shame, they were good," Ben added.

"Is that a lead we should follow?" the policeman asked.

"I wasn't offering it as such," Sam said, "It was just that your reference and Bernie's original name put it into my mind."

The policeman made a note on a pad, "We'll run it through the process anyway and see what comes out."

At the end of the session the room emptied of people as they went back to their work. Max and Barry sat quietly and looked across the large table at each other, "It's dire isn't it," Barry said miserably. "It's a real bugger's muggle Max, a real mess and I don't know why," Barry said in a shaky "What do you think?" Barry asked.

"I think I need a large whiskey," Max answered, "and then we need to do some thinking.

Barry reached across the table and touched the intercom, "Gillian? Will you bring two whiskeys in please?" Max shook his head and gesticulated urgently to his brother, "You'd better bring the bottle in Gillian," Barry added.

"It does sound as if this Bernie has changed his name in order to deceive you, doesn't it?"

"Could be," Barry agreed, "But why?"

"I don't know," Max said, "what evidence or clues have you got?"

"To be honest Max, nothing worth my spit, it's a bloody disgrace. Three deaths and one attempted murder and now Rosie and Harry have been kidnapped and the only thing we can raise is that Bernie Thorpe had the same name as some consultant in Dorset, who trained my senior team a few years ago. I mean, please!"

"I remember the team coming down for that course because they called into my gallery and one of them bought a painting."

"That was Ben Charles; he's got it hanging in his office. It's an interesting piece."

Max laughed quietly, "It's alright Barry; I know what you think about my work, so you don't have to spare my sensitivities."

Barry chuckled for the first time in a long while, "It's crap, but it's still hanging in his office."

Max frowned, "Remind me, what this man changed his name from?"

"Garnet. Bernard Garnet."

"I've never heard of him, but I might know the consultant you're talking about."

"How come?"

"Well, if it's the same chap, his wife used to buy paintings from me. I think she bought three or four over the years. She saw them as an investment," he said pointedly and indicated that his glass was empty.

"He did a lot of training for us, leadership, teamwork, personal development, that sort of thing."

"You know, it probably is the same person. I knew him through his wife but he came in to the gallery a few times. He bought one of the paintings as a birthday present for her one year. His name was Nigel, or Martin or something like that."

Barry shrugged, "Well whatever. Look, tell me, how did you get here you old grisly?"

"Gillian called me and told me to come up. She even sent the helicopter for me," Max smiled.

"Did she indeed? She's taking more and more responsibility upon herself,

"Barry commented, "Thank God. I don't know how I'd run this business without her and Rosie."

"It's obvious that she is very good. And she cares about you and this business."

"Shut up you lush," Barry chortled, "Have another whiskey."

At that moment, the door flew open and Gillian burst in gasping, "Pick up your telephone, it's Rosie, she's ok!"

Barry ran to his desk and pressed the speaker function on his telephone, "Rosie?"

"Uncle Barry!" Rosie's voice was full of emotion and adrenalin.

"Are you alright?"

"Yes I am, but Harry is still captive!"

"Are you injured or hurt in any way?"

"No, I'm fine. I wanted to let you know you don't need to worry about me, but poor Harry is in real danger! Oh, Uncle Barry, it's horrible!"

"I'll send the helicopter to come and pick you up, where are you?"

"I'm not sure, somewhere between Bracknell and the M4 motorway, but don't do anything, I need to get back to help Harry."

"No don't get yourself into any more danger, you done enough, we'll get the police onto this," Barry insisted.

"There's no time for that, I think they're going to leave very soon and I need to be there to follow."

"Ok, but stay at a safe distance and telephone to tell us where you're going."

"My telephone's useless, dead battery.
"So how are you calling me now?"
"From a pay phone. I'll call when I can, don't worry."
"Of course I'll worry, and so will Uncle Max, he's here."
"Oh, bless his heart. Hello Uncle Max! Look after Uncle Barry will you?"
"Hello Rosie, my dear, of course I will, that's why I'm here."
"I've got to go. I love you both. Bye," and she was gone.
Barry and Max sat and looked at the telephone, "That's quite a girl," Barry said.
Max scratched his head, "Indeed."

CHAPTER 23

Saturday 24th September

arnie@arniecottrell
We had all the boys together to plan the run-in and we are ready. We feel we are on the right road!

The journey seemed rugged and bumpy as he bounced painfully against the hard and sharp parts of the seats and various items in the foot well. Between bouts of pain and aching Harry wondered where Rosie had gone. One stream of common sense suggested she had gone to the police but, by the time they returned, Bernie would have fled. A second stream suggested she would be hiding and then following them by car to their new destination. Harry hoped she had gone for the second option. At the top of the dirt track Bernie turned right down Drift Road and drove until he reached the A330 where he turned right towards the M4 corridor which, of course, gave him several possible escape routes. Harry could see nothing of this through the sackcloth, but he could sense the turns and hear the traffic, plus he had some knowledge from his time working at the research centre at Jealotts Hill. He tried to visualise where they, knew they had turned right and driven for some distance before turning right again, There was a lot more traffic on this road so Harry estimated they were probably on the A330 Ascot Road headed towards Maidenhead, but it was all speculation, he could easily have got it wrong by missing a turn or just not sensing things accurately. There was a definite change in the quality of the sound from outside and Harry guessed they had just driven into an area of open space. He searched his memory of the road and, if this was the A330 then the only place he could think it might be was the village of Holyport which had a very large green. Bernie slowed the car and turned off the road onto a gravel drive and stopped sharply. Harry could hear Bernie moving around between the car and what he presumed was a building. Eventually, he was dragged roughly from the car and pulled across the gravel on his back, up two stone steps and through a doorway, and as his heels came over the threshold he heard them catch a metal strip. He heard a knob being turned and a latch bolt released, the feel of cold air hit his body and then he was rolled through a doorway and tumbled down a wooden staircase onto a concrete floor and then he heard the door close.

Silence fell; Harry rolled over and groaned as various parts of his body complained about the treatment it had endured over the last eighteen hours or so. The sacking was extremely rough and Harry had been sweating profusely so that it was scratchy and wet on his face. Added to this was the fact that the light was switched off making the cellar a dense black place. His breathing was so heavy and hoarse that it filled his head and obliterated all external sound, so he lay still and tried to control it so that he could listen to the sounds in the house and after a minute or two he had slowed and softened it, so that other sounds could get in. He could hear a clock ticking upstairs; he thought it might be a grandfather clock or something of the sort. After a few minutes the clock dominated Harry's world and a flood of anxiety swept over him so that he was filled with the thought that this could be the end for him if he didn't find a way of getting out. With this came a complete inability to think straight or plan what to do and as Harry desperately attempted to marshal his thoughts, the images of 'what might be' got in the way of the thoughts that could change them. Every time he managed to focus his mind on how he might escape, thoughts about what the world might be like without Harry Marsh swept in and swamped them. The clock upstairs chimed one giving Harry his first notion of the time of day. Would Bernie want to sleep or would he have things to do through the night? Harry had no idea. He rolled his head to one side and banged it against something hard; so now he knew that the cellar was not empty! This knowledge energised him and his mind took on some discipline, by wriggling and squirming, he was able to move around the floor like a cartoon worm. In the course of this exploration he bumped his limbs on many items and when he found something that was both sharp and curved and he manoeuvred his head in such a way that the sack snagged on it. After several unsuccessful attempts, when the sack slipped off it's anchor, Harry managed to catch it securely and he was able to pull the sack so that it rode up to his chin, then with great difficulty and some pain he scraped it over his chin and nose until it sat on his head like a Rastafarian Tam.

He discovered that the cellar wasn't quite a pitch black as he first thought and that he could see vague shapes that suggested that there was a light source somewhere other than the crack under the door up the stairs. Over the next ten minutes he continued to travel around the floor like a giant maggot and deduced that there were quite a lot of boxes stacked roughly in rows at different angles. The floor was reasonably clear of dirt and dust suggesting that it wasn't just used for storage. If that was the case, maybe there was a light switch somewhere. He thought that the obvious place for that would be by the door at the top of the stairs but he hoped that there might be another one downstairs. Harry got himself into a sitting position with his back against some boxes and ran a risk assessment through his mind. If he tried to climb the stairs with his hands tied behind his back and his feet tightly bound together, one of two things were most likely to happen; one; he might fall and hurt himself badly, although, he had already fallen down them; and it did really hurt, or two; he might make so much noise that he attracts Bernie's attention and that just meant real trouble. An alternative was to stumble blindly around the room in darkness in the hope that he might find something he could use to release his bonds. Bumbling about might be ok if he had unlimited time, but that was not the case, any time now, Bernie was going to bring trouble to him anyway. There was a third scenario in which he made it to the top of the stairs, turned on the light and found something to release himself. He decided that was the one he liked best.

Harry thought that the stairs would probably be in line with the door at the top of them. He could see the outline of the door where the light was coming in so he shuffled carefully towards where he estimated the foot of the stairs would be. All in all, it was not a bad effort and he took more satisfaction than was justified from finding the bottom step. He turned and got himself seated on the floor, laced his hands on the second step, pushed up and shuffled his bottom on the first step. This was much easier than he anticipated so he got into a pattern of repeating the process with two short resting periods until he reached the short landing at the top. He sat on the edge of the landing feeling a real sense of achievement but knowing that the next bit was going to be genuinely risky. How took get onto his feet in such a small space without falling back down the stairs? He twisted around onto his knees, faced the door and saw in the low illumination that there was a banister to protect people from falling the whole height of the stairs into the cellar. Harry could feel his heart beating in his chest as he placed his forehead on the wooden handrail and lifted his knees off the wooden platform, taking his weight on his neck, forehead and toes in a strange 'S' shape teetering on the edge of the landing. The banister creaked as he managed to move his feet awkwardly under his body and with a controlled, slow and extremely strenuous effort he managed to straighten into an upright position by shuffling his feet under his body. Harry tried to stay calm as he recognised that this was the riskiest moment of all as he stood swaying slightly on the very edge of the top step. Slowly and smoothly he inched his way to the wall and leaned against it with a deep but silent sigh. To his delight he found a light switch by the door and using his nose he pressed the rocker switch into the down position. Bingo! A piercing and dazzling light filled the room and for a few seconds he was unable to see anything. When his eyes grew accustomed to it he could see that he was indeed in a cellar that was used to store neatly stacked boxes and also as a games room for teenagers, for there was a table tennis table, a pool table, a sofa in front of a large curved screen television and a PS4.

Harry got himself back down the stairs using the same method he used to ascend them. Once down he set about finding something that he could use to release his bonds. Eventually he found a metal stanchion that held some of the heating pipes in place. It offered enough of an edge for him to rub the cord around his wrists up and down its length and although it wasn't sharp, it was galvanised and therefore had a rough edge which, after a few minutes, tore and melted its way through the man-made fibre of the cord. Freed from his bonds, Harry stretched and flexed his stiff and aching body and then went back to the top of the staircase where he turned off the light and listened attentively. All he could hear was that damned clock ticking loudly and he began to think that maybe Bernie might not actually be in the house at all and he was just about to take hold of the door knob when he heard Bernie's voice shouting obscenities at someone right outside the door making Harry jump with surprise. Not only was he there, but someone had made him very angry indeed, "You can do that if you think it's hard and clever, but you've just signed Marsh's death warrant!"

"Shit," Harry whispered under his breath as he stood behind the door, not more than a few feet from his would be killer, wondering what to do next and probably more importantly, wondering what would Bernie Thorpe do next? Harry concluded that Bernie must be talking to someone connected with paying the ten million pounds and was finding them less than cooperative. Bernie's voice faded as he went back into another room and then he heard a door close and his voice was just a muffled sound.

There was space behind the door which when opened was sufficiently large for him to stand hidden from view. There were some boxes and plastic bags stacked there so he moved them downstairs as quickly as he could and then settled himself in the gap he had made behind the door. He started to think about where Rosie could be and what she might be doing. Given that nothing had happened, he thought it best to assume she wasn't close by. So, where was she? Even if she had told the police they wouldn't know where to go because Bernie had vacated the house before the police had arrived there, so they weren't going to come riding over the hill to rescue him. Harry tried to work out whether it was better to wait for Bernie to come to him and tackle him on the top of the stairs when he would almost definitely be carrying the shotgun. Alternatively, he could go through the house and tackle Bernie out there and, if he were quiet enough he would have the element of surprise on his side. The next thought was abruptly sobering, whatever pro-active idea he pursued depended on a single and pivotal requirement, the cellar door needed to be in an unlocked state. Harry felt a cold wave rise up from his stomach, sweep through his chest and settle like bubbling water in his throat. He placed his hand on the door knob, pushed the door against its frame to release the tension of the latch bolt on the strike plate so that it would not make a loud click as he brought it through the hole in the plate. He felt it ease open as he gently let the pressure off and felt the knob turn back to its starting position. His intention was to close it again once he knew he could open it, but that seemed pretty risky now he had it open, so he decided to go through and deal with whatever he found.

He needed to get an idea about Bernie's whereabouts, so he carefully opened the door until the crack on the hinge side was big enough to see through. There, right behind the door, was the bloody clock completely obliterating everything! Not only could he not see, but the infernal mechanism was so loud that he could not hear anything either. He had to get further out to see anything and that meant exposing himself. Praying that it didn't squeak, he eased the door a little wider and as soon as he could get his body through he slid out into a hallway and quickly recognised that the kitchen was to his immediate right and empty. In three silent steps he reached the relative safety of the kitchen, saw the back door, tried it, found it unlocked, opened it, stepped outside and walked casually around the corner of the house. Harry leaned against the rough brick wall and waves of relief swept over him making him feel light headed and nauseous. Fighting this feeling down he looked around and could see the property, most of the gravel drive and the road outside. He couldn't visualise himself crossing over that space undetected, so he ducked into the bushes that grew alongside the property and made his way through the enormous garden until he reached a head-height wooden fence. Without hesitation, Harry clambered over it and dropped into an area of shrubs and rhododendrons that created a dense covering that ran down to a paved drive. He lay on the ground feeling sick with relief and breathing heavily and shaking violently; he shuffled his body into a sitting position with his back against the fence and tried to get his heart rate down. After a few minutes he ventured through the complex network of branches until he felt well hidden, sat down and started to plan his next move.

CHAPTER 24

Saturday 24th September

arnie@arniecottrell
Thinking there's a chance we can catch Poole and Wolverhampton if we give chase with real effort!

After a few minutes Harry gathered himself together and climbed through the bushes until he got to a path at the side of a large house in about an acre of land. He trotted round the front of the house and rang the doorbell, feeling strangely surreal and incongruous. A smartly dressed woman of around sixty-five years or so opened the door until it jarred against the security chain on the inside, looked at Harry from head to toe and, based on his appearance, quickly formed an unflattering opinion of him. Harry was dirty, dishevelled and, to an old lady alone, extremely threatening.

"Can I help you?" she asked with a cultured but shaky voice.

Harry could see fear written across her face and felt guilty, but he managed a pleasant smile and said, "Please excuse my appearance, my name is Harry Marsh and I am trying to find a telephone so that I can contact the police. I don't wish to alarm you, but I have been the victim of a kidnapper from whom I have just escaped. I am in grave danger and would like to get out of sight before my kidnapper discovers my whereabouts. Can I come in and use your telephone?"

The woman was not at all convinced by what sounded like an outrageous story and refused to let him in, "Wait here while I get the telephone for you and please don't try to get in, there is a security chain and several CCTV cameras. She moved back into the house and Harry stepped closer to the door in order to gain some benefit from the substantial porch. A minute later she returned and offered him a portable telephone, "Here you are, make your call."

"Thank you," Harry said taking the handset, "Please don't be afraid, I am telling the truth and I wish you no harm." He dialled 999 and was put through to the police service to whom he gave all the information he could recall and had to check with the woman with regards to the name of the village and the address. There was a ten minute period of dead time while the police checked Harry's identity and story against their records. When they were satisfied that Harry was telling the truth they assured him that a patrol car was on its way to the address.

While Harry had been engaged in the conversation with the police, the woman, realising the truth of his tale, went back into the house and came back with a glass and a carton of orange juice and when he had finished his call, she handed both to Harry. "Here you are my boy, you have obviously been through a terrible experience."

Harry drank gratefully and finished the whole carton in a very short time, "Thank you Mrs..?" he tailed off wiping his mouth on his sleeve.

"Mrs Carter," the lady told him, "you haven't had a drink for a while have you?"

Harry shook his head, "No, you're right, I haven't. It was yesterday sometime."

And so a strange scene developed on the front step of the house as Mrs Carter brought out some flapjack which Harry devoured until he jolted his mind back to the danger next door. Harry said, "There's one more call I need to make to my girlfriend," he told Mrs Carter. He didn't have much faith that she would have gone back to the cottage to get her bag, but he called anyway. It rang a few times and then Rosie answered it, "Rosie! It's Harry!"

"Harry! Where are you? Are you ok darling?"

"Yes, yes I'm fine. How are you?"

"I'm fine too," she reassured him, "but where are you now?"

Harry told her and asked how she got her phone back. Rosie told him that she went back to the Chimney where he caught us and there it was! "I couldn't believe he hadn't found it."

"I don't think he noticed that you had it, let alone dropped it," Harry said, "tell me where you are now."

"Looking for you," she answered. "I'm on the roundabout under the M4 at Maidenhead just about to start back. I've just filled up with petrol, bought a magazine and a drink. I'm about five or six miles from you and on my way. See you soon."

Mrs Carter was very sympathetic towards Rosie's situation, "That poor girl, she must have been distraught."

Harry agreed but said, "I should keep an eye on what's happening until the police get here," he said. "I think you need to go in and stay there until it's over."

Mrs Carter agreed and went straight up to the master bedroom where she could get a grandstand view of the whole drama and phoned her daughter to tell her what was happening.

Harry jogged across Mrs Carter's lawn to the fence and walked along it until he found a panel that had some damage and through which he could easily see the front drive of the house where Bernie was hiding. Within a minute, as he watched, the house door slammed open and Bernie ran out onto the drive looking around wildly and clearly trying to find Harry. He turned and ran back into the house only to reappear within five minutes with a briefcase and the shotgun, both of which he threw into the Honda before running back into the house and emerging with two boxes of what Harry suspected were the files he needed to track the money through the different bank accounts. Bernie got into the car and started to drive towards the entrance. Harry felt panic rise in his chest and throat, if he lost Bernie now, it would a disaster of life threatening proportions for some unsuspecting innocent. He ran towards the entrance of Mrs Carter's property to at least see which way Bernie went and as he arrived he saw the Civic turn past him and drive down the Ascot Road out of Holyport. By instinct, Harry crouched behind a bush to remain unseen, but Bernie was watching traffic coming from his right and so didn't see him. Harry ran out into the road and watched Bernie speed away then leapt with fright as Rosie's Ford Focus approaching from the other direction screeched to a halt in front of him and spun in an untidy hand brake type turn to face the way Bernie had driven, "Was that him leaving?" she asked casually as she leaned her elbow on the edge of her open window.

Harry blinked, "Yes."

"Well then, you'd better get in here before the traffic decides to overtake me and get between us and Bernie. Harry opened the passenger door and flopped into the seat. To Mrs Carter's delight, Rosie left some rubber on the road, which she would show friends and family for over two weeks until it wore away.

CHAPTER 25

Saturday 24th September 2016

arnie@arniecottrell
We are just beginning to see how good Frankie Chivers is. It's like watching a duck turn into a swan!

Chief Superintendent Law sat straight backed with his hands on his thighs as he waited in the Bulldogs Board Room. As usual it was a busy and intense environment as people worked on various projects that were designed to discover who the kidnapper was, where he was, how to pay him, how to avoid paying him, how to rescue Rosie and Harry and how to find them. Barry Leech and Gillian came in and made their way across to him, taking time to say hello, encourage and sympathise with members of the team.

"Good afternoon sir," the policeman said formally.

"Afternoon," Barry replied, "have you got anything for us?"

"Yes, I believe I have."

"Right, well let's get on with it," the businessman said.

"Well as you know, we left here after the last meeting saying, given the fact that Bernard Garnet or Thorpe had the same name as one of your suppliers, we would run that through the system and see if anything of interest came up."

"Yes, yes, get on with it," Barry said in irritation.

The policeman looked at him calmly and completely under control, "Yes, I will sir. The supplier, Michael Garnet ran Management Training Courses for several large clients, one of which was Leech Logistics, which we understand is a part of the Leech Group."

"Yes."

"Mister Michael Garnet is the brother of Bernard Charles Garnet, that same Bernard Charles Garnet who has recently changed his name to Bernard Thorpe," the policemen stated and then paused to allow it to sink in.

"My God," Gillian whispered.

Barry Leech sat forward and leaned his elbows on the table, "Go on," he urged.

"Michael Garnet's company was called Next Step Management Training limited and supplied services to your company for some twelve years and in that time won a National Training Award for the leadership courses that they ran for all of those twelve years. In summer of 2015 their business suffered a series of financial blows in the form of clients cutting costs and consequently cutting their training requirements; one of these companies was Leech Logistics. Michael Garnet then became involved in the exchange of a series of letters with, initially the Finance Manager of Leech Logistics and latterly the Finance Director in which he requested payment of two invoices that the company had not paid for services provided." He pushed a photocopy of the letter across the table, "You will notice that this is a neutral sounding letter in which he simply states the dates of the services and the sums owed." The policeman then slid another photocopy of a letter across the table, "This is the company's response to his letter. It is a standard holding letter informing him that the invoices missed the deadline for that month's cheque run and that it would be included in the next months."

Barry was visibly agitated, "The revelation that Bernie is related to Michael is remarkable, but do we need all this detail about the letters?"

"Excuse me sir. I am also a very busy man, I do not waste time on things that don't matter. However, it is my judgement that you need to hear all of this if you want to understand how this situation has developed to this point," the policemen said carefully, "Now, may I continue?"

Barry nodded shortly to indicate that he agreed.

"In this letter he is on the edge of threatening the company. The response from the Finance Manager recommends that Michael Garnet should address himself directly to the Finance Director. Up to that date, this cycle had taken five weeks," he held a photocopied letter out for Barry to read, "this is a letter from Michael Garnet's bank manager stating that, due to him exceeding the limit, the company overdraft facility had been frozen. Mr Garnet wrote to your Finance Director, Brian McDermott asking that his invoices be paid immediately and spelling out the consequences for his company if this were not done. Six days later, Mr Garnet's business went into liquidation as a consequence of not being able to pay its debtors." The policemen paused to let the information settle into the collective consciousness and then went on, "Three days later Michael Garnet committed suicide without leaving any note. As you know, two weeks later Brian McDermott was killed by a hit and run driver as he walked his dog along the country lane outside his home."

"Are you suggesting that Brian was killed deliberately?" Barry asked.

"I'm suggesting that we might have a genuine motive now that places Bernard Thorpe in the centre of the investigation. Additionally, Bernard Garnet has the opportunity to go with the motive. His skills set is ideally suited to this kind of activity given that he became trained sniper in the British Army."

"I don't understand," Gillian said, "I can see how a sniper's skills are good for shooting people, but how would they help with the other forms of death?"

"The role of a sniper extends beyond shooting people," The policeman told her, "They are scouts who carry out reconnaissance and intelligence gathering while remaining undetected. They are trained hunters with advanced navigation skills, a steady, patient and calm demeanour, experts at camouflage, able to gauge shooting parameters and calculating in their planning abilities and specialist stalking skills which includes surviving in and moving around different terrains. In essence, he knows how to stay undetected and how to kill with a gun. I'm not sure whether unarmed combat is a skill set taught to snipers, but I would assume as a soldier he would have received some tuition in that." Chief Super Intendant laid a photograph of Bernie on the table, "For those of you who do not know what he looks like," he looked around the group, "We are treating him as a very dangerous man who will not hesitate to kill if that what he feels he needs to do."

Barry asked, "What are you going to do?"

"We have already visited his home with a view to arresting him, but he was not there. We are now working on the basis that it is he who has kidnapped your niece, Rosie Higgins and Harry Walsh and I have alerted the police forces of the four surrounding counties to arrest him if they encounter him." Chief Super Intendant Law looked around the group, "Do you have any questions?"

The people in the room sat in a silence heavy with dread for Rosie and Harry.

When the policeman had left, Max turned to Barry and asked, "Can all this about Michael Garnet be true?"

Barry picked up one of the letters, "You heard what he said and look at these," and he let the letter fall to the table top. "It seemed pretty damning to me. It sounded as if the company ignored Michael Garnet's pleas and delayed payment of his invoices."

"These situations are complex, you can't simply connect the two events in a causal relationship," Gillian said.

Max shook his head slowly and said, "They are intricately connected. But I can see that this is not the moment to open it up, but there will come a time when it will have to be faced."

"Bernie's making us face it right now," Barry replied, "He's killed three people already and he's threatening to kill my niece and her boyfriend next. If his intention is to make me suffer, then he's achieved it, but it's going to stop right now."

CHAPTER 26

Saturday 24th September 2016

arnie@arniecottrell
Ty Woffinden is a legend! What an honour to work with this great rider as he shows us all how to compete at this level

Rosie drove with a very light touch on the steering wheel and simple clean gear changes that demonstrated her skill and economy of effort. Harry thought, if she had been a speedway rider, she would have been in the same mould as Barry Briggs or his dad's favourite, Peter Craven. Rosie sat relaxed, but stern faced and concentrated on catching the Honda. Harry phoned Barry Leech and told him about the developments, current location and the danger Bernie now represented. Barry assured them he would alert the police and then let them know what help they could expect. Harry told Rosie that some kind of relief was on the way, but the only sense of relief they felt right then was akin to nausea. And then Rosie's mobile battery ran out.

Harry looked at the blank screen, "Shit! That's helpful" he said testily.

Rosie glanced at him and back to the road, "It was on for God knows how long in my bag at the first cottage and I haven't had time to recharge it since. It's done bloody well considering," she said as if it needed defending, "At least Uncle Barry knows where Bernie is at the moment, so he can tell the police."

"Yes, but who knows where we will be half an hour from now?" Harry replied knowing it wasn't helping, but feeling the need to say it anyway. As this conversation took place they arrived at the huge Braywick Roundabout, just outside Maidenhead, which has a spur going up to the M4 junction or four other exits.

"Which shall I take?" she asked Harry.

"I don't know!" he answered.

Rosie found herself stuck in the outside lane of the roundabout and thus forced off at the M4 exit anyway, so they had to drive up to the motorway junction and onto the roundabout where Rosie got into the inside lane and circulated three times while debating what Bernie might or might not have done.

"We've got to do something," Harry said, "we can't just keep doing this."

"If we drop on to motorway, we are committed until the next junction and we don't even know if he took the motorway!" she responded.

"It's the best bet for him and, if I were him I'd head for London," Harry stated.

As they came around for the fifth time past the entrance where the 308(M) joins the roundabout, they thought they saw the Honda Civic waiting in traffic to get on. "Harry swivelled in his seat, "It's him!" he shouted, "I'll watch him and see where he goes."

Bernie joined the circus on the roundabout and exited onto the M4 in the direction of Wales. Rosie took the same exit about thirty seconds behind him, "Nice deduction Sherlock, it must be wonderful to understand the criminal mind the way you do," and she blew him a kiss.

They had to exceed the speed limit by more than a little in order to catch Bernie, but by the time they had reached the elegantly designed Winnersh Wokingham junction, they had him in their sights and with Bernie driving just under the speed limit, they settled into following from a good distance behind. With no way of telling Barry or the police what was happening, they were rightfully concerned about how anyone, other than them could know where they were.

"What do you think he's doing now?" Rosie asked.

"Not really sure," Harry answered, "but given how well planned this whole affair has been, I can't see this being any different. My guess is, he's got another property to go to as a backup."

"Yes, I tend to agree," Rosie concurred, "in other circumstances I might admire his ability for planning."

"I think we are on our own Rosie," Harry said out of nowhere.

"Me too," Rosie agreed.

"We mustn't lose him."

"No. I know."

Then Bernie signalled to leave the motorway and pulled into the inside lane.

"Now what?" Rosie asked.

"This is Chieveley Services, so he could be getting fuel," Harry speculated.

"Hmm. Not a bad idea," Rosie observed glancing at the fuel gauge, "We're between empty and a quarter full."

They followed the Honda into the complex and realising the impossibility of remaining anonymous on such a small site, they stopped in the lorry park in the lee of an articulated container truck and Harry got out to keep an eye on their target.

Bernie casually refuelled his Civic, wandered into the service station building and paid for his fuel. He then drove across to the food hall, bought a Daily Mail sat for fifteen minutes over a cappuccino and read his paper before visiting the toilets and climbing back into the Honda.

When they saw Bernie's intention to rest, Rosie took the opportunity to refuel the Focus and both used the toilets there before returning to their hiding place at the back of the truck in the lorry park. The exit back onto the M4 doubles back on itself at the Chieveley Services and this was the undoing of Rosie and Harry's anonymity. As Bernie accelerated up the long straight road that runs at a higher level for the entire length of the site he looked down and saw Harry and Rosie moving away onto the road below him. Anger and panic surged through him and he pushed the accelerator to the floor to put some space between his Civic and the Focus.

"He's seen us Rosie! He knows we're here!" Harry said with urgency, "Let's catch him now or we'll lose him." Rosie drifted the Ford around the long left curve and onto the straight seeing the Civic going into the left curve at the far end and onto the roundabout.

"Keep an eye on him Harry and tell me which exit he takes." Rosie gunned the Ford up the straight whilst Harry concentrated on keeping Bernie in sight.

"He's stuck at the lights!" he yelped, "put your foot down Rosie!"

As they came out onto the feeder road and joined the general traffic, so the lights changed to green and they all started moving. Harry pointed at Bernie's car so that Rosie could see where to go, for there was no room for error at this stage of the chase. Bernie took the Civic down onto the feed road to motorway but he did not want to be stopped by the police and he knew that whatever speed he might dare to drive Rosie would easily keep up, so he kept it to a steady seventy miles per hour which meant that Rosie could sit on his tail now that she was unconcerned about discovery.

The situation remained in a steady state until they approached the Hungerford exit, when Bernie veered from the middle lane and dashed up the exit, but Rosie stayed with him and as they sped down the A338 at seventy miles per hour the whole chase suddenly became much more dangerous. They flashed past the junction of Gipsy Lane and Denford Lane as they blazed up Eddington Hill towards Eddington town. Harry was holding onto the armrests as they approached the cross roads in the town centre. Rosie was feeling very concerned about what might happen if Bernie decided to disregard public safety, and hey, what did he care?

"Don't take any chances Rosie," Harry said as they closed in on the junction.
Bernie's brake lights stabbed on, off and on again as he slowed for the bend. He clearly didn't want to stop for anything, including killing a pedestrian. They accelerated into Bath Road and turned left down Charnham Street as people stopped to look at what was happening in their sleepy little town. At the junction of Bridge Street Bernie clipped a mini clubman whose driver thought he had the right of way at the roundabout and sent the car spinning onto the pavement. Rosie and Harry sped past relieved that there were no people around the incident who could have been injured. All the way down Bridge Street and the High Street Bernie began to take more and more chances as they sped through the built-up area that was the main part of the town.

Rosie and Harry backed off to give him some space in the hope that he might slow down, but that didn't seem to work particularly. With more luck than judgement the two cars shot past the last buildings and onto the open road again without killing anyone. The A338 is a long road with gentle bends, but it is not a smooth road, so both drivers fought to keep their vehicles on the road as they hit the dips and rises that were emphasised by the speed. The occasional cars that came in the opposite direction were forced to pull over or take to the edge of the road to avoid the oncoming danger.

As they approached a T-junction that sits in a kink in the road by La Bellezza, a white van coming the other way appeared and found the road taken up by Bernie Thorpe driving over the centre line. With lightning reactions, the driver wrenched his steering wheel to the right and swerved down a B road to the right, rode up a grass curb and through a fence on the corner, landing in the field beyond. Rosie took the Focus very close to Bernie as he slowed sharply to avoid the van, but Bernie accelerated and avoided being rear-ended as they screamed through the junction and took the long right hand curve. Both cars swept through the junction, clipping the grass verge on the left and hurtling on to East Grafton and then Burbage. Bernie was trying everything he could think of to throw Rosie off his tail, but she would not be shaken. On the Burbage bypass she tried to overtake the Civic with her greater power and, as they came alongside, Bernie ruthlessly turned his car into theirs and tried to force them off the road. With the great concrete supports of Westcourt flyover coming towards them rapidly, Rosie hit the brakes and pulled in behind the Civic again.

Bernie lost the back end as he negotiated the narrow bridge over the railway line, which caused him to hit the wall and ricochet across the road to collide with the wall on the second and equally narrow bridge spanning the Kennet and Avon canal at Burbage Wharf. Because both collisions were glancing blows at obtuse angles, rather than head on at acute angles, the Honda continued to travel forward at speed and as it left the second bridge somewhere near the middle of the road, its right front wing caught the large rounded front bumper of a Volvo truck that had stopped to allow the oncoming traffic through. This put Bernie on course towards the high hedge protecting the narrow boats in the wharf thirty feet below which he hit side on again taking off his mirror and spoiling the paintwork, but not hindering his progress significantly. Rosie took the bridges with much more control but still travelling faster than was safe and the Volvo truck driver flashed his lights and sounded his horn at her as she went through.

"We can't keep this up Harry," Rosie said, "We'll save one innocent victim, but we'll kill a car full of people."

"I know," Harry agreed, "we'll just have to slow down when we think it's getting too dangerous. On the other hand," he added, "I don't want the bastard to get away."

"Me neither," Rosie said with her voice full of determination.

The drive through Savernake Forest was nothing short of terrifying as the road dipped and rose sharply without warning. Rosie was up for another overtaking manoeuvre, but the oncoming traffic made it impossible, "Let's hope the truck driver was angry enough to telephone the police," she said through a tense jaw.

"Let's hope any of the poor sods we've seen off the road have done the same," replied Harry.

"If they had, you'd think we'd have seen some evidence of it by now wouldn't you?"

Harry agreed with that and refocused on the road ahead. The Focus crashed to the bottom of its suspension as it flew across a dip and landed heavily and bounced through before taking off over the sudden rise and flying past the thousand year old Big Bellied Oak.

"It's said," Harry offered, "that, if you dance around that oak naked the Devil will appear."

"Not tonight darling," Rosie replied, "anyway, we're chasing the Devil"

They sped through Cadley and dived down the long hill into a dip and swooped up the other side at around ninety miles an hour. It was now three o'clock in the afternoon and the traffic was getting heavier, Bernie slowed right down to the speed limit as they went through Marlborough, giving Harry and Rosie some hope that they might be able to gain some advantage, but the local traffic meant that none was forthcoming.

"You know," Harry said to Rosie, "Bernie's plan is in tatters, he's failed to get the money because as long as we keep doing this, he won't be able to lose the money, so it'll be traceable. That's assuming that Barry has paid the ransom."

"That's a very big assumption, my Uncle Barry isn't the kind of man who let's anyone push him around."

"Anyway, whichever, Bernie's blown it."

"Well, technically he could use a smartphone, but not at this speed and with the complexity of the transactions. I think you're right. He's failed."

"That's going to make him very angry, I should think," Harry suggested.

"Very." Rosie agreed.

Bernie was angry and he put his foot down again as they hit the top of Herd Street and gunned the Civic all the way down Port Hill overtaking three cars in the face of oncoming traffic and leaving Rosie a long way behind and in traffic. Harry and Rosie were frustrated by this all the way through Ogbourne St George, where one vehicle turned off. They then managed to get past the last car on the long curve up to the Golf Club and pumped up the speed as they entered the old Roman road that ran to Swindon. This road was a nightmare, with it dips and mounds that created sensations akin to air turbulence in a plane. This made the steering either very light or very heavy accordingly and made overtaking very difficult due to the blind spots.

The Focus was gaining all the time on Bernie's Civic and the oncoming traffic made the whole affair extremely dangerous for everyone and drivers were now routinely sounding their horns in protest. Bernie was getting more and more liable to take reckless risks in order to stay ahead of his chasers and to their horror Harry and Rosie watched as he attempted to overtake vehicles only to be faced with vehicles appearing over the crests of the undulating road forcing him to squeeze back in behind vehicles missing them by inches. His third attempt ended in disaster as an oncoming car veered left to miss him hitting the grass verge which then threw the vehicle across the road towards Rosie and Harry's Ford. At seventy five miles per hour, Rosie twitched the wheel right putting the left front and rear wheels onto the verge on her left, producing an almighty bang as the front spoiler was torn off and crushed beneath the car.

A second later, as the Focus bounced in the grass, the rear dipped into a drainage ditch and tore the back box off the exhaust which caused the whole car to bounce even more manically. Both Harry and Rosie shouted with the shock of the jarring impact and Rosie fought with the steering as she tried at seventy miles per hour to keep from going over and into the fence that bordered the huge field on their left.

Inch by agonising inch she eased the Focus back towards the road and then saw the concrete fence post approaching. Any exaggerated movement would have resulted in disaster, so Rosie applied an almost undetectable amount of extra pressure on the steering and felt the car begin to move to the right a little quicker, but it would be touch and go as to whether it was enough. "Brace yourself!" she shouted at Harry.

The front of the Ford kept coming round and as they passed the post they heard the loud metallic scraping sound as the whole side of the car made contact with the rough concrete. The impact threw the car back onto the road and Rosie had to correct the steering to stay on the left and then continue to give chase, "That'll buff out, won't it?" she asked staring hard at the road.

"I fear not. I think you've probably blown the excess." Harry answered.

Then suddenly, and with tremendous skill, Bernie hung a left turn, raced up the Ridgeway and headed towards the open farmland on the narrow road. Rosie managed to slow and turn in pursuit but had lost some ground. They drove at speeds of seventy to eighty miles per hour along the narrow twisting road. Rosie and Harry both felt that it was unlikely that anything would come from the other direction given that Bernie would have encountered any vehicle before they did. They came to a long straight section and saw Bernie about a hundred meters ahead. Rosie pressed her foot to the floor and felt the Focus accelerate still more. As they began to close the distance between them Harry let out an incoherent shout as a tractor and trailer pulled out in front of Bernie and turned up the road ahead of him. The driver, wearing earphones and listening to who knows what, and not expecting anyone to be on the road, let alone travelling at around eighty miles per hour, never even looked to his right or thought to slow down. It's not recorded anywhere whether he ever knew what happened behind him, but he drove on oblivious to Bernie's existence. Bernie, of course, was living a different reality, one in which he was required to swerve to avoid a collision, and attempt to overtake the tractor, which he did instantly.

Had he been successful in actually overtaking the tractor, he would have been clear and away from Harry and Rosie, but travelling at eighty miles per hour on a road that was just wide enough for two cars, but not a giant tractor and trailer that sat right in the middle of the road and a car, Bernie was only ever going to fail. He clipped the huge tyre on the trailer with his left wing causing the Civic to leap and then career off the road. Beyond the initial trees and bushes that lined the road, a deep ditch lay in wait for anything that tried to get through and apart from Albert Bettis, who fell into it as he rode drunkenly home on his bicycle from The Patriots Arms in Chiseldon on a midsummer Friday night in 1934, nobody else had ever tried.

At seventy miles per hour, Bernie wasn't troubled by the ditch as he sailed over it, passing through the hawthorn hedge on the far side. Harry's mouth gaped open as he watched the car punch a hole through the dense bushes and disappear, missing the three trees that could have created a wreck. Rosie went past the scene, pulled over and stopped by a gate at the bottom left corner of the field. She and Harry leapt from the car and with stiff legs ran as fast as they could to see what had happened to Bernie. They saw the tractor go out of sight around the corner half a mile down the road then rushed to the gate to see what they could see. To their astonishment they found that The Honda had landed on its wheels and, hitting the gently upward sloping field of curly kale, bounced and then cut a deep, fifty metres car-wide scar across the beautifully ploughed surface, eventually coming to rest some three quarters of the way up the field with its nose in a shallow hollow and its rear wheels sticking in the air some three feet off the ground.

CHAPTER 27

Saturday 24th September 2016

arnie@arniecottrell
We're ready to execute the last part of our strategy now but we need Swindon to lose as well.

From their position in the car and by the gate, Harry and Rosie saw Bernie climb out of the driver's seat, collect the shot gun and briefcase and start to stumble and jog diagonally across field towards the dilapidated five bar gate in the far right corner. Harry leapt over the bottom gate closely followed by Rosie who shouted urgently to him, "Wait Harry! There's far too much cover up there and none down here, plus he's armed and we're not."

"Right," Harry agreed, "let's go up there through there," and he nodded towards a similar gate at the opposite side of the top hedge.

"Two things," Rosie observed. "One; if I was him, I would be waiting for us to follow him and I'd use that shot gun, two; he has the high ground at the moment, so he can see more than us and we can see nothing. So, if we go higher," and she indicated a copse at the top of the hill beyond the field, "we should be able to look down on everything giving us the upper hand."

"Excluding the weapons issue," Harry added.

"Yes excluding that."

Harry saw the sense in this and readily agreed, so they climbed back over the gate, trotted the short distance down to the gate into the next field, climbed over it and ran up to the top under cover of the hedge. When they arrived at the gate, they stopped, "He went on to this path further along, so he might be covering it with the shotgun," Harry pointed out, "so, I'll go over first to see if that's what he's doing. If it's clear, you can come over. Cross the path and go straight up to the copse. Got it?"

"Got it," Rosie confirmed.

Harry slid over the gate and down onto one knee in the shelter of the thick hedge trying to see through the foliage and up the path. Very slowly, he inched his head round the end of the barrier expecting at any second to have it blown off. In the event, Bernie had run in the other direction and to Harry's profound relief, the coast was clear, so they crossed the path and ran up the hill into the copse.

Nothing happened and they didn't see any sign of Bernie Thorpe. Sitting on a log at the edge of the tree line, they looked down on the scene and searched for movement, but saw none. The Honda sat in an awkward manner with its rear end sticking in the air, while their Ford was parked untidily at the entrance to the field by the road. Both cars seemed to be undisturbed and were not attracting attention.

"Have you got the keys to the car?" Harry asked suddenly concerned that Bernie might see an opportunity for escape. Rosie held them up between her fore finger and thumb and dangled them in front of his face with a look of utter contempt on her face.

"Ok, just asking," Harry said defensively.

The small wooded area was not a managed piece of land so there were lots of dead trees rotting on the ground where they had fallen. As the two made their way through the copse they were acutely aware of the noise this debris made when stepped on it, so they placed their feet carefully amidst the tangled woodland. They tried to follow the edge of the treeline, without exposing themselves, still able to view the landscape below them. They could see the gate where Bernie had left the field and they stopped to take stock when they reached the point directly above it. What lay below them was unpromising from a search point of view and, with its disorganised array of fields, hedges and several derelict buildings, it offered ample opportunities for hiding.

"What do you think?" Rosie asked.

"I don't know," Harry replied honestly, "he could be anywhere."

"Not only that, but I think he's quite close, because we can see a good distance from here and he didn't have enough time to make a break for it before we got up here."

"Good point," Harry said, "if he had been on the move, I think we would have seen him."

"That means," Rosie added, "we need to take great care as well. If we make a move on open ground, he'll see us too."

Harry scanned the scene, "We should be able to see him if he moves, unless he moves in the shelter of the hedge rows like we did."

Rosie bit her lip and considered what Harry had said, "Perhaps we should wait here and watch to see if he loses patience before we do and gives his position away."

Harry agreed with this strategy, "Given that we are unarmed, we can't afford to be caught by surprise."

They made themselves reasonably comfortable by lying on a bed of mossy ground behind a fallen log. Even in these circumstances Rosie noticed the beautiful smell of the summer foliage and earth, "Hmmmm, smell that, isn't it just gorgeous?" she said.

Harry inhaled audibly,"Yes, nice, but nature can't compete with the deliriously intoxicating smell of methanol as it leaves the exhaust of a speedway bike."

"You Philistine!" Rosie whispered hoarsely.

They fell into a silent watchfulness as they systematically scanned the landscape; Harry left to right and back again, Rosie right to left and back again.

After thirty minutes nothing had changed and Rosie whispered, "Maybe he's waiting for darkness and will try to get out then."

Harry considered this for a moment, "Yes that's a definite possibility. So maybe, we need to make something happen to prompt him to reveal himself."

"I suppose," Rosie said, "It'll be dark in about four hours, so we don't have a great deal of time."

They fell silent again and continued to observe until Rosie remarked, "We should get the police here really and let them deal with it. We've got Bernie trapped at the moment, so we've got time to alert them and get them here."

"That makes good sense to me," Harry replied.

There were a few complications that needed to be planned for, such as the mobile phone was dead and the nearest public telephone could be miles away.

Harry continued to watch the landscape but said, "You should take the car and drive to the nearest house and ask to use their telephone or get to that Esso petrol station at the top of Plough Hill on the Marlborough Road."

Rosie looked at him as if to say, "Why me?"

"It's got to be you; you're the only one with a license to drive a car," Harry explained.

"And what will you do while I'm doing that?"

"I'll be making sure that Bernie doesn't leave here." Harry replied.

"And what would that entail?" Rosie pressed.

"Nothing," Harry said weakly, "just watching."

"And if he should attempt to run for it?"

"I'll follow without making contact."

"Promise?"

"Promise."

Rosie pulled a face that said, "I don't believe you," but she said, "Ok, I'll go back the way we came and take the car."

"I'll skirt down there," Harry said pointing to the opposite side of the field, "I'll be able to see you from there and make sure you're safe."

"That's you doing nothing is it?" Rosie shook her head in disbelief, "And if Bernie's down there?"

"Well, I've already said what I'll do about that," Harry said.

"I'm not happy about it. Why don't you stay here where you can see everything?"

"Just in case," he replied.

"Harry, it's dangerous because that's where we think he's hiding. I don't like it."

"Ok, ok. I'll stay here and watch, but you don't break cover until you are certain the coast is clear. Get it?"

"Got it,"

"Good."

There was nothing else to be said, so Rosie started back through the copse and retraced their steps, cutting down the slope after waiting a long ten minutes to see if Bernie was around and deciding he wasn't.

Harry broke his promise within two minutes of Rosie's departure and dropped down behind a low undulation in the side of the hill and made his way down the slope in a crouching lope. When he reached the hawthorn hedge behind which, they thought Bernie could be hidden, he lay in its shadow and scanned the ditch and surrounding area, but detected nothing. After a few minutes he satisfied himself that it was safe and stood up slowly until he could see over the hedge. He found that he was about thirty meters from one of the many derelict buildings that now served as shelters for sheep in the worst of the winter weather. Harry determined he would try to get to it and use it for cover. From where he was, he couldn't see any evidence of Bernie's presence in the building, so he made his move. He slid over the dilapidated gate onto the path, crossed it whilst looking both up and down its length, threw himself over the equally ramshackle gate into the next field, landing awkwardly on his hip, rolling amongst dried cow pats and sheep droppings and coming to rest in a bone hard and deep tractor tyre track. He then lay very still expecting to hear the sound of a shotgun. He was now two fields away from that which Rosie should be crossing shortly, but he was also in full view of anyone who might be in the derelict building. Wincing as his sore hip complained about moving he clambered to a crouching position. Still no adverse activity, so he scrambled untidily across the dry uneven ground and sat with his back against the exterior wall of the building. He sat trying to control his breathing so that he could listen for any sound that would tell him if he was in immediate danger but could detect nothing that gave him either comfort or concern.

He began to feel very uneasy about Rosie, who would be making her move to cross the path and head down the field and he wanted to be in place to observe her in case she got into trouble. With his heart in his mouth he stood up and moved down the wall until he could see through the space where there had once been a door. He saw a single room with a broken staircase tenaciously hanging onto the wall and running up to a single room upstairs. It looked empty, but that didn't mean it was. Harry felt alert and alive as every molecule in his body tingled as he crouched and quickly threw himself through the doorway scaring a sheep that bleated loudly and scurried past him through the door into the field, leaving Harry lying on the floor in a state of high anxiety. With heart beating like a drum so that he could hear it in his ears he rolled over to look around the room. There was a basic fireplace that hadn't seen a fire in years, a badly chipped Belfast sink that had been pulled off the wall and abandoned, half a charred chair leg that was a left over from a fire, but no Bernie. Well, no Bernie downstairs.

Harry's eyes wandered to the stairs and up to the first floor which was only partially visible through the hole in the ceiling. There was only one way to know if that was vacant or not, so he very slowly started up the rickety stairs step by rotten step keeping his back pressed against the wall not wanting to put any stress on the few screws that still held it up. The room above gradually came more and more into view. With legs like rubber bands and his heart in his mouth, he reached the heart stopping point where his head was going to be exposed at floor level of the upstairs room and consequently at its most vulnerable to being shot off by a waiting gunman. He went up another step turning his back and forth to scan the whole room with what he supposed was the taste of fear in his mouth and found the space was 'sans Bernie.' Harry exhaled and realised that he hadn't been breathing at all for about a minute. He thought he might actually be sick but managed to swallow the gobbet of bile that had risen to burn his throat. He sat on a wooden box that he found and looked through the large hole where the stone tiles had slipped down the roof. He had a good view across the field where the Honda still balanced on the edge of its shallow grave, as if it were waiting for some kind of service to begin when it could be tipped in.

After a while Harry saw Rosie move out of the field below the copse, dropping over the gate onto the path halfway up the hill where she then crouched behind an outcrop of hawthorn hedge by the gate. She stayed there for about five minutes before darting across the exposed path and slipping athletically over the five-bar-gate, crouching and looking around to sense any movement. Harry watched her and his heart filled with love and compassion as she slid from view behind the hawthorn hedge that she was using as cover He really did not want anything to happen to this wonderfully beautiful and brave woman. Even as these thoughts washed around his mind a small movement caught his eye and he was back in the 'now' watching the hollow where the Honda was suspended. Nothing else happened for another minute so Harry took a second or two to look for Rosie again. She had moved only ten metres more when he caught a momentary glimpse of her dark hair where the hedge was thinner and lower; and there was the movement again!

This time Harry's eye was straight onto it and sure enough it was Bernie! He saw him crawl very slowly on his stomach between two bushes that grew on the bank of the hollow next to the Honda and make his way towards another clump that skirted the top edge to the left of the car, keeping him hidden from an unsuspecting Rosie. Harry looked back to where she was but could not see her. He felt a rising energy that seemed to throb in his chest, it was much more than a heartbeat, it was as if his heart was trying escape the vice like grip of his chest muscles. He swallowed and tried to control it by slowing his thoughts and focusing on Rosie's whereabouts. He saw her, she was about a hundred metres from the road and the Ford Focus, but there were two distinctly bald patches of hedge where she would be clearly visible to Bernie. Harry looked back at Bernie who had now chosen a prime sniping position in the bushes at the top of the hollow. To his horror, Harry saw that the gunman had what appeared to be a rifle with a telescopic sight on it. It must have been in the car and that's why he had gone back there. The situation had just got much more dangerous and serious for Rosie and Harry felt instinctively that when she passed the first of the two 'sight points' in the hedge that Bernie would waiting for her.

Harry calculated that, if he sprinted, it would take him twenty to thirty seconds to reach Bernie. If he sprinted, he would almost certainly by heard and become the target, but that was better than Rosie being the target. Plus, accepting that he would always be at a disadvantage because of Bernie's greater strength and ability to fight, if he sprinted that distance at that speed and got there undetected, he would be adding to the existing disadvantage, however, that would alert Rosie and she would then be safe. He concluded that, given all the negatives, he still needed to make the run and get to Bernie before he could get a shot at Rosie, but he had to do it silently.

He slid away from the hole in the roof and descended the stairs as quickly and smoothly as possible for fear of bringing the whole structure down and alerting Bernie. Stumbling and regaining his feet he fell out of the ruined building and scraped his knuckles on the sharp, concrete like ridge of a sun dried tractor tyre track. Cursing, he skirted the building and came out with a hedge between him and the gunman. He had to go through the broken gate, cross an exposed stretch of uneven field and get above the contour of the hollow and thus, hopefully out of Bernie's sightline. Given he was in a grass field, he was banking on a reasonably quiet approach and also, given that Bernie had his back to him, he hoped that he could remain unseen until he was on top of him.

Trying to run in a way that didn't involve his feet actually touching the ground, Harry rushed through the tumbledown but open gate and turned up the hill in a diagonal line to clip the top of the hollow. He tripped twice on tufts of grass and fell sprawling and looking anxiously in Bernie's direction to see if he had been disturbed, but it appeared not. He made it safely to the top rim of the hollow and crouched behind a large tangle of brambles to catch his breath. From this position Harry could not see Bernie and decided that he should move carefully until he knew exactly where he was and what he was doing. He crawled slowly on all fours around the edge of the bramble bush and then quickly to the next bush, peeking round the edge of this one and spotting Bernie's feet as he lay under the cover of a Blackthorn and an Elder bush.

Harry stood up into a crouched position, slowed his breathing down, calmed his racing mind, visualised how he was going to subdue Bernie and stepped forward onto a dry twig. It snapped with the sound of a starting pistol and Harry saw Bernie's feet twist as he attempted to turn his body and bring the gun round onto this new threat. Harry rushed forward and grabbed Bernie's feet and heaved on them to pull him out from the bushes. Bernie squirmed and grunted as he tried to pull the gun through bushes, but both the butt and the barrel snagged in the tightly tangled small branches and, in so doing, the rifle discharged with a loud crack that echoed across the fields.

With Bernie at a disadvantage, Harry managed to heave him clear of the bush hoping that he might get the rifle from him before he turned it on him, but this was not an issue because it jammed in the branches and was torn from his hands by the force of Harry's pulling. When Bernie let go of the rifle he came out like a cork from a bottle and the sudden release of resistance caused Harry to stagger backwards, trip and roll down to the bottom of the hollow where a mess of leaves, twigs, branches and cuttings from the hawthorn hedges momentarily entangled him. Harry's predicament was further complicated when Bernie also rolled into the crater and landed on top of him and quickly swung a right hook which flattened Harry's nose and broke it with a loud pop. Harry was on his back and taking blow after blow, trying to protect his face with his arms and trying not to swallow his own blood. Bernie sat astride his chest and rained blows down. In a moment of sheer desperation and instinct Harry threw out a fist amidst Bernie's series of blows and by a fluke made a connection with Bernie's temple and stunned him for a moment. In the two seconds it took Bernie to clear his head, Harry heaved him off his chest and rolled away from him.

As they lay on their backs directly under the suspended Civic in the deepest part of the hollow Bernie looked up and made a grab for the front of the car. Harry saw the danger and leapt at his adversary, catching him in his midriff and pushing him back, but Bernie had already got a grip on the right hand air vent set into the bumper. Harry's weight took Bernie backwards into the earth bank and this was enough to alter the balance of the car which dipped its nose menacingly and then with an animal like groan began to slide downwards towards the two men. Bernie saw it coming, placed his foot in Harry's chest and pushed himself up the bank and in so doing pushed Harry back onto the opposite bank of the crater. The Honda slammed down between them bringing with it a shower of twigs, leaves, grass and earth, leaving Bernie on one side on the top of it and Harry on the other on the underside. Both scrambled away from the vehicle and emerged simultaneously to confront each other. Bernie slid down the bank onto the bonnet and then dropped onto Harry who was struggling with some of the debris that had fallen onto him under the car. Bernie Garnet stood over him, raised his foot and brought it down hard into Harry's groin. The howl that Harry emitted was animal like and the pain he felt was beyond description, "I should have crushed your head when I had the opportunity Marsh," Bernie snarled, "but let's not waste this one." And he pressed his foot deeper into Harry's groin.

A voice came from above them, "Kindly take your foot off my boyfriend's genitals, I'll be needing them later," Rosie said calmly from the rim of the crater.
Bernie looked up and his shoulders sank as he realised that his own rifle was being trained on him, but his foot didn't move from its position. "I'm going to have to insist that you remove your foot Bernie, or I'll be obliged to blast your acorns from their grizzled bag." Rosie added.

Bernie disengaged his foot and stepped away from Harry, who lay in agony emitting a low groan interspersed with occasional high pitched whimpering sounds. Rosie nodded towards Harry, "Get him out of there and pretend you're a paramedic by taking really good care of him." Bernie complied by lifting Harry to his knees at which point Harry indicated that he needed to rest there and curl into a ball, so Rosie pointed with the rifle to show Bernie where to go, "Sit there and don't move."

It took a good five minutes before Harry felt like communicating. When he did, he looked up from his lowly position and smiled weakly, "You're a welcome sight, "he gasped, "but I think I had him."

Rosie pulled a hankie from her pocket and threw it at Harry, "Of course you did. Now wipe your nose Rocky, you look a mess. Is this your version of, I'll stay here and I won't do anything?" she mimicked him more than adequately, "I promise. What was all that about?"

Harry buried his nose in the handkerchief trying to ignore the rebuke and deciding that he would be better served by hurt silence than vigorous defence.

Bernie sat half way down the bank of the crater looking defiant and angry while taking some enjoyment from Harry's plight.

"Do you think you can walk?" Rosie asked Harry.

"It's very painful," Harry said in a nasal drone.

"Yeah, it will be, you nose is broken and goodness only knows what he's done to your normally tiny penis."

"That's more than compensated for by my grapefruit sized bollocks."

"That's true, we should thank Bernie really."

Harry felt his nose tentatively, "I'm going to lose my looks, aren't I?"

She laughed out loud, "On the contrary, it could be an improvement."

Bernie made a small movement up the bank, "Don't even think about it Bernie" Rosie told him moving the rifle in line with his head.

Eventually, Harry decided that he might be capable of moving, so they walked slowly down towards the Focus with the intention of taking Bernie to the Police Station in Swindon. Rosie kept the rifle, not trusting it to Harry while he was distracted by his intimate and disabling injuries, she also stayed behind Bernie so that she could keep a close eye on him. Bernie had said nothing since Rosie appeared preferring to watch and wait for his best opportunity to reclaim his dominance, so as the three of them made their way down the field in the fading light, Rosie and Harry were keenly aware of the danger he still represented. Harry's progress was slow indeed and, although it was only some two hundred and fifty metres from the hollow to the gate, his discomfort was such that he had frequent rest stops to allow the pain to subside before continuing. Each time they stopped, Rosie demanded that Bernie sat five or so metres away, on the ground while she kept the rifle trained on him. Eventually they reached the car and were faced with a problem they hadn't foreseen.

The Focus they had was a hatchback and where there should have been a detachable shelf to cover the boot space, there was nothing. In Rosie's mind, she had planned to put Bernie in the boot, but that was no longer feasible. They considered every configuration they could think of but could not come up with one that they considered safe. In the end they put Bernie in the boot space and instructed him to stay in a crouched position. Rosie decided to empty the ammunition all but one round on the basis that she would probably be able to get one round off if Bernie tried anything, but if he got the upper hand, he would not be able to shoot them. So, with the ammunition thrown into the hedge and Bernie in the boot area, Rosie knelt sideways on the rear seat, the rifle held awkwardly with the tip of the barrel resting on the rear backrest, the butt under her armpit, finger on trigger, with Harry as driver, who groaned with every movement of his legs. If it hadn't been so serious and dangerous, it would have been funny.

The truth is, it was never going to work, any more than any of their other plans were going to. Harry put the Focus into reverse and as he attempted to engage the clutch, the pain of moving his left leg was such that he had to twist his body to make more space for his poor swollen testicles. In so doing, his left foot slipped from the clutch peddle causing the car to jolt backwards dropping the left rear wheel off the raised edge of grass verge, upsetting Rosie's balance and throwing her sideways. The jarring action caused her to discharge the rifle with a deafening explosion, missing Bernie and hitting the rear door with a loud thump. In an instant Bernie came over the rear seat like a cat, grabbing the gun from Rosie and smacking her across the face. The car stalled and Harry at first tried to turn but could not, so he tried to open his door and get out, but Bernie was much quicker and he threw open the rear door and rolled out onto the grass.

He leapt to his feet opened the front door, "Ok, both of you get out of the car," he ordered.

As Rosie eased herself across the back seat towards the door her hand came into contact with a glossy magazine she bought at the service station just before Harry called her from Mrs. Carter's house. She grabbed it and rolled it into a tube holding it like a dagger. A mental picture of her middle aged, slightly overweight and not quite coping with getting older self-defence teacher called Pauline flashed through her mind, as the she demonstrated how a magazine can be used as a weapon. God bless the Women's Institute for putting on those sessions.   Rosie bounded from the back of the car as Bernie focused his attention on Harry's feeble attempts to get out of the front seat. He half turned as he detected her movement presenting his face to the oncoming attack. Rosie brought the end of the tube down into the middle of his mouth with sickening effect. Bernie let out a cry of pain as blood and teeth spilled from his battered gums and split lips, but he managed to swing the rifle like a baseball bat as he fell against the side of the car and caught Rosie a glancing blow across the side of her head, sending her tumbling sideways onto one knee.

"You bitch!" he spluttered as he straightened up and took a step to run towards her. Harry pushed himself so that he fell in front of Bernie's feet, thus tripping him so that he staggered and half fell towards Rosie. She took full advantage and leapt on his back hitting him with the magazine while Harry lay in the foetal position moaning in the background. Bernie flipped her off like a rag doll, rose and kicked her with all his might in the kidneys, "Try getting up from that you cow!" he growled. As he passed Harry, he gave him a strong kick in his right thigh which brought a sharp yelp of agony out of him followed by a long miserable groan.

All Harry heard as he buried his head in his arms as he lay in the damp grass was the slamming of the two car doors, the engine start and the car reverse onto the road before making its getaway down the road.

They both lay in pain for a long while before Rosie crawled over holding her side and flopped by Harry who hadn't dare move since Bernie kicked him, "Harry? Are you ok?" she asked.

"Yeah, great," came the muffled answer, "'triffic. What about you?"

"Same really."

"Good. I'm glad we're good to go." After a period of silence, Harry said, "I'm going to try to move with a view to standing up eventually. I may make quite a bit of noise, but don't worry about it."

It took a slow and depressing series of moves with periods of rest to allow the pain to subside before starting again, but after five or so minutes Harry was on his feet and leaning against the gate.

"Now what?" he asked

"We need to get you to a hospital quickly," Rosie answered.

"I'll be ok soon, stop worrying about me," Harry complained.

"I hope you're right, but if you have torsion of the testis, you need to get it seen to as soon as possible."

"A what of the testis?"

"Torsion," Rosie repeated, "a twist in one of the tubes that carry sperm. It's very serious because if you don't get help, you may be sterile and the testicle can wither and you could lose it."

"Which right now would be a blessing," Harry said weakly, "but ok, I've got the message."

"You stay here and I'll walk to the nearest house and call Uncle Barry." Rosie suggested.

It sounded like a good idea to Harry, so Rosie helped into a sitting position against the gate and went off in search of the nearest house.

In order that she didn't let him know how concerned she was, Rosie walked away from him until she was out of sight and then began to jog painfully. She was very apprehensive because he could go into shock very quickly and had nothing to use as a warm cover. Rosie's kidney was very sore from the kick it had received as she half ran, half stumbled down the dark lane using the gap between the tree tops to show her the middle of the road.

At a T junction she stopped and was close to tears as the consternation of having to make even a relatively easy choice began to overcome her. She forced mind to slow down and think sensibly and became aware that she could see the headlights of motor vehicle about a mile, maybe a mile and a half, away and reasoned that it must be the Swindon to Marlborough road and then, as she looked up the road to the left, she saw what she thought might be a light from a house, but it was behind trees. She jogged a couple of hundred metres along the road in the moonlight and to her eternal relief she came to a house and knocked on the door.

An elderly bent lady in a grey dress, grey cardigan and with a grey tea towel in her hand came to the door and was shocked to see a battered and exhausted Rosie standing there, "Oh my good gaud, what's happened to you my lovely? Bring yourself in, has you had an accident? Edgar! Edgar!" she called out, "put that kettle on and make some strong cup of tea with plenty of sugar in it!"

Rosie was ushered into a cosy living room where a warm coal fire burned in the hearth casting a glow over old wooden furniture that had clearly been here for many years. "My boyfriend needs help," she told the woman in a weak voice.

"Yes of course, there, there, you just sit yourself down here on the settle and tell me all about it," the woman said.

"Have you got a telephone I can use to call for help?" Rosie asked.

"Yes, we've got one that my daughter bought for us last year when I had my fall," the woman said, "Edgar! Get that handset thing that Julie got us and bring it in here." She turned back to Rosie, "She got us a modern one that works in any room and even in the garden. It's very good but we don't use it much because it's a bit complicated for us and we keep forgetting what to do."

Rosie smiled at the woman and winced with the pain, "Thank you. My name's Rosie Higgins."

"I'm Winifred Reed, Winnie to you me dear. That's my hubby Edgar in the kitchen, he'll be in in a minute, but he's slower nowadays," and she laughed, "aren't we all?"

A minute later, Edgar entered with a mug of hot sweet tea and the telephone. Rosie rang Barry Leech who was shocked and distressed to hear what had happened, "I'll get a helicopter up there straight away. Can you get to an airfield?" He turned and called over his shoulder to someone, "Find out where the nearest airfield is just South of Swindon," and then he came back on the telephone, "it's in hand, now give me your number and I'll get back to you and tell you where to go. I'll send a taxi for you."

Rosie handed the handset to Winnie and said, "Tell my Uncle what your address is and he'll send a taxi to collect me."

Winnie took the receiver muttering, "A taxi indeed, do you hear that Edgar, a taxi. Oh think of the expense of it and all the way from Swindon!" Barry got her attention and she gave their address on the Draycot Road,

Edgar came over and leaned on the back of Rosie's chair, "I got an old Morris that goes fine if you want to save the money on the taxi."

He caught Rosie in a fragile moment and she started to cry and wondered why it was so often the people who had so little who were the most willing to offer it to help others, "Oh thank you Edgar, but there's no need for that, my uncle can afford it."

"Well if you're sure, I wouldn't want to see him out of pocket when there's no need."

"You are so sweet," Rosie said taking his hand in his, "will you take me to get Harry? He's hurt and it's cold out."

"I'll reverse the car onto the road now," Edgar said taking his coat off the peg by the door.

"Take a hot drink for him," Winnie said bustling into the kitchen to make one.

"I'll take a coat for him as well," Edgar called back to her, "and here's one for you girl," he added throwing another old coat onto the back of the settle. Rosie pulled it towards her, wondering what some of the stains might be, "Thank you Edgar."

The telephone rang and Winnie picked it up and listened, nodding occasionally and assuring whoever it was that she understood, "Your uncle says they will fly into Draycot Farm airfield in about an hour. He says they're going to open it up special like," she said with undisguised surprise, "I've never heard the like of it, have you Edgar?"

"No, never," Edgar agreed, "They're usually very strict about that sort of thing, cos of them terriers and the like."

Rosie stood and up and put on the coat that Edgar had found for her, "My uncle is a very persuasive man," she commented noticing that her hands hadn't appeared out of the end of the sleeves of the coat.

Edgar laughed quietly, "You look a picture you do." And he went to get the car.

Winnie came back into the room, "Here," she said sliding a vacuum flask into the voluminous pocket of the jacket. Rosie buttoned up the coat, "I only know of one sort of coat that has pockets this size," she said not looking up.

"Aye, well, that's as maybe," Winnie responded, handing her a pair of gloves and ushering her out of the door. Rosie heard her muttering to herself as she stepped out of the way of the Morris Minor as it reversed out of the ramshackle wooden garage.

When the Morris Minor drew up opposite Harry, he was just beginning to fall asleep. Rosie and Edgar got the spare coat onto him and gently encouraged, persuaded and carried him to the car and eased him into the front passenger seat. Fifteen minutes later he was propped up next to Rosie on the settle drinking warm broth that Winnie had conjured up from somewhere. He and Rosie wrapped their hands around the steaming mugs and gloried in the taste of potatoes, onions, carrots, leek and chicken. Rosie had a picture of her grandmother at her cottage on Birchy Hill just outside Sway in the New Forest with a saucepan of broth continually on the range, being added to and consumed in roughly equal measure. This was the way of poor country folk and she thought it was a shame that it was dying out.

"Hmm, this is lovely," she called to Winnie, "is this fennel I can taste in the background?"

"What's that me dear?" Winnie called from the kitchen.

"I said; is this fennel I can taste in the broth?" Rosie repeated.

"I dunno love; I'll check the ingredients on the tin." Winnie called back.

Rosie sank into the settle a bit more and didn't look at Harry, but she could hear him chuckling next to her. In years to come, "Is this fennel I can taste in the background?" became a stock phrase that came back to haunt her when either of them was in danger of appearing pretentious.

Not long after that, a taxi drew up outside, the driver hooted his horn and Harry and Rosie were loaded aboard and left for the airfield bidding farewell to Winnie and Edgar as if they'd known them all their lives, promising to visit whenever they came up to watch the Robins on a Thursday night and meaning it. The helicopter took them both by prior arrangement to The Manor Hospital at Oxford where they were treated for their various injuries. It was a private hospital, so as long as someone paid the bills, the pair were kept there in comparative luxury . Rosie was generally checked and administered to for her bruising and aching body, whereas Harry underwent a thorough examination of his swollen testicles. An Ultrasound was taken and the doctor was satisfied that there was no permanent damage and proposed the application of alternate hot and cold direct treatment, either in the form of home-made pads or bags or a purposely designed testicular support pouch. In addition, she suggested the gentle uplifting support that is best provided by close fitting underpants or indeed, the aforementioned testicular support pouch; all of this together with four or five days of paracetamol for pain relief.

Sunday 25th September 2016

Rosie awoke on this sunny Sunday morning to aches and bruises. She sported a black eye that spread down her cheek, a black and blue blotch engulfed her hip and waist over her left leg and her shoulders felt as if they had been welded together.

Harry awoke around noon and couldn't move at all without stabbing pains radiating all over his body. His genitals were the size of small lemons and had taken on a bluey, yellowy, greenish, dark brown blotchiness that resembled a piece of abstract art that came from a collaboration between Claus Oldenburg and Wassily Kandinsky. He kept looking under the sheets at them to check that they really were like they were and each time he resurfaced with the same sense of shock and disbelief. He was sure that the nurses were making far more frequent visits to monitor them than was required because they always seemed to be accompanied by a second or even third nurse who seemed to be attending as part of their training or in an observational capacity, whatever that might mean. In addition to the feature injury he also wore a half face transparent mask that protected his broken nose. When Rosie showed him this in a mirror they both giggled like children, "You look like a superhero who can't make his mind up about having a secret identity or not," Rosie teased.

About three in the afternoon Barry Leech's helicopter landed on the roof of the hospital and he was greeted and ushered around by obsequious sycophants who derived at least some of their self worth from being seen with people who arrive in helicopters. The flowers that he brought with him were arranged in expensive vases in Rosie's room by the nurses.

When he saw the bruises, he was stunned, "What the hell happened to you two?" he asked as he sat in the Stirling High Back Winged Chair by Harry's bed, while Rosie sat on his bed. They told him everything from being trapped in the gym, to Mrs. Carter's porch, about the car chase across Berkshire and Wiltshire, the crash in the field and the stalking in the copse, to the fights in the hollow and the car balanced on the edge of the hollow. They dwelt on the care they received from Winnie and Edgar and told Barry about those sweet people and how they just welcomed two strangers into their home and offered love and compassion to them.

"I'd like to meet them," Barry said, "I'll get my people to bring them down to London and we'll give them a day to remember."

"I've got a better idea," Rosie said, "we three will go to see them at their house and take them out for the afternoon to a place they know. I think they'll be able to cope with that."

"You're probably right," Barry agreed.

When he left at six o'clock, both Rosie and Harry were exhausted and the doctor insisted that they get some sleep, which is exactly what they did.

Monday 26th September 2016

When Rosie awoke at 0900 she discovered her eye and cheek had turned into a yellow ochre, black and purple splat that looked dreadful. Harry's genitals were reduced to the size of two passion fruits, but maintained their colourful presence. His nose seemed to be very large still, but he knew that it wasn't like that at all because he could see it through the mask. Both ached less than the day before and felt able to get about a bit more and both started thinking about their work and the need to get discharged from the hospital, but were told to forget any such ideas. They spent the time watching day-time television, playing scrabble and surfing the internet.

Tuesday 27th September 2016

When Rosie awoke at 0800 she was pleased to see a distinct fading in the colour of her cheek and eye, so that now there was left a pale yellow hue with a blended redness that created an interesting tinge of orange. Harry was relieved to see that his genitals had reduced in size to about the dimensions of two large strawberries. His nose didn't hurt anymore, although he supposed it would if someone touched it. They decided that they would discharge themselves and get back to Battersea and back to work. There was much to do before they set off for the 2nd leg of the semi-final of the play-offs.

Their arrival at the stadium however was greeted with genuine concern and warmth and as a consequence of regular visits from well-wishers, concerned, curious and simply nosey people, plus the relating of their experiences to all of them, neither Harry nor Rosie got any work done at all, so that when they finally got away that evening they resolved to go in early the next day before motoring down to Swanage and onto the 2nd leg of the semi-final at Wimborne Road.

CHAPTER 28

Sunday 28th September 2016

And so it was that they picked up Uncle Max from his studio just after two o'clock and took him straight to the Portsmouth Hoy, where they ate delicious crab sandwiches which Harry, Rosie and their security officers washed down with tea and Max complemented with whiskey. He was shocked to hear the details of their experiences and it distressed him to see the damage that Bernie had wrought on their bodies, "My dear children, it must have been appalling. Doesn't it scare you that he is still out there?" he asked them.

"It petrifies me," Rosie responded, "I just feel on edge all the time."

Harry agreed, "Yes, it's pretty scary, but we both feel that we have responsibilities to others and we don't like the idea of Bernie bullying us into hiding from him."

"And on a very personal note," Max paused and looked around the room to see if the three security officers were in earshot, "how are your, your, you know."

Harry blushed bright red, "getting better thank you."

"I noticed you were moving with care," Uncle Max said.

"Yes, they're still tender, much better than they were, but I wouldn't want to run anywhere."

"No, no, I don't suppose you would," and he turned to Rosie and placed his hand on her arm, "and what about you my dear?"

"I'm fine Uncle Max, "she touched her face, "this will be completely gone soon."

They discussed the various pluses and minuses of private hospitals which provided a platform for the elderly artist to rail against capitalism.

Harry listened to Max's impassioned ranting and then asked, "Since we met for the first time and you told me about working 'not for profit' I've often thought about how you reconcile your philosophy with Barry's, I mean, his is about as opposite to yours as anyone can get."

"You're right," Max agreed, "the truth is we don't agree and we have had some serious arguments about it. We didn't talk for about fifteen years because of it and because of our own foolishly belligerent egos."

"Have you reconciled it now?" Harry asked.

"No, not reconciled, but we have agreed not to get on each others case about it. I think we both realised that our love for each other is far stronger than any differences we have. But I still think he is a very greedy man"

After their late lunch they drove across to Wimborne Road and parked in the stadium car park and took some comfort from the fact that the Dorset Police Station was next door.

"All the years I've been coming here and I've never noticed it was there," Harry said. As they walked through the door into the foyer it became clear to them that the Chief Superintendent's concerns were well founded. There were so many people that Bernie could easily blend into the background unnoticed until it was too late to do anything about his presence. The security officers were also clearly unsettled by all the uncontrollable elements they had to attempt to manage. Every second seemed to be potentially the last one and eventually Rosie said, "This is ridiculous, we can't go on like this. Either we find a way to relax and enjoy this or we should just get out of here."

Harry thought about this and said, "Bernie's argument is with Barry personally, not with Poole or Wolverhampton, so there's an argument to say that he would go to the other semi final rather than this one."

"Unless he transfers his hatred from Barry to us," Rosie pointed out, "in which case, he would come here."

Harry couldn't argue against that logic, "What about if we go to the pits and then up into the office area, there's small anti office next door to the referee's room where we can sit and watch the races. I can get any interviews I want and we are away from the public areas and Bernie won't be allowed in to those areas."

Uncle Max, Harry and Rosie, along with one security officer, squeezed themselves into the very small anti-room, while the other two guards positioned themselves one at the top of the stairs and the other at the bottom. The group borrowed some hard folding chairs to sit on and crowded in front of the window that gave a magnificent view of the track.

One guard accompanied Harry when he excused himself, ostensibly to join the general chaos and get some interviews, but actually to ease the ache from sitting with his legs together on a hard chair. He walked gingerly down into the pits where he found the excitement and tension to be crackling with energy. Engines revving, bikes on stands with back wheels spinning, mechanics tweaking engines to find that extra bit of speed for their riders, people sorting the tyres to find the best grip, riders stretching, sitting in meditative silence, cleaning goggles, polishing helmets, arranging and rearranging their personal gear on the tables in their stalls, managers having words in the ears of riders, promoters, and mechanics, television crews seeking the best shots, interviewers from local and national television and radio looking for that attention grabbing interview that would differentiate their broadcast from the others, all mounting in intensity, noise levels and focus as the time for the start of racing came closer and closer.

All of this was televised by Sky on large screens both at Wimborne Road and The National Speedway Stadium in Manchester and broadcast live to Australia, New Zealand and every country in Europe to give the Elite League worldwide exposure. The laboriously slow, and much looked at, clock eventually ticked round to seven thirty and both the semi finals started together.

CHAPTER 29

Thursday 22nd September 2016
    Harry and Rosie got back to Notting Hill at about three in the morning, rose later around lunchtime and potted about in their dressing gowns doing only what was minimally necessary to prepare and consume drinks and food. They both felt wasted and rung out, both, at different times awoke on the sofa to discover the other asleep with the newspaper draped over their knees. At six thirty they decided they couldn't be fussed to cook anything for dinner and wouldn't it be a good idea to get pizza delivered. They rang in their order and sat down to watch one of those programmes where people participate to keep in an act that has always dreamt of making it into the big time and now desperately needs your votes.
    When the pizza arrived at seven thirty they were both asleep and awoken by the insistent ringing of the bell and the frustrated calling of the deliveryman. Harry found a DVD that was one of Rosie's great favourites and which he could happily watch with her, so they settled with a bottle of wine to watch Notting Hill in Notting Hill, but by the time Hugh Grant was walking through the market while the seasons changed around him, they were both asleep in each other's arms.

Friday 23rd September 2016
They awoke with a few stiff joints and made ready to go over to the Barns' house in Guildford, arriving just before eight o'clock and were waiting when Tony and Irene Fuller pulled up in their minibus. When Dorothy opened the door to their ring she was surprised to see Tony and Irene, but when Rosie introduced them as their friends, she invited them in with a welcoming smile, "I do hope I've made enough sandwiches," she said in a worried voice. "Rosie, you naughty girl, you should have said something when you rang."
    Rosie laughed shortly, "I couldn't; I was afraid that you would make some excuse not to meet us."
    Dorothy looked at Rosie under furrowed eyebrows, "You're probably right about that," she said ruefully as she ushered them into the living room.
    When they were all seated Rosie coughed quietly, "Peter and Dorothy let me tell you who Tony and Irene are and why they have come here with us." She could see that that Peter and Dorothy were unhappy and felt as if they had been manipulated into an unpalatable situation. "Please don't think badly of me," she exhorted, "I am pretty sure if I had asked your permission that you would have refused and I wasn't willing to allow that because I think that this is too important to leave with any stone unturned." She took a deep breath. "I have asked Tony to come here to talk to you about his experiences and I have asked Irene to come so that you can meet her and see what Tony has done, and what the results are."
    She opened her laptop and hit the keys to start the DVD, "Let me show you something that I hope will inspire you as much as it inspired me." She turned the laptop round so that they could all see the screen saying, "The summer of 2016 has been remarkable for the performances of the athletes in the Paralympics in Rio, but I want to show you the Special Olympics which are organised for people with 'learning disorders.' These scenes are from a promotional video as well as some personal

footage from Tony who was at the 2012 Special Olympics in Leicester. It's non-elite and open to all abilities for people above eight years old and while it does have an element of competing against others, it is much more about doing your best, beating your best and being your best."

They watched the promo disc first which described the background and history with images of competitors engaged in activities that stretched them both physically and intellectually. When this was finished, Harry put on Tony's personal disc.
Rosie said, "You'll see competitors including Irene, She looked over to where she was sitting and smiled gently. Irene grinned broadly back at her. Rosie went on, "Some suffer from severe physical difficulties, others with problems with their brains that hinder their thinking skills and still others who suffer from both, but, above all, they are trying and succeeding."

They watched as the home video showed Irene participating with hundreds of others in a highly organised series of events at the athletics stadium in Leicester. They saw people with incredible problems of coordination and control racing each other, each started by their own volunteer and each greeted by welcome arms of volunteers as they crossed the finishing line regardless of their position and the time it took. As they watched, they were moved by the sheer joy and pride of the competitors as they received medals for taking part.

It was a highly charged and emotional viewing as they saw the evidence of the pleasure, pride, dignity and sensitivity shown and felt by everyone involved and eventually Harry turned it off and everyone sat in silence. "The last time we were here you both told us what the future looked like to you when you thought about Davy, it was bleak and cold, without any pleasure and warmth. You see a disabled Davy who cannot do things and cannot achieve things in her life. That's not the way we see the future for him. It doesn't have to be like that, we see people who can achieve significant things if they are given the opportunities. One day Davy make wake up and we discover he is like the worst affected people we saw in the film, perhaps he is unable to walk properly or control his movements without erratic convulsions. Perhaps he can move ok but has the kind of brain damage that affects him in other than physical ways." He turned to Tony and nodded, then back to Peter and Dorothy with tears in his eyes, "Please listen to someone who has lived through what you fear. Tony?"

Tony Fuller cleared his throat and gulped back a lump that had formed there during the DVD, "Let me say first; I understand what you are going through, the feelings, the torture of making a wrong decision, the love you feel for Davey, the stressful and protracted process, the pain. I know you are concerned about your beloved son and also about yourselves and the quality of life that lies ahead for all of you. I know about the guilt that comes with even thinking about what you might or might not have to do. My wife and I went through something similar ourselves. WE questioned whether we could cope as parents, we worried about whether Irene would be able to manage the worst of what other people might say or do. We were very anxious about the impact it would have on our lives and we were extremely worried about the money involved and how we could afford it. So, you see, you are not the first to agonise over this. Far from it. I can't advise you or try to persuade you about what you should do, but let me tell you what it is really like, not pessimistic or optimistic fiction, just the way it is for us in our lives and what you can expect if you let Davy live and he wakes up disabled."

Peter and Dorothy say silently, listening, so Tony continued, "Our daughter, Irene suffered a couple of life threatening episodes before she was born and doctors advised us that she had an extremely high risk of cerebral palsy. We were offered, and in fact, encouraged to abort the pregnancy. After a period of painful and emotionally draining discussions, we decided to go ahead with the birth." He paused and took hold of Irene's hand, "We have never regretted that decision even though things have sometimes been difficult and depressing. Irene needs constant assistance which my wife and I provide along with the vital support from various agencies, family and friends. Providing that support to her is not the ordeal that we thought it might be. Yes, at two o'clock in the morning when she needs to be turned, it is not the most fun you can imagine, it is just the way it is. That's the deal, not the ordeal. Having said that, some of the time it can be an ordeal, most of the time it is a matter of routine, but all of the time it is a privilege. I don't know if you have something that you believe in that makes you treat life as the most precious thing in the universe; we do, and we have come to understand that this life cannot look after itself and it has fallen to us to nurture it and look after it. No matter what the cost to us in time, money, effort or emotional stress, Irene gives us far more than she could ever take. She gives us something that is very precious and more than repays us for what we do," he squeezed her hand and she smile lopsidedly at him. "She loves us. We know it, feel it and cherish it every day. If we had aborted that pregnancy we would have extinguished the very purpose for living, to love each other. What do you think?" he asked looking at Irene. Irene's mouth contorted mouth struggled to form the words she wanted to use, but she persevered until she was able to tell them what she thought, "I see things in simple ways,"she said, "would I prefer to have not lived at all or live this life the way I have to live it? My dad is right, there are lots of things I am not going to experience in my life because of my disabilities, but there is one thing that I am experiencing that millions of able bodied people never do. I know what it is like to be loved and to truly love someone else. I watch television and see people who have a lot, or do a lot, they go to wonderful places, own marvellous houses. I can see their unhappiness in their desperation to be well thought of. I read about their divorces, the way they waste love. They have all that and miss the point." Peter and Dorothy leaned forward and took Tony and Irene's hands in theirs and they all sat with moist eyes in an emotionally charged silence.

As they stood by Tony's minibus, Rosie hugged him and sniffled into her hanky, "Thank you Tony, thank you so much. You'll never know how much that meant to me"

Harry shook his hand and thanked him from his heart, "You are one remarkable human being Tony Fuller. It's a privilege to know you. Bless you for what you've done tonight."

Tony smiled, "You're one of the good guys too Harry. See you tomorrow morning," and he climbed into the driver's seat.

Harry slid open the side door and Irene grinned at him, "I want to say thank you to you Irene. What you did tonight was so kind and brave."

Irene pointed a wobbly finger at him, "It was my pleasure," she said, "I like you very much indeed Mr. Walsh. Have you got a girlfriend?"

Harry put his arm around Rosie's waist, "I afraid I have Irene, I knew I loved her, but it wasn't until tonight that I realised just how much I love her." He leaned forward and kissed Irene on the cheek and whispered in her ear, "But I'll always keep a corner of my heart especially for you Irene Fuller. You are a very special person."

Rosie pushed him away, "What did he say to you?" she smiled,

"He said I could be his girlfriend as well." Irene answered.

"Well, I suppose I could share him with you," Rosie said, "How would that suit you?"

"It would suit me well." Irene replied and they both laughed together.

CHAPTER 30

SEMI FINAL PLAY-OFF 2nd LEG

Wednesday 28th September 2016

arnie@arniecottrell
Heady days. Let's do it for the people we've lost this year!

WOLVERHAMPTON 19 (58) V (46) 11 POOLE

Heat 1	Karlsson	Lindgren	Holder	Kurtz	5-1	5 - 1
Heat 2	Ellis	Newman	Howarth	Clegg	1-5	6 - 6
Heat 3	Harris	Masters	Tungate	Kurtz	5-1	11 - 7
Heat 4	Howarth	Proctor	Newman	Buczkowski	5-1	16 - 8
Heat 5	Ellis	Clegg	Karlsson	Kurtz	3-3	19 - 11

The match got off to an exciting and competitive start with four 5-1 wins in the four heats with Wolverhampton taking three of them so that by heat 5 they were 19-11 in the lead. Wolves lost Jacob Thorssell and replaced him with Chris Harris who put in very steady 7 paid 8 on the evening. Poole's efforts to replace Antonio Lindback were much less successful with Rohan Tungate suffering engine failure, a tapes violation, a fall and delivering a second place somewhere in the middle of all that. The only ray of sunshine for the Pirates was the relative strength of their reserves compared with those of Wolverhampton, but in every other respect Wolves looked dominant.

POOLE

C Holder	1	2	1	2*	1	1		8+1
B Kurtz	0	0	0					0
Rider Replacement								
K Buczkowski	0	0	1					1
R Tungate	1	R	2	T	X			3
A Ellis	3	3	1	X	1*	1*		9+2
K Newman	2*	1	3	3	3	2	0	14+1

WOLVERHAMPTON

F Lindgren	2*	2*	3	3	2*	12+3
P Karlsson	3	1*	1*	0		5+2
C Harris	3	1	1	2*		7+1
T Proctor	2*	3	2	3	3	13+1
S Masters	2*	3	0	2*		7+2
M Clegg	0	2	2	0		4
K Howarth	1	3	0	3		7

SEMI FINAL PLAY-OFF 2nd LEG

Wednesday 28th September 2016

arnie@arniecottrell
Heady days. Let's do it for the people we've lost this year!

BATTERSEA 22 (63) V (57) 8 BELLE VUE

Heat 1	Sundstrom	Dudek	Zagar	S Worrall	5-1	5 -1
Heat 2	Bjerre	Chivers	Jacobs	R Worrall	5-1	10 - 2
Heat 3	Woffinden	Cook	Neal	Fricke	4-2	14 - 4
Heat 4	Ljung	Chivers	Nicholls	Jacobs	5-1	19 - 5
Heat 5	S Worrall	Bjerre	Sundstrom	R Worrall	3-3	22 - 8

This was possibly the best meeting that the Bulldogs have ridden since they were formed. The aces came with an 8 point lead which was demolished by the end of heat 2 and then they experienced a bombardment of points. The Bulldogs won every heat other than heats 5, 9 and 12 which were drawn leaving heat 6 as the sole 4-2 victory for Belle Vue.

BATTERSEA

P Dudek	2*						
L Sundstrom	3	1*					
J Neal	1						
P Ljung	3						
T Woffinden	3						
K Bjerre	3	2					
S Chivers	2*	2*					

BELLE VUE

M Zagar	1						
S Worrall	0	3					
M Fricke	0						
S Nicholls	1						
C Cook	2						
R Worrall	0	0					
J Jacobs	1	0					

SEMI FINAL PLAY-OFF 2nd LEG

WOLVERHAMPTON 34 (73) V (77) 26 POOLE

Heat 6	Proctor	Holder	Harris	Tungate	4-2	23 – 13
Heat 7	Masters	Lindgren	Holder	Buczkowski	5-1	28 – 14
Heat 8	Newman	Proctor	Ellis	Howarth	2-4	30 – 18
Heat 9 rerun	Newman	Clegg	Karlsson f/remounted	Ellis	3-3	33 – 21
Heat 10	Newman	Holder	Harris	Masters	1-5	34 - 26

Heats 6 through to 10
The middle section of the match was much more balanced sharing two 5-1 heat wins each, two 4-2 heat wins each and one 3-3 drawn heat. Poole will thank their reserve Kyle Newman for his three wins during those heats and Chris Holder's two second places were a strong support. Wolves' greater strength in depth ensured that their opponents could not capitalise on their individual strengths and so by heat 11 they were able to maintain their eight point lead.

WOLVERHAMPTON

F Lindgren	2*	2*	3	3	2*	12+3
P Karlsson	3	1*	1*	0		5+2
C Harris	3	1	1	2*		7+1
T Proctor	2*	3	2	3	3	13+1
S Masters	2*	3	0	2*		7+2
M Clegg	0	2	2	0		4
K Howarth	1	3	0	3		7

POOLE

C Holder	1	2	1	2*	1	1		8+1
B Kurtz	0	0	0					0
Rider Replacement								
K Buczkowski	0	0	1					1
R Tungate	1	R	2	T	X			3
A Ellis	3	3	1	X	1*	1*		9+2
K Newman	2*	1	3	3	3	2	0	14+1

SEMI FINAL PLAY-OFF 2nd LEG

BATTERSEA 41(82) V (69) 20 BELLE VUE

Heat 6	Zagar	Ljung	Cook>	Neal	2-4	24 - 13
Heat 7	Dudek	Woffinden	Fricke	Nicholls	5-1	29 - 14
Heat 8	Ljung	S Worrall	Chivers	R Worrall	4-2	33 - 16
Heat 9	Nicholls	Sundstrom	Bjerre	Jacobs	3-3	36 - 19
Heat 10	Woffinden	Neal	Zagar	S Worrall	5-1	41 - 20

The lead after heat five was 14 points and by the end of heat 10 it was 21 as Battersea relentlessly turned the screw and crushed the energy out of a surprisingly fragile Aces side. But, that was not why the score was so unbalanced, the truth is, that the Bulldogs were supreme across the board offering such strength in depth that Belle Vue offered little by way of resistance.

BATTERSEA

P Dudek	2*	3						
L Sundstrom	3	1*	2					
J Neal	1	0	2*					
P Ljung	3	2	3					
T Woffinden	3	2*	3					
K Bjerre	3	2	1*					
S Chivers	2*	2*	1					

BELLE VUE

M Zagar	1	3	1					
S Worrall	0	3	2	0				
M Fricke	0	1						
S Nicholls	1	0	3					
C Cook	2	1						
R Worrall	0	0	0					
J Jacobs	1	0	0					

SEMI FINAL PLAY-OFF 2nd LEG

WOLVERHAMPTON 55 (94) V (86) 35 POOLE

Heat 11	Lindgren	Tungate	Ellis	Karlsson	3-3	37 – 29
Heat 12	Howarth	Newman	Ellis	Clegg	3-3	40 – 32
Heat 13 rerun	Lindgren	Masters	Holder	Ellis Tungate tapes ex	5-1	45 - 33
Heat 14	Proctor	Harris	Buczkowski	Newman	5-1	50 – 34
Heat 15 rerun	Proctor	Lindgren	Holder	Tungate	5-1	55 - 35

Heats 11 through to 13
Poole held out for two more heats before Wolverhampton completely overwhelmed them with three 5-1s in a row as a magnificent finale. A powerful combination of a transcendent Ty Proctor, Freddie Lindgren, currently the eighth best rider in the world and Kyle Howarth providing all of the heat winners to dominate and decimate the Pirates.

WOLVERHAMPTON 55

F Lindgren	2*	2*	3	3	2*	12+3
P Karlsson	3	1*	1*	0		5+2
C Harris	3	1	1	2*		7+1
T Proctor	2*	3	2	3	3	13+1
S Masters	2*	3	0	2*		7+2
M Clegg	0	2	2	0		4
K Howarth	1	3	0	3		7

POOLE 35

C Holder	1	2	1	2*	1	1		8+1
B Kurtz	0	0	0					0
Replacement								
K Buczkowski	0	0	1					1
R Tungate	1	R	2	T	X			3
A Ellis	3	3	1	X	1*	1*		9+2
K Newman	2*	1	3	3	3	2	0	14+1

SEMI FINAL PLAY-OFF 2nd LEG

BATTERSEA 63 (104) V (77) 28 BELLE VUE

Heat 11	Dudek	Sundstrom	Cook	Fricke	5-1	46 - 21
Heat 12	Jacobs	Chivers	Bjerre	R Worrall	3-3	49 – 24
Heat 13	Woffinden	Zagar	Dudek	Cook	4-2	53 – 26
Heat 14	Neal	Ljung	Fricke	Nicholls	5-1	58 – 27
Heat 15	Woffinden	Ljung	Zagar	Cook	5-1	63 - 28

Heats 11 through to 15 was simply more of the same as Battersea rattled off three 5-1s, and a 4-2 while, in a moment that came out of no-where Joseph Jacobs grabbed the most unexpected win of the night, but for all his efforts, he was only able to hold a rampant Battersea to a drawn heat.

BATTERSEA 63

P Dudek	2*	3	3	1				9+1
L Sundstrom	3	1*	2	2*				8+2
J Neal	1	0	2*	3				6+1
P Ljung	3	2	3	2*	2*			12+2
T Woffinden	3	2*	3	3	3			14+1
K Bjerre	3	2	1*	1*				7+2
S Chivers	2*	2*	1	2				7+2

BELLE VUE 28

M Zagar	1	3	1	2	1			8
S Worrall	0	3	2	0				5
M Fricke	0	1	0	1				2
S Nicholls	1	0	3	0				4
C Cook	2	1	1	0	0			4
R Worrall	0	0	0	0				0
J Jacobs	1	0	0	3				4

240

CHAPTER 31

PLAY OFF FINALE 1st LEG:

Monday 3rd October 2016

arnie@arniecottrell
Steady nerves needed now. Must do the business properly.

WOLVERHAMPTON 54 V 36 BATTERSEA

Heat 1	Dudek	Lindgren	Karlsson	Sundstrom	3 - 3	3-3
Heat 2 rerun	Howarth	Bjerre	Clegg	Chivers	4 - 2	7-5
Heat 3	Masters	Thorssell	Neal	Woffinden	5 - 1	12-6
Heat 4	Proctor	Howarth	Ljung	Bjerre	5 - 1	17-7
Heat 5	Howarth	Sundstrom	Karlsson	Bjerre	4 - 2	21-9

Two 5-1s and two 4-2s landed a heavy blow on the unprotected chin of the Bulldogs as Wolverhampton stamped their authority on this first leg. Kyle Howarth was a notable contributor with two wins and a second in the first five heats imposing his fast growing reputation as a rider of developing talent. Meanwhile, his team mates deliver solid points by dispatching Battersea riders to last place in each heat. World Champion and ex Wolves captain Tai Woffinden was relegated unceremoniously to fourth place on the track that had been his home for so many years.

WOLVERHAMPTON

F Lindgren	2							
P Karlsson	1*	1						
J Thorssell	2*							
T Proctor	3							
S Masters	3							
M Clegg	1							
K Howarth	3	2*	3					

BATTERSEA

P Dudek	3							
L Sundstrom	0	2						
J Neal	1							
P Ljung	1							
T Woffinden	0							
K Bjerre	2	0	0					
S Chivers	0							

PLAY OFF FINALE 1st LEG:

WOLVERHAMPTON 54 V 36 BATTERSEA

Heat 6	Woffinden	Proctor	Thorssell	Dudek	3 - 3	24-12
Heat 7	Masters	Ljung	Lindgren	Neal (N)	4 - 2	28-14
Heat 8 rerun	Sundstrom	Howarth	Woffinden	Bjerre	3 - 3	31-17
Heat 9	Ljung	Clegg	Karlsson	Chivers R	3 - 3	34-20
Heat 10	Sundstrom	Dudek	Masters	Thorssell	1 - 5	35-25

Heats 8, 9 and 10 saw the Bulldogs staunch the flow of points away from them and pull back 4 to end with a 10 points deficit. Improvements from Sundstrom and Ljung were the stabilising factors in this period, but the general feeling was that Wolverhampton had plenty of strength so the Bulldogs would need to find further improvements from more riders if they were going to get closer to the very impressive Wolves.

WOLVERHAMPTON

F Lindgren	2	1	2	3	1			9
P Karlsson	1*	1	1*	1*				4+3
J Thorssell	2*	1*	0	3	3			9+2
T Proctor	3	2	1*	2*				8+2
S Masters	3	3	1	1				8
M Clegg	1	2	1*					4+1
K Howarth	3	2*	3	2	2			12+1

BATTERSEA

P Dudek	3	0	2*					
L Sundstrom	0	2	3	3				
J Neal	1	N						
P Ljung	1	2	3					
T Woffinden	0	3						
K Bjerre	2	0	0	0				
S Chivers	0	0						

241

PLAY OFF FINALE 1st LEG:

WOLVERHAMPTON 54 V 36 BATTERSEA

Heat 11	Woffinden	Lindgren	Karlsson	Neal	3 - 3	38-28
Heat 12	Bjerre	Howarth	Clegg	Chivers	3 - 3	41-31
Heat 13	Lindgren	Woffinden	Masters	Dudek	4 - 2	45-33
Heat 14	Thorssell	Proctor	Bjerre	Ljung	5 - 1	50-34
Heat 15	Thorssell	Woffinden	Lindgren	Sundstrom	4 - 2	54-36

Heats 11 through to 15 simply provided Freddie Lindgren, Kyle Howarth and Jacob Thorssell the chance to lead a Wolverhampton attack that squeezed the threat out of the Bulldog team. Robust backing from Ty Proctor and Sam Masters ensured no leakage of single and double points behind the leaders and therefore any thought of a 'come-back' that might have briefly ignited in the Battersea team were quickly and effectively extinguished. Joe Neal's painful and awkward fall during a heat 7 battle for second place with Freddie Lindgren left him with a very sore wrist and he looked to be in a lot of discomfort when he finished last in his third ride, leading Arnie Cottrell to use Kenneth Bjerre to replace him in heat 14. Joe is optimistic that he will be available for the second leg. So the Wolves were to take an 18 point lead to the second leg of this Play Off final. No team had ever overcome a 12 point deficit from a first leg defeat until Wolverhampton did exactly that in the semi-finals of this competition, so the prospect of surmounting an 18 point shortfall caused an ominously heavy cloud that cast a deep shadow over the Barry Leech Stadium as the two teams headed south to the capital.

WOLVERHAMPTON

F Lindgren	2	1	2	3	1		9
P Karlsson	1*	1	1*	1*			4+3
J Thorssell	2*	1*	0	3	3		9+2
T Proctor	3	2	1*	2*			8+2
S Masters	3	3	1	1			8
M Clegg	1	2	1*				4+1
K Howarth	3	2*	3	2	2		12+1

BATTERSEA

P Dudek	3	0	2*	0			5+1
L Sundstrom	0	2	3	3	0		8
J Neal	1	N	0				1
P Ljung	1	2	3	0			6
T Woffinden	N	3	3	2	2		10
K Bjerre	2	0	0	0	3	1	6
S Chivers	0	R	0				0

PLAY OFF FINALE 2nd LEG:

Thursday 6th October 2016

arnie@arniecottrell
Steady nerves needed now. Must do the business properly.

BATTERSEA 18 (54) V (66) 12 WOLVERHAMPTON

Heat 1	Dudek	Lindgren	Sundstrom	Karlsson	4 - 2	4-2
Heat 2	Chivers	Howarth	Bjerre	Clegg	4 - 2	8-4
Heat 3	Neal	Thorssell	Masters	Woffinden	3 - 3	11-7
Heat 4	Chivers	Howarth	Ljung	Proctor	4 – 2	15-9
Heat 5	Karlsson	Sundstrom	Bjerre	Clegg	3 - 3	18-12

Wolverhampton and Battersea put on one of the most dramatic play off finals in the history of the Elite League. The meeting started well for the Bulldogs with three 4-2 heat wins giving them a 6 point lead after five heats. The best Wolverhampton could do was to squeeze a couple of 3-3 draws to slow them down. Frankie Chivers decided to have the meeting of his life and delivered two heat wins from his first two rides looking every bit the end product as he showed his back wheel to highly regarded Kyle Howarth in heats 2 and 4 as if to make a point about the ability of British youngsters to thrive in the fast track system.

BATTERSEA

P Dudek	3						
L Sundstrom	1	2					
J Neal	3						
P Ljung	1						
T Woffinden	0						
K Bjerre	1	1*					
S Chivers	3	3					

WOLVERHAMPTON

F Lindgren	2						
P Karlsson	0	3					
J Thorssell	2						
T Proctor	0						
S Masters	1*						
M Clegg	0	0					
K Howarth	2	2					

PLAY OFF FINALE 2nd LEG:

BATTERSEA 37 (73) V (77) 23 WOLVERHAMPTON

Heat 6	Neal	Lindgren	Ljung	Masters	4 - 2	22-14
Heat 7	Dudek	Woffinden	Proctor	Thorssell	5 - 1	27-15
Heat 8	Chivers	Karlsson	Clegg	Ljung	3 - 3	30-18
Heat 9	Sundstrom	Proctor	Howarth	Bjerre	3 - 3	33-21
Heat 10	Neal	Lindgren	Woffinden	Karlsson	4 - 2	37-23

Steady progress for the Bulldogs saw them stretch to a 14 point lead by heat 10. Joe Neal took the opportunity to impress by storming to two excellent heat wins and take his score up to 9 points to match Frankie Chivers, who thrilled the large crowd with a heat win over Peter Karlsson who pushed the young rider all the way to the flag. Things were beginning to look hopeful for the Bulldogs and unsettling for the Wolves as the aggregate score closed to only 4 points as they went into the final section of the meeting.

BATTERSEA

P Dudek	3	3						
L Sundstrom	1	2	3					
J Neal	3	3	3					
P Ljung	1	1	0					
T Woffinden	0	2*	1					
K Bjerre	1	1*	0	0				
S Chivers	3	3	3					

WOLVERHAMPTON

F Lindgren	2	2	2				
P Karlsson	0	3	2				
J Thorssell	2	0					
T Proctor	0	1	2				
S Masters	1*	0					
M Clegg	0	0	1*				
K Howarth	2	2	1*				

PLAY OFF FINALE 2nd LEG:

BATTERSEA 53 (89) V (91) 37 WOLVERHAMPTON

Heat 11	Masters	Dudek	Thorssell	Sundstrom	2 - 4	39-27
Heat 12	Chivers	Howarth	Clegg	Bjerre	3 - 3	42-30
Heat 13	Dudek	Woffinden	Lindgren	Masters	5 - 1	47-31
Heat 14	Neal	Proctor	Thorssell	Ljung	3 - 3	50-34
Heat 15	Woffinden	Howarth	Lindgren	Chivers F	3 - 3	53-37

The twists and turns of this meeting surprised, tantalised, shocked and delighted in equal measure. The ending was so dramatic that, had it been the stuff of a novel or a film, we would have condemned it as fanciful and ridiculous. At the start of heat 14, the Bulldogs had pulled the Wolves back to within 2 points and seemed to have the momentum to go on to win the title, but that's not what Wolverhampton had in mind. Heat 14 was a 3-3 draw and then heat 15 produced the most incredible resolution seen in speedway Elite League history.

Going into the last heat the Bulldogs needed a 5 -1 heat win to take the championship, a 4 -2 heat win, to draw, while the wolves needed only a 3 – 3 to win the title, it could not have been more tantalising. Or could it? Tai Woffinden found the form we thought had left him to make a lightening start as he hit the first bend in the lead closely followed by Frankie Chivers who was having the night of his life and the Bulldogs fans erupted and filled the Barry Leech stadium with a noise that could be heard down in Clapham and Balham. Together they rode the track like a moving barrier that, for all their skill and mastery, neither Kyle Howarth nor Freddie Lindgren could penetrate. This state of affairs lasted for three and a half laps until, when the fans were just beginning to celebrate winning the title and Woffinden and Chivers were comfortably holding off Howarth and Lindgren on the final bend and the whole thing seemed over, that's when the unthinkable happened. Frankie Chivers was just starting his rush for the line when he literally fell off the back of his bike, bounced twice and slid on his back, stopped just short of the finish line and lay perfectly still. Howarth and then Lindgren sailed past him to finish second and third and Wolverhampton were the Elite League champions. The referee ruled that the result should stand and the presentations and celebrations began with Wolves Mechanics and riders giving vent to their elation and surprise. Peter Karlsson celebrated his last appearance for Wolverhampton in a jubilant display of Champagne spraying as the trophy was held up by the captain. The Bulldogs were devastated by the sudden snatching away of the title as they were beginning to party themselves. And so, the most remarkable final that one can imagine was over and Wolverhampton Wolves were the Champions in circumstances that they could never have predicted.

BATTERSEA 53

P Dudek	3	3	2	3				11
L Sundstrom	1	2	3	0				6
J Neal	3	3	3	3				12
P Ljung	1	1	0	0				2
T Woffinden	0	2*	1	2*	3			8+2
K Bjerre	1	1*	0	0	0			2+1
S Chivers	3	3	3	3	F			12

WOLVERHAMPTON 37

F Lindgren	2	2	2	1	1*			8+1
P Karlsson	0	3	2					5
J Thorssell	2	0	1	1*				4+1
T Proctor	0	1	2	2				5
S Masters	1*	0	3	0				4+1
M Clegg	0	0	1*	1*				2+2
K Howarth	2	2	1*	2	2			9+1

TITLE RESULT

BATTERSEA 53 (89) v (91) 37 WOLVERHAMPTON

CHAPTER 32

Thursday 6th October 2016

Bernie Garnet sat on a bench in Battersea Park quietly reading William Craig's *Enemy at the Gate*, drinking soup through a straw and eating the soft centre of freshly baked white bread so that he didn't have to use his still sore and painful teeth and gums to masticate crispy or hard food. His mouth had scabs and scratches around it which made it painful to speak, smile or, if the mood had come upon him, to whistle. He took all of this philosophically, it came with the territory, it was just part of the way things happen when you enter the world of violence. Bernie knew this, accepted it and kept moving towards the objective, that's what it is to be a professional he told himself. It was five o'clock in the early evening and the Elite League final second leg was only two and a half hours away. Bernie just had to wait patiently until work had finished for the day on the building site next to the stadium when he had only to worry about the security presence. Beside him was an Urban sniper rifle bag that looked similar to a sports bag so that, when Bernie decorated it with brand labels for tennis equipment, it appeared as if he were on his way to some kind of sporting event. In the bag was one of the best sniper rifles ever designed, a L115A3, which is a large caliber bolt-action rifle equipped with a 5-25 x 56 Schmidt and Bender Telescopic sight and a few rounds of 8.59mm ammunition, although he hoped he would only require one.

At six forty-five he rose from the bench, picked up his bag by the handles and casually wandered along the path beneath trees that were beginning to display their Autumnal colours. He stopped and watched two squirrels chasing each other and smiled pleasantly at a young mother who stood with her little boy while he took enormous pleasure from the same squirrels. He strolled out of the Queenstown Road entrance and crossed to the other side and made his way down to Sopwith Way, where he turned left and walked to the bottom and turned right past a parked van and an empty flatbed trailer. There was no-one around so Bernie unzipped the straps he had sewn to the rifle bag and swung them over his shoulders to convert it into a back-pack. He then squeezed through the gap between a high wall that separated the yard and the railway Victoria station line and a decomposing fence that gave him access to a lower part of the wall where he was able to climb down a stanchion onto the roof of a double train shed and from there it was equally easy to climb down the diagonal angle iron bars that formed part of the framework for the shed wall.

Once on the ground Bernie checked the shed, found it was empty and stepped inside to get his bearings and check that the course was clear. Once satisfied that no-one had spotted him, he explored the shed and found, what he assumed was a long jemmy that someone had left leaned against the back wall, so picked it up and carried it with, what he hoped, would been seen as a workman like manner. He then walked diagonally south at a leisurely pace across the five sets of railway lines occasionally stopping to tap the occasional clamp with the jemmy, inspect a fishplate or kick pieces of stray ballast back between the sleepers in the hope that this would place doubt in the mind of anyone who might happen to be looking at the security film footage. After a minute he reached the metal gantry that supported the signals for the fifth line and crouched behind the metal cabinet that held the control board. The gantry butted up against the perimeter fence and Bernie simply had to climb through the metalwork of the structure and drop over the fence onto the roof of some industrial workshop units that faced onto the main building site. The workshops were of such a design that there was a gap between them that, a climber or mountaineer would call a 'chimney' and down which Bernie could descend by placing his feet against one wall and pressing his back against the opposite wall and, using a walking motion, make his way carefully to the ground.

Once there, he found himself on a large and complex building site that was cramped in between the western set of railway tracks to the eastern set that came in to join them and form the final approach to Victoria Station. Bernie spent a minute scanning the site to check for security cameras and any clue to the presence of security officers. Again satisfied that it looked clear he made his way under cover of vans, bulldozers, tippers, lorries, porta cabins and various other bits of machinery until he came round the side of a Ford Transit, saw the site office and found it occupied. He froze in his tracks waiting and watching like a cat and saw two men through the rectangular window in the hut. One was seated with his back to the window so that Bernie could only see the back of his head; the other seemed to be making tea as he walked back and forth until he sat facing his colleague and talking animatedly.

Bernie needed to get beyond that office to the self-supporting tower crane that overlooked the Barry Leech Stadium on the old Battersea Power Station site. He spent a few minutes exploring the surrounding terrain and concluded that the men would be unlikely to see him if he skirted the portacabin and stayed behind the plentiful cover. He turned and looped back around the Transit, dodged behind two large cement mixers that stood together and from there was able to slide down the side of the office, spend an anxious moment passing the entrance and let the pleasant feeling of relief wash through him when no one came out before he was away and headed for his objective.

When he reached the crane, he looked up at it and felt the thrill of the anticipation of danger hit him like a strong gust of wind causing him to momentarily wonder if this was after all the best plan. The crane was eighty meters in height and Bernie could not see the cabin as it was way beyond the reach of the site lights and sat somewhere up there in the darkness that had now descended. The ladder was a tubular metal framework that fitted into the square section framework that formed the body of the tower. Daunted somewhat by the height, he started up the vertical metal ladder carefully and after six or seven meters realised that this was not going to be an easy venture. Due to the general beating his body had taken over the last few weeks he was breathing heavily after fifteen meters and his arms and legs were complaining at the exertion he was demanding of them. At thirty metres he rested and leaned back against the metal cage structure, blowing hard. He could see across London and down into the speedway stadium, but not enough and not from a stable position. The circular bands of metal that were spaced approximately a metre apart contrived to snag the barrel section of the rifle bag and stop Bernie's progress on a regular basis causing him to backtrack a step of two before disengaging. He continually caught his knees, banging them against the rungs because his body was too close to the ladder due to the back pack preventing him from leaning further back. He found himself reciting, "It is what it is; now get on with it",as a kind of mantra to keep himself going upwards. He rested one last time at about sixty-five metres and marvelled at the fitness of crane drivers who did this climb every day. "You wouldn't want to discover you'd forgotten something important after climbing to the top of here," he reflected, and that sparked a momentary attack of panic as he thought about where he'd put the ammunition until he calmed himself and remembered it was in the centre pocket of the bag. The whole climb took Bernie twenty minutes and left him with a feeling of disappointment at his current level of fitness. He stood on the small platform that sat under the cabin and looked at the magnificent view. It was a fine almost cloudless night and the lights of London were spread out before him. A light breeze blew through the framework of the crane and he could feel a slow gentle swaying motion that he decided to stop thinking about, although he logged the thought that it would be a factor in his calculations when aiming.

Bernie climbed up the short ladder to the cabin, broke the lock on the door, stepped inside, slipped the rifle bag off his back, stored it at the back of the cab and sat in the driver comfortable chair with a sigh. He sat for four or five minutes with his eyes closed and slowing his whole body down so that he was calm and controlled. Eventually he began to take an interest in the stadium below him. It looked magnificent from this viewing position and he could clearly see the home straight and the two bends in their entirety, but it was not the case for the back straight, which was partially obstructed by the stadium roof so that he could only see half of its width. He was sitting contemplating this issue when he noticed that the jib was protruding out towards the stadium. Surely, if he could get along its length, he would get a full view of the back straight. Time was beginning to press now and he could see the track being prepared, the crowds were filling the stands and the meeting was getting close to starting. Bernie didn't feel rushed about this because he wanted to carry out his mission towards the end of the meeting anyway.

The jib was constructed of steel tubes forming a triangular section down its length like a large Toblerone chocolate bar with a metal plated walkway running down its base for the entire length of the jig. Bernie took a thin wind proof jacket out of the rifle bag and put it on over his fleece, then climbed the short ladder that took him onto the platform that gave access to the jib. It was a little tight and the two and a half metre width felt very narrow as the whole structure moved around in the wind. Carefully, Bernie made his way down it length carrying the rifle bag in his hand until he got to the end where two tubular poles ran from the walkway corners to the central beam at the top forming a barrier. He looked down to the stadium and smiled to himself as he viewed the whole track from this amazing perch. It was cold at eighty metres in the October wind and he was pleased with his forethought to bring his windproof jacket. There wasn't much room on the jib, but he managed to lay down so that he could rest the rifle barrel on the junction of two stanchions and angle it perfectly to achieve a stable position in a maintainable attitude.

The meeting had been running for about fifteen minutes by the time he was properly settled, and comfortable. He wore a fur lined cap with ear muffs and a pair of warm mittens, he did not want any distractions such as feeling cold, he would need to have maximum sensation in his hands when the moment to squeeze the trigger came. He could hear only a muffled version of the distant PA announcements, but from that and knowing where the track maintenance breaks are in a meeting, he was able to pinpoint exactly which heats he was watching. It became evident to him that there were several real issues surrounding aiming that needed detailed consideration.

Bernie stretched and flexed his arms, shoulders and torso feeling the twinges that still hung on from his tussles with Harry over a week before. He slotted the 12 inch Gemtech suppressor on the end of the rifle barrel and assumed the prone position and placing the barrel in the crook of the jib frame. He inserted a round of ammunition. He shuffled and made tiny alterations to his posture until he felt he had his 'natural point of aim' which allows the rifle to point at its target without any muscle tension and he scanned his body bit by bit to lodge the details in his memory so that he could recall it at will later. He had already sewn a soft pad into his jacket where the hollow of his shoulder would be when he was wearing it to reduce any disturbance from the beating of his pulse or his breathing. He took a considerable time getting the butt positioned in the pocket of his shoulder; he gripped the small grip at the back of the trigger with his non firing hand and then on the fourth attempt that he exerted a small pulling movement to place it exactly where he wanted it bedded into the pad and in the pocket of his shoulder. He then placed his index finger on the trigger and made a tiny adjustment to his shoulder and elbow to ensure that his finger did not touch the stock and would not disturb the rifle when he pulled the trigger. He felt his elbows settled into their pads and was confident that they would move. He gently placed his cheek on the stock, held his head in an upright position and, keeping his eye away from the tube, he looked down the sight, set the distance to one hundred and fifty meters, set the zoom to maximum magnification, focused the eyepiece until he had a sharp image, checked that the natural point of aim was still maintained and squeezed the trigger until the rifle gave a moderate kick and emitted a quiet 'fut' sound.

He had aimed to take out one of the roof lights that ran along the length of the Barry Leech stand, but he was not surprised when his target continued to shine brightly. "You lucky, lucky man," he muttered to himself as he noticed the light to the left of the target go out. With the rifle aimed at the original light he rotated the windage and elevation turrets until the cross hairs moved were centred over the actual light that he hit. With his scope set he tried again, this time choosing a light at the end of the stadium with the third and fourth bends. He went meticulously through the same procedure and this time hit the light at which he was aiming.

He knew that they were about to start Heat Twelve and that this would be a good time to start. Bernie was a realist and he knew that he would probably miss with the first couple of shots due to the fact that he was shooting a fast moving target over a great distance from a gently swaying platform. From that distance he couldn't identify which riders were on the track, but he could distinguish between the Battersea and Wolverhampton colours. He chose to follow a rider down the back straight and travel with him until he felt he could hold him steady in the sight. His first attempt was unsuccessful and he saw the spurt of dust some two meters in front of the bike and he made adjustments to the sights accordingly. His second attempt was actually worse but he thought that the wind had changed suddenly. His continual concern was that someone would notice that shots were hitting the ground, but he really needn't have worried for the frenzy of activity obliterated any small disturbance that the bullet made. His other concern was with regards to ricochets, but again this seemed minimised as the bullets seemed to penetrate the shale instead of being deflected. Bernie reasoned that this might be to do with the velocity of the bullet by the time it reached the stadium for it seemed that they were also lodging in the safety fence on the start and finish straight. He decided against shooting on the bends in case he hit the air fence and punctured it, thus revealing what was happening. All of this though was so much froth and spit; what he needed to do was hit his target.

When the final heat started, he knew he had just four rounds left and four laps in which to finish the job. He could see that the Bulldog riders were headed for a 5-1 heat win, although he had no idea what that meant in terms of the meeting score. He trained the sight on the second placed rider, who he thought looked like the young reserve Charmers or Chiltern or something. Bernie tracked him down the last part of the back straight, round the third and fourth bends and into the first part of the start and finish straight as this involved the least movement of the rifle, but, not being happy, did not shoot. On the second lap, he allowed his anxiety to overcome his better judgement and he squeezed a shot out that splintered the thick wooden barrier just after the fourth bend. When they came round again on their third lap, he was much more controlled and placed a round that must have gone through the boy's rear wheel spokes without doing any damage.

Bernie consciously slowed his breathing and consequently his heart beat as the riders started their last lap and picked the young Bulldog rider up again as he came down the back straight. Almost immediately Bernie fired and missed leaving himself with one round and one bend left to do the job. He had the sight right on the rider's torso as they passed the apex of the bend and allowed it slip off as they came into the fourth bend, a surge of panic leapt into his throat and he forced it down while keeping a smooth transverse of his weapon. As the cross wires moved slowly onto the torso again he allowed it to go past and ahead of the target before he squeezed the trigger very smoothly and the final round left the barrel and travelled along its deadly arcing vector through the night air arriving at a point in space at exactly the same time as Frankie Chivers helmeted head. Bernie saw the figure fly off the back of the bike and slide on his back, and he thumped the air, "What a shot," he said with satisfaction.

He packed his rifle away made his way stiffly back to the driver's cab where he sat for a few minutes watching the activities in the stadium and considering his options. He decided to leave his rifle and bag in the cab rather than struggle back down the ladder with it. He had written a letter to leave here anyway in order to taunt Barry Leech and make his suffering even worse. The descent of the ladder was much less troublesome than the ascent so that Bernie found himself at ground level in minutes and making his way towards the entrance to the building site. He went with care and stealth for he did not want to be discovered at this stage when all the important stuff was finished. He was crouching behind a low wall while he surveyed the final dash to the gate and had reassured himself that the coast was clear when he rose to start across the space and turned into the form of an enormous security officer who was equally surprised to bump into Bernie.

"What the fuck?" the guard gasped.

Bernie smiled at the man and put his finger to his lips saying, "Shh." He watched the guard's eyes follow the movement of his finger and as this happened he raked his instep down the man's shin. The large man let out a wail and folded up as he grabbed for his leg, as he did this Bernie brought his knee up firmly into his chin. With a cracking of breaking teeth and a groan of agony, the guard fell to the ground and Bernie made a break across the yard to the gate. It was the work of a moment to mount and vault the gate into Prince of Wales Drive from where he simply stepped out purposefully, turned left onto Battersea Park Road and strolled down to the Battersea Park overland station where he boarded the first train that came in and went to Victoria Station.

CHAPTER 33

Friday 7th October 2016

arnie@arniecottrell
Shocked by the news of Frankie's shooting. He is still unconscious, but alive, thank the Lord. But Why? Why?

It didn't seem worth going home, so Barry Leech, Arnie Cottrell, Rosie and Harry had spent the night at the stadium attempting but failing to sleep on the large sofas and armchairs in the board room. As the first rays of weak autumn light crept through the wall of windows that looked down on the stadium Rosie stretched and swung her legs off the sofa and put her feet into her flat shoes, "Coffee anyone," she yawned. A general groan let her know that she should make lots of it. She freshened up in the ladies toilet, went into the kitchen at the back of the secretarial office and busied herself preparing cups and saucers while the coffee dripped into the glass jug. When this was done, she went on line and found a greasy spoon café that was open and would make bacon and egg and sausage sandwiches and deliver them by 0700; she ordered more than she thought was required and arranged to meet the young woman at the main gates instructing her not to provide two bottles of ketchup.

By 0730 the group had comprehensively demolished the extensive pile of butties and dealt with two jugs of coffee; if ever a group was going to be ready to tackle this difficult day, they were ready.

Barry appeared to be in a determined mood as he sat at the head of the board room table. The truth was that he was holding it together by sheer will-power and was in fact on the ragged edge of emotionally falling apart, but this he kept hidden from the others, "This problem is now far bigger than just the Speedway Team. I checked last night to see what the Japanese were saying when the NIKKEI opened and it was not good, there are a couple of companies circling to see if they can grab some early meat and we are in their sights. At 0230 when the Bursa Efek opened, we were being talked about in terms of crashing and failing. Ten minutes ago Germany and France were much the same. I'd say that we may have a week, possibly a fortnight to get out of this, if it's possible to get out of it."

"What could you do?" Arnie asked.

"I'm going to separate the Speedway Team from the rest of the group today. That mechanism was built into the Articles of Incorporation and should raise no objections. That will protect the Bulldogs from any flack that could start flying any time from now and we'll run it as a separate business. With all this in mind, I have to go in a minute and make a meeting with the Group Board at 0830; the LSE will have been open half an hour by then and we can try to manage things in real time from the headquarters; whichever way it develops, it's going to be very messy."

Barry's words left a battered group feeling even more battered, but he had left them with a small light at the end of a dreadful tunnel.

Rosie went to a flip-chart and threw over a sheet on the pad, "Let's look at what we have to do over the next few days," she charted the ideas from the team and asked for offers of who should do the tasks: They listed seven things that needed doing.

1/ Visit Frankie (Arnie and Rosie)
2/ Visit Frankie's family (Arnie and Rosie)
3/ Talk to the police (Rosie)
4/ Speak to Security (Rosie and Arnie)
5/ Plan with personal security officers (All)
6/ Release something to the press (Arnie)
7/ Release a reaction on Social Media (Arnie)

The 0900 Security officer's shift change offered the perfect opportunity to discuss how they saw things in the light of Bernie's fresh initiative, so all relevant personnel were gathered in the Board Room for the briefing session. It was agreed that Bernie now offered a greater threat than he had before, and that security should be tightened and that each of Rosie, Harry and Barry should have two officers each allocated and that Arnie should be immediately added to the list of prime targets thus receiving the same security attention.

By 1000 the group had split to pursue their individual duties and Harry found himself sitting with Arnie Cottrell in his office and drinking his coffee.
"It's just struck me that we lost the Elite League Championship last night," Arnie commented, "It seems remote somehow, almost like it never happened."
"Yes, I know what you mean," Harry agreed, "I'm going to do a show this afternoon and it's bound to be the topic everyone will want to talk about, but it seems surreal to me, disconnected and detached."
Arnie took a sip of coffee and clasped the mug in his two hands watching the steam rise in front of him. He spoke but his voice choked, he coughed and started again, "Yeah, one moment you're cheering and shouting in ecstasy because our team is seconds away from winning our first ever Championship and the high is so extreme you think you'll explode with pleasure, the next second you're devastated because it's been dramatically torn away from us by a terrible mistake and your emotions change into despondency and despair, and then the awful reality that one of your friends has been shot and is close to death overtakes it all and everything shrinks back into an insignificant perspective, leaving you feeling physically sick but also empty."

That afternoon Harry broadcast a programme that was both volatile and sombre. Many contributors rang and tweeted with sympathy for Frankie and his family, others were horrified at the violence that Bernie was inflicting upon the Bulldogs and still others were saddened by the failure to win the Elite League Championship. He flew for an hour and a half on automatic pilot as he fielded all these points of view with an efficient professionalism but without any feeling of conviction. When he came off the air Johnny Matthews put his arm around his friend's shoulder, "Are you going to be ok," he asked with concern.
Harry looked at him, "Yeah, of course I am. I'm down at the moment, didn't get any sleep worth talking about last night and I'm emotionally drained. Give me a few days and I'll be back."

"I think you right," Johnny agreed, "You need time to get over this. Take two weeks off and then let's review how you are."

Harry shook his head, "No need for that, I can carry on and you can't afford to lose me at the moment."

Johnny walked over to the small coffee table and sat in the armchair, "You're wrong about that on two counts. One, you cannot carry on. That show was not good enough and you know it, and you also know that what you are experiencing requires quiet and calm time for you to centre yourself again. Two, we can do this without you. Jenny and Bethany are happy to do extra hours for a while, so we can cover you in the short term. If you carry on, I think you will fall over and then need longer to recover. That then gives us a bigger 'cover' problem to handle. On that basis, it's pretty obvious to me that you should go away and have time off." Harry agreed that the logic was good and that Johnny had a point.

Johnny stood up, "Damn sure I've got a point, now come here and give me a man hug,"   Harry went over and put his arm s around Johnny, after a few seconds his head lay on his shoulder, he gulped down the first sob but his shoulders convulsed and he quietly cried while his friend held him.

. .

Rosie approached Frankie's bed trying to see if he was awake and found him asleep. Apart from his bandaged head he looked ok, but of course she knew that couldn't be the case.   She turned to the nurse who was checking his notes at the end of the bed, "How is he, has he been awake at all?"

The nurse looked up from the clipboard and hung it on the hook at the end of the bed and replied, "No, the doctors are keeping him sedated for the time being because he is very poorly indeed."

"How bad is it?" Rosie enquired.

"I can't say," the nurse answered, "Are you a member of the family?"

"No, I'm…" Rosie hesitated feeling the answer would rule her in or out in this nurses eyes, "I'm his boss."

"I see, let me ask the doctor and see if he will come out to see you."

Rosie thanked her and sat on the chair by Frankie's bed and a few minutes later Doctor Longi came onto the ward and walked over to Rosie, "Miss?"

"Higgins," Rosie responded standing up.

"I understand you are Mr. Chivers' boss, is that correct?"

"I am the Personal Secretary to the Chief Executive of the company that employs Mr. Chivers."

"I see," the doctor said, "how can I help you?"

"We are obviously very concerned about Frankie after his accident last night and before I go on from here to visit his family, I wanted to get the latest information about his health."

"Yes of course," Doctor Longi saw Rosie's motives were laudable and became less defensive, "He is very poorly. His head wound is quite serious. Fortunately, the angle of entry was acute and therefore will have travelled through much less of his brain matter than an obtuse entry. Our hope is that the damage will be minimal, but that doesn't follow automatically."

"What will you do?" Rosie asked.

"After the swelling has subsided enough, I will perform a craniotomy, which just means that I will make a hole in Frankie's head in order to access his brain. I will find the bullet and decide whether we can remove it safely, I'll also remove any blood clots that may have formed in Frankie's brain and repair any damaged blood vessels. Once I've stopped any bleeding inside his brain, removed any pieces of skull bone, I'll either replace or reattach them using small metal screws. Of course, this is important stuff but it is somewhat peripheral compared with the damage the bullet will have done, and there no way, yet of knowing what that is."

Rosie listened with growing awe and horror, "My goodness," she whispered, "and you do that every day?"

The doctor smiled, "Yes, well, nearly every day and I wish I could report a higher rate of success than I actually achieve, but we can only do what we can do, but we are learning more with every operation," he paused and then asked, "Tell me, who was the paramedic who treated him at the scene?" the doctor asked.

Rosie thought for a moment and said, "That would have been Julia Raglett, she's our senior St Johns attendant. Why do you ask?"

"I would like to congratulate her on a superb job done," he answered, "It is perfectly possible that she saved his life right there on the track."

"Really?" Rosie said.

"Certainly. The application of ice in a tea towel kept the potential swelling down and prevented more pressure than there was. It also means that we don't have to wait so long for the swelling to subside.

"I'll make sure that she hears that."

There was a general disturbance at the entrance to the ward and Rosie saw a middle aged man and woman talking to the nurse at the desk. She walked over to them and introduced herself, "Hello. Are you Frankie's parents?" she asked.

The man looked round, "Yes, I'm his father. Who are you?"

"I'm Rosie Higgins, I work for the Battersea Bulldogs."

"Oh, I see. Well, it's good of you to come here," the man responded, "I'm Bob Chivers and this is my wife Alice."

They all three shook hands, "I am so terribly sorry that this has happened to Frankie," Rosie ventured.

Alice Chivers answered, "Well you expect them to get hurt when they're flying round on those motorbikes, but to be shot?"

"I know," Rosie said sympathetically, "It's just awful. I wanted to come and see him and you so that the club can offer any support that is needed."

"I don't think we need anything," Bob Chivers answered, "we just want to be with our son, nothing else matters does it?"

"I understand," Rosie said, "Why don't you go on in and I'll get out of your way." She handed her business card to the man and smiled weakly at him.

He softened a little, "Thank you very much," he said quietly, "we're so worried you see." He took his wife's hand in his, "he's such a good boy, we can't belie…" and a great sob escaped him. They both wept openly as they stood there, and Rosie reached out and took their hands in hers. As they stood there she felt her eyes filling with tears, that sat on her lower eyelashes and then overflowed to run down her cheeks and chin.

When Rosie got back to the stadium, the police were waiting to see her, so she took a coffee with her to the Board Room where they asked her a few questions, but mostly briefed her about their investigations.

"I've spoken with Mr. Leech, Mr. Marsh and Mr. Cottrell, so I wanted to see you before getting back to the station," Chief Superintendent Laws said, "In short, there's no doubt about who the gunman was. We found a suppressed firearm and carrying bag with Bernie Garnet's fingerprints, and this." He held out the letter that Bernie had left for Barry Leech. It read:

> You'll be relieved to know that it is coming to an end now. Your pain is now almost as great as it can be, but not quite. Your business is sinking under the pressure, like my brother's did, (so good to find a punishment that fits the crime so beautifully, your beloved Bulldogs lost their prize, you have death and destruction all around you and deep inside, you know you cannot relinquish responsibility. You have used and abused people and cast them off like unwanted clothes. And all for what? Lots of money? No, because even though you've got more wealth than anyone could spend in a single lifetime, it's still not enough is it. It doesn't buy the one thing you crave more than anything else, does it. For what then? To prove to yourself that you are worthy? To satisfy your ego's insatiable appetite for recognition, praise and love!
> **Enjoy the power Mr Leech – I hope it's worth it!**

"It seems," The policeman said, "that he is not finished yet. He refers to the pain being 'nearly over'.   It is my opinion that you are all still in danger."

Rosie read the letter again with a horrified look on her face, "He's completely mad isn't he?" she said handing the letter back to the policeman.

"That's a copy you can keep," he said.

Rosie folded it and put it in the back pocket of her jeans, "He is insane isn't he?"

"I don't know Miss; I'm not a psychiatrist, my opinion doesn't count." He thought for a moment and then said, "I met people who were certified as insane and I've met people who I thought were insane, but weren't certified. I remember a doctor defining insanity in court once and he said, 'Insanity was to be in a state of mind which prevents normal perception, behaviour, or social interaction.' To be perfectly honest," and he smiled thinly as he spoke, "as far as I can see, that definition encompasses most of the population."

Rosie looked at him, "And what's normal?"

"Ah, that's where you should talk to a Zen Buddhist or someone, not to me."

"And not a Western psychologist either?"

"I couldn't possibly pass an opinion on that," the Inspector said, standing up, putting his hat on and putting his hand on the door knob, before turning with a smile and saying, "I'll bid you good day Miss Higgins, please let our security officers take good care of you until we get Mr Garnet."

"I will Chief Superintendent, and thank you."

CHAPTER 34

Friday 7th October 2016

It was late in the evening and Harry was working late on an article to celebrate Peter Karlsson's career at Wolverhampton and the marvellous finale that winning the Elite League Championship had been. This was going to be one of the best things he'd worked on and could establish new standards for the station, so he was not going to rush it and he was paying attention to very small details that, on other occasions, he would have disregarded. Much as he was keen to do this work and much as he was enjoying it, it seemed that he was wading through treacle to get anything accomplished. He took a drink of his coffee hoping the caffeine would kick in and spark an energy surge. The defeat two days earlier had left a strange, dull lack of sensation and drive akin to that which follows the bereavement of a favourite relative and it hung like a heavy dark cloud over the whole stadium.

He was editing the post meeting interview with Peter Karlsson which he knew was particularly good because, not only did it present Peter in a professional light, but also showed him for the thoroughly pleasant, kind and utterly polite man that everyone loved. The single desk lamp that illuminated his workstation created an island of bright light in an otherwise darkened room and he felt like a character out of *The Third Man*, and if Orson Wells had walked in at that moment, Harry would not have been surprised. However, he was surprised when a voice spoke quietly from just behind him and he felt something hard and cold gently press against his temple.

"Don't turn your head Harry, it is a gun and I will shoot you here and now if I have to."

"Bernie?"

"Correct. You must have been expecting me?"

"Yes, but that's why we've got Don standing outside."

"The Silver-back in a suit downstairs?"

"Don, yes."

"Even a Silver-back can't overcome a bullet in the side of its head," Bernie said with humour in his voice, "funny isn't it, no matter how big and tough they come, they can all be beaten by a good brain."

"And a gun?" Harry added.

"And a gun." Bernie agreed. "Now, what I want you to do is telephone Rosie and get her over here now."

"On your bike you psycho. I'm not getting her to come over here."

Bernie pressed to gun harder into Harry's temple, "Then I have no further use for you so I'll just kill you here and then I'll go over there and get her myself."

"Well then, that's what you're going to have to do Bernie because I'm not putting her in danger just to make it easy for you,"

There was a dull 'thwack' very close to Harry's ear as Bernie fired the suppressed hand gun and then the Laptop exploded into several pieces and leapt off the table top making Harry jump with the unexpected violence of the act. He stayed calm however and turned his head so that the gun was pointing right between his eyes, "It's still a no, I'm afraid," he said in an even voice.

"So, you're not scared to die then?"

"Yes of course I'm scared of dying, but I would rather die than be the cause of pain to Rosie."

"I believe you Harry and that makes you a brave person." There was silence for a few seconds and Bernie stepped back two paces, "You don't like me, do you?" he said to Harry.

An involuntary smiled spread across Harry's face at the incongruity of this remark and he said, "You sound like a 1950's war film; what's your next line?" Harry adopted a stereotypical Gestapo Officers voice, "Cigarette Harry, you know, in other circumstances we might have been friends, I too went to Oxford." He relaxed into his chair and dropped the fake German accent, "but in these circumstances Bernie, well, you're just not giving our potential friendship a fair chance to blossom. I think it might be the gun and the death threats that are taking the pleasure out of it."

If Harry had got this right, Bernie was re-evaluating his plan and he was not quite on his guard. Bernie went over to the door and threw the switch to turn on the main light and, keeping the gun levelled at Harry, he sat down on the other office chair and let out a short laugh, "Strange how things work out isn't it?" he asked rhetorically, "All of this was never in my plan you know. I've never hurt anything in my life. Just the opposite, I save lives and take pain away."

"Hang on a minute," Harry said, "Please don't start the, 'I'm just misunderstood and it's the system that made me like this,' because that's just not going to wash at this stage."

Bernie shook his head, "I know that," he conceded. "I had a plan and it was going well until you and Rosie got involved and then I had to start improvising."

"Haven't you wreaked enough havoc and grief for one lifetime?"

"When I see Barry bloody Leech crying like I did, that's when I'll stop. But he's a heartless bastard and he doesn't yet connect all this with his own actions."

"From what I've heard recently, I'd say he's beginning to," Harry said.

"Don't give me that bollocks Harry, I'm not buying that," Bernie shifted his weight on the chair, "but he will when he loses his precious Rosie."

"And me," Harry added.

Bernie burst out laughing, "Oh bless your heart, do you think he cares about you?"

"Well he......"

"Nope! He doesn't care about anyone outside of his family and a 'care-light' for anyone who helps him make more money, and then when the day comes that they can't help him make more money, he dumps them too."

"That's a harsh judgement."

"You have no idea, do you? Did you ever meet my brother?"

"Michael?"

"Yes Mike. He worked for Barry Leech and did a bloody good job for him too. He never cheated anyone, never cooked the books and never claimed anything that he shouldn't have claimed. He was the best man I've ever known, hard-working, honest, diligent and fair. And Barry Leech killed him and took him away from me."

"How did he do that?" Harry asked

"By being greedy and encouraging his staff to be greedy. By treating people as if they are things. Things that can be thrown away when they are not wanted any more. Or in the case of Mike and his little company, just ignore the contract that he had with him. He created the culture where it's legitimate for his large company to take advantage of the vulnerable smaller companies and save money by delaying payment, calculating that the smaller company could not possibly dare to challenge it for fear of losing its contract and knowing that it could not afford legal action. It's so easy to do as well. The finance department just have to write an apologetic letter and fabricate an excuse which exonerates them, 'your invoice just missed this month's cheque run,' 'unfortunately, our finance manager has been away on holiday, a conference or a course, but we'll make sure it makes next month's cheque run'. And then just ignore that and make a different excuse so that two months go by, maybe even three. And even when they knew that Mike's company was suffering from cash flow issues and that it was on the edge of failing, they still delayed payment calculating that they would go out of business before they would have to pay."

"Barry didn't do all that," Harry responded.

"He created the monster that did, he's the one that sets the rules and he's the one that questions the bottom line, and the budgets, and the targets when they're not met. He's the one that creates the fear and the mean-minded greed."

Harry's natural disposition was somewhat sympathetic towards this reasoning as a socialist, but the thought of murdering innocent people as a response appalled him. "How did you choose the victims on the basis of that rationale?"

"The first was very easy; Brian McDermott was the Finance Director so he was directly responsible for the delay. Sonny Brett became a target because I had easy access; I just had to wait for a crash that had enough of a possibility for killing the rider."

"How did you kill him?"

"Smothered him before anyone could get there, it was straightforward enough given that he had injuries that prevented him stopping me. John Sinclair was not a target, he just happened to be around when the explosion happened, but the effect was enhanced by his death. Sarah Johnson was opportunistic and just increased the pressure because her role meant that BSR and FIM would bring massive pressure to bear on the club."

"And when are you going to be satisfied?" Harry asked him.

"Not until he weeps as his company collapses."

"But you killed five people to avenge one."

"That's irrelevant, that's not going to get to him. I lost the thing I most loved in my life and he needs to lose the thing he most loves in his life; and that's not a person, it's his ego and that means it's his company and via that, his reputation."

The door opened and Rosie stepped into the room, "Hi, I finished early so I....." she stopped in her tracks.

Her bodyguard walked into her back knocking her forwards. Bernie raised the gun quickly and fired one shot into the man's throat, Harry stood up and Bernie levelled the gun at him and simultaneously pointed his finger at Rosie to indicate that she should stand still as well. The frozen tableau posed like this until Bernie said, "You'd better sit down and make yourselves comfortable."

Rosie was horrified; "What about him?" she asked pointing at the bodyguard, "he's dying, listen to him." The officer lay on his back gripping this neck and emitting gurgling sounds as he tried to gulp in the air he needed to live.

Bernie looked down at the man and saw that he was indeed struggling, "You're right, it's a bit of a distraction isn't it?" Bernie said, and he swung the gun towards the prostrate man and shot him once in the head, "there, that's settled."

Rosie shrieked, "You animal! You monster! You are insane"

"Yeah. Yeah. I know how you feel," Bernie said dismissing her.

Harry wondered what he could do but the distance to get at Bernie was too great to take him by surprise, plus he was seated on this office chair that offered no purchase because of the wheels. Harry's dad had been dead for nearly six years, but he had given Harry the single most useful bit of advice he had ever been given. Whenever he or Harry made a mistake he'd say, "We'll make it into a feature son. But how?"

"Rosie, you move over here next to Harry," Bernie said waving the gun to indicate where he wanted her to go and glancing in Rosie's direction as he did so. In that instant, Harry twisted off his chair, grabbed both the arms and pushed it with all his strength towards Bernie. As the chair spun towards its target, Harry grabbed his mug of coffee and threw it towards Bernie's head watching the arc of brown liquid as it travelled through the air hitting Bernie across his face. Harry threw himself at the distracted gunman as the first shot fizzed passed him and hit the wall. The mug missed its target but was close enough to cause Bernie to dodge it and thus the second shot shattered the window that separated the anti-room from the studio. Harry crashed heavily into Bernie and both of them tripped over the dead security officer and fell in a tangle of arms and legs. Another thwack as Bernie squeezed out a shot that tore into underside of the office chair that lay on its side next to them, Harry fought desperately to get a hand on to Bernie's gun rather than just his wrist. Rosie danced around the two men trying to get involved but having constantly to watch the direction in which the gun was aimed, the dead officer and the furniture, apart from the impossibility of gaining any grip on the writhing mass of arms and legs. Grunting, gasping and wheezing, both men were getting slower and slower as exhaustion began to take its toll and as it did so, Rosie saw more opportunities to get a few blows in that irritated Bernie more than it hurt him. As he appeared on top of Harry's squirming body for a few seconds, she delivered a sharp rap to his head with the heel of her shoe in response to which he looked round pulled his right arm way from Harry's grip and fired the gun three times as it traced an arc around the room. Rosie let out a loud rasping grunt as one of the shots struck her and ripped through her upper chest, tearing her right pectoral muscle, passing through her right lung, under the right subclavian vein, shattering her right shoulder blade and lodging itself amongst the mess it made there. Her body twisted as she was thrown against the wall where she slumped in a sitting position issuing bubbling guttural sounds as she tried to draw breath into her one good lung.

Harry let out a deafening roar when he saw Rosie go down and, in one of those moments when a person can find strength they didn't know they had, he rose up and grabbed Bernie's gun hand with both of his and wrenched it downwards with such force that his assailant lost his grip on the weapon as his hand made contact with Harry's shin bone. Both howled with the pain as the gun skidded across the floor and under the desk where Harry had been sitting. Bernie slapped his hand across Harry's face knocking his head backwards against the wall with a thud and causing flashing lights to appear before his eyes. Bernie launched himself across the floor to grab the gun but fumbled the move and knocked it further away where it lodged against the wall and radiator input pipe. Harry recovered grabbing Bernie's right foot and heaving him back across the floor and away from the gun. Bernie rolled over and kicked Harry hard on the side of his left knee raising a cry of pain from him and causing his grip on Bernie's leg to release. Before Harry could recover, Bernie was on his feet and landing a clean punch on Harry's nose spreading it excruciatingly across his face for a second time and sprayed blood everywhere.

Harry crashed back against the wall as Bernie threw a second punch that landed painfully against his cheek. Harry grabbed whatever he could as he desperately struggled to breathe through his mouth. He got a handful of cloth and yanked it furiously to his left side feeling Bernie go with it. He kept the momentum going and forced Bernie further along the wall and slammed him against the corner unit hearing the glass in the doors shatter while the contents crashed against each other. Glass shards showered down upon them bouncing and tinkling on the floor, in their hair and clothes. Harry put his left hand down on the floor to push himself back onto his feet and felt several pieces sink deep into his palm and fingers. Bernie rolled away, sprang to his feet and immediately launched a fresh attack at Harry as he struggled to get up, but as he drove off his right foot to drop on his victim, the broken glass caused him to slip and lose his momentum so that he landed short of Harry and landed painfully on his knees in the shards.

Harry struggled to his feet and stood over Bernie who looked up into his face and grabbed for his clothing in an attempt to raise himself off his lacerated knees. Harry brought his knee up with tremendous force into Bernie's chin and heard the cracking and splintering as his teeth came together, the loud clunk as his jaw dislocated and the splatter of blood as his lower teeth came through his lower lip. Bernie fell back holding his face as Harry skidded across the glass strewn floor to retrieve the gun and slump on the floor holding his left hand out flat as the pain washed over him. He pointed the gun at Bernie, who didn't look like a man who wanted to fight any more, and then he looked across to Rosie and saw that she was in a very bad way. Her chin was on her chest and she emitted low gurgling sounds as blood seeped into her punctured lung and air leaking into her chest cavity through the gunshot wound both acted to collapse her left lung in a haemopneumothorax condition. Harry knew enough to know that Rosie needed medical help urgently, so he stood up and pointed the gun at Bernie, "Don't fucking move, just don't fucking move," he said in an exhausted but determined voice. He found his mobile on the floor and carefully dialled 999 with his left hand and asking for an ambulance first and the police second. He went over to Rosie and sat beside her, facing Bernie put his mouth close to her ear saying. "Rosie, it's Harry, the ambulance is coming so just sit here darling, don't try to move, don't try to speak, just concentrate on breathing."

Bernie was sitting slumped against the opposite wall and mumbled with difficulty through his broken teeth and mangled mouth, "put something over the wound."

"What?"

"Get something, handkerchief, a napkin, a piece of paper or just use her hand and place it over the wound so that the air can't enter that way."

Harry found several napkins that he got with his coffee at the local coffee house and laid most of them over the wound on Rosie's chest. He dabbed the rest on his injured hand but stopped when the small shards were pulled and disturbed by the soft paper sending sharp piercing bolts of pain through his being. "Stick them down with some sticky tape so that it doesn't fall off," Bernie muttered, spitting some blood onto the wooden floor.

Harry did this, and it held the pad in place and he heard an immediate improvement in her breathing.

Bernie altered his position slightly so he could see better, "She looks very pale, feel her skin and tell me if it feels cold."

Harry did this, "It does feel cold.

"Can you find a pulse?"

Harry took her hand and fumbled around, I can't find anything," he said.

"Don't worry, you can try her neck," Bernie suggested, "just press your second and third fingers on the side of her neck in the soft hollow area just beside her windpipe."

He watched Harry placing his fingers on Rosie's neck, "Ok, what's it like?"

"I don't know," Harry said in frustration, "I can hardly feel it."

"I thought so, she's gone into shock. Move her slowly and carefully so that you can get her feet higher than her head, loosen any tight clothing, get something you can wrap around her to keep her warm?"

"How bad is it?" Harry asked.

"It's very bad, so do it quickly. Be gentle though, any pain will make it worse."

Harry did all this and felt a dull ache of despair washing over him with the prospect of Rosie not making it.

The three slumped on the floor, each in their own desperate, painful realities and each not wanting to move, Rosie because she couldn't, Harry because the pain associated with it was too much to bear and, he wanted to hold the gun steady, and Bernie, because the gun that Harry was trying to hold steady, was pointing at him. This state of affairs stayed the same until the ambulance and the police arrived almost at the same time to take control.

As they entered the room Harry said calmly, "Don't be concerned about the gun. I'm the good guy," he nodded towards Bernie, "He's the bad guy and the woman on the floor is in desperate need of assistance."

The paramedics busied themselves with their priorities to get Rosie stabilised, into the ambulance and away to hospital. The police established Bernie's identity, arrested him and then, after the paramedics did what they could for him, took him to hospital in their vehicle. Harry was allowed to travel with Rosie in the ambulance and also required some treatment for his cuts and bruises.

Rosie was rushed into A&E at the Chelsea and Westminster Hospital as a Type 1 patient and seen immediately by the trauma team and then into Intensive Care, whilst Harry was sent down to wait in A&E as a type 3 patient, where he sat in a queue for over two hours and then had his nose reset, three small staples in a scalp wound and a hard hearted nurse extracted the shards of glass from his hand with tweezers and made unsympathetic tutting sounds when he reacted to the piercing pain. When he walked out of the cubicle he wore another face mask, but this time black, hairs sticking up in clumps around his staples and a large bandage on his hand.

He found his way back up to the waiting area at post-op where he found Barry Leech sitting alone. Barry told him that Rosie was still in surgery and there was no information about her. Barry questioned Harry about the fight and the shooting and was horrified to hear how close to death both of them had come. Harry related the tale that Bernie had told him about with regards to his brother Michael and Barry grew silent as he heard Bernie's version of the events that led to Michael Garnet's suicide. Harry made the point that, although the delayed payment forced the issue for Michael's business, his suicide was an extreme response which must have had other, deeper causes and Bernie's response was still more extreme and surely waiting like a time bomb to explode over something. While Barry agreed with this, Harry could tell that a worm of guilt had started eating into Barry and he thought that perhaps he should keep an eye on him for a while to make sure he came through this.

They slept fitfully on the plastic covered chairs not wanting to leave in case someone came looking for them with news of Rosie. Just after 0500 a doctor walked slowly into the waiting area looking exhausted and drained and asked, "Are you family of Rosemary Higgins?"

Both Harry and Barry get stiffly to their feet slowly, "Yes we are," Harry answered for both of them. "How is she?"

"She's very poorly," the doctor said, "but out of immediate danger."

Barry sank back into his chair, "Thank God," he whispered hoarsely, "Thank you so much Doctor erm?," and a tear squeezed through his closed eyes.

"I am Doctor Mittal," the doctor responded; "I operated on Rosemary."

"Rosie," Harry said, "we call her Rosie," and Doctor Mittal nodded. "How poorly is she?" Harry asked.

"She has suffered a trauma that would have killed someone less fit than she. The injury was sufficient to have killed most people, but the bit of stabilising surgery that we have performed has also been punishing, so she is going to need a few days before we can finish the job and then after that she will need time to mend and get well."

"How long?" Harry asked.

"Three months or so should see her pretty active again, but don't be beguiled by the apparent mobility, it could be a year before she is back to her best."

Barry looked up at them, "She'll get the best that money can buy," he said.

"That's good," the doctor agreed, "but it's only part of her overall recovery. She's going to need people who will look after her, nurse her, help her, have patience with her."

"She'll get that," Harry said, "We'll be there for her; just tell us what we have to do."

"We'll get private nurses, as many as she needs. Is there some kind of equipment she needs, a special type of bed?" Barry enquired.

The doctor looked irritated, "Don't worry about that, we'll let you know about all of that when she's fit enough to leave here."

"Do you have a feel for when that could be?" Harry asked.

"Not really. Weeks at best I should say."

"It sounds as if she's been through it," Harry said.

"She has, she really has," Doctor Mittal confirmed, "Whoever covered the chest wound with the wad of napkins probably saved her life. I don't think she would have made it here without that bit of first aid, or if she had, she would have been in such a bad state that I doubt that we would have been able to do much to save her."

Harry nodded thoughtfully, "Bernie suggested that."

"Bernie?" Doctor Mittal asked.

"The man who shot her. The one who went there to kill her."

"That doesn't seem to make much sense does it?" the doctor said.

"Not immediately, no," Harry mused.

At the point, Barry stood up again and asked, "Did you fix everything that needed fixing?"

"No, no. We operated for four hours and worked on all the vital injuries in order to stabilise her. That done, we must let her rest now and continue when she is capable of more surgery."

"What else do you need to do?" Barry questioned him.

"To date, we have given her some blood; she lost quite a bit before she got here. We also treated her collapsed lung which involved 'needle aspiration' to suction out any air that was in there, but because the pneumothorax was so large, we had to employ percutaneous chest drainage to get it all out of the thoracic cavity and eventually that enables the lung to reflate on its own. We mended the entry wound and the torn pectoral muscle; an x-ray showed us that the bullet passed right through and we found the exit hole in her back, level with her shoulder blade."

Harry looked concerned, "How bad is it?"

"It's bad enough, but I've seen worse. It's in two separate pieces with some small fragments. I think it's going to need plates and screws maybe just some wiring, but that will become clear when we operate after the weekend. It's unusual for the shoulder blade to break like that," the doctor said, "usually a bullet will just pierce the bone without doing too much damage, but not this one."

"My goodness," Harry said. "Is there anything else?"

"Yes, but nothing as serious." Doctor Mittal answered, "a couple of broken ribs, torn muscles. Fortunately, the bullet missed some large veins, like the subclavian artery for example, which, if hit would have caused a dramatic loss of blood, so, although there is a bit of nerve damage, it could have been a lot worse."

Barry said, "What do we do now?"

"Go home, get some rest and come back this evening."

"Will we be able to see her then?" Harry asked.

"Yes, but she may not be very receptive."

"We'll be here whenever she needs us," Harry promised.

The doctor smiled at Harry, "That's what she needs from you; leave the physical stuff to us and you give as much love as you can."

"I will," Harry answered, then looking at Barry he said, "We will."

CHAPTER 35

EPILOGUE

Saturday 8th October 2016

arnie@arniecottrell
Our thoughts are with Rosie today. She is very ill and needs lots of care. Operations today will start her recovery.

When Harry returned to the hospital at midday he found Peter and Dorothy Barns were sitting by her sleeping form, holding her hands and speaking to her. Harry stood in the doorway and watched them for a full minute before Dorothy looked round and saw him there.

"We came over as soon as we heard," she said crossing the room and putting her arms around Harry.

"Thank you," he replied, "I know she would appreciate it, as I do. Has she been awake?"

Peter smiled warmly at him, "No, no but we have faith that she can hear us."

Dorothy took Harry right hand in hers, "We've been telling her that we have decided to keep Davy in treatment and continue his feeding and sustenance."

Harry smiled at the both, "She'll be delighted and grateful to hear that news."

Peter explained, "We saw Doctor Hammond two days ago and talked the whole thing through with him. We talked a lot about you and Rosie and especially about Irene and that influenced us greatly. The doctor respects our decision and is supportive of our decision."

Harry listened to them talking through their change of heart and thought that he would call in at Tony and Irene's house in the next few days to tell them about it all and update them on Rosie's condition.

Just after three o'clock when Harry was sitting alone with Rosie, holding her hand and keeping a personal vigil by her side, he felt a gentle tap on his shoulder and a girl's voice said, "Mr. Harry?"

He looked up and met Irene's concerned eyes, she was sitting in her electric wheelchair and behind her stood Tony Fuller. "Oh, Irene, how nice of you to come," he was touched very deeply by their visit and found it hard to speak for a few moments.

"We wanted to come," Tony told him, "Irene was very taken with you both when she met you and hasn't stopped talking about you two ever since."

Harry smiled, "It's great to see you. I was going to come to your house tomorrow, but this is even better."

"Can I say hello to Rosie," Irene asked as she steered her wheelchair round to the other side of the bed.

"Go ahead," Harry replied and smiled wanly at Tony.

He and the Health and Safety Manager watched as Irene unselfconsciously put her unsteady hands out to take Rosie's in hers and tried to lean forward to get her face as close as she could, her head occasionally jerking and wobbling uncontrollably, "Be careful not to hit her," Tony cautioned her.

"I know that dad," Irene answered not looking at him.

She gently stroked the back of Rosie's left hand, "Rosie? Rosie, this is Irene Fuller. Do you remember me? Do you remember I came to see some people about Davy? I've come to tell you to get better because I want you to be my friend."

Harry told Tony all about the events with Bernie, the injuries and how they had been treated and what was still left to be done by way of operations while Irene sat talking to Rosie for about half an hour.

Barry came back to the hospital just after four o'clock. He had showered and changed somehow between leaving, attending two business meetings and returning with Uncle Max in tow.

"I found the old bugger walking around in Gastroenterology making a nuisance of himself, if I hadn't taken him away they would have given him a colostomy as a matter of course," he told Harry.

A pattern of events became established for a few days. Each day Harry arrived and ate breakfast in the burger bar on the ground floor, sat with Rosie until he took lunch at the burger bar and then sat with Rosie until he had dinner down at the burger bar after which he would sit with Rosie until he was asked to leave. Each day people visited to see how she was and sat with them both. They were long tiring days that seemed endless as they waited for Rosie's body to stabilise enough to perform further surgery.

It was Monday when Doctor Mittal announced himself satisfied that he could operate on her shoulder. And so, Rosie went into the theatre at 0700 and was wheeled out into the recovery room at 1330. Half an hour after that, Doctor Mittal sat with Harry, Barry and Max and sipped tea from a polystyrene cup as he explained the different stages of the operation.

"Even though it was reasonably along affair," he told them, "in many ways it was a straight forward operation, but there were a couple of tricky bits that absorbed the time. Rosie was shot at close to point blank range and that meant that there was scorching around the wound and that the gases from the gun had also entered the wound which always gives us concern, plus we had to use antibiotics to take care of any infections that come from bacteria on the clothing fibres that inevitably follow the bullet into the wound. With regards to the bigger stuff, I'm pleased with the way her lung is coming on, her shoulder blade is repaired and will be sore for a while, but fine, her ribs will just have to mend naturally, but there's nothing to be concerned about there." He swallowed the last of his drink, rose slowly from his chair and dropped the cup into a waste bin, "She's going to be fine," he reassured them, "Don't throw her tennis racket away just yet."

As the sun dipped behind the buildings on the Fulham Road the sky was red, blue and orange with only a few lonely clouds to pick up the colours and absorb them into their folds. Max Leech stood by the window in Rosie's room and gazed across at *Boots* and then further down the road, "There's a French restaurant on the corner of Seymore Walk, an Italian just opposite or a Tesco Express if you just want a sandwich." No-one responded and he looked across the roof tops to where he could see the roof of Earls Court looking red under the last of the sun and just catch a corner of the Brompton Cemetery. "I couldn't live here in London," he said suddenly wanting to be back in Swanage.

"We love it," Rosie said in a husky voice.

Max turned to face her, "I know you do my dear girl and I don't pretend to understand it all."

"But we love Swanage too," she added.

Uncle Max sat down beside her bed and took her hand that lay limply at the side of her exhausted body, "You know, we been very anxious about you this last week. You're very precious to us and the thought of losing you made us despondent beyond description." Rosie tried to raise her head from her pillow and Max leaned forward, "No, no, just lay still and rest.

As for Bernie Garnet, he predictably manipulated the system all he could before pleading guilty at his last opportunity to do so without losing his discounts on his sentence. The judge spent an hour summing up and attempted to guide the public towards keeping objectivity as a central consideration in their thinking and not allowing subjectivity to cloud the important issues. He covered each attack in detail, dwelling on the forensics especially around the ballistics and the killer's modus operandi. Finally, he urged everyone to ignore all the publicity that had surrounded the case for, as he said, "Much of the output from the press had been speculation, assumption and hearsay all of which has been presented as fact in order to sway public opinion."

Bernie was ordered to return to the court at a later date for sentencing, but he was also informed that he should expect to be placed in custody for a considerable period of time. He returned three weeks later to hear that he had been sentenced to serve at least 30 years in prison before any consideration of parole. Harry, Rosie, Barry and Arnie sat in court for every minute of every day of the trial and observed the justice system unfold in its tedious, logical and adversarial manner and announced their own satisfaction with the result. Bernie accepted the sentence with equanimity, showing no sign of emotion until, as he left the court in handcuffs he looked across at Barry Leech, grinned broadly and blew him a kiss. Two years later, while attending a programme in prison, he revealed to a psychiatrist that he had no regrets and that he hoped that bastard Leech was haunted by the ghosts of each of his victims. He may well have been satisfied with the effect that the whole terrifying and disastrous episode had on Barry Leech.

Barry Leech went downhill rapidly after the court case and withdrew from his businesses to such an extent that the Group Board felt they were left with no alternative except to propose a vote of no confidence in his leadership, which saw him defeated and ignominiously replaced as the Chief Executive. Shortly after this, with the exception of his beloved Bulldogs, he stepped down from any participation on any of the Boards of the companies he ran. Over the next two years the Group was ravaged by hostile takeovers for the various component parts until the description of 'group' was rendered moot and the entity was dissolved.

Within a few months of the first of these events, Barry presented himself at an exclusive private psychiatric clinic near South of England where he stayed for three weeks, was diagnosed as suffering a form of Clinical Depression known as Dysthymia. He was prescribed selective serotonin re-uptake inhibitors and then returned home, from where he became an outpatient and helicoptered to their helipad once a week for psychotherapy. Over the period of two years he was able to make progress and eventually got back to a position where he could take pleasure and joy from the everyday things in life and particularly speedway. He can still be found in the Brent Sinclair Stand at Battersea laughing, cheering, complaining about the management and berating the riders with all the other fans, where he is well loved and respected. This is enough for him and he is content to be an older and wiser man of simple tastes.

Rosie recovered and was back to full health within a year. She took on more and more responsibility for the day to day running of the Battersea Bulldogs when it became clear that Barry was ill. Her promotion to the Board in 2018 was supported by all the Board members, employees and fans alike and she soon became a challenging and creative presence within the business. Her combination of leadership and benevolence earned her the reputation as 'the iron fist in the velvet glove,' from which she took some quiet satisfaction.

Uncle Max continued to show no signs of respect for the ageing process. He continued to paint in his studio in Swanage, getting others to organise exhibitions and sell his abstracts for phenomenal prices. He added speedway to his very short list of leisure activities and became a regular enthusiastic presence at Wimborne Road and feeling bereft during the close season. He painted a large canvas entitled 'Speedway' although few, if any people would have recognised the subject from the finished piece. He just laughed of course.

Harry was just Harry. He and Johnny continued doing the jobs they loved and broadcasted from the small studio at the Bulldog's stadium every day. The only reoccurring physical effect from his exploits with Bernie Garnet was the occasional rheumatic ache in his ankle when rain threatened. When Johnny decided to make Speedway FM into a limited company, he offered Harry an equal share which was accepted with enthusiasm. Harry's relationship with Tony went from strength to strength and he and Rosie would regularly visit the Fuller household to see Irene and spend time in her radiant presence. Tony managed to get the occasional Health and Safety insert into Harry's Wednesday programme, but Harry resisted all suggestions that it should become a regular feature, let alone a programme unto itself.   Harry's feelings for Rosie matured into rich mixture of respect, compassion, pride, affection and loyalty; which he called it love and it was the best thing in his life.

BULLDOGS FIXTURES AND RESULTS 2016

A 23rd Mar 5 – Coventry 50 v 40 Bulldogs CH
H 24th Mar – Bulldogs 55 v 35 Coventry CH
H 31st Mar – Bulldogs 56 v 34 Swindon ELA
A 3rd Apr – Wolverhampton 52 v 38 Bulldogs ELA
H 7th Apr – Bulldogs 47 v 45 Belle Vue ELA
A 8th Apr – Coventry 50 v 42 Bulldogs ELA
A 9th Apr - Belle Vue 51 v 41 Bulldogs ELA
H 14th Apr – Bulldogs 61 v 29 Leicester ELA
A 17th Apr - Kings Lynn 44 v 48 Bulldogs ELA
H 21rd Apr – Bulldogs 47 v 43 Kings Lynn ELA
H 28th Apr – Bulldogs 50 v 40 Wolverhampton ELA
H 5th May – Bulldogs 48 v 45 Belle Vue ELA
H 12th May – Bulldogs 47 v 42 Poole ELA
H 19th May – Poole 54 v 30 Bulldogs ELA
H 26th May – Bulldogs 52 v 38 Swindon ELA
A 3rd June – Coventry 49 v 41 Bulldogs
A 4th June – Wolverhampton 57 v 37 Bulldogs ELA
H 9th June – Bulldogs 56 v 34 Leicester ELA
A 12th June – Swindon 54 v 41 Bulldogs ELA
H 16th June – Bulldogs 47 v 45 Lakeside ELA
H 23rd June – Bulldogs 54 v 36 Belle Vue ELB
H 30th June – Bulldogs 48 v 38 Wolverhampton ELB
A 1st July – Leicester 45 v 45 Bulldogs ELA
A 2nd July – Coventry 51 v 41 Bulldogs ELA
H 7th July – Bulldogs 40 v 50 Swindon ELB
H 21st July – Bulldogs 44 v 48 Swindon ELAB
A 29th July – Belle Vue 57 v 35 Bulldogs ELB
H 4th Aug – Bulldogs 61 v 29 Kings Lynn ELB
H 4th Aug – Bulldogs 52 v 41 Swindon ELB (rerun from 6th July)
A 5th Aug – Coventry 45 v 45 Bulldogs ELB
H 11th Aug – Bulldogs 43 v 47 Lakeside ELB
H 18th Aug – Bulldogs 58 v 32 Leicester ELB
H 25th Aug – Bulldogs 25 v 11 Coventry ELB (abandoned after Heat 6)
A 27th Aug – Wolverhampton 50 v 42 Bulldogs ELB
A 1st Sept – Bulldogs 42 v 32 Kings Lynn ELB
        (abandoned after heat 12 – result stands)
A 3rd Sept – Swindon 50 v 40 Bulldogs ELAB
H 8th Sept – Bulldogs 52 v 38 Coventry ELB
        (Rerun from 25th August)
H 15th Sept – Bulldogs 41 v 51Coventry ELB
A 17th Sept – Kings Lynn 35 V 57 Bulldogs ELB

A 21st Sept – Semi Final Play off 1st Leg
        - Poole Pirates   51 v 39 Wolverhampton

        - Belle Vue Aces 49 v 41 Battersea Bulldogs
H 28th Sept – Semi Final Play off 2nd Leg

- Wolverhampton   55 v 35 Poole Pirates (agg 94 – 86)
- Battersea Bulldogs 63 v 28 Belle Vue Aces (agg 102 – 77)

A 3rd October – play off final – first leg
- Wolverhampton 54 v 36 Battersea Bulldogs

H 6th October – play off final - 2nd leg
- Battersea Bulldogs 53 v 37 Wolverhampton (agg 89 – 91)

SUMMARY OF THE LEVELS OF SPEEDWAY
Speedway Grand Prix (SGP) is the format for the World Championships. Run over 11 international events, all but two in European countries, with New Zealand and Australia usually holding the first and the last of the series.
Elite League – The top league in the UK
Premier League – second level in the UK
National League – third level in UK.

THE BASIC LEAGUE RULES
Each race is over 4 laps from a standing clutch start.
Riders score point according to their performance in each race:
1st = 3 points, 2nd = 2 points, 3rd = 1 points, 4th = 0 points.

Riders wear coloured helmet covers for identification: Home riders wear red and Blue covers, while visiting riders wear white and yellow/black.

There are several flagged track signals:
Yellow & Black Diagonal Cross = Riders entering last lap.
Black & White Chequered = Race finished.
Black with accompanying disc - Rider Excluded.
Red = race stopped
In addition, red lights are used to let riders know that the race has been stopped.

Each meeting has a referee who views the proceedings from a room looking down on the track. The referee tosses a coin to decide which team get first choice of the starting gate positions before the first heat. The captain who wins that coin toss can either choose gate positions for Heat 1 or Heat 15.

In order to keep the excitement alive when one team is dominating a match, a Tactical Ride (TR) is permitted. This can only happen after Heat 4. It can be used only once, when a team is 10 or more points in arrears - any rider from the team can then be nominated for this Tactical Ride. The TR rider starts from the starting tapes and, providing he beats an opposing rider, any points he scores are counted double. A rider can only take a TR once. TR is not permitted after Heat 11 in the Elite League or Heat 12 in the Premier League. Tactical rides are not permitted in the National League.

All 7 riders in each team must have a minimum of three rides prior to Heat 15, unless a medically ratified injury prevents this; this will be done by the official Medical Officer at the track.

The team reserve, number 7 can have a maximum of 7 rides, and be used as a Tactical Substitute, Rider Replacement as well as in their normally nominated races which will count in the maximum rides allowed.

When a rider touches or breaks the starting tapes, the Team Manager may either, use the number 7 reserve in the original starting position, or re-instate the rider who infringed the starting gate to start with a 15-metre handicap. In the case of this happening in heat 15, the rider can go off 15m or be replaced by another rider who is eligible for heat 15.

BONUS POINTS (in league meetings)
Because riders are paid per point they score and to avoid riders needlessly competing with their team mates for race positions, when a rider finishes a race one place behind his team mate (other than 4th) he will be awarded a 'paid point' that does not count towards the match score, but does allow the rider to be paid for the point that he may well have allowed his team mate to score. This paid point also counts towards the rider's total points when the league officials calculate the riders' average scores per ride, per meeting, per season.

At the start of each season, the British Speedway Board publish the overall point total to which Promoters and Managers must adhere when building their team ready for the coming season. The 7 riders' averages from the last season are aggregated and must be under or equal to (but not over) the official declared total for that season.

NOMENCLATURES: (seen in race results section)

X = Excluded
T = Excluded, tapes
M = Excluded, missing the 2 minutes deadline or delaying start
R = Engine failure or retirement
N = Fell, non-starter in the rerun
> = Tactical ride (points doubled)
< = Tapes or 2 minutes offence, handicapped 15 metres

LEAGUE SCORING SYSTEM
Home loss by any amount of points = 0
Home draw = 1
Home win by any amount of points = 3
Away loss by 7 points or more = 0
Away loss by 6 points or less = 1
Away draw = 2
Away win by between 1 and 6 points = 3
Away win by 7 points or more = 4

TERMINOLOGY AND SLANG

BSPA British Speedway Promoters Association.
SRBF Speedway Rider's Benevolent Fund.
Spanner a pits mechanic.
Filled in a rider's goggles are covered in so much wet shale that he cannot see.
Low siding This is a crash that results from a loss of traction so that the bike lays down or drops and slides along the track.

High siding The high-side is a crash that results from a loss of traction by the rear wheel, followed by recovery of traction which, in turn results in the rider being flipped off the bike.

Green sheet Average A list issued periodically by the BSPA, of rider's Meeting Average.

SOPs Standard Operating Procedures – A Health and Safety requirement for every limited company and PLC.

LIST OF CHARACTERS

Harry Marsh – reporter for Speedway FM
Rosie Higgins – PA to Barry Leech
Barry Leech – Promoter of Battersea Bulldogs
Johnny Matthews – MD of Speedway FM
Tony Fuller – HSE Manager at Battersea Bulldogs
Bernie Thorpe – Paramedic
Johnny Sinclair – Jimmy Parsons' mechanic
Steve Hildegarde – Sonny Brent's mechanic
Sonny Brent – Reserve rider for Battersea Bulldogs
Arnie Cottrell – Battersea Bulldogs Manager
Davy Barns – Rosie's comatose fiancé
Peter Barns – Davy's father
Dorothy Barns – Davy's mother
Mary Lambert – admin nurse – St Boniface
Paul Worrall – St Boniface nurse in reception
Doctor Hammond – Helen's doctor in hospital
Jim Norman – HSE Manager at Torquay
Julia Raglett – Head Paramedic
Susan Hawley – Dirt Track Studios Manager
Geoff Falk – Mechanic
Jenny Howard – Harry' fellow broadcaster
Kevin Hinchcliff the Rebel's Health and Safety Manager
Sarah Johnson – Dead referee
Doctor Rogers – Battersea Bulldog's doctor
Andy White – Rider for Southampton
Jason Priestly – Rider for Southampton
Frankie Chivers – Bulldog's new reserve
Sarah Johnson – Referee for Kings Lynn match
Officer Pollock – investigating Harry's attempted murder

THE AUTHOR

Luke Eden lives on his boat on the Shropshire Union Canal where he wrote his novel DEAD HEAT after many years of wishing someone else would do it. He has been a speedway fans since 1965 when he first went to see the Sheffield Tigers compete in the Provisional League and like many other fans, fell immediately in love with the sounds and the smells of the sport. Like all kids he idolised the undoubtedly brave riders and collected their autographs, diligently filled in the programmes, started taking the Speedway Star, bought a PVC jacket in the belief that if looked like leather and stuck a large Tiger's head on it. Since then he has worked all around the UK and travelled the world for his job as a consultant to many large corporations, but where ever he was, his first piece of research about the area has been discovering the nearest speedway track. He has supported, Cradley Heath, Swindon, Poole and Belle Vue as well as his first love, the Sheffield Tigers.

Luke has always written and worked as an artist through his life and he is currently building a Website to represent these activities. You will be able to become familiar with his short storeys, poems and songs as well as his drawings, paintings and collages when the site is running in the Spring of 2019.